Finding
Albert
Strange

(A Day to Remember)

C C CANNING

Acknowledgements:

Quotations from 'The Herald' refer to The Sydney Morning Herald issue

of Thursday, April 25, 2002. 'The Crossword' is Cryptic Crossword 16534

from the issue of the same date.

Published by the author

ccanning@xtra.co.nz

ISBN 978-0-473-22130-0

For Hugo

1.

Roger Saville

Roger Saville left his Mosman house at 7.15am. It was a beautiful, sunlit morning that promised a perfect day; a morning that might normally have inspired him to open his car sunroof and sniff the scent of his wife's garden as he drove down the tree-lined driveway and out the sandstone pillared gates.

The sun had been up for nearly an hour and was already forming rainbows in the sprinklers that watered the lawns, adding lustre to the golden real estate that perched above the still, deep waters of Sydney's Middle Harbour. Rosellas swooped between the palm trees as he passed and a kookaburra, which started each day in the Moreton Bay fig on the street corner, stretched its neck and laughed hilariously.

None of this registered with Roger. His nostrils were closed to the honeyed scent of the late-flowering daturas, his ears deaf to avian salutes and his eyes blind to the yellow and red bracts of heliconia glowing in the emerald green shade of Frank-the-Gardener's Balinese border. His focus was obscured by the bitter, green flavour of his own bile, the source of which he hadn't yet identified.

Like the sun, he'd been up for nearly an hour already, but unlike the sun he had not warmed to the day. Anxious not to disturb his wife, he'd slid out of bed like a cat burglar making a silent escape, tip-toeing his way to the shower with the unresolved anxieties of the night still clinging to his skin. He'd taken those anxieties to bed with him so he shouldn't have been surprised to find them still there when he arose.

For the second time in eight hours he'd stood with his head bowed in supplication while stinging jets of hot and cold water pulsated through the massaging shower head, sluicing his hair and skin, but still the elusive odour had clung to him. What was its source? Not guilt, for God's sake? With obsessive care he'd scraped each newly-emerged hair from his neck and chin and sprinkled after-shave over his chest and arms before buttoning them into a crisp white cotton shirt. He'd brushed his thick black hair away from his high forehead and squinted down his aquiline nose for any facial imperfections in the mirror, but all to no avail. Nothing had made him feel better.

The house had been silent. His wife's head had lain, light as fairy down, on her pillow, breathing invisibly through half-opened lips. There was no sound from his daughter or from his father-in-law in the guest room, and with luck, he'd thought, he could escape the house without having to speak to anyone. He'd knotted his silk Armani tie, slipped on his black Bally shoes and descended quietly to the kitchen.

He'd thought about eating something, because he knew he had a big day ahead, but he was anxious to get on the road. His cell phone had sat in its charger on the kitchen bench and, spurred by an ill-defined unease, he'd checked to see whether there had been any missed calls before opening the outside door to retrieve the morning paper as usual from the back step.

That's when the source of his displeasure had revealed itself. It was Anzac Day. He'd momentarily forgotten. On the front page of the newspaper there was a colour photo of an old man in the last stages of decay, his parchment-dry skin stretched thinly over atrophied flesh and illiquid veins, his dry crusty eyes and mouth devoid of life. 'Gallipoli's last man standing', read the caption.

Roger had shuddered in distaste. Why did they have to shove this crap in people's faces every year? And why did the world have to stop for it?

To make matters worse Joanne had suddenly swept into the kitchen, carrying with her an air of unfinished business from the night before.

'At least let me make you some breakfast,' she argued, taking up from a conversation he must have chosen to forget. 'You can't go off on an empty stomach.'

And despite his impatience he'd surrendered and let her make tea and toast.

'Listen to this crap,' he'd exclaimed, spreading out the front page of The Herald in an effort to direct conversation into a neutral corner: '*Price fixing executives deserve jail, says Fels*'. Have you ever heard anything like it? Who does this bastard think he is? He's supposed to be a consumer watchdog, not the head of the FBI. How the hell can you sell petrol if you can't agree on the price? Business is such an easy target for politicians and academics. It makes me sick.'

Not that price rigging in the petrol industry had anything to do with him.

To which she'd replied: 'I don't understand why you need to go to work early when it's Anzac Day and the whole country is on holiday.'

And he'd snapped.

'You just don't get it, do you, Jo? Business doesn't stop just because the fucking Government calls a public holiday. Business never stops. It's time you got used to it.'

Then he'd pecked her hurriedly on the cheek and left before she could think up some other complaint.

So it hadn't been a good start to the day, yet, as he stopped at the lights waiting to get onto Military Road, he knew she wasn't the source of his annoyance. She'd been justifiably angry that he'd forgotten her father was coming to dinner the night before and had arrived home late. What could he say? Business was business, for God's sake. Surely everyone understood that? He may have been late, but at least he'd made it in time for the main course. Besides, they'd all be seeing each other tonight at the Anzac Day charity dinner. There was a lot riding on that dinner and it was no small thing that he'd included his family – not to mention the fact that it was costing $1,000 a head.

There, that was it; that was the explanation for his mood. It was the argument that had ensued yesterday when he'd presented the bill to Lawrence Beck for payment and Lawrence had tut-tutted as though it was a gambling debt that he was being ordered to settle, rather than a measly $10,000 tab for the year's most important charity dinner. If the city's top property developers couldn't afford to buy a table, then who in God's name could? What was it with Lawrence? Yes, that was why he was pissed off. It had been building for a long time.

The traffic along Military Road was lighter than usual and he made good time on the approaches to the bridge. Anzac Day falling in the middle of the week was a bloody inconvenience but at least the lack of congestion was one positive he could take from it, and because he'd left home early he'd be at his office before they started erecting the barricades for the morning street march. Alright, he wouldn't dwell unnecessarily on Lawrence, and he wouldn't allow himself to feel guilty about Jo, either. It was meant to be an agreeable day, a day filled with high expectations, for if things went as planned it might easily turn out to be the defining day of his business life.

At 7.35am, therefore, as he pulled into the basement car park of his office building in Phillip Street, Roger Saville's distaste for life had somewhat abated. He parked his Jaguar in the usual space next to the elevator, turned off the ignition, checked his reflection in the rear view mirror and reached behind him to retrieve his briefcase from the back seat where he always placed it before going home. That's when he was forced to recall the reason he'd returned home late the night before; the reason he'd scrubbed his skin so vigorously in the shower.

2.

Albert Strange and his granddaughter, Samantha Saville

'It's a beautiful day, Grandpa.'

'There's no denying that.'

Fine after early morning fog and mist, was what they promised in the morning paper, then warm and sunny with a light north to north-easterly wind. And that is what it was. Already the mist had evaporated from the western bays and the harbour proper. All that remained was a pale white sprinkling of fog in the eastern side of Mosman Bay where the sun had not yet reached.

It was almost laugh-out-loud beautiful, so blatantly picturesque that it was difficult to resist even for a man who had come to this morning burdened with misgivings and not quite sure that what he was doing was right.

'It doesn't seem,' he murmured, 'like a day for celebrating war.'

The teenage girl beside him, alert and attentive in her crisp blue and grey school uniform, lightly held his sleeve as they boarded the ferry at Mosman and searched his face for more meaning, but he wasn't going to give any as he allowed her to protectively lead him to an empty seat near the stern. Sunlight skipped across the surface of the water and he narrowed his eyes against it - feigning a myopia which, in truth, related more to his current view of life than to his eyesight.

He'd brought the front section of the morning newspaper with him at Joanne's insistence and proceeded to lay it open on his knee before thinking better of it and folding it up again.

It was Anzac Day: a day for remembering the dead. At his age, and with his history, that was something he seemed to have been doing for an awfully long time, but it was something he had grown used to resisting, resenting even, so for the moment he chose to focus instead on the present.

'It could be a lot worse,' he ventured with a sweep of his hand, 'going to work each day on the ferry like this, reading the paper at leisure, sitting in the sun, watching the boats and the people. It could be very pleasant I imagine.'

He smiled reassuringly at his granddaughter, looking around at the other passengers for evidence of such contentment and quickly realising these were not commuters heading to work. Like him, too many were branded with the grey hair and shrunken bones of age, their clothes too big for them, eyes too cautious of the next accidental fall. Oh, God, he thought, not wanting to catch an eye, is that really what we've come to?

He looked at his watch - not quite 8 o'clock. They had an hour to get to Martin Place for the start of the parade, but he wouldn't mind too much if they were late. It was more Samantha he was thinking of. She seemed so excited by it all and he didn't want to disappoint her.

'Is that what your father does,' he continued cheerfully, giving her a little dig with his elbow to let her know they were in this thing together; 'read the paper and plan his day on the ferry each morning?'

'No, he takes his car to work.' She wrinkled her nose in mock disapproval.

'Can you imagine it, across the harbour bridge with all that traffic every night and morning? Like, he's always complaining about it. I don't know why he doesn't live in town because he's hardly ever home.'

She shrugged. What could you say? There was something so familiar in the way she played with her hands in her lap, as if manipulating an imaginary loop of string, that her grandfather was hit by an unexpected pang of nostalgia, so intense that it caused his eyes to water.

'He works late a lot,' she explained, without conviction, 'says he can't have his life ruled by a ferry timetable. You tell me.'

Albert Strange nodded without responding. There was something in her turn of phrase too, that prodded his memory and he peered more closely at her profile, not wanting to be caught doing so, but looking for clues. She was, of course, not unlike her mother, but that similarity was not what he was intent on examining; it was something else that he couldn't put his finger on. Perhaps it was the unmuddied view of life that she displayed.

'Did you used to commute to work?' she asked, turning suddenly and catching him looking.

'No.'

He straightened up and awkwardly adjusted the folds of his suit jacket. Christ, his hands were old. When had that happened?

'No, I was not a city man, myself, unlike your father. It never appealed to me much, the idea of working in an office, being cooped up with all those people. It's as bad as prison.'

He put on a funny voice.

'Not that I was ever in prison mind, oh no, I was too quick for that.'

And she giggled politely. If she noticed his hands, now in his own eyes so inflamed with deterioration, and the thinness of his knees as he gripped them beneath the loose folds of his trousers, she made no sign of it. Perhaps it was the brightness of the light, or the incongruity of seeing his hands sticking out from the sleeves of a dark suit jacket that made him so suddenly aware of what she might be thinking. If she could see through her father so clearly, what chance would he have of getting through the day without being uncovered?

With a much deeper sense of certainty he felt that what he was doing was a mistake. He could have avoided all this and made his peace with Jim Percy some other way - privately, without risking exposure of his guilt and shame.

'It's hard to imagine,' he said, turning to the newspaper in his lap, 'that tomorrow it will be raining - unless the paper has got it wrong, of course.'

3.

Lawrence and Marjorie Beck

The early sun shining through the window of their Rose Bay kitchen reminded Lawrence Beck that time was moving on and if he didn't leave the house soon it would take him at least twenty minutes longer than usual to get into town.

'Have you finished yet?' he asked his wife.

He made no attempt to disguise his impatience. Christ, it was like this every morning. Why, after so many years, could she still not make an allowance for him? It wasn't like she was the one who needed to be somewhere else.

No, she sucked on her pen and furrowed her brow over the worn thesaurus, his thesaurus, with one hand cupped over the ever-present pack of cigarettes which would one day kill her.

'All I ask is to be able to see the front page,' he said, measuring his words so there would be no doubt about the extent to which he was being tried. 'Is it too much to ask that I might at least learn what the headlines are before I start the day? Or should I pay for two papers to be delivered: one for me so I can actually read the news, and one for you so you can do the effing crossword.'

'You can have it in a minute,' his wife mumbled, scribbling in the margin of the paper.

If she scribbled in his thesaurus, he thought, that would be it.

'I just need to get this first clue, then ...'

Her voice trailed off as she sucked more deeply on the pen. Clearly what Marjorie Beck wanted was another cigarette, but not while he was in the room.

'What I don't understand is why they have to put the crossword on the back of the news section,' he complained. 'Why can't they put it on the entertainment pages, or the back of the classifieds?'

'Perhaps you could write to them and suggest that. The news is always the same anyway, so I don't know what you're carrying on about.'

He took a deep breath. As usual, he thought, this wasn't the time. Unfortunately there never was a time - a right time - so he tried a different tack.

'What is it, then, that is so much more important than what's happening in the world? What is the clue whose answer stands before my going to work on one of the most important days of the year and, incidentally, earning the money that allows you to spend your mornings doing crosswords? Would you like to tell me?'

'Oh, don't be so...' she began, and then, changing her mind, she read aloud: '*Bury the deeds in mutual engagements.*'

'Is that a proposal you're making, or is that the clue?'

'One across: twelve letters.'

'Well, I suppose deeds is like documents; wills, contracts, agreements.'

'Naturally, you would think that; you're a lawyer. You plan for death. It might also be an act of kindness, as in 'good deeds'. I do this for you and you do this for me. We work together for our mutual good. We are mutually engaged.'

'Right! Can I have the front page now, please?'

She lay down her pen and picked up the cigarette pack, then thought better of it.

'Lawrence, I told you I wanted to get this first clue. It starts my day. You're just annoyed because everything doesn't happen exactly when you want it. It doesn't make any difference if you're five minutes late. It doesn't even make any difference if you're a whole day late. The world doesn't end.'

'What the hell does that mean?'

He could feel his gorge rising.

'Nothing.'

Oh, yes, it did. It meant that she dismissed the importance of what he did. Well, maybe she should try living without the substantial fruits of his labours and see how that felt. How easy it was to demean the responsibilities of others if you didn't have any yourself.

'It means,' she said sweetly, returning to the thesaurus, 'that the world will not end if you're a little bit late because of the Anzac parade, because everyone knows how important your work is and how just one hour of your time is worth a whole month of someone else's. So why don't you learn to ration it out? Make people appreciate it more. That's what I'd do if I was so essential to the success of the business; I'd ration myself out.'

Yes, he thought, ration yourself right out, so that someone else ended up doing the work and covering everyone's butts. A great appreciation for the realities of life that showed.

'Because,' she continued, 'people can end up taking you for granted and not really noticing how hard you work. So then, if you're not careful, you start resenting it and, before you know what's happened, the only thing people notice is your resentment, and not how hard you work. So that's why I'd ration it out a little.'

'By 'people' you mean Roger Saville, presumably? Is that what you're trying to say?'

'People, Lawrence. People!'

This was, he knew, a deliberate provocation.

'The word you're looking for,' he responded coolly, 'is *disagreement*. It has, I think you will find, twelve letters.'

And if she wanted a clue to start her day she couldn't have found one more appropriate, he thought. Without giving her time to write the answer down he reached across and snatched the paper from in front of her, softening the severity of this action by flashing a mock smile of triumph.

'*Disagreement*,' she said, pushing back her chair and picking up her cigarettes, 'is the opposite of *mutual engagements*.'

She opened the kitchen door and lit up while he turned the paper inside out and then made a very thorough show of reading the front page news.

'Besides, it can't be *disagreement*', she said, over her shoulder, 'because the word ends in S and *disagreements* is too long.'

Not for the first time, he wondered how someone who smoked forty cigarettes a day could have avoided death for so long.

4.

Joanne Saville

Returning from dropping off her father and daughter at the ferry, Joanne Saville walked across the sun-lit courtyard from the garage, paused to remove the rosehips from the climbing rose at the kitchen door and took a slow, deep breath before going inside to make a cup of tea.

The house was filled with silence and the silence spoke of emptiness. She watched the kettle boil and listened to the kitchen clock, then took her cup of Earl Grey tea up to her bedroom to shower, as she did every morning at this time. In the bedroom, she placed the tea on her dressing table, sat down on the bed to remove her Nike trainers, then – out of habit - lent across the bed to reach the radio on Roger's side. The assured and reassuring voice of 2GB had momentarily been taken over by a skirl of bagpipes and she quickly turned it off, then stood and removed the casual clothes she'd hurriedly thrown on before the trip to the ferry.

In her dressing table mirror the reflection of her pale skin flashed briefly as she stooped to retrieve her track pants and knickers from the floor, dropping them in the laundry basket on her way through the dressing room to the bathroom vanity. Though she had no need, having removed her make-up before going to bed the night before, she painted her face and neck with a thick, white facial cleanser, working it meticulously into her hairline and around her eyes and mouth, like a player in the commedia dell'arte. Her large hazel eyes stared back at her from the bathroom mirror, expressionless.

In the shower, the expensive French *Lait du matin* dissolved on her upturned face and ran in milky white rivulets down between her breasts and around her toes before swirling down the drain hole. Her pale skin flushed and darkened as she stood motionless, eyes closed, beneath the hot pulsating jets. After ten minutes she shampooed and conditioned her hair. After twenty minutes she stepped out of the shower, wrapped herself in a cotton bath sheet from the towel warmer and returned to the bedroom to retrieve her tea which had now grown cold.

It was 8.30 and this was the time when she always called Prue.

She returned to the dressing room to consider what she would wear. A shaft of morning sunlight had found its way in through the overhead skylight and as she unwrapped the bath sheet and dropped it to the floor, turning to the drawers on her side of the dressing room with the intention of selecting a matching pair of bra and briefs, she unconsciously stepped into it.

Perhaps it was the contrast with the chestnut panelling of the wardrobe doors behind her, but the bright ray of sunlight fell on her blonde body like a spotlight falls on a darkened stage, creating an ineluctable image that leaped out from the bathroom mirror in front of her and caused her to stop.

Magnified and illuminated, her body, with which she had long ago established a mundane and distant relationship, unexpectedly claimed her attention. Well, viewed in such a glaring light and at a remove, distanced by the focal length of the mirror, it was not quite her body anyway. It was that feeling; that the flesh that surrounded her thoughts and emotions, and which she generally ignored, was only distantly related to the image before her, that roused her curiosity and she began by looking at it in a painterly way. There was a bone that ran out along each shoulder from the bottom of her neck which, being top-lit, cast a small shadow that caused her to frown. Above the bone, her shoulders sloped smoothly downwards into her arms. She raised her arms in front of her as if preparing to dive and then wrapped them across her body beneath her breasts. The shadows from the bones disappeared.

Sitting on her forearms, bathed in sunlight, her breasts were larger than she remembered. Was it the light? She unwrapped her arms again, closing her eyes momentarily, knowing her breasts would fall, then leaned forward and placed her hands upon her knees. No, they were not larger they were ... looser. The face reflected back at her from the mirror looked on dispassionately as she straightened, running her eyes from her breasts down across her belly to her pelvis where a shadow line, similar to the one beneath her shoulder, ran out sideways from her pelvic hair on each side till it blended away into the high muscles that shaped her hips. The shadow was formed by a layer of thickening that stretched across her abdomen beneath her navel and was accentuated by the line of Willie's, and then Samantha's, Caesarean scars. So, it *was* her body after all. She breathed in and held her belly firm. The shadow disappeared and she stepped back out of the sunlight and away from the reflection in the mirror to resume her search for suitable underwear.

The last time she'd examined herself was prior to her annual mammary scan. Looking for unwanted lumps had destroyed any lingering illusion that breasts manifested sexual allure. They were glands that required careful dressing and – increasingly – monitoring for health. Besides, Roger had long ago made it clear to her that he liked flat-breasted women. There wasn't much she could do about that. You took what you were born with. And she was happy enough not to have them fondled. She'd find her own lumps, thank you very much.

Finding the underwear she wanted, she slipped her breasts comfortably into their C-cups and tucked them away out of sight. But what if Roger's attitude was different, she suddenly thought. What if he wanted to fondle her breasts and play with her nipples? Would she respond to his desire by feeling arousal too? Why had their sex become so perfunctory when once it had been filled with passion? It wasn't age. At forty eight they were both still within their prime, so where had his desire been redirected? On work alone?

Joanne had long ago demythologised love, she liked to believe, moving closer to the church's version of patience, compromise and commitment; but there were times when she stumbled, despite her prayers for help, tripping over her own distrust. It would be different if he shared the effort to make things better, but he didn't even try. He'd let her down last night without any apparent show of concern or regret, returning home hours late as if it hadn't mattered, knowing full well what it meant to her.

What mattered more?

She tried to resist the thought - told herself it was not in her nature to pursue it - but her own naked body, that she'd observed so dispassionately in the mirror as if it belonged to someone else, had aroused a feeling of apprehension that, despite herself, was heightened by a frisson of sexual jealousy.

Trying not to think, she turned away from the clothes racks on her side of the dressing room and slid back the doors on Roger's wardrobe. He'd worn the charcoal grey Hugo Boss suit the day before, the double-breasted one, and it hung now on the end of the rack. Half-pretending to herself that what she was doing was what she always did before taking his clothes to be dry-cleaned, she methodically turned out his pockets.

They were empty. She held the suit briefly to her nose and then returned it to its rack. His suit, like everything else in his cupboards, smelled faintly of the dried rosemary she'd collected from the garden and tied up in muslin sachets; just as her clothes smelled faintly of lavender harvested in the same way. But she couldn't stop there.

The woman in the bathroom mirror continued to watch her but she avoided her gaze as she lifted the lid on the cane laundry basket and reached inside for Roger's shirt. Her heart was racing and her breath was short as she held it up in the bright sunlight that now filled the entire dressing room, turning it round to examine the collar and then holding it firmly against her face for a long, lonely moment filled only with the silence of the empty house.

Nothing.

Her breathing was still short and anxious as she put on a housecoat and returned to the bedroom to telephone her friend Prue.

5.

Willie Saville

Floating in that semi-conscious space where dreams can be observed, Willie Saville watched in amazement as the flaming torches which he'd tossed into the night air tumbled over and over like slowly spinning Catherine wheels, lighting his upturned face so clearly that he could see his own mouth opened in awe.

Where was he? Somewhere on Oxford Street; high iron railings at his back, a broad pavement for his stage; traffic, lights, horns: it seemed familiar. Then, in the dream, he must have reached down between his legs and picked up the clear glass bottle of kerosene that was standing there and taken a flamboyant swig from it for, as he opened his mouth to breathe, the flaming torches reached out like electric eels, flicked out their tongues and plunged them down his throat.

He gasped in horror, giving the kerosene that he'd swallowed in the dream the oxygen it needed to burn. And he burned all the way down to his lungs.

He could see the faces of the street crowd as they hovered above him, illuminated by the blue flicker of flames, their eyes gleaming with excitement. They seemed to be whispering. What the fuck were they saying? He needed breath to silence them. He needed light to drive them back. He needed to be able to stand up. This was no fucking way to die.

Surprisingly there was no problem with his limbs, other than an inability to move them. They lay like mounds of jelly flopped on the ground and what he needed, he felt, was a calm examination of the options available for solving the mechanical problem of how to pick them up. Like some pathetic fucking Scots' College Initiative Course for the Duke of fucking Edinburgh Award, or something.

This was a start. Behind their charred lids his eyes began to search about, probing the dark, looking for anything useful, and in their search beginning to find light. At first orange, the colour of flame, then white, a pale grey-white like watery milk stains on a pane of glass. And, as it does, light elbowed aside the fangs of darkness and the howls of night surrendered to the sounds of morning.

Somewhere nearby a radio was playing. In the street outside, a passing car sounded its horn. He couldn't remember what he'd taken; only that Luke had thrust them on him late in the evening. He hadn't even asked what they were, but he did recall the water he'd poured in, too late, and the feeling that his stomach and intestines wouldn't be able to hold enough of it and that he'd burst like a worn out fire hose. Which he had; for his thighs were cold and it was a damp cold so he knew without looking that his bladder had drained of its own volition, not having had his conscious presence to control it. Or had he deliberately watered the ground around him? Did he lie there under the golden shower of his own urination as the result of some orgiastic sacrifice of self and dignity, now clouded by the fog of exhaustion and dead brain cells?

Whatever.

He was going to have to get up. The fire was still smouldering in his throat and chest and he needed to damp it down while there was still a chance that the fragile tissues lining his oesophagus were intact and might be prised apart to allow the intermission of air. Aware now of his nakedness, and feeling vulnerable, he channelled his focus into his right thigh, heaving it across his left leg so it lay heavy but protective over his crotch. Eyes still shut (he wasn't yet ready for extra confrontations) he threw his right shoulder in a similar direction to his leg until he was as close as could be to the position where, with one massive shove, he might end up kneeling.

Now his head began to throb but it was like the head bang that disguises another pain and through its pounding he was able to swing his buttocks into the air and gain his knees. Yes, he'd live. This was good. He could rock like a baby in the arms of the Lord. He could hum gently in self-contemplation, a void waiting to be filled with Tantric light, ready to accept that which is yet unknown.

The radio, he realised, was set to 2GB, the same radio station that emanated from his parent's bedroom each morning. He couldn't hear the words but he could hear the tone. Shit! Now he had no choice but to open his eyes.

6.

The Rose Bay Kitchen

'Who said it ends in *S*?'

'Seven down: *shellfish*.'

Lawrence reluctantly interrupted his reading of the lead story and turned the paper back to the crossword again. If she already knew it finished in *S*, she shouldn't have wasted his time.

''*The lady will drop a line to an aquatic animal*'. So what's the nine letter word beginning with *S*? *Shellfish*? Isn't that a little bit obvious for an aquatic animal? Why couldn't it be something like *trevally* or *terakihi*: something beginning with *T*?'

'She will fish ... She'll fish ... *Shellfish*. It's obvious.'

'You don't drop a line to catch shellfish. You drop a line to catch finned fish. You drop a line to a friend thanking him for a whale of a good time. If you were a writer of crosswords wanting to be tricky you wouldn't be so obvious as to use the word fish; you'd pick an aquatic animal that wasn't a fish. The whale is a mammal; perhaps there's a whale with a name like Moby Dick that a lady might drop a line to.'

He turned the front page and folded it back, beating it into place for emphasis. Now that he had possession of the paper he had a duty to read it, irrespective of how much the individual stories might engage his interest. To his mind it was a duty of care.

'Perhaps,' she conceded from the doorway, 'it *is* a little obvious, but sometimes they put simple ones in and sometimes the ones you think are incredibly hard turn out to be very obvious when you read the answer the following day.'

She stubbed out her cigarette butt in the kitchen sink (how he hated that) and came and leaned over his shoulder, reaching for the pen that lay on the table.

'Caught up with the news?' she asked, knowing damn well he hadn't had time to read it. Her breath made him sway away from her, giving her the space to reclaim the paper.

'The petrol companies have been colluding on prices,' he said primly.

'That isn't news.'

'It's news if they can prove it.'

'They won't.'

'Well, if that's the case, I'd better phone and tell them not to waste their time. Madam has spoken. No matter what the Competition and Consumer Commission may think, there will be no action on price fixing. And just for good measure, I'll phone The Herald as well and let them know that you do not consider this story constitutes news. Perhaps they should move the crossword to the front page where it would be easier to find for those who don't need to go to work and who aren't interested in what's going on in the world. I'll get onto it as soon as I reach the office.'

'Don't be silly.'

He pushed his chair back and left the room to clean his teeth of the acid which he suddenly felt rising up his oesophagus into his mouth. He wasn't being silly. Silly was not a word that could ever describe him, but he didn't trust himself to reply so he made noises instead, grabbing his jacket and briefcase from the chair in the hall with such a righteous force that the chair clattered across the parquet floor into the glass-panelled front door. Momentarily chastened, he paused at the internal garage door to call goodbye despite knowing he couldn't be heard.

The same sunlight that had filled his kitchen also bathed the 18th green and clubhouse of the Royal Sydney Golf Club as he passed, rolling slowly down Kent Road in his BMW, snugly nestled within the familiar cocoon of leather and burr walnut that fitted him so well, adjusting the bass for the Rondo movement of Beethoven's

Pastorale on the audio system as he did every morning, before turning onto New South Head Road. He had no trouble moving to the outside lane as he passed the Rose Bay Marina but he was not fooled by the light traffic; it was a school holiday after all, so the usual convoy of Pajeros and Jeeps, delivering sons and daughters to Cranbrook and Ascham, was bound to be missing. But sure enough, once through Edgecliff and past the schools, the traffic was backed up from the Kings Cross tunnel and barely moving at all so he knew he was in for a slow run to town.

The Rondo movement finished and the first movement of the Pathetique began. He sighed audibly. He'd known this would happen. In the rear-view mirror he exchanged a glance of acknowledgement with himself, lips compressed in resignation. For a brief moment he tapped his fingers on the leather steering wheel and considered his options for evasive action. Filter left and avoid the tunnel? No, that could be even worse. Take his punishment then. Relax and enjoy the music. Know better next time. But the bitter flavour of resentment overpowered the bland taste of acceptance.

The first movement soon finished. Another seven minutes and sixteen seconds had passed. He wished there was someone he could tell, but who was there who could be made aware of his sense of helplessness? Marjorie? He took a deep breath. He could hear his own words falling in a clatter on the kitchen table while she continued to frown at the crossword.

Then the second movement, Adagio Cantabile, finished with the tunnel traffic still not moving. He pressed the stored numbers button on the dashboard keypad of his car phone and counted the ringing tones that would be echoing through his house, wondering if his wife was now in the shower. When she answered on the seventh ring he wanted her to know that all was not well with him.

'The traffic is bloody diabolical,' he complained. 'Just as I knew it would be.'

'Oh, poor darling!'

Silence.

What else did he want to say?

'I think you're becoming obsessive about this crossword thing. Isn't there something else you could turn your mind to?'

'Did you have something you wanted to suggest?'

'It's just that ...'

No, he didn't.

'The answer to one across was *interactions*,' she cut in; 'a deed being an action and mutual engagements being ... well ... *interactions*.'

'I prefer *disagreement*.'

'Yes, but it doesn't fit.'

'Because of *shellfish*. By the way, you won't forget the RSL dinner this evening, will you?'

For no discernible reason, the traffic suddenly started to move through the tunnel and he turned the phone off as the cell dropped out. By the time he emerged from the tunnel ten minutes later his mind was well and truly on other matters and he didn't bother phoning back. She had all day to finish her crossword, while he had more important things that needed to be done. Besides, in his heart of hearts, he knew how the conversation would go.

7.

The Offices of Saville Corp

Roger Saville looked down from his corner office high in the Colonial Centre at the orderly throngs filing into Martin Place from Macquarrie Street. With the benefit of his bird's eye view he could see patterns in the movement of the crowds below, both civilian and military, as if they were being directed by an invisible hand, drifting into loose formations, already instinctively dropping into step even though there was still an hour to go before the march began. There would be nine thousand people lined up in George Street soon, maybe more, old soldiers and young, and among them somewhere his fourteen year-old daughter and her grandfather.

Impatient with that thought, he turned away from the window and returned to his desk.

Bloody Anzac Day! When were they going to wake up to the fact that it was a political con? Still, if it suited the politicians to keep it going he was happy to play along. Whatever they wanted, as long as he got what he wanted in return. He'd dressed the part and he was ready. But, by Christ, nothing had better go wrong. He'd already made one mistake, leaving his briefcase behind last night - that was recoverable – but he didn't want any more. The day was too important.

Unable to sit still, he stretched and checked his reflection in the mirror that backed the credenza which lined the wall opposite his desk. Being a tall man he had to bend slightly to see himself. Perhaps it was his mood, but today he found his nose a little too long and thin, his forehead too high and tilted. He pulled back his mouth to expose his teeth. It took some effort because he wasn't in a mood for smiling.

Despite the sound-proof double-glazing of his office, he could hear the familiar roll of marching drum beats and the high-strung reel of distant bagpipes. It was designed to be stirring stuff and even from his height he could tell it must be lifting the feet of the old soldiers forming up into platoons down below ready for the parade. It was a sound that could destroy all reason and lead men to their deaths. He hoped his daughter understood that.

Meanwhile, where the hell was Lawrence? He'd told him they'd meet first thing. Didn't he realise the importance of what had to be done? How was Roger meant to operate if the Company Secretary was showing all the signs of menopause? Should he force him to stand down on medical grounds? He was serious; some of the things Lawrence had been saying lately, particularly in front of the Board, suggested he had completely lost his way. He was becoming a danger to the company.

Saville took a deep breath and shook his head at his own reflection in the mirror. It was the same damn story over and over.

So, the year-end result had undershot their forecasts. What had they expected? It was nothing more than timing. If developers could guarantee the sales and leasing markets then everyone would be in the same game. He shouldn't have needed to explain that, not to the Board and certainly not to Lawrence. And so, the share price had fallen. Of course it had; because investment managers, who hadn't the nerve or energy to be developers themselves, hadn't the brains to realize that timing sometimes defied prediction.

The mistake Lawrence made was in listening to these idiots and then coming out with nonsense about tight ships and corporate restraints like he was some sort of corsetiere. What the investment market wanted was for him, Roger Saville, to pull off another deal so they could all pat themselves on the back for having invested in Saville Corp in the first place -- and that was precisely what he was going to do. And if it took a $10,000 dropkick for a charity dinner table because the most influential member of the State Government had suggested it, then that would be *his* call.

Fuck the investment analysts and fuck the media. Any more of this crap from Lawrence and Saville swore he would take down that Jeffrey Smart painting from Lawrence's office wall and smash it over his head; the Jeffrey Smart for which Saville had bid $200,000 at the Premier's Fund Raising Dinner before turning to Lawrence in front of the whole room and presenting it to him as a personal token of appreciation for all that he had done for Saville Corp, a gesture which not only Lawrence, but everyone in the room it seems, got wrong. So now, whenever his own wife - or some other ill-informed dinner guest from that night - popped in to admire 'Lawrence's Jeffrey Smart', Saville had to bite his tongue and refrain from explaining to them that the motivation for the purchase was to demonstrate to Sydney society, and the Labour Party inner sanctum in particular, just how fucking civilised and successful Roger Saville was.

Because, dear Lawrence, success did not reside in your sanctimonious fixation on detail, no matter how you tried to pretend. Detail could be bought, but fortune, as every fool should know, only favoured the truly brave.

So here it was, gone 8.15 already, and who was it that was on duty, thinking ahead, planning the defences of the company while the rest of Australia took the day off to get drunk? And if *he* could get here in time, why the hell couldn't Lawrence Beck?

His mood growing darker with every second, Roger abandoned the examination of his image in the mirror, picked up his desk phone and dialled one of his stored numbers.

'Where are you?' he demanded. 'Yes, I did ... Well, of course they are, it's bloody Anzac Day ... If I could get here on time from Mosman, you should have been able to make it from Rose Bay for Christ sake ... Are you through the King's Cross tunnel yet? ... Then dump it. Get out, lock the door and walk away ... Of course I'm serious; we've got work to do here ... I'm not going to talk about it over the phone but you should know by now that if I say it's important then it's fucking well important ... This is make-or-break time in case you hadn't realized it ... I'm worried, and if I'm worried I want you to be worried, too ... So, welcome to the chocolate factory, Charlie.'

With that, he switched off the phone and, whistling softly to the tune of 'Amazing Grace', went off to the boardroom kitchen in search of coffee.

8.

The House in Mosman

It didn't happen when she said her prayers. She said her prayers beneath her breath. It happened when she opened her mouth to speak and found her lungs so full that she was breathless and she couldn't get the words out fast enough to make room for fresh air. It was as though she'd been running.

It was happening to her now.

'There are days when I hate this house,' she said brightly.

She had to say it like that because otherwise she might sound sorry for herself, which she wasn't. For heaven's sake, how could she be?

So why had she said it at all?

The sun streamed in through her bedroom window as it did on most days in this gorgeous, lucky city and she put down her nailfile and looked at the speaker-phone on her dressing table, as she did so often at this time in the morning, with an expression that said, 'Well?', but which of course Prue wouldn't have been able to see on the other end of the line.

'Well?' she asked finally, because clearly Prue hadn't heard.

'Oh, sorry, Darl, I missed that - busy looking for the ferry. We've got friends over for the day and I like to wait until I can see the ferry coming in before I drive down to pick them up. What were you saying?'

'Oh, it was nothing ...'

Because it didn't bear repeating.

'I'd forgotten you could see the ferry,' she lied. 'That must be awfully handy. We face north, of course.'

'Hmm, you get the sun, lucky thing.'

'Samantha went off on the ferry this morning,' she hurried on, 'to the Anzac parade. She went with her grandfather ...'

'Oh, how lovely for her. Did Willie go, too?'

'... Though we have to be careful now; she's not our Samantha anymore, she's *Sam*, apparently. We're all having trouble getting used to it. When I think of that little thing I used to drop off at kindy, so bouncy and feminine, and the way we used to envy her natural curls which she wouldn't let us cut off, and now she's Sam, and all the curls have gone of course, and there's no way in the world she'll let me drop her at school, or even be seen with her in the street. It's little Miss Independent now, and public transport everywhere, even on weekend sports days ...'

'That's because of the boys, of course.'

'... So I suppose we should allow her to pick her own identity if she needs to.'

'Of course, didn't *we*?'

Yes. But it wasn't that. It was how quickly it had all happened. That's why, as she looked out beyond her dressing table mirror, beyond the garden and the pool with the Phoenix palms framing the sparkling blue waters of Middle Harbour, up the coast past Narrabeen and Newport, and Palm Beach and beyond, glistening and shimmering in the distance, the view which, when she'd first seen it, had convinced her that this was it, this was home, that's why ...

'I know,' she laughed, 'I'm being silly. So who are your visitors?'

'Kiwi cousins. Everyone's got Kiwi cousins - they're all coming to Sydney. These ones are white, *not* unemployed, and quite nice actually. They're looking to buy on the North Shore so we've offered to drive them around. It *is* Anzac Day, after all.'

Jo smiled. How very Prue. Then, remembering something she'd read, she got up to retrieve part of the morning paper from her bed.

'I don't know how anyone can afford a house these days,' she shouted over her shoulder to the speaker-phone.

The item she wanted was in the Domain section, the one part of the paper she always enjoyed. Where was it now?

'Listen to this. *Northern exposure*, it says. This is about Balgowlah. *Price range: From about $550,000* (and that would be a two bedroom shack!) *to more than $4 million*. We're talking Balgowlah here, right? Remember that girl, Julie Cleary, who used to live in Woodland Street and their toilet wasn't connected up to the main sewer so they had to use the long drop in the garden shed and you said bugger that and ...'

'Don't say it!'

'... We all felt so sorry for her? Well, there are two houses for sale here in Woodland Street and they say, *These are expected to sell for more than $900,000*. By which they mean, *more than $1 million*, you can be sure. And that's the other side of the Spit Bridge and absolutely nothing special to look at you can be certain of that. I mean, how on earth do people do it?'

The thing is, it did genuinely amaze her. Wasn't one million dollars an awful lot of money; let alone the three, four and five million that people were prepared to pay in her street?

'Well, the thing is, they do,' said practical Prue. 'You're in or you're out. You do or you don't. And if you don't put your foot on the rung of the ladder at some stage then you'll never be able to afford it, 'cause it's not going to go down. So there.'

No. Everyone was saying that. And how must it be for the young? Would they ever be able to afford to buy a decent home, or would they just give up? What about someone like Samantha when she was ready to get married and they wanted to buy a place and start a family? What a daunting prospect it was. While all Roger would say on the subject was, 'It doesn't matter whether a house is worth one million or ten million, because at some point either the price is wrong or the dollar isn't worth what people think it is.' Or something like that. Very comforting! And what about someone like Willie, who one day would have to become a breadwinner? What did he think about a lifetime which could, if one was absolutely honest, be described as nothing more than servicing a mortgage? If only he would talk about the way he saw his life. If only he would just call her and tell her where he was.

'Anyway, you've got nothing to worry about,' Prue added chirpily, 'you're sitting on a fortune there.'

'Hmm.'

It wasn't something she liked to talk about. Though Roger had told her the house was now worth six and a half million, she wasn't going to admit that to people because, quite frankly, she didn't think that would be in good taste. Or maybe it was because she felt it would invite disaster, talking about that sort of money when so many people had so little. As if that would be like inviting someone to burst in and take it; a violent and envious thief who would casually shoot her or her children on the way out. Which was a silly way to think, she knew, for God would not deliberately punish property inflation in that way, but she couldn't help her feelings. And that's why she'd been so reluctant to listen to Roger last night when he was telling her that he'd re-valued the house and was putting it in her name only, because that made better sense what with the business being a public company and everything.

She could never admit it to him, but she had a dreadful premonition about having too much money and she couldn't put it out of her mind. It made her, quite literally, breathless.

9.

The Domain Carpark

What annoyed Lawrence Beck was the utter predictability of all this. He'd known that being fifteen minutes late in departing for town would result in a thirty minute delay in completing the journey. Hadn't he said so? And sure enough, here he was, having to abandon his car in the Domain Car Park, miles from the office, when he had an abiding distrust of underground public garages. To make matters worse, he now had a stiff fifteen-minute walk in front of him, for he'd parked at the wrong end of the car park, not being familiar with it and it being so bereft of sign-posting. Couldn't they at least get that right? How much did sign-posting cost?

Once again, knowing was not enough. When was he going to take control of his life and listen to himself for a change?

There was a simple lesson in this: break a habit and it will surely find a way of undoing you. That was the lesson. He had sat longer over breakfast despite the nagging belief that he would regret it, and yet, he had done so from worthy motives; because it was a public holiday; because it seemed appropriate to linger a while with his wife on a day not normally assigned to work. (Though strictly speaking it was not a day *un*assigned to work, quite the contrary. But perhaps that was being too literal.)

However, none of that justified being spoken to by Roger Saville as if he were some sort of layabout who couldn't be bothered getting up in the morning; as if all the years of being first into work had somehow been credited to someone else. He didn't need to be told that it was his own fault; particularly by Roger, of all people. Maybe he should adopt the Saville approach to punctuality for awhile. 'Do unto others as they do' etc. Forget appointments. Ignore undertakings. Break his word at will. No, that was being petulant.

He couldn't compromise his own behaviour in order to highlight the shortcomings in another. Besides, for Roger, that would be far too subtle. No, the time had finally come for some plain speaking; to point out the vast difference in standards, of performance and consideration for others, which existed between Roger and himself and which was, if anything, only highlighted by this single exception arising from Lawrence's rare miscalculation about the density of traffic on this particular morning. Yes, it was time to speak out.

Thus resolved, Lawrence Beck set out across the concrete wasteland of the Domain Car Park in search of an exit. Behind him, his BMW, acting on his key ring's microwaved signal, immobilised its engine, emitting a plaintive beep like a pet dog whimpering after its master.

The trick now was to hold on to this resolve, to keep the fire of resentment burning in his breast while still maintaining a cool head, for nothing undid the justice of one's complaint like the single intemperate word that could leap like a spark from a fanned fire unless one was fully in control. His stride lengthened and then, because he was not a tall man, his footsteps quickened as if, independent of this mood of righteousness, they were anxious that he should not be any later. The irony was not lost on him, that he was hastening to meet a man who was, himself, never on time. Perhaps that was the cause of his resentment now. The fact was that he was thrown. Not for one moment had he imagined that Roger would make it to the office before him. On today, of all days, there must have been any number of excuses for him to have failed to show.

So, in this way, little by little, Lawrence Beck began to surrender self-righteousness in favour of self-recrimination. Perhaps, after all, it really was his fault. He'd miscalculated. It had nothing to do with the obligation he'd felt to linger with his wife over breakfast on a public holiday; he'd simply lacked faith in Saville's resolve to work on a public holiday and had taken his time accordingly.

As he made his way out of the underground car park via the steps next to St Mary's Cathedral, and crossed the road towards Macquarrie Street, he wondered what it could be that was so urgent that it needed him to be there without delay. Now his pace was driven by an urge to get there. Clearly he was needed. Despite their fundamental differences in temperament and philosophy, Saville must have known that he couldn't - shouldn't - act without reference to Lawrence. For – even though it was seldom acknowledged - that was the strength of their relationship; that was the factor that added surety to the management decisions affecting Saville Corp: the very reason, ten years prior, that Saville had lured Lawrence away from Mapleton and Thorpe in the first place.

As he crossed over Phillip Street, a little sweaty from the exertion, he began to feel better. Passing the chambers of Mapleton and Thorpe, he reflected on the risk he had knowingly undertaken when Saville had persuaded him to give up 'the desiccated life of professional practice for the real business of making money'. Was it really only ten years ago? It seemed a lifetime.

10.

A House in Newtown

Kneeling stark naked on the floor, Willie's eyes fell first on a thin grey carpet, once laid out and tacked down but now peeling away from the edges in rolls, like slack skin on an old person's corpse, and along the ridges of the rolls were drips and drops and stains of God knows what. Apart from the carpet there was little else in the room; two wooden beer crates turned upside down as a table for a mini stereo, and CD cases scattered against the wall. Bean bags; two purple and one brown, arranged in a way that suggested they may, at some stage, have been his bed. An orange lava lamp oozed light like a lazy squid drifting in the currents. (Was that the light he had seen?) And on the wall directly in front of him, a full scale anatomical chart of a woman, stripped of her skin and sub-cutaneous tissue, like a skinned hare waiting to be jugged, with her head turned away as if in shame at the wanton exposure of her internal organs. To make matters worse, someone had drawn upon her. With a black felt marker they'd given her a penis and balls, pubic hair and a furry chest.

Willie slowly got to his feet, his heart beating erratically. The room was not big, two more bean bags and it would have been full, and the absence of daylight was not a factor of the hour but of the architecture. At one end of the room a dim passage with two rooms off it led to a frosted glass door backed by wire mesh. The glass was partially broken and through it Willie could see a shard of sunlight in the street beyond. The other end of the room opened to what he presumed, or hoped, would be a kitchen.

Of course, if Willie had no prior memory of any of this he could have been excused for an overwhelming feeling of anxiety; cause disconnected from consequence; time's continuum fractured, perhaps never to be rejoined. But he was not totally without memory; he was merely sheltering himself from too much sensation. He needed water and then he needed sleep.

There was no sign of his clothes, but at his feet was a crumpled blanket which, from its touch, had seemingly absorbed the bulk of his night's urine. He took it with him and tiptoed across the creaky floor to the kitchen, avoiding the spilled wine glasses and saucers filled with cigarette butts, not entirely sure of his nakedness.

All this because he hadn't wanted to be chicken, he thought. And why hadn't he? Could he answer that, Willie the man boy, standing over the chipped concrete tub in the kitchen that was barely big enough for him, cupping his hand under the cold water tap, bending to suck the water in, bare arse bumping on the painted wooden cupboard that held the cups that he hadn't the patience or care to take down because his need was too urgent?

'Pretty Boy wants to play in the ugly end of town,' Luke had crooned as he left the room the night before. 'Pretty Boy wants to show how bad he can be. So take your pills Pretty Boy.'

Sucking at the water like a greedy lion cub slurping on blood, he began to feel his heart slow down, felt recovery begin to flush through his young body until, finally relaxing, he could lean his weight on his hands and ease the air from his lungs in a long, slow sigh.

'Oh, Lordy, Lordy, Lordy, man,' he whispered softly to himself, 'let me live.'

11.

The Mosman Ferry

It wasn't quite what Samantha had expected. All around them there were men wearing medals. All except her grandfather who, despite his polished shoes and old-fashioned suit, showed no outward sign of being a participant in the event at all. She wished now that she'd ignored school instructions and not worn her uniform. If he didn't want to look like he was part of it, then neither should she.

Albert sensed this disappointment but felt powerless to respond. She'd been fishing for stories, hungering for words that would validate him and he couldn't find them within himself. He guessed she wanted what they all wanted; a mythical man, glorious in victory, tragic in defeat. That's what time and misinformation had done. Every year the sanctification of the Aussie digger grew more absurd. What he might have said, if pressed, was that they'd been digging bloody latrines, for heaven sake. They'd been digging graves for young men who, it turned out, would rather have copped a bullet than die of dysentery; young men who, if they'd still been at home in Ballarat, would have been happy to throw themselves down a dirt road on a motor bike at a hundred miles per hour without a crash helmet on, because they lacked a sense of mortality. How could he possibly explain that?

And how could he ever explain about Jim Percy, the shadow of shame and regret that had followed him all his adult life: the one reason he'd finally agreed to come to an Anzac ceremony?

Was now the time to try and explain, or would he cock it up and regret it even further?

As their ferry came up the harbour towards the Bridge and Sydney Cove he could see Goat Island in the distance.

'There,' he said, pointing and desperate to give her something – anything. 'That's Goat Island. I remember loading ammunition there, back in 1942. It was back-breaking work that was. We felt just like the convicts who'd built the place a hundred years before us. There was no sun block to protect us in those days, no 'slip-slop' commercials to remind us of the dangers of ultra violet rays. I'll never forget that place.'

Six months later, lugging munitions ashore at Salamaua he'd been thankful for the muscle tone earned at Goat Island, but the sun tan hadn't helped much as by then his neck was raw and peeling and his back was soon to become infested with maggots.

'Did you feel like heroes then?' Samantha asked ludicrously.

'Oh, yes, absolutely!'

God, why must there be heroes? Jim Percy was a hero, but he couldn't talk about him without also explaining the many forms of cowardice that existed. Neither of them were equipped for that sort of conversation so, instead, he smiled and looked around as if to be sure they were not being overheard.

'And none of us ever believed we'd die,' he whispered.

As their ferry started to turn in a slow arc towards Bennelong Point, heading in towards Sydney Cove, the harbour water slapping against their sides in the cross-currents created by the early morning traffic queuing up to get into Circular Quay, Albert had a sudden recollection of another sea; but in contrast to the bright light and rushing waters of the busy harbour, his memory was of total darkness and the smell of tension mixed with ozone on the tropical night air. Looking over the ship's side into the waters of the Huon Gulf where some of his platoon had nervously peed as they waited to board their landing craft, he had seen tracers of phosphorescence, bright as arc lights, being pursued by small excited fish.

But now they were there and Samantha was already on her feet. The harbour waters, beaten into a white foam by the full thrust of the reversing propellers, surged against the jetty piles and bounced back angrily at the ferry, sending Albert, who believed himself to have been balanced nicely while eschewing the help of a handrail, tumbling forward into the man in front of him, quite out of control.

In that instant it was difficult to tell who was the more angry; the thirty-something victim whose heel suddenly hurt and whose shoe had come off, or the seventy eight year-old who prided himself on his balance and alertness and who, in one moment of distraction had failed to anticipate the proximity of the wharf and its likely effects, so was now being steadied by a rush of hands from concerned strangers when really he didn't need them.

'Alright, mate?' the victim graciously enquired, his anger immediately abated on checking Albert's age.

This was a day when age would be deferred to nationwide.

'Grandpa?'

He nodded and mumbled. It could have happened to anyone. Shaking his arms free of support, and with his jaw firmly set, he concentrated on holding his ground while the berthing lines were hauled tight and the bucking ferry was brought under control.

'Should stay seated,' he said to Sam over his shoulder by way of explanation.

The same on aeroplanes and buses, he thought: everyone wants to stand up and be the first off. Won't get there any quicker, so why do we do it? We do it because everyone else does it. Just another example of how stupid we are.

His step was measured as they moved forward across the gangplank and up the ramp to the Circular Quay concourse. For him, coming from the country and being unused to the pace and direction of crowds, he needed to move slowly, checking himself mid-stride as he miscalculated the speed and course of those who crossed his path. For Samantha, the city girl, this was not a crowd at all and she raced on ahead, seemingly in anticipation, so that he quickly lost sight of her and began to worry that they might be separated, which he would have to explain to her mother. When she appeared again, therefore, out of the doorway of one of the concourse shops, he was too relieved to be irritable with her. She was tearing at a packet of peppermints, the object of her anticipation apparently, and extending it to him as an offering, as if it were just the thing to help get over a stumble, and beaming in encouragement.

'Go on,' she urged, 'take one.'

'Where do you get the money?' he asked, but she didn't understand the question, so he took one of the proffered sweets and popped it into his mouth, an act so foreign to him in public that he immediately felt like they were on a day outing, to a country fair perhaps, or a football match, rather than a veterans' march in honour of the dead.

'I think we'd better stick together,' he suggested.

Rolling the peppermint around in his mouth, its sweet astringency coating his palette and his gums, enlivening them like strong toothpaste in the early morning after a night spent sleeping in the bush, he wondered why he never thought to buy them himself.

They emerged from the concourse onto the Albert Street pavement where he allowed her to take his arm as they crossed the road to the Customs House. Here they paused to get their bearings and consult the newspaper about the proposed route for the march. Traffic had been stopped and people walked openly in the street. It was not unlike a football match, he supposed, there being a general direction to the flow, and a common purpose being followed. He wasn't a member of an RSL and had no designated rendezvous in mind, nor did the paper give any indication of where and how those who were marching should gather, but it seemed quite reasonable to join the flow and be led by events. In any case, Sam seemed to know the way. Guided by a familiarity whose origins lay in day trip shopping, the teenager led him confidently in the direction of George Street, dismissing the activity in the side streets in favour of the main event.

In Pitt Street, and further south in Bridge Street, there were uniformed platoons of khaki, blue and white lined up, and bands playing, and behind regimental placards, men of his age and older, their reefer jackets and suit coats tightly buttoned, were already forming rows shoulder to shoulder. Medals and ribbons sparkled like jewels: red, blue, green and gold.

'What's your regiment, Grandpa?'

'Oh, there's no point in bothering with that. They'll all be dead.'

12.

The House at Mosman

'What do you think of Glenn Murcutt?' Joanne asked, suddenly changing the subject.

'Glenn who?'

'Murcutt. There's an article about him in this morning's paper. You either like his work or you don't. He's the one that received the Pritzker Prize. He uses a lot of corrugated iron and is something of a national treasure. I think I quite like his work.'

'Do you mean those big cut-out elephants and giraffes and things that they set up in paddocks? I've always wondered what they'd be like once they started to rust.'

'No, no, this is architecture, Prue; tin-shed architecture, and very, very prestigious. Have a look in The Herald. Those sculptures you're thinking about are by Jeff Thompson - a Kiwi.'

'Ah! Silly me! So why the interest in tin sheds?'

'There's just something so beautifully simple about them, so unpretentious and down-to-earth, like a house should be, and yet filled with beautiful light and space and such a wonderful appreciation of the bare essentials of living, pared back to only those things that really matter. His houses are like those Japanese poems, you know the ones, which express one perfect idea in five sparse lines.'

'Their poetry sounds like their food.'

That's what she wanted: simplicity.

'You're too much, Jo,' her old school friend continued cheerfully. 'Only *you* would know about Japanese poetry that has to be told in five lines. I bet you can quote some, too. So, why the interest in this architect?'

'I don't know. I was thinking how nice it would be to build a pure and simple house by the sea; at Palm Beach, maybe, or somewhere even further.'

'A beach house ...?'

'... Or a house by the beach.'

They weren't the same thing at all.

'I can't keep up with you lot. Here we are battling away to pay the school fees and you're off to Palm Beach with the nation's treasure to build a tin shed. At enormous cost, I presume. Saville Corp must be doing well.'

Good old Prue, always down to earth and willing to instil a dose of reality. But where had this idea come from all of a sudden?

She picked up her silver hairbrush, tilted her head to one side, and began to methodically brush her hair, counting softly under her breath in what now was a daily ritual that she'd maintained for over twenty years, since the day her mother had died and Jo, grieving heavily, had determined that of all the few but treasured possessions Gwen Strange had left behind, the Victorian dressing table set would be the one thing she would keep with her every day of her own remaining life. One hundred strokes a day; how many did that make? Three hundred and sixty five times for twenty something years; it must be at least a million, not counting all the years when her mother had done it for her. And now she did it for Samantha; not every day, but on those days when her daughter didn't quite have the courage to admit her own doubts out loud and instead would arrive in the kitchen with the hairbrush and demand of her mother, 'Brush me.' So one day her daughter would inherit the dressing table set, too.

'Prue,' she asked, 'do you think sometimes it would be better to lead a simpler life?'

'Is that the big question for the day? How much simpler could it be? I get up and cook breakfast that no-one eats. I swear at the children because they're going to be late for school. They swear at me because it's my fault. I give the leftover breakfast to the dog, make a cup of coffee and phone you to complain about it. Then I go out and restock the fridge for tomorrow's breakfast. This life is so simple that no-one even notices I'm living it. You, meanwhile, sit on the Board of the art gallery buying million dollar paintings, have a husband who builds towns and cities and can probably afford to buy Thailand, and now you are about to build a house at Palm Beach. Why would you want simple?'

'I mean ...'

She paused. Was that thirty strokes, or only twenty?

'... *Prue*, your life's better than that. Your children adore you. Tom adores you. You all do things together, on the weekends and during the holidays. You go camping and running. You have a wonderful life. Don't make it sound like that. I count on you.'

There was a pause of ten strokes before Prue answered.

'Alright, what's the real question?'

There was a small plane flying up the coast, just out to sea from Long Reef, glistening silver in the early morning sun, scuttling along like a happy dog on a beach, relishing the freedom and the fresh, bright air over the South Pacific.

'I had my father here last night.' Breathless again, she put down the brush and paused. 'He came to stay so they could make an early start for this morning's parade. It's just so difficult. He's growing old now and it's up to me to make the effort, but I can't help myself. I just can't let go of it, and I should, if only for the children's sake. As soon as we're together I feel myself being wound up tighter and tighter, like a guitar string, until I'm stretched to the point where I fear I'll break. But it's not anything he does, it's me that's doing the winding, and I can't stop myself. It isn't what he says or even what he doesn't say. At times I feel he's looking at me wanting me to know that there are a thousand things he has to say, explanations he wants to give, but he's waiting for me to give him permission. And I can't.'

'You have to, Jo. You'll regret it if you don't because he isn't getting any younger and what's past is past. Grandparents are very important to young people and if you're not careful you'll be taking Sam and Willie to your father's funeral with them knowing you were never reconciled. Whatever the rights and wrongs, Darl, it just isn't worth holding on to.'

'But I can't. Not after the way he deserted my mother.'

'And deserted you?'

'And he's never ever offered an explanation.'

'He probably doesn't know how. At least he's here now. Give him the benefit of the doubt.'

So she took up her hairbrush and started brushing again, rubbing with her left hand that spot below her breasts and rib cage where the small pocket of air that sustained her life struggled to be absorbed..

Then, almost to Jo's relief, her friend had to go. The ferry was turning into Mosman Bay and she needed to be off to pick up her Kiwi cousins. So they promised as usual to talk again later, though that was unlikely as Jo had forgotten to tell her that she would be going to the charity dinner, and knowing how those men could talk, it would probably end late.

She switched off the speaker phone and continued to brush to a hundred, glad that the call had ended when it did and relieved that Prue hadn't asked about Willie again, which, if they'd continued to discuss her father, she inevitably would. The last thing she wanted to admit was that Willie had not gone to the Anzac march with his grandfather because Jo had found no way of contacting him; that his cell phone had gone unanswered now for three weeks and that when she'd rung his hostel and University Admissions it was to be told that Willie hadn't been seen and there was little point in leaving a message with them. And so, though it was Willie who over the years had volubly called for the right to have a relationship with his grandfather, it was Samantha who was taking that step alone, while Roger simply made a joke of it.

'Little bugger's probably shacked up with some bird and lost his battery charger,' he said. 'He's nineteen for God's sake.'

As if that was how all men were expected to behave.

13.

The House in Newtown

Behind the painted wooden cupboard that held the crockery, and through an opening cut in the brick outer wall, was a lavatory bowl, sheltered only by a beaded curtain. Willie needed to take a pee, and having completed that process and splashed some water on his face he took the only towel on view, tied it precariously around his waist and returned to the room with the bean bags.

His nervous system was calling to him discordantly, like an irritating cell phone. He needed something: a cold beer, maybe, or a shot of nicotine. But the cans scattered across the floor with the wine glasses were all empty and the dead stogies were beyond reviving.

His memory of the night before didn't contain anything that alarmed him, but that might have been because his memory wasn't complete. Where were his clothes and wristwatch, for instance? He was sure he'd find a cigarette in his jacket.

Pausing before the poster of the life-sized skeletal woman, he tried to remember whether he had been involved in the graffiti additions but could see nothing in their execution that spoke of his hand so he tip-toed down the passage to the first of the two rooms, easing open the half-shut door while trying to adjust his eyes to the gloom.

The floor was littered with clothes including, to his relief, his own. A blanket was tacked up above the one window, blocking outside light. Through the window he could hear the radio from the house next door, but there was no other sound. The only furniture in the room was a bed, a queen sized mattress base sitting on bricks, facing a wall with a fireplace that had been boarded over. Propped on the painted mantelpiece above the redundant fireplace was a cheap wooden mirror and in large capital letters, written in a similar black marker to the one used on the poster in the other room, was the phrase *ICH BIN*.

As the bed was partly obscured by the door he stepped inside and closed it silently behind him. The explanation for his sleeping on the carpet with the bean bags started to become clear. The bed was without sheets but covered with a quilted doona. From beneath the doona, closest to him, a foot overhung the side of the bed, and on the side furthest from him, a girl's bare arm and breast were exposed, the head hanging over the edge out of sight as if she were on the point of sliding out. She was tall and, lying diagonally, monopolised the mattress.

Willie paused, wondering if she was fully asleep, then he lifted the corner of the doona exposing her leg. There was no response, so he pulled it back further until, on one side, she was exposed to the waist. The girl stirred, raising her other knee, whether consciously or unconsciously he couldn't tell, kicking away the covering completely. Again, he paused, waiting for any sign of her awareness, then he knelt gingerly on the end of the bed and tugged gently at the quilted fabric held lightly under the weight of her arm until slowly it came free leaving her fully naked beneath his gaze, arched back across the mattress, her dark hair touching the ground.

Discarding the towel, he carefully stretched out beside her, propping himself on one elbow with his chin cupped in one hand, his free hand invisibly tracing the shape of her body back and forth a bare centimetre above it. He could feel the radiant warmth in his palm, could sense her magnetic aura as it flowed point-to-point along her limbs. Her skin was drum tight, white, the texture of parachute silk, barely holding her in. Beneath the silk, little rivulets of dark blood flowed close to the surface, rhythmically pumped from her slow breathing heart and lungs, trickling through her organs, flushing them with life.

Her legs were as long as Willie's and her hips just as slim. She had a flat, lean belly beneath a broad rib cage and square, high shoulders. With one arm back above her head her breasts were pulled tight, the nipples small and hard, pointing irresistibly to the ceiling. Around each nipple and between her breasts there were stray black hairs like wild seeds taken root in a smoothly manicured lawn. In the pit of her thrown back arm the hair was thicker, longer, black and curling, and beneath the mound of her pelvis soft dark strands of hair strayed down the inside of her upper thighs, black on white, outrageous and alluring.

Willie felt the blood flow to his cock, watched it lengthen and strengthen; touched it with his hand; moved his hips until he could feel the touch of the girl's body. He breathed softly, slack jawed, listening to the sound of his own blood, closing his eyes and feeling himself floating giddily in circles in the whirlpool of a dark river before being washed away downstream into quicker water, pulled suddenly towards the rapids of deep narcotic sleep.

14.

Martin Place

Lawrence Beck made his way purposefully into Martin Place, frowning in concentration as he pushed through the crowds assembling for the Anzac Day march, mildly impatient that so many people should be filling the streets. The terrace in front of the main entrance to the Colonial Centre was blocked by a congregation of teenage boys in tartan kilts, wheezily tuning bagpipes and adjusting uniforms, using the plate glass windows as their mirror.

Suddenly his shirt collar was moist and uncomfortable and his briefcase had grown heavy. Placing it on the ground, he searched his pockets for the swipe card that would admit him to the building, fearful that he had left it in the car. Then, remembering that he had a spare in the side pocket of the briefcase, he hurriedly let himself in and made his way to the elevators.

All things considered, perhaps, Lawrence should have been a contented man; a man who had chosen to devote himself to work and who had been rewarded by it, now standing in the marble-lined foyer of one of the city's temples of commerce waiting for the high speed lift to carry him up to the ivory tower where he was privileged to be able to perform at his best. Yet, he was not content. On the contrary, as he watched the elevator number its way downwards from the thirtieth floor he felt a heaviness descend upon him.

So, when had things begun to go wrong?

He couldn't think of any single event; it was an accumulation of minor annoyances, doubts and dissatisfactions which, taken in isolation, sounded petty. Yet, just like the unspoken complaints of marriage, they had festered, so that successive irritations had become increasingly more painful to bear. The analogy with marriage being appropriate when applied to a business partnership (which is how Lawrence viewed his relationship with Roger even though it was not a partnership in the legal sense), so, just as in marriage, Lawrence had begun to question whether he had failed to understand Roger's true nature at the outset or whether that nature had altered during their time together.

The tone of their conversation on the phone twenty minutes earlier had been a case in point. Would Roger have spoken that way to a Senior Partner at Mapleton and Thorpe? And if he had, would Lawrence ever have agreed to leave the practice and go and work for him? Was this just the product of familiarity, or of disrespect, for if it was the former, it revealed an unpleasant nature which must always have been there and which Lawrence had failed to detect for nearly nine years? But if it was the latter, then it suggested a rejection on Roger's part of Lawrence's judgment and values, the same values which had made him attractive to Saville Corp in the first place, and the judgment which, if anything, had grown even more reliable with time. God knows, the papers were brimming with examples of the consequences of poor judgment and injudicious behaviour; surely he didn't have to spell it out?

Perhaps it was time to prove his point.

It was no accident that Lawrence had chosen property and financial law as his areas of specialisation. They both relied on fact, rather than interpretation. To be properly informed was to be right. To be always right was not a conceit, it was merely a product of learning and attention to detail. This was something he had tried on occasions to explain to Marjorie, without great success. Perhaps it was difficult for those unfamiliar with the nature of Law to comprehend, but for Lawrence it was not ego on which he relied for confidence, it was facts. He had examined his performance over the last decade at Saville Corp and was confident, on the basis of fact, that it could not be faulted. Roger had no grounds, therefore, for disrespect and when the moment was right, Lawrence intended showing him.

Still, it was probable that he was being over sensitive. This was Lawrence's problem, not Roger's. He must learn not to take things so personally. Emotion had no place in business, only reliance on the facts.

The boys outside the main entrance began to practice on their drums, the harsh beat echoing in the marble chamber like a submachine gun. Then the elevator arrived and Lawrence hastened forward, stepping quickly as if to avoid the imaginary bullets.

15.

George Street

They moved with the herd in a mood of suppressed excitement up George Street, the crowds growing denser until eventually, by unspoken consent, their ranks began to divide into those who by entitlement or assumption intended to march and those who'd come to support and approve. As the latter drifted towards the pavements, so Sam and Albert found themselves instinctively forming line abreast. She still held his arm and in this she was far from alone for the young were strongly represented, and girls as readily as boys, their eyes bright with anticipation.

For Albert, still getting used to so many people, there was a confusion of thought that left him stumbling for focus.

'I couldn't have done this without you,' he said.

The buildings were so tall, giant monoliths of granite and glass that must have each housed more than the population of a country town. Were they always so tall? And where had all these people come from with their generations and their intricate lives of which he knew nothing? How many streets full of houses with garden paths and sideboards crammed with memories in suburbs whose names he'd crossed and long forgotten had spawned those around him? And where was his hard won anonymity to hide on a day like this when the sun shone like an arc light on the bald and greying heads of men who were deemed to have committed deeds worthy of celebration? Big eared, close shaven, men of his age eyed each other warily, balancing in their expressions an outward nod to comradeship and an inner fear of memories that could no longer be trusted. Did they realize, like him, that it was only chance that stood them there; only chance for one and all, young and old, short and tall; a random seed that germinates; four years following orders out of a life of seventy eight; bullets that missed and boats that didn't sink?

'Grandpa,' Sam asked. 'Your father was at Gallipoli, wasn't he?'

'Absolutely!'

'Did he get a medal?'

'He got a lot of medals -- heaps, as you would say.'

'How many?'

'Oh, I don't really remember. Why?'

'I put it in my school essay that he'd swum ashore at Anzac Cove and been wounded, and I got twenty out of twenty for it.'

'Twenty out of twenty? You can't do better than that.'

I'll march for him as well as for Jim Percy, he thought suddenly. Yes, I'll bloody well march for him.

Up ahead a series of side-drum rolls followed by the metronomic boom of the base drum signalled that the march had started. The crowd around them stood in silence as the melancholy wail of the brass band and bagpipes filled the George Street canyon, and then, little by little, like a growing whisper, the sound of footsteps swept back towards them so that they all lifted their heads erect, waiting for the off, and Sam grabbed Albert's hand.

Some put their left foot forward, and some put their right, but they all smiled awkwardly together and a few even called out loud, 'Quick march!' The young played heel-and-toe, skipping to get into step while the brass band crescendo bounced from wall to wall.

Albert should have known it would be like this. A brass band and uniforms, a cultivated reverence focused on a very special day, the last survivors dying, their skin and organ cells long ago ceasing to replace themselves, small deeds made into myths and the sun swinging up over the horizon to warm the dawn as it had and would forever long after they were gone: how else would it be? No wonder he'd stayed away in the bush, working with his trees all these years. But he didn't regret it, and possibly, in the trusting lightness of his granddaughter's hand he sensed that this was not about war at all, but about generations and, in particular, the rare chance for one generation to say to another, though far removed by age and custom, that they were capable of the same feelings.

Then, he'd go along with it, if that's what it was. They could throw torn up paper at him out of the department store windows if they wished (not considering who would have to clean it up), but maybe out of this he could bring himself to tell his granddaughter some of the things she wished to know; the things she didn't know.

'Oh, he could swim alright, my father,' he said, beaming down at her. 'He could swim for Africa.'

16.

The Boardroom of Saville Corp

'I'm not giving them any more of my equity as security, Lawrence, that's final. I sometimes wonder who the fuck you are working for, me or the Banks? Go back and tell them that if I hear any more bullshit about breaching covenants we'll take our business elsewhere. Melbourne and Hong Kong are all over me like a rash. They'd kill for the chance of being lead lender on a deal like this. That's what Banks are for, for fuck's sake. How do you think they make their money? It's because pricks like us put our arses on the line to earn it for them. It's not even their money they're lending in the first place. Their money doesn't exist. Their money only gets created when we stupid schmucks walk in the door and agree to put our arses on the line. Isn't that what we are, Lawrence: stupid schmucks? You should know. Tell me what it's called. Come on, you're the learned one around here; you know how it works.

'And what gets me is they have no risk. Zilch! They've got our land. Everything we add to our land, they've got that, too. What do they think is happening to the land? Is it going down in value? In the whole of Sydney, land and housing, offices and factories are being fought over like bread scraps in Belsen but uniquely, incredibly, *our* land, Saville Corp land, two hundred and eighty fucking hectares of prime zoning that Lend Lease and Mirvac would be drooling over like unfed dogs, is going down. *Down!* What's with these people? Do they think we're stupid, or something?

'And on top of that they've got fifty million of my equity in escrow. How did I ever let you persuade me to do that? What was I thinking? To let them have security over my shares; I must have been out of my mind. Had you drugged me? Was I hypnotized? You're a lawyer and you let me do it. Did you check whether I was of sound mind? Obviously that question answers itself. Nobody could be of sound mind to let the Banks take security over their shares. Tell Mapletons to check their fucking indemnity policy because they let me do it, too. I'm serious, Lawrence. I'm deadly fucking serious.'

But cool with it; deadly fucking cool: that's the portrait that Roger presented. It was important that Lawrence took him seriously, and equally important that he shouldn't be misled into thinking he might be exaggerating. The beauty of the raised voice and the uninterrupted flow was that when it stopped the silence in the room was palpable. No matter how fast sound might travel it still took a clearly identifiable moment to leave the room, an echo like a rifle shot in an ice canyon that the brain picked up and retained where a recording device would fail, framed by the ensuing silence. Into that silence Lawrence would have to step, if he was to be the first to speak, choosing his words carefully and without help.

Far off the wail of bagpipes rose like wood smoke in the city air. The march must have started down in George Street. Saville turned his back on the board room table, swivelling his chair to gaze out the window at the harbour view, so clear, so blue, so unlike any other and across which at any moment he could expect a squadron of Skyhawks to fly, drawing white vapour trails, completing the picture of beauty.

Lawrence cleared his throat.

'You volunteered the equity,' he said. 'You might recall that I wasn't asked for my opinion. I wasn't even present.'

He cleared his throat again. This time his voice was stronger.

'You came back from the conference at Hayman Island and didn't even tell me. I only found out because Greg Cummings told me as if I knew. He couldn't believe that you'd suggested it. I presumed you were drunk. Once the offer was made there was no taking it back, so don't blame me, don't blame Mapletons; we're only doing our job.'

God, how Saville loathed that injured tone. It always missed the point.

'The point is, Lawrence, that it was up to me to convince them to commit to the loan. It's always up to me. We wanted five hundred million from them. All they could see was some scrubby bush and swamp land. What the fuck would bankers know? So I had to show them I was serious. But the point is ...'

What was the point? You pull off the biggest land banking deal of the century; big enough and bold enough to keep every parasitic banker and trust fund manager fed for decades; a deal like no other because the city is growing at the rate of eighty thousand people a year and the only land available is owned by the State Government which is why every hot shot corporation in town is working over their cronies to try and get the inside track but it turns out that Roger Fucking Saville has his foot well and truly on it. Oh, yes! *'Saville Corp Snares Whiteman's Creek'* announces the financial press. *'Govt Anoints Roger Saville with Massive Land Release'.* So suddenly the phones are ringing off the hook and everyone has got these great ideas and there aren't enough restaurants to feed all the Merchant Wankers who want to make Roger Saville rich and there aren't enough shares to satisfy the Funds Managers' order books and every lending institution in Sydney is suddenly throwing corporate golf days for 36-handicappers (because the word is out that Saville can barely hit the ball) and ... He treats them all as partners.

'... I treated them all as partners.'

He swivelled his chair around to face the room, head back and looking sadly down the length of his nose as if sheltering at a distance from a hurt which he expected but couldn't avoid.

'I was a fool, I know. I should have known better. Partnership is such an outmoded concept. I treat our shareholders as partners, but all they want is a quick profit no matter what. They buy for a dollar and sell for a dollar twenty. They're not interested in what you say or do in-between. That's their right. The fact that I'm a shareholder, too, that I do all the work as well, that it's *my* shares that are in escrow, that's lost on them. So they deserve what they get. And the Banks; what right do they have to tell us how to run our business? When did we ever fail to pay their interest? Has this company ever defaulted on a loan? Have you put this to them, Lawrence, or do you just play patter-cake with them in your monthly get-togethers?'

Lawrence was barely paying attention it seemed, distracted by the newspaper which Roger had been reading while killing time waiting for his colleague to drag himself away from the domestic bliss of the Rose Bay breakfast table and get his arse into the office to focus on things that mattered. Worse still, Lawrence appeared to be amused, which was the direct opposite of the effect that Saville was trying to have.

'I'm deadly serious about this, Lawrence.'

He leaned forward, pulling his lips shut over his teeth so there could be no suspicion of a smile, an effort which caused the muscles in his neck and cheeks to become distended and made him feel perhaps grimmer than he looked. A brief flicker of impotence passed over him, so quickly that he had no time to react to it, like an insult shouted from a passing car.

'Deadly serious,' he repeated.

From the bottom of Barrack Street and Martin Place the insistent thump of a marching drum wound its way between the granite columns of the GPO to reverberate against the sandstone façade of the Commonwealth Bank and in through the silicone seals of the Colonial Centre's curtain wall where it took hold lightly of Roger Saville's attention, causing him to look away. His daughter was out there somewhere marching to that beat. Funny the things that grabbed them.

'Talking of partners,' Lawrence said; 'how would you like to pick up the CBD column of The Herald each morning and read what your erstwhile colleagues have to say about you now that things have gone sour? It seems to me it's dog-eat-dog when business goes wrong. I'm sure there's a lesson in that for all of us.'

With which he tapped the newspaper like a sanctimonious priest pointing at a passage in the bible.

'*Left, left, left, right, left*', went the drum in the distance, worming its way into Roger's head like a maddening tune from *The Sound of Music*.

'What exactly are you trying to say,' he demanded: 'that you think our business is in trouble because the Banks want us to cut back our borrowing? Is that where you're at ..?'

He reached forward and grabbed the newspaper, forcing Lawrence to give him his attention.

'Because if that's the case, it explains a lot.'

Gripping the arms of his chair, he pushed it backwards so he could stretch out his legs and lean his head back, like his father used to do, looking to the heavens in exasperation and in search of help. The effort in taking people along with him was sometimes overwhelming. Of all the burdens of business, that was the worst; something his father must have known. It would be easier to do it on his own. After all, that's how Saville Property Holdings was created; just his old man in a dingy office on York Street with Rita Hartman collecting the rents and a Letraset sign on the door that his father never bothered to get engraved. He should have taken the lesson; instead he'd listened to some other mantra. 'Surround yourself with good people'. Where the fuck had he learned that?

'Of course we're not in trouble,' Lawrence replied calmly. 'We haven't breached our covenants but we could, if we're not careful, get very close to doing so. All the Banks are saying is that they want to see some sales and the capitalization of interest needs to stop.'

'And do they have any suggestions, these banking friends of yours, about how you sell swamp land before it's developed and how you meet interest costs before you start collecting income? No ...?'

'No.'

'Oh, how surprising!'

Roger observed a moment of silence before allowing himself the pleasure of whispering, 'Well, luckily I do,' but so softly that it was only to himself. Maybe it was a matter of acknowledging that, like his father, and despite all the corporate trappings - the Legal Counsel, the Board of Directors, the Project Managers, Financial Controllers, Building Supervisors, Agents, Consultants and Hanky Wankers - he really was completely and absolutely on his fucking own; acknowledging it and acting accordingly.

17.

The House in Mosman

Feeling that she still had things to say, but knowing Prue would be preoccupied with her guests, Joanne Saville decided to ring Marjorie Beck instead and ask her what she planned to wear that night.

They weren't bosom friends, but neither, after ten years, were they distant acquaintances. Jo had decided early on that although Marjorie was very different ('unusual' was how she had described her after first meeting), she rather liked her. 'Odd', was how Roger had always dismissed her, but there was nothing wrong with that. 'Odd' was not a pejorative in Jo's vocabulary, it was pretty much an essential ingredient in every worthwhile artist and writer she had ever studied, so she didn't mind if her husband chose to say that, though whether Marjorie was in the same realm as those artists and writers she couldn't say. The jury was out.

In the hour or so since Jo had ended her call with Prue she hadn't moved from her seat at the dressing table, her eyes dissolved in the blue middle-distance of the Northern beaches, following the opaque images of daydreams that lay beyond; a nagging, persistent ache in her chest which no amount of self-admonishment or rubbing had succeeded in reducing.

She didn't need help in reading the banner headlines of her concerns; they were only too obvious. That she was despondent over Willie's 'phase of rejection' towards his parents; that she always felt angry and numb at her powerlessness to deal with the demons that regulated her relationship with her only remaining parent; that she felt herself to be alone in coping with these issues: these were not matters that she needed to have pointed out, they were universal. If she but knew it (and probably she did), they were the common concerns of women of her generation: not worthy of self-pity, only resolution.

Why, then, this deep azure tide that she would suddenly feel ebbing out within her; this seductive passivity that unexpectedly coated her limbs and anaesthetised her resolve, luring her to a place she knew she had never been. Why now? Was it God's way of telling her to surrender more fully to him?

'I don't seem to be able to get started this morning,' were the first words she said to Marjorie.

'Well, that doesn't sound like you,' was the response.

That was right, it didn't sound like her at all. Time to snap out of it.

'Perhaps you've been overdoing it,' Marjorie suggested vaguely.

She had a strong voice, matronly and no-nonsense, yet she often sounded vague on the phone, as if she were doing something else at the same time.

'I have a bit, I suppose. The whole of yesterday I spent on my feet doing the church flowers on behalf of the Friends of St. Agnes ready for today's services, and then I had the most trying night dealing with my father who'd come to stay, which is always tricky, and needless to say Roger didn't get back until late, so this morning I've just been sitting around like an old hag with dementia.'

'I can't see that description ever fitting you, Joanne, but I'll let it pass. Tell me about the Friends of the Gallery. Last time I saw you the Committee was getting excited about a Japanese exhibition you were bringing out from the British Museum. How's that coming along?'

'Good. Not exactly my cup of tea, I suspect. I've never quite got the hang of Japanese painting, but they tell me it's going to be very good of its type and it'll be here in June so you must come along. But what about you?'

'Me?'

Marjorie sounded surprised, as if she had just put down the thing she was doing in order to concentrate on the question.

'Well ... this and that. I can't pretend to be as busy as you, but I muddle along.'

This was the point where their relationship usually got stuck and failed to go further, but for some reason, on this occasion, Jo had a sudden intimation of the cause.

'There's something I've been meaning to ask you,' she said quickly, 'without the men being around. How does Lawrence manage to put up with Roger? I mean, it must be awfully difficult for him, coming from such a disciplined profession to find himself in a completely unstructured business, because it seems to me nobody knows from one day to the next whether these property development schemes are going to make money or lose it. I remember so clearly when Roger took over following his father's death how cavalier he was and uncertain of what he wanted until Lawrence joined him. I don't think he realises how lucky he is, and yet it must be hard for Lawrence. You don't have to tell me if you don't want to.'

Marjorie began to laugh. She had a laugh that started softly before becoming full blown and throaty at which point, because she was a heavy smoker, it turned into a cough and then ceased.

'Oh, dear,' she wheezed, 'you've brought tears to my eyes. It's the thought of Roger being uncertain of what he wanted. I simply can't imagine that.'

'It's true ...'

'Well, maybe for an instant, but knowing Roger I'm sure the moment would have passed whether Lawrence had joined the company or not. Look, honestly, Joanne, we don't talk about business so I have no evidence at all that Lawrence has a problem with it. He sometimes complains to me about how hard he works and how little he's appreciated, but that's just for my benefit to rub in the fact that I don't work, despite not having children, and to remind me how lucky I am to have him paying for everything.'

'But you have your tapestry.'

'I have my tapestry, and if he wasn't paying for everything no doubt I would go out and work as well, which might then give rise to a situation where *I* could complain about how hard I work and how little appreciated I am, and so it would go. The thing these men forget is that they have a choice. If they don't like it, then stop. They're doing what they want to do. In the absence of war, and hunting with bows and arrows or playing footy, these men have taken up business: different styles maybe, but the same game. Roger's one thing, Lawrence is another. They only work hard because they can't think of anything else to do, and they think it's important because they're the ones doing it, and because they're men. Don't worry about it.'

So it wasn't that. And if it was true that they didn't talk about business at home, then it occurred to Jo that Marjorie was fortunate. Business, and making money, was the life that Roger led and somehow, even when he wasn't talking about it, it filled the air around him and engulfed those who were in his company, so even if she wasn't privy to the detail, she was a party to the mood. It was a mood that she found debilitating. Worst of all, to her shame, she realised that Roger did talk about Lawrence and he did so habitually in a way that was graceless and unappreciative, like a spouse gone sour.

'I know what you mean about the constant working,' she answered. 'We don't have holidays anymore.'

'But you all went to Bali, just a month or so ago.'

'Yes, but it wasn't a proper holiday,' she was quick to explain. 'With Roger on the phone all the time, and refusing to be away from the fax machine, we might just as well have stayed at home.'

Holiday! Once the word had filled her with such anticipation she became greedy for it. It held so many connotations: excitement, glamour, mystery, sex, friendships, discoveries, children, love. If the entire world turned to ash, where would your memory fly except to holidays? There, on the silver sands of Phuket or Nusa Dua, eyes half-closed, shadows of the palm trees shading her face, drifting dreamily in and out of sleep to the tinkling sound of Samantha and Willie's laughter at the water's edge, her husband's voice a distant murmur from the poolside bar, happy with friends, happy with family, happily in love: that was where she longed to be. Or better still, sailing on the Hawkesbury like they used to do when the children were little; just the four of them.

'Did the children have fun?' Marjorie asked sympathetically.

'No.'

God, had she really said that? Could she dare admit it? They'd outgrown buckets and spades. They'd outgrown each other. Dare she say it, but they'd outgrown their parents as well. Samantha, only fourteen and now wanting to read undisturbed in her room, to be covered up when walking on the beach, to eat or not to eat as she wished, to be left alone to stare at the sinking sun and the blazing torches being lit on the water's edge and not have to say what she was thinking, not have to bear the flesh-tearing agony of questions. Her sweet Samantha, who she'd once believed would be forever her close and constant companion.

And Willie! Well, Willie: he simply disappeared. 'Friends', he said; not that they ever saw them. He was never in at night, never joined them for dinner, failed to turn up for the mountain village tour and arrived late at the airport as they were leaving having lost both his camera and his wallet. All of which Roger, permanently wrapped around his cell phone, apparently thought was perfectly normal.

Some holiday! But if the message Willie took away was that he was now excused from participating in the family, it certainly explained why they hadn't heard from him since.

'What a shame. They want to be with their friends now, I suppose. That'll be sad for you.'

The nagging, persistent pain in the chest was still there. This woman who had no children of her own had spotted it. But who would massage it away?

'It comes to all of us, I suppose, but I hadn't expected it to come so soon. I'm not sure that I'm ready for it. In two years time I'll be fifty, and I still haven't worked out my own relationships. I don't want my children to head off into the world incomplete, yet they make it so hard to help them.'

She gave a bright and brittle laugh. All this on a sunny day with money in the bank, as Prue would say.

'Fifty,' Marjorie announced emphatically, 'is the time of your life. That's what I've decided and that's how I'm going to treat it. I can barely wait.'

'Is yours soon?'

'Next January, but I'm not waiting 'till then, I'm starting now. It's already my fiftieth year.'

'How wonderful! What have you got planned?'

Already she felt envious.

'The first thing I've done is join The Purple Hats.'

'What on earth's that?'

'It's our version of The Red Hat Society. The Red Hats wear red hats and purple shirts. We wear purple hats and red shirts. For some reason the first members got it back to front and that's how it's stayed; middle-aged women determined to be absurd because that's the only intelligent response to life: no men, no children, no pretensions, no anger, no restrictions or inhibitions and *no* embarrassment. You should join. It would do you a world of good.'

Jo couldn't imagine what was being described to her.

'Is it a luncheon club?' She had more than enough lunch commitments, what with the Gallery, church and school.

'Not necessarily. Breakfast, lunch, coffee, tea, Champagne suppers, knicker parties. Was it the activity you remember from when you were young, or was it the fact you were having fun? For many of us the fun stopped when we chose to live life with a man. I'm not saying it's the man's fault; probably the fun stopped for him, too, if he thinks about it. Women have an enormous capacity for fun when they are together and nothing suits us better than silliness, which is, after all, the proper response to life. When were you last completely silly; I mean giggling at absolute nonsense because it just felt good? Not in the company of men, I'll warrant.'

'I don't know.'

Perhaps she was right; but, silly hats?

'So what else are you planning to do?'

'I'm going to live in France.'

'Really?'

This *was* a radical pronouncement.

'Does Lawrence know?'

'Not yet. I've been thinking about it for years. I've always wanted to see the Bayeux Tapestry, and working on the Federation Tapestry in Melbourne last year and hearing people talking about it and the wonderful ateliers in Normandy and Paris I realised what a fool I was to let life pass by and not go there and see for myself. It's not as if I have children to worry about, so what have I been sitting here all this time for? No-one forces me to stay caged in Rose Bay, waiting to die. So I've decided to go with a friend. She worked on The Globe Theatre tapestries and is a weaver like me, and we thought we'd possibly rent a place, maybe in Paris, or maybe in the country. We'll see.'

'What will Lawrence say?'

There was just the briefest pause, but that may have been because Joanne could hear her lighting a cigarette.

'Is that the issue?' Marjorie asked.

The question was rhetorical; certainly that's how Jo chose to take it. She was not at all sure how to proceed, having reached a point in the conversation she never would have expected, and having arrived there so suddenly. She felt like she was an inappropriate recipient of such information, and yet she couldn't put her finger on why that was. Was it a confidence that would now test her loyalty to Roger? Was she embarrassed on Lawrence's behalf?

'It sounds terribly exciting. I envy you,' she said feebly. Then, looking for a way out, she remembered why she'd rung. 'I can't wait to hear more but I really should fly. It's such a gorgeous day outside, and I've got a thousand things to do before tonight, so I just wanted to check what you are planning to wear to the dinner. Not a red shirt and a purple hat, I hope.'

'Why not?' Marjorie laughed.

'Well ...'

'Men in uniform like ladies in hats. For that reason alone I will not be wearing my purple hat. Sombre and contrite is how I will dress, so that the old fogies as they drift off to sleep later in the night will be happy in the belief that all is right with the world, women in their proper place and the fight was worth fighting.'

'No colour?'

'No colour.'

'Done!'

Returning to the view from her dressing table, out to the distant beaches of the North Shore, Jo pondered the significance of the friend who had been chosen to share the adventure in France and wondered if the source of Marjorie's 'Oddness' could now be emerging, and that what she had described in herself might simply be a lesbian 'coming out'. God forbid, she thought; that is so trite of me, even to think it. Whether she is, or whether she isn't, all that matters is that I should be happy for her, pray for her, pray for everyone, men and women alike, that they should be alive to the joy of living. Isn't that all that matters?

But that ache in her chest she now began to recognise as panic. She was not by nature a melancholic, yet she felt herself slipping into a state of aloneness; a place in which, if she allowed herself to go there, she might well become increasingly content to lie. She looked at her watch. Phone Prue. But tell her what? This was a state of feeling, and feeling could only be sensed, not described. 'Alright, what's the real question?' Prue had demanded earlier that morning, but the question she had posed had been a substitute for the real one which she had not yet had the courage to formulate, and the answers that would be given, she knew, would not even be capable of describing the colours that made up the palette of her feelings.

18.

The Boardroom

'The issues,' Lawrence went on stoically, 'are fairly well known to everyone. The Banks want to know whether the government's Home Start loans will be granted for town houses built on leasehold land. We need to clear that one up fairly quickly because all the other housing developments in the area are freehold and forty percent of new home buyers are applying for the loan. We may have to re-think our leasehold strategy. They're also looking for something definitive on the Windsor Road upgrade. There's a strong rumour that the government will be looking to developers to fund that and Alison Pyke in her monthly report to the banking syndicate has flagged the possibility that we, as the largest land holder in the area, will be asked to make the biggest contribution. They want to know how that will be funded.'

'We are not changing our leasehold strategy.'

'We may not have a choice, Roger. The Project Home business is highly competitive. Take away the Home Start loans and sales could quickly dry up.'

'We are not changing our leasehold strategy.'

Roger thumped the table angrily. That bitch, Alison Pyke: he should have guessed she needed to be minded. Always watch the women, particularly in banking. They may seem quiet and contrite, taking the notes, pouring the coffee, blushing when the men get vulgar, but all the time they were working to a hidden agenda and, one way or another, you could guarantee that it wasn't designed to be helpful.

'I agree it would be a shame to have to revert to freehold,' Lawrence continued, 'and I'm confident we'll find a way round it.

That's what I've told them: that I'll get a definitive ruling on the issue within a week.'

'Make them wait.'

It was typical of Lawrence to want things to be definitive, black and white and incontrovertible. Where were the opportunities in that? A definitive ruling might allow him to move on to the next issue confident that he'd acted with the utmost efficiency and correctness, but it might also expose them to a fucking disaster. What if the government said no, you can't qualify for loans for perpetual leases? Why would you rush off to tell the Banks within the week when you hadn't figured out a way around it? And what would the jittery Banks' reaction be to that news when they were already talking potential breaches in the lending ratio? Somewhat more hysterical perhaps? And whose fault would that be? Not Lawrence's, you could be sure.

But now he was on to the Windsor Road issue; Alison Pyke's explosive device. What was her motive for raising that issue at this time? Did she get her kicks out of looking for the worst, or was this a more sinister bent that she portrayed; a power play using the very tools that others, men in particular, had condescendingly given her? Yes, that one was important alright; she knew that. It could explode at any minute. Maybe that's how she got her kicks, like an Arab suicide bomber who goes to an Israeli nightclub and smiles seductively at the arrogant Army boy sitting with his mates in the booth, longing for the moment when his hand would ride up her skirt to find the snap on her suspender belt (so innocent, so feminine, so irresistibly seductive that quaint old device on a young girl), knowing that the minute his fingers succeeded the explosives in her waistband would be detonated and they would all spread their blood across the walls and ceiling; smiling; smiling in anticipation and willing the moment.

Christ, she'd done that very thing to him at Hayman Island, the smiling.

Every time he looked up, it seemed, her eyes had been on him. When he stood at the lectern talking his way through the Whiteman's Creek slide presentation - the artists' perspectives of shopping malls, factories, offices and schools, streets teeming with happy, multicultural people, the park land and grid plans, the sales stats and projections so compellingly drawn that you could swear you had already been there – in the darkened room, filled with middle aged bankers and the smell of the imminent buffet lunch wafting in through the doors from the room next door, one face, one pair of eyes, always. And when he met her eyes, even though accidentally, she would smile so briefly and discreetly that anyone who was not meeting her eyes at that same moment would have been unaware of it, so turning it into a secret; a secret between two people who had not at that stage even met.

'These events are hard for a woman,' he said to her when he found her standing beside him on the pontoon later in the day while the conference delegates were waiting for a boat to take them across to Hamilton Island for the afternoon; 'all the men want to do is play golf and go sailing.'

'I play golf,' she replied. 'I sail.'

The nature of her smile in the bright sunlight suggested she'd said something completely different, but he couldn't tell what. That evening she sat next to him at dinner. There were ten men and only two women, neither of whom occupied senior positions, but out of political correctness, and probably because the conference manager was a woman, it had been decided that he, as the host, should have the lead banker on one side and Alison on the other. The conversation encompassed the whole table. That was how he liked it; a round table for twelve people so that when he talked about his plans and the exciting prospects for Saville Corp it wasn't just wasted on the person next to him. At the same time he could draw the best out of Lawrence and his other key people. It was like conducting an orchestra. He was in good form that night, enjoying the audience and sharing his enthusiasm with them. Why not? Whiteman's Creek was one of the most exciting projects these bankers would ever be exposed to. He could tell they loved it.

As usual they drank their way through the wine list without regard to cost. This was what bankers particularly liked; to go away to luxury resorts and drink wine that cost more than the weekly salary of their secretaries, all paid for by clients to whom they were lending the money. It was one of the rules of the game. When the '92 Grange ran out (surprise, surprise) it was up to him to pick a replacement. He couldn't go down in quality, but how could he match it, let alone do better? So he threw the *problem to Lawrence.*

The mood of the party was delicately poised, bright eyed, smiling, mellow but wanting more. While Lawrence looked from one side of the wine list to the other, matching prices to names like a spectator watching a game of miniature tennis, Saville decided to ask the million dollar question.

'So, now you've all seen it, who would like to have equity in the Whiteman's Creek development?'

He knew the answer, otherwise he wouldn't have asked the question. Hands rose, mouths opened, chairs were pushed back and some even got to their feet fumbling in false bravado for bank notes and credit cards. Lots of laughter of the bloke-y sort filled the room and even the resort wine waiters, waiting for Lawrence to make a fucking decision, joined in the fun looking like they'd be keen to buy shares, too. But it went on too long and started to go flat because it needed to be followed quickly with another great wine; something that would at least sustain their spirits, if not lift them.

'Come on, Lawrence, for Pete's sake!' he cried, but the more he was pushed the more determined Lawrence was to take his time. Then from beside him Alison said:

'Hill of Grace.'

'Hill of Grace ...?'

''96 or '98?' asked the wine waiter.

''98.'

'A good choice, Madam.'

Well, bugger me, thought Roger, not having a clue, but taking comfort from the wine waiter's attitude that they would not be embarrassed by it, and rather pleased that Lawrence had been left floundering. Not just a pretty face, then.

When the wine was brought and she had, at his insistence, confirmed that she was satisfied with it, he turned and raised his glass to her eye-to-eye.

'A good choice,' he said quietly, for her alone, and she gave that same smile that he had seen earlier in the day, the one that you might not have noticed if you hadn't been looking her directly in the eye. Whether it was the wine, or the smile, or just because enough had been said already that

night and anything further would have been superfluous, his mood suddenly changed and he excused himself from the table, encouraging everyone else to stay and continue enjoying themselves. His influence on the table, the effect of what he had said, would only be heightened by his absence, so he took himself for a stroll on the beach. He was not a drinker and the golfing stories bored him.

'So, what has been your response to this roading issue?' he asked now, some months later.

'Oh, I've been very non-committal. Said it was built-in to our assumptions already; nothing new in developer contributions; we had excellent relations with State Government; a level playing field was all we asked; no surprises: that sort of thing. I naturally presume you'll be taking it up with Bob Summers, seeing we make such healthy contributions to the State Labour Party. Didn't say that to them, of course.'

'Why not? Don't you think the Banks know the value of political donations? They're the masters at it.'

'You're probably right. I'm just not sure how it would sound if it found its way into Alison's monthly report.'

How's that for power, he thought? Who needed to be a man, Head of Lending, twenty years of kiss-arse on the corporate ladder, when a twenty eight year-old girl with a PC and a pot plant behind her mid-height partitions on the open plan floor of Level 6, Corporate Banking, could slip a few words into her monthly newsletter for syndicate members that could not be challenged for fact but, more importantly, once published, could never be withdrawn? As she sat down to write each month could she feel those fingers creeping up her thigh towards the suspender clips? Did she shiver in anticipation at the thought of the ensuing detonation?

Standing on the foreshore with the warm waters of the Whitsunday Islands lapping at his feet he had expected to be mildly exhilarated by the success of the day, but instead he was overwhelmed by the enormity of what he faced. Building Whiteman's Creek was going to take a decade of effort, every day bringing more and more problems dressed as challenges to his desk. Was that what he wanted? There it was; there was the great scheme, created by his own hand: it would never be more admirable and exciting than it was at that moment. Let others have it, he thought. Yes, yes, yes.

Naturally he feigned surprise when Alison tip-toed out of the black night in her black dress trailing her shoes in her hand. Why is it that on calm nights when the ocean breathes softly, laying itself rhythmically at your feet, and the sky is starless like a photographer's darkroom, people standing on the shore tend to whisper like children at the key-hole of an adult room?

'It's so dark,' he whispered.

'No city lights,' she whispered back. 'The warm air above the ocean rises and meets the cold air descending, creating a condensation that blocks out the stars.'

'Hmm.'

He'd turned away and started back to the hotel, feeling uncomfortable with the setting. She followed. At the door of his room she said, in her normal voice, 'You believe very much in this project, don't you? Enough to risk your own equity if it doesn't succeed?'

Well, of course he did, he'd replied, because no-one should expect to succeed if they weren't willing to put themselves on the line and that was the nature of the business and he wouldn't be where he was today if he hadn't been prepared to show that commitment throughout all his dealings. Above all else, he had said, believing it implicitly, property development is not for the faint hearted. How this conversation, held under the low voltage down light in the passageway outside his executive suite, turned up at breakfast time the next morning as an assumption that he was offering equity as security, took some explaining.

What the hell: it was water under the bridge now.

'Forget Alison and her monthly report, Lawrence, our problem is that the Banks are fixated on an imaginary number. The number is sixty, as in sixty percent. It is a stupid, pointless, meaningless fucking number as we all know, but for the little salaried weasels on the credit committee who have nothing else to do but sit and watch a ticking clock it is the number that causes the alarm bells to ring, and when the alarm goes off the old boys upstairs stir in their chairs and shout down the intercom to the little salaried weasels on the credit committee ...'

'That they're not doing their job.'

'Do we care?'

'Certainly! I hope so, yes. We have a good relationship with them. The thing is it's not the sixty so much as the hundred percent that we should be concentrating on. At the moment, the hundred isn't big enough in their eyes, and that's partly because we've been capitalizing interest for the last six months, partly because your security is being valued at a forty percent discount and partly because, well, they are unsure about the valuations given these questions that have been raised.'

'Why is my security being discounted? I gave them fifty million dollars worth of shares.'

'Which are trading at sixty cents.'

'With an asset backing of a dollar.'

'As I'm sure we will one day be able to demonstrate.'

Roger stood up and walked to the window. The marching bands that had been waiting in the side streets were in full cry now, the wailing and thumping coming from all points of the compass. It was going to be a long parade. The white lighthouse above Watson's Bay was bathed in full sunlight which hadn't yet reached the houses on the near side of the hill at Vaucluse, and a small yellow plane, also glinting in the sunlight, was testing the air above Bondi.

'We have a lot to do today,' he said. 'This meeting with Astor United Holdings is absolutely critical.'

'You've told me very little about it. Do they want to invest?'

'Oh, yes. The reason I want you here now is because I need to brief you. Butch Astor is arriving in Sydney this morning and Greg Cummings is bringing him as our guest to tonight's RSL Dinner. I want you and me to be reading from the same script. By tomorrow

I'll be wanting a heads-up, so you're going to have your work cut out.'

'Do they want land or equity?'

'Both. I'll explain the whole deal to you.'

'Then we'll need those valuations.'

'Don't worry, Lawrence, I received them yesterday. All your problems will soon be over.'

Oh, yes. Did they really think he would not be prepared for them? This was how it would always have to be. Like a magician pulling rabbits from the hat it would always be him, Roger Saville, standing alone on the stage in the spotlight having to perform, plunging his hand in one more time. Who would remember the rabbits that came before if eventually his hand came up empty? Fuck that. Fuck them. He wasn't going to come up empty, he was going to come up full of rabbits, and today was the day when they would be hopping everywhere.

'Once the analysts see these valuations our shares should rise. They make nonsense of the Banks. They can't argue with our asset values unless they're willing to dismiss the entire valuation industry and if they go down that route it will be the end of property banking forever.'

He smiled. Lawrence wasn't such a bad old fart.

'When do I get to see them?' Lawrence asked.

'They're in my briefcase …'

He started for the door and then he remembered, of course, he'd left the briefcase at the city apartment the night before. Somehow he was going to have to find time during the day to go and pick it up.

19.

The Mosman House

When she entered the room, Joanne had no objective in mind. She was wandering the house, just as one might wander the garden, waiting for a purpose to crystallize. Well, after all, the house was her responsibility, the way it looked and functioned and how people felt about it. Without ever having made a formal pact with herself she probably made a point of checking its wellbeing two or three times a day. That was all she was doing, just checking in with the objects and spaces that represented, in their absence, those for whom the house had been created. Sometimes she might be disturbed that something was out of place. At other times she might be disturbed at how a familiar object now gratingly cried out to be moved. Men wouldn't understand it.

She didn't come to Willie's room expecting it to be in any way different to previous mornings or for any purpose related to change. Perhaps she came to test the strength of its familiarity, to concentrate upon it like a fading memory that she was reluctant to let go. Willie in his body and voice, eyes, hair, feet and hands was not there, of course. Even when he'd last slept in the room at the end of January, after returning from Bali for the week before varsity began, she'd felt that he was no longer there. He had failed to take possession of his room, the setting for his teenage years, treating its contents as if he were a stranger to them. As if in response, those same objects which had always seemed to be imbued with his spirit now failed to speak at all of his presence.

Standing at his desk and scanning his bookshelves she suddenly realized that she, of all people, had aided this departure. Unable to help herself, she had gone to his room the day after he moved into the university hostel and set about tidying it. At the time it was her way of dealing with her shock. How could she have known, who could have warned her, of the grief that she would feel after eighteen years, of losing a son? So she'd gone to his room as soon as she was alone in the house and set about tidying it, something she told herself she had been dying to do for all his teenage years, and in the process of touching every object, hoping, praying that she could recreate his presence. What she had done instead was to destroy his presence for, at its simplest, a teenager's room was not a tidy place. More importantly, where she placed a book was not where he placed that book. How she stacked his CDs was not how he had left them. Not only had the sifting and ordering, the fondling and perusing, failed to retrieve him, it had cemented his absence.

How futile the whole process had been. Like any mother she had only wanted to prove the value of tidiness. Well, she had failed. And why had she wanted to promote tidiness: because that was a happier way to live? Did tidiness make other people happier because it made for them a more attractive environment, or was it just a way of demonstrating control over that environment and, by extension, over life itself? In the absence of anything more worthy being proved, was it the only visible proof of her effectiveness at mothering?

Her eyes moved from the bookshelf to the poster on the wall beside it. Liam Gallagher in a filthy acrylic tracksuit had his hands down his pants mimicking an erection; Liam Gallagher the disgusting, drunken, head-butting 'role model' from *Oasis* whose vile ranting played at full volume had trashed the carefully nurtured peace of her house so that she had dreaded Willie's return from school each day, panicked at the tension and resentment she would feel at 4.00 o'clock each afternoon, knowing how it would affect her: Liam Gallagher who, among others, had made her wish her son to be gone. Turn it off, she would shout at Willie, wanting to smash his music system with an axe, hiding behind the kitchen door so no-one could see her contorted face at that moment taken over by the ugliness of rage. *Turn it off*, she would scream again and again: that was the style of her effective mothering. So he would turn on Eminem instead, and Eminem would deliver obscenities directed at his own mother.

As she looked at that poster now, the futility of her idealized love numbed her. What had been the point? It had turned her instead into a screaming harridan. That's how he would remember her.

Calmly, she reached out and scrunched Liam Gallagher's head slowly in her hand until the poster began to peel from the wall. Slowly and deliberately she compacted it into a ball of trash which she then dropped on the floor. Where the poster had been there were now six ugly patches of broken plaster where the blue tack, used at her insistence, had set hard and pulled the Porters lime wash from the wall.

How futile: how utterly futile. 'Use satin enamel in the children's rooms', her decorator had said, but she didn't want satin enamel, she wanted soft plaster because it was a home not a kennel, a haven of soft colour and warmth and fondness with which she could surround her children and which, if she was right, would help determine the sort of people they would become. Was that all a nonsense, too? Were the Jim Thomson silks, the Baker mahogany bed sets, the pure wool carpets and the Smidge of Ivory walls in fact the perfect incubator for parental rejection; a training ground for Formica tastes and acrylic emotions? Oh, someone had better tell the editors of *Trends* and *Vogue Living* the consequences of what their readers were doing. Tell them they were not creating a home; tell them they were engaging in a complicated, hideously expensive self-delusion. This obsessive home-making was not the palliative that would alleviate the pain of inevitable desertion; it was nothing more than a useless placebo. Bare bulbs and linoleum floors performed better.

Next she grabbed Eminem by the crutch and crunched him violently into a mashed up ball as well. More holes appeared in the wall. Who else was there? 'Ms Dynamite'; that fat, black rapping animal form in army fatigues: how could any intelligent person take her seriously, let alone listen to her drivel at full volume?

The holes in the wall stared at her in mute shock as if they had no answer to her questions and she returned their gaze obdurately. No emotion or resolve rose within her towards them other than a dull, fatalistic suspicion that she might never have the energy or will to repair them; she, who had so meticulously nursed every aspect of the creation of this house, might simply let these weeping sores go untreated. She no longer had the energy.

'Oh, Mrs Jo, is Willie home?'

Joanne turned, startled, to the bedroom door.

'Sophia! I didn't expect you to come today.'

She looked at the plaster dust and screwed up papers on the floor and fleetingly considered a lie.

'No, Willie isn't home. I'm the guilty one.'

She shrugged apologetically.

'I couldn't stand those posters any more. It's a bit of a mess I'm afraid.'

Sophia bustled forward to claim command and Joanne stepped back surrendering the room to her.

'You didn't have to come today, you know. It's a public holiday on Anzac Day: no-one works.'

'Mr Roger is at home?'

'Oh, no, he works, he always works; but you didn't have to.'

'I don't like holidays for war. There is too much war. It is stupid.'

Sophia's Slovenian dogmatism brooked no contradiction, not that Joanne felt inclined to disagree.

'People should forget war and keep their eyes and cheeks to themselves. Believe me; an eye for an eye only makes the world blind. I seen it.'

'Yes, 'An eye for an eye and a cheek for a cheek'. You're right; it's in the bible. It can cause a lot of sadness.'

'You ask me this Anzac Day is stupid. All they want to do is go tell lies and get drunk in the pub. You don't need to have a holiday for that. I rather work.'

Plugging the vacuum hose into the Centravac wall fitting, her broad hips like a stone buttress that had withstood a thousand years of Balkan bombings, Sophia simultaneously swept the plaster from the carpet and cleared the room of self pity. Joanne felt the cloud lift and was pleased that she was there.

'I'll have to get the walls repaired I'm afraid,' she admitted sheepishly. 'I didn't realize the damage it could do.'

'Poof! It no problem. Mr Roger do it?'

'Oh, no, Roger would never do a thing like that; he wouldn't know where to start. No, I'll have to get a plasterer and a painter in. The room needs redecorating anyway.'

Though every speck of plaster had disappeared Sophia kept sweeping, sucking air from the room into the pipes within the walls where it whistled along the hallway and down the central duct into the giant dust bag in the basement garage which it was Sophia's job to empty on Thursdays for rubbish collection on Friday. Momentary bursts of over zealous cleaning were Sophia's way of signalling that she had something to say. She switched off the vacuum and straightened up.

'You no need to decorate. Look at this room; you waste money. Little bit filling stuff and it beautiful again. Beautiful! I do it myself. You get me some what-you-call-it ...'

'Plaster?'

'... and I do it myself. You still got paint the same colour, must be somewhere in the garage or some place, and no-one know the difference. No need to spend good money for this little thing. Save your money for when the rain comes. Believe me, I know.'

Joanne held her hands up in front of her and started to back towards the door, shaking her head with a disbelieving smile but no words to justify it. Just minutes earlier she had had the feeling she would never be able to summon the energy or resolve to deal with decorating again, and now here was her middle-aged and impoverished housekeeper offering to do it for her. Sophia, the grandmother who left her home at 6.30 in the morning to catch the train from Emu Plains in order to earn fifteen dollars an hour cleaning a house in Mosman, was willing to repair Joanne's walls for her in order to save her money. It was no problem, she said. So why did she want to shout out, 'NO'? Why did she want to get them both out of the room and close the door behind them? Perhaps she'd wanted to deliberately damage Willie's room and leave the visible scars for him to see. Perhaps this was the only way she could speak to him of her anger and hurt. From the second he was born she had strived to do everything right. Talk about cheeks; she had turned her cheek a hundred thousand times to take the casual, uncaring blows of Willie's disinterest in her love. He'd plucked out her eye with his withdrawal of contact. Now let him see the scars on the wall for what they truly were: tears in the flesh of her heart; irreparable lesions on her soul. No, she would not allow Sophia to repair them.

'My father is staying in the spare bedroom,' she said, changing the subject. 'I wonder would you mind making the bed and putting out a fresh towel. He may be staying another night.'

Sophia shrugged and strode off down the hall to Albert's room, not bothering to press her offer any further. Joanne hung back in her wake, breathing in with shallow, uneven breaths. Yes, it was good that she had been shaken from her black mood but that mood had been clamouring to be confronted and couldn't be put off forever. Even Marjorie had sensed it. A moment had been reached in her life for which she'd had no warning or preparation and which, when she considered the strength of its impact upon her, she doubted her stock resources of religion and friendship would be able to counter. She had lost a child. She, who had lived only for the purpose of luxuriating in the security of family bondage, had woken to find the ties undone and the family gone. If Willie could go so freely, what was there to tie Roger and Samantha? Who could be sure they had not already gone?

'Your father sleep here?' Sophia called disbelievingly down the hall and Joanne hurried to catch up.

She'd put him in the room with the Warwick fabrics, believing he'd be more comfortable with the navy fleur-de-lis and Regency stripes. It was a masculine room, not austere and certainly not simple, but closer to what she imagined his generation might prefer. Through the French windows was the potager garden which she herself had designed and which Frank the hippie gardener loved to maintain, and down the railway sleeper steps were banks of rosemary, thyme and sage; solid old-fashioned herbs that had stood the test and which surely - if he happened to find them - he was bound to appreciate.

'He's a very tidy man,' said Sophia approvingly.

The bed was already made and all she could do was pretend to fluff the pillows. His bath towel had been unfolded and spread across a chair back to dry. Joanne crossed the room and opened the French windows giving Sophia time to remove the towel and go in search of a replacement. The sun was already on the herb garden, which was why it grew so well. There were clumps of basil as fresh and vigorous as if it was early summer rather than autumn, and the lavender was trying to flower again after its late summer pruning. Did he notice any of this? He never said.

She returned to the room looking for some trace of him. The en suite bathroom was clean and dry without even a toothbrush to mark his presence. The writing desk hadn't been used, nor the TV and DVD controls. Beside the desk was a small suitcase sitting ready for departure. As with his whole life, Albert Strange was leaving her little to go on.

She crossed to the bed and turned down the cover exposing the pillows which Sophia had just plumped up. Only one pillow case could be judged to have been used and even that one was barely creased. Did he not move his head at night; not dream and bury his face, pulling the pillow around him? She picked up the pillow and held it to her face, taking a long deep breath through her nose and holding it, perfectly still, with her eyes closed.

Perhaps she detected a hint of lemon or of pine; maybe there was a flavour of age, a musty smear of hair tamed each day with water and soap. More likely what she detected was detergent and the smell of linen that had lain on the unused spare bed throughout the summer. Of Albert Strange there was nothing.

In her prayers she asked that her selfish concerns be forgiven and that she be made accepting of God's will. She'd never asked for comfort or plenty, nor even that she be made the recipient of others' love, for love must be given without reciprocal demands. But it didn't work. It wasn't working now.

Having already once transgressed her own rules of acceptable behaviour that morning she now moved one step further towards the unthinkable by picking up the suitcase and laying it on the bed. If Albert, her father, could so successfully hide himself from her all these years then he must have a hiding place. Right or wrong, she would find it; for that, she had convinced herself, was her birthright.

The suitcase was made of a hardboard material with a dimpled blue finish that imitated leather. It had two metal catches with key holes that resisted the pressure of her thumbs so that at first she thought they must be locked. The thought that he would find it necessary to use the locks while staying in her house spurred her to attack them again. This time they sprung open with a loud snap, prompting her to pause and check for sounds of Sophia. If she expected at that moment to feel guilty she could not have realized the strength of anticipation that would spur her pulse and grip her breathing as she opened the lid and laid it back upon the bed.

On top was a small sponge bag of the type given out by airlines, and beside it was a wooden hairbrush. She removed these and placed them carefully on the suitcase lid. Next she removed the top clothes which were the ones he'd arrived in: serge trousers of a donkey hue and a brown tweed jacket that had been turned inside out before folding. There were two shirts, both a little worn, a ball of dark brown woollen socks and a pair of brown shoes in a tartan cloth shoe bag. All these she laid out on the suitcase lid one by one in the same order as they had been

---

packed. His pyjamas were on the bottom, together with a plastic shopping bag containing underwear. That this might be a clue, perhaps as to his intentions that night but certainly as to the timing of his packing that morning, was not considered by Joanne as her attention was taken by the black leatherette folder that lay on top of the pyjamas. She picked it up and straightened, holding it in both hands.

The cover was stamped, 'CSIRO Conference 1996' in white lettering that had been worn through repeated handling. Larger than a Filofax, it was big enough to hold a writing pad and exercise book as well as a diary. A press stud clasp held its contents in place and a blue and white ANZ ballpoint pen had been slid into its spine.

It was not yet 11.00 o'clock so there was well over an hour until the Memorial Service in Hyde Park. Samantha had promised to phone from the ferry in good time for Joanne to pick her and her grandfather up. In the next three hours all she had to do was refresh the flowers at St Agnes' Church. She laid the folder down on the desk and returned to the suitcase, replacing its contents in the same order that she had removed them. Then she closed the case, returned it to its original position on the floor, smoothed down the bedspread and took the black folder out into the garden before Sophia returned.

20.

George Street

The march had started well, lifted by an initial burst of enthusiasm and self-imposed order, but it soon deteriorated as the irregular pace of the front echelons swept back through the ranks of those following, creating hesitancy. By the time they reached the Town Hall the Doppler Effect had taken root, sweeping through the marchers in increasingly frequent stop-start waves that frustrated the general desire for militaristic style which had motivated them thus far. Out of step, they were unable to sustain a common rhythm. Those in front became an obstacle and those behind became an irritation.

Albert's resolve, which he'd struggled to maintain for Sam's sake, now began to crumble. The buildings oppressed him. The tar seal drained his legs of energy. There was something missing from the air which caused him to breathe too hard: it was city air, air without life, used by too many people before him.

'I don't like crowds,' he explained to Sam for fear that his growing agitation was being transmitted to her.

Nobody liked crowds; that wasn't the point: he didn't like people. Their very presence disturbed his senses. How could he hear clearly with so much noise? How could he see distinctly when surrounded by a blur of faces? What was a safe and certain direction when his path was crossed by others whose intentions were oblivious to his own? If he just stopped and closed his eyes he would see more clearly and breathe more freely, but there was no stopping for he was a prisoner of the crowd, shackled to it, a victim of its purpose. Though no-one was touching him he felt as though invisible hands constrained his arms, hurting him. His arms, in turn, ached from the unrealized desire to strike out and slash a path through the jungle of faces and hostile limbs to a safe clearing of silence and solitude; the place from which he had come.

Somewhere along the way he'd let go of Sam's hand, or perhaps she'd withdrawn it. The fondness he'd felt for her minutes before rose up out of him and departed, like a bird that had appeared to be tamed only to lift its head and suddenly fly away. A light flickered in the bird's eye, revealing in its yellow and brown opalescence an instinct for freedom that had flashed within and had to be obeyed. The bird, being Albert, flew to the treetops where the sun shone in air that shimmered from the cymatic waves of the breathing earth.

'I think I need to stop,' he said.

The volume of his voice was at odds with the proximity of the people nearest him, Sam in particular, and, combined with a hint of desperation it revealed the distance to which he'd withdrawn. He believed he'd spoken loud enough but perhaps he'd only spoken to himself, the person who knew best the response he sought.

'I don't want to go on.'

His free hand, the one that had held Samantha's from Martin Place to Park Street, involuntarily took off, describing a parabola above the heads of the encircling crowd and, before returning to his side, inadvertently disturbed the precision of the parting in his hair as if afraid to be caught making a gesture without purpose. He looked down sharply at the girl beside him and realized she was oblivious to him, caught up in the shared emotions of the march.

Not only did his feet hurt in their unaccustomed shoes, but they were no longer wide enough to support him. He felt himself losing his balance, swaying like a dizzy top. He blinked in frustration and clenched his jaw, ripples of determination running up his cheeks and into the steel-grey hairline of his temples. It was absurd – he was fitter than all of them. He strode through forests and climbed the hills every day of his life. His heart rate was that of a young man. He could chop a cord of timber in an hour.

'Did you think it would be like this?' he asked.

This time he really did speak out loud, tapping his grand daughter on the arm to be sure she heard him.

'It's not what I expected.'

He offered this as an explanation for his withdrawal. Whether she'd noticed or not, he felt it was important to point out that he was not withdrawing from her so much as from the rapid deterioration of the event.

'It's a shambles,' he protested.

People now were beginning to curse, resenting the lack of progress and the unavoidable jostling as the marchers concertinaed from behind. Ahead of them the leading columns had turned left into Bathurst Street heading for the park. The glass façade of the Energy Australia building loomed above them and every blare and thump of the military band ricocheted off it straight into Albert's ear.

'It isn't very far,' she pleaded. 'We'll soon be at the Park.'

Her eyes radiated life with such substance that they were like steadying handrails in the maelstrom that raged around him.

'Take my arm,' she added, now the adult to his tentative child, 'and when we get to the Park we'll find a place to sit down.'

So he allowed himself to be led, furiously thinking about what he could say to her, for it was too late now to opt out. He'd stayed silent for sixty years, convinced that words were unreliable. But, of course, with every day that had passed a new reality, falsely manufactured as it was, had become stronger and safer for everyone to adopt. Those who knew the true reality were dying and eventually would all be gone. Even while still alive, they were mostly gone; living out their last days in a fudge of the truth, memories too weak to wrestle with the created myths of those who had the energy to promote them - politicians and romanticists in particular.

If he'd spoken out, would he have remained true to the reality they'd all understood sixty years ago, or would he have allowed that to be re-written too? Perhaps he was fooling himself. Even sixty years ago there were lies and misrepresentations, both deliberate and accidental, but the subject at least was understood by all. The subject was deliberate death; death deliberately inflicted; means of death deliberated upon at length: the death of one's own species.

In the first few years a consensual silence had fallen upon them all, a kind of shame as if the beast had been viewed through the window at night and its image, blood dripping at the mouth, had been uncannily like the reflected image of the viewer looking out. Picture books of Belsen were published and put away quietly in bookshelves.

The silence of the women was different to the silence of the men. Perhaps women were wise enough at that time not to dwell on the nature of men. When men broke the silence it was to question their manhood.

How to explain all that?

21.

The House in Newtown

Willie was awake and feeling anxious. His heart beat rapidly as though it was responding to a blockage somewhere along the arterial highway leading to his limbs. He had a strong urge to shake his arms and legs to loosen the blockage but they were too heavy to lift. His neck ached and so did his left wrist for he had fallen asleep propped up on one elbow and then tipped forward trapping his hand awkwardly beneath his head.

Wherever he was he sensed it was unfamiliar. Cautiously he opened his eyes. The bed, to his relief, was his alone. The light within the room was dim but beyond the blanketed window it was bright. He lay back and looked at the ceiling, wondering why his heart was racing; trying to remember what had woken him. The girl had gone and there was no audible hint of her within the house. The radio he'd heard earlier was still playing next door but he no longer recognised the announcer's voice. His clothes were still on the floor in a pile and a wardrobe that he hadn't noticed before stood open revealing a sparse collection of dresses and skirts, the shelves stuffed with papers and text books.

His mouth was still dry but no longer on fire. Remembering the empty fridge and the cold tap in the kitchen he was not motivated to get up and slake his thirst, contenting himself instead with whatever saliva he could conjure up with his tongue to moisten his palate. He guessed he must have slept deeply or he would have been woken by the girl getting dressed and yet he felt as though he hadn't slept at all. The pounding in his chest was erratic and when he lifted his hands they trembled. If he tried to raise his head the pounding immediately transferred itself to his temples and the back of his cranium felt like it was being prised apart with a crowbar.

Her name was Nicole; he recalled that without having to search. He was in the house in Newtown where he and Luke had returned after an afternoon drinking in the bar on Broadway because, as Luke had said, he was fucked if he was going to piss up against the wall all night and fall into some dark hole stinking of alcohol. They should go look up Ari, he had said, because Ari was a true white man and he knew the way to the land of hope and light. So next thing they were going up King Street in this cab with a Lebanese taxi driver who seemed to be at war with the entire world, scowling and cursing at everything that moved including them, which Luke seemed to find hilarious. Then the road branched at the top into a Y junction with traffic coming from both directions at once, or so it seemed, and without any prior warning to Willie, Luke had suddenly started carrying on in a high pitched voice screaming like a faggot queen about which way to go, left or right, so the cabbie started shouting back until they were both screaming, and Luke went mad, scratching at the Arab's head and pouring filth at him. Stalled in the middle of the intersection and hemmed in by angry honking cars, Willie was shitting himself but Luke suddenly flicked a switch and, calm as could be, informed the driver that he had noticed that the photograph on the taxi licence was not a photo of the driver at all and, besides, he had used one foul epithet too many and they were not going to travel with him any further, with which he grabbed Willie's arm and they got out of the stalled cab and calmly walked away. Well, Luke was calm anyway: he'd apparently achieved his purpose, which was not to pay, and didn't give it another thought. Luke was an actor, that much was clear, but his mock rage had been highly convincing.

The house had been somewhere nearby in one of the back streets filled with brick terraces and rubbish bins and doors that opened onto the street. The single window, barely a meter from the pavement, was barred and boarded. The door of the adjoining cottage was lit by a bare bulb in a broken fitting and a cardboard sign had been pinned to it saying that refugees were welcome there. When Ari answered the door Willie made a presumption that somehow he was associated with the sign, and that presumption had stayed with him all night even after he had learned enough to know it was not the case.

Ari was small and black and softly spoken – Indian, Sri Lankan, Malaysian or thereabouts, Willie guessed – and, as he opened the door Luke greeted him with the boisterous enthusiasm normally bestowed on welcoming dogs, patting him on the back and pushing past into the hallway in a clear demonstration that this was familiar territory to him while Ari checked the street as if wondering how many other unexpected visitors were waiting outside before firmly bolting the door behind them.

All this he could remember clearly. They'd sat on the floor on bean bags and smoked dope that Ari produced from his bedroom at Luke's urging, rolling it very carefully as if the leaves were delicate shards of glass and smiling at Willie and Luke in turn as if everything they said was so very fucking interesting, which it wasn't. Luke had grabbed at the first roach and sucked on it greedily as if there were no such thing as courtesy and Ari had just smiled as if that was Luke's need and Luke could do whatever he wanted. Shit, but the dope was good, he'd thought, though he hadn't said so in case Luke thought him inexperienced or too easily impressed. It went straight down into the wall lining of his gut making him feel like he was opening up and surrendering his body. A giant zip ran down his front from the top of his head to the crack in his buttocks and he pulled it down slowly and laid himself out on the bean bag as if offering his entrails to the sunlight and the wind.

'Good skunk,' Luke had said. 'Ari always has the best.'

Ari just smiled and nodded. Willie had smiled and nodded, too. For the first twenty minutes he was barely holding on, then he started to come to grips with it and on the next round he sucked on to it just as greedily as Luke had done, trying to reach back up to the same place as he'd begun. They smoked and talked and lay about listening to music and drinking Ari's beer which soon ran out and then moved on to the white wine that Luke also found in the fridge, overriding Ari's protests because apparently that belonged to his flatmate, Nicole.

Whether it was the TCP in the skunk or the mix with the alcohol, Willie had found it harder and harder to speak. He wanted to talk about the *Bhagavad-Gita* and the Tibetan book about living and dying which he had tried to memorise for times like this because they were so full of great stuff and so not where the fucked-up world was focused, but he couldn't remember a single phrase. It was like someone had put an electric wire into that part of his brain where all the words were stored and had numbed it. His tongue had a tight rubber band around it.

Luke did most of the talking. He told Ari he was a black cunt and he shouldn't have been allowed in the country. He smiled at him and told him he loved black cunts; said he was the only man in Australia who knew that one day white cunts would be feeling what black cunts felt today, because what goes around comes around and white people were like snow tigers: pretty but outnumbered; pretty but soon to be extinct; stuff like that. Ari just nodded and smiled. It was hard to disagree.

That was all fine, he remembered that, but he couldn't put a time frame to it. How long had they been smoking and drinking? Was it around midnight when Nicole arrived home? She must have let herself in very quietly, just standing there in the semi-dark unannounced so that when Willie looked up and noticed her he had the impression she had materialised and he was in the front row of Hoyts Cinema watching *Star Wars*. She was tall and dressed in black with very thick short dark hair which made her white skin look Gothic. Something about the plainness of her clothes and the satchel she was carrying made him think she must be an executive of some type, a lawyer maybe, and he was filled with an irrational rush of guilt. But she was wearing black rubber-soled boots, he remembered: lawyers wouldn't wear boots like that. She turned and disappeared into her bedroom; the bedroom where he now lay. It was what happened after she came back to join them that he was struggling with.

She came back in bare feet and black pyjamas. Maybe it was a track suit. Neither Luke nor Ari acknowledged her, let alone made an introduction, so he had no idea who she was or how she fitted in. That was yet to emerge. The three of them were lying on the floor in a fairly liquid state doing a fair imitation of the flotation oils in the lava lamp. She sat down on a bean bag, too; back against the wall and legs extended so Willie had a close view of the under soles of her white feet which were very close to the elbow on which he was propped. It seemed to him at that moment as though her feet were the only objects in the room. He passed her the roach.

There were times when life seemed to Willie like a dangerous creature lying at rest. It could suddenly awaken and catch him with its claws. The knowledge of that speed and ferocity of awakening was like a peptic bug buried deep within his gut and as he lay on the bed now, trying to reassemble the pieces of the previous evening, he could taste it in his mouth.

'Nicole from Auschwitz,' Luke smirked eventually.

He looked at her as if challenging for a fight. After having let silence build to the point where it was becoming a deliberate statement, anything said was bound to have sounded like a challenge. Maybe it was just that they were pissed and their timing was out, but with Luke and the taxi incident still fresh, Willie could not be sure.

'Katowice,' Ari corrected apologetically. 'This is Nicole my flatmate from Katowice whose wine we have drunk and which we will have to replace tomorrow. Please forgive.'

'Fuck forgiveness,' Luke protested. 'I want to be punished. We all need a damn good hiding. Beat us up, Nicole. Give us a thrashing.'

Yes, he'd wanted a fight. Ari must have sensed it, too, for he pressed on solicitously, addressing himself to Willie but with the message intended for his flatmate.

'We are both at the same TAFE together and Nicole is the champion of computer sciences while I am just a poor unworthy specimen by comparison who one day will be very lucky to know her when she is extremely rich. So you will be very lucky, too, if you know her. At Enmore we call her Lady Gates.'

Luke sniggered, for what reason was not clear; perhaps for all reasons.

'Where is Katowice?' Willie asked.

'Poland,' Ari replied.

Her feet were the colour of boiled white potatoes and beneath the translucent skin of her ankles her veins were a pale milky blue.

Her toenails had been filed into perfect crescents and coated with clear lacquer. The presentation of her legs and feet in such proximity created an unfamiliar feeling in him; a perspective he had never encountered before. He felt as if he must find a way to communicate with these objects that had been thrust in his face if he was to have any form of communication with their owner, so he reached out and took her toes in his free hand. They were cool and the bones were flexible, more like sinews than bones, and between her toes the skin was warmer and more slippery, opening to his thumb without resistance; private, unseen and silent. His ears rang with the silence and his eyes clouded over. Time was suspended and his arm became frozen.

'Nicole is a business lady,' Luke had proclaimed loudly, 'right Nicole? Way it should be, too. See women in their high heels trotting off to work, cell phones ringing, 'ting-a-ling-a-ling'; it's all fucking good stuff. Cell phones were invented just for women, right Nicole? You couldn't live without them. Gotta take the money from the man, take the money from the man, take the money if you can. And you *can* take the money from the man 'cause the man says you can. Right Nicole?'

She didn't move her legs at all, or her feet, or her toes. It seemed to Willie that if he could stay like this, so intimately attached, something would flow back along his arm that would reveal itself as the most important message he might ever hear, too important for words. He could see that her legs were long and strong, not as muscled as his own but almost the same length. He liked his own legs; they were athletes' legs.

Being unsuccessful in prompting a response to his Tom Waits impression, Luke switched his point of attack to Ari.

'You like the sound of the 'ting-a-ling-a-ling', Ari? You've got a cell phone; didn't you know they were invented for women so they'd never be alone with their own thoughts? Do you know how dangerous thought can be? Haven't you seen them on the buses with their fucking hands pressed to their ears? You must be a bit of a woman yourself I reckon. Way to go! You're never alone with a cell phone. You're never at home with a cell phone. You're a dog with a bone with a cell phone. The radiation is already killing our sperm cells you know, Willie. That's why Nicole's taking her pills, so she'll be the last man standing.'

He had a demented laugh like a stand-up comic, not funny, but effective in getting the response he wanted.

When Nicole spoke for the first time her voice was very matter-of-fact, bored even, and only slightly accented so that if Poland had never been mentioned Willie wouldn't have picked it up.

'Get fucked,' she said.

Willie took his hand away from her foot.

'Your friend is a prick. Is he your friend?' she asked. 'You should tell him he is a prick.'

Having taken his hand away, Willie couldn't think how to put it back again. The spell of invisibility had been broken. He closed his eyes and feigned sleep.

Recalling all this now, Willie wondered whether the reason he'd resorted to sleep was because he couldn't think quickly enough to stay in the conversation. There was Luke sniping away like an angry magpie at anything that moved, and the girl who could clearly hold her own, and Ari with his conciliatory self-effacement, and they all seemed to know each other well, which gave them the freedom of knowing what they could get away with. Whatever first word Willie might have chosen would have fallen awkwardly amongst them, so he closed his eyes instead and listened. He listened to Ari lamenting the burden of study and his seeming inability to cope with it, and to Nicole showing no sympathy, and to Luke searching half-heartedly for any comment that might provoke outrage; and he wondered above all else how they viewed him. Did they look across at his body stretched out on the floor and see him as a person they wanted to be there, or were they indifferent to him? How could he provoke them into revealing their judgement?

Eventually he must have fallen asleep because he remembered waking with a start and finding Luke standing over him, leaning down and trying to pull him upright with one hand behind his neck; cackling in his usual way and, with his free hand, trying to shove something in Willie's mouth.

He fought free – hell, there was no way he was going to be man-handled by anyone – and spat the object out, forcing Luke to step back.

'It's a pill,' Luke protested.

He could see that.

'What the fuck's going on?'

The room had changed: no music, no lights, only the orange lava lamp. No Ari. Luke kneeled down and whispered.

'One for the money, two for the show - you'll thank me.'

He held out his hand with two more pills in it. Sitting with her back to the wall and her feet level with his chest Nicole had watched him impassively. In the glow of the lava lamp her skin was strangely tinted and her eyes were those of a resting cat, saying nothing. Willie looked at the pills and then looked up again at her watching eyes. There was no movement in her face or body. The watching was more like waiting, as if waiting for him to act; so he took the pills and put them in his mouth. Her eyes still did not move while Luke left the room. He remembered reaching over and taking her foot in his hand again, the daring that it had taken and the rush of intimacy that almost forced a groan from him; remembered looking up at her eyes fearful of what he would see in them and, finding nothing still, remembered swallowing the pills.

Now he lay on the bed with the alkaline taste of anxiety filling his mouth, realising that he'd lent his body and soul to oblivion and, now that he had them back, he had no idea what oblivion had done with them in the interim. He remembered waking in his own pool of urine, naked on the floor; remembered finding his clothes in the bedroom, climbing onto the bed and falling asleep again; but he remembered nothing in-between. He touched his cock searching for clues, felt a soft erection and toyed with himself, contemplating a quick ejaculation. His head pounded and the thought was abandoned. Then he heard the sound of a key being inserted in the front door followed by the door closing. Firm footsteps strode towards his bedroom and he quickly pulled the doona over his naked crutch.

22.

Hyde Park

Roger was not the sort of person who would willingly close his eyes in public. It went against his survival instincts. So, with eyes wide open, he was able to take in the crowd around him.

There must have been eight or ten thousand of them, many in full regalia, gathered together in silence in the April sunshine and it was surprising how, at the first mention of God, so many had closed their eyes and dropped their heads as one, intoning the Lord's Prayer with perfect clarity as though God was giving marks for elocution.

Not that anyone observing his lack of participation would have taken it as a gesture of disrespect, for his solemnity couldn't be faulted. As his gaze took in the celebrity group around him, he was for all appearances at another level of piety. It had taken him a while to get there, however.

Crossing the park from his office his concentration had been upon pinning the red poppy to his lapel, straightening his tie and buttoning his jacket; little housekeeping jobs that allowed him to brush the lingering dissatisfactions of his morning meeting with Lawrence out of his system. The dark blue Zegna suit that he'd chosen to wear that morning lacked a button hole in the lapel and he'd spent a fruitless ten minutes scouring the office in search of a pin before finally resorting to using a stapler to attach the poppy. Sure that he'd be late, he then scooped up the VIP invitation from his desk only to realise that the poppy, which had been thoughtfully enclosed with the invitation, came with its own gold safety pin and red ribbon still enclosed in the envelope. Blaming his distraction on Lawrence and his fucking nit-picking, he dashed from the office and strode off to Hyde Park ripping the staple out of his lapel as he walked, tearing the wool and mohair cloth in the process. Blame that on Lawrence, too.

He knew the park walkways well - they led to The Connaught building on the far side which housed the company apartment – and knew he had to hurry if he was to be on time at the mustering point beside the Pool of Reflection at 12.20. The park was filled with over-dressed people, serious and intent, hurrying across the lawns like extras in a European movie and by the time he reached the Archibald Fountain his thoughts had turned to behaviour and protocol. He'd never been to an Anzac ceremony before, let alone as a VIP, and he had little idea what to expect.

In the event, when he crossed over Park Street and approached the cordon of the VIP section, the radiant silver hair of Bob Summers immediately caught his eye and in that instant Roger's role became defined. There, too, was the large head, all chin and ears, of the State Premier bent reverentially in seeming awe at the importance of the occasion as if Anzac Commemorative Services hadn't already been held in tens of thousands of venues for the last eighty seven years.

'So glad you could come,' murmured Bob, pressing his hand in passing. The skin that covered the saturated fat of his neck and jowls was still tanned in late autumn. His suit was pale grey, almost the colour of his hair, and his shoes were grey also.

The protocol became easier, Roger decided, if he watched and copied the Premier. When he walked, he clasped his hands behind his back. When he stood still, he clasped his hands together in front of him. If he should lose the thread of what was being said by the Duntroon voices over the loud speaker, he would look thoughtfully up at the sky. When he'd recovered the thread of what was being said again, he would look solemnly down at his feet, moving his weight from one foot to the other, stirring one foot occasionally as if quietly stirring memories.

Pretty soon he had the hang of it. He knew why he was there and what needed to be done. They were all there to honour the great sacrifices that had been made. In his case the sacrifices were monetary ones in favour of the NSW Labour Party. He sure as hell wasn't there because of the great sacrifices made by generations of

Savilles in the Great Wars (which wasn't to say they wouldn't have made them if called upon.)

As the prayers finished, and the crowd opened their eyes to listen to the address, Roger began to steel himself against the rhetoric. What made the dead so glorious? Why did defeat define a nation? Was anyone else questioning this? Wasn't it contrary to the winning ethos? It seemed to him to be a bit of an emotional wallow - which might explain why Samantha had become caught up in it. (Females did have that tendency.) Would she ever be inspired to write the Saville family history for her class with the dedication and fervour that she had devoted to the Gallipoli Campaign? What was wrong with schools that they preferred death and defeat over survival and victory?

It occurred to him then that Samantha hardly knew the Saville family history. He'd never discussed it with her. He'd allowed too much of the family ethos to come from Joanne, as if acknowledging that there was only one type of history that bestowed legitimacy on Australians. She, after all, was an Anglo. Her grandfather and father had fought in the Great Wars. How could the Savilles compete with that? (Well, apart from anything else, there hadn't been the opportunity. His father had arrived on the first plane into Darwin carrying refugees from the Hungarian uprising in 1956; too late for the Second World War; too late for the Korean War even. They couldn't be blamed for that.)

Perhaps there was another reason why he'd been reticent. When his own father talked of their family history he never spoke of bravery and sacrifice for all; he spoke of survival of the individual and the seizing of opportunities. These were values implicitly rejected in the Anzac creed. When Russian troops had poured into Budapest to crush the uprising in November '56 it was, according to Janek Slavjil, the smart ones who used the opportunity to get out. He and Roger's mother had been planning their escape from Communism for months anyway and under the cover of exploding guns and Molotov cocktails they slipped across the Austrian border and into a United Nations camp, leaving the foolhardy (mostly criminals, according to his father) to fight their bare-handed battles with the Russian tanks on their own. What would the true Aussie have done? He'd have stayed and been killed as well, if the legend was to be believed.

No, he'd never properly discussed it with his children; they'd have wanted a dead hero and been confused by what he was offering them instead. As a child even he had been confused. It had taken him a long time to realize that his father never considered for one moment that it was necessary to embellish his story. If history had chosen to re-write some of the atmosphere surrounding events it had to be blamed upon the Australian propensity for siding with the underdog. Janek Slavjil was first off the plane (in case they changed their minds and flew them back to Hungary, he used to joke). Somehow Slavjil metamorphosed into Saville (because it was easier to spell, perhaps) and the caption to the photograph of him standing on the steps of the aircraft in Darwin - head bandaged and arm in a new white sling because The Telegraph journalist had wanted a scoop before the first plane load of wounded evacuees arrived - described him as a student freedom fighter. 'That's what they wanted,' his father said. He never disguised the facts. They gave him a university grant and he studied accountancy. In no time at all they became Australians. There was no shame in any of that. He must make a point of talking more about it.

The address droned on. So now Janek Slavjil's son stood in the VIP enclosure at the Anzac Memorial Service forty six years later. In a single generation they had traversed the demographic arc from Matraville to Rydalmere, East Ryde to Randwick and Bellevue Hill to the northern slopes of Mosman. Surely that defined a nation more clearly than death on a foreign beach eighty something years ago?

He breathed deeply of the mild autumn air and watched the golden yellow leaves tumbling from the plane trees. The light aircraft which he'd seen earlier in the day over Bondi had finished its work and left a powdery white inscription in the sky: 'Lest we forget.' He thought of his house with its sweeping views of the northern beaches and the Phoenix palms leading down the garden to the pool, and he thought of his office boardroom lined with cherry wood panelling high above the city's financial district with its commanding view of the harbour that not even the Renzo Piano building could better. And he thought of Alison Pyke.

It never had been Roger's intention to invite her to his room. She'd walked back with him from the beach and stopped when he stopped at his door. Her question about his commitment to Whiteman's Creek was a business question. His answer was serious. Of course he was bloody committed. He put his key in the door and opened it. It wasn't his job to ask where her room was and seek assurance that she knew how to find it. She was a grown woman for God's sake. Goodnight, he said formally, and then he stepped inside. When he turned to close the door again she was still standing there. He presumed she wanted to say something and he waited, hand on the door knob. But she didn't speak. Her eyes held the same look that he had seen when they stood on the jetty earlier that afternoon, as if she'd spoken but for some reason he'd missed the meaning. He hesitated, then he took his hand off the door knob and she stepped past him into the room.

He lay down on the bed and put his hands behind his head, removing neither his shoes nor his jacket. This was her script. He looked at the ceiling and waited, expecting to hear the rustle of her black dress as it drifted to the floor, the clunk of her shoes as she kicked them into the corner, the snap of her bra strap and the creak of the bed as she knelt beside him. He closed his eyes. There was a fan that sliced the air as though it was cutting through jelly. He was tired. She would place her hand on his waistband and undo his belt, pulling on it sharply to release the buckle; and then she'd slide open his fly and slip her hand inside his underpants. His belly was firm. Her hand would be cool and dry. If she sucked him with a wet mouth his erection would grow and grow. If her mouth was hard he would struggle to respond.

A minute passed. It seemed like ten. He let out a heavy sigh, expelling all the tired air of the world, and turned his head towards her. It was a world that he alone carried on his shoulders, a weariness that only he alone could comprehend.

'*The CEO gets a bigger suite than everyone else,*' *she said, as if filing a report.*

All that time she must have been looking at him.

He frowned. What was this? He didn't like being on his back. He didn't like her standing over him.

'*Is that a question?*' *he asked.*

She shrugged.

'A fact.'

The same smile returned.

'Which is as it should be...' he got off the bed and stood up, towering over her, for she barely made it to his chin. '... The CEO should have the biggest fucking suite in the house. He should have the biggest bed and the biggest bath and the biggest tray of midnight chocolates and the biggest bottle of champagne and, if he feels the need, the biggest bevy of maidens to massage away his cares because ...'

'He has the biggest ego ..?'

'Because human beings have always lavished comforts on the condemned man and no-one is more quickly condemned when things go wrong than the CEO. It is purely a matter of kindness.'

She smiled openly, this time with her teeth, and he turned her around and lowered the zip of her black dress from the nape of her neck to the small of her back. By the time he'd pushed her dress down over her hips to the floor, removed her bra and brushed his hands over her nipples and down to the elastic band in her pants he had the beginnings of an erection.

It wasn't his script. He hadn't invited her there. How was it, then, that he'd found himself later on his knees, back straining, arms beginning to weaken, pushing his pelvis harder and harder as if he had some Goddamn obligation to create the orgasm of the century? Why was he doing all the work? What the fuck was her contribution? As he strained unsuccessfully to extract some joy from her body she watched as if she were a police witness on the other side of a one way glass screen. It wasn't even as though she smelled that good. She was young; she should have smelled better. Fuck the little bitch!

Roger recovered with a start. The wreaths had all been laid. The recitation had begun.

'At the going down of the sun, and in the morning, we will remember them.'

The Premier's head rose and his large jaw shot firmly forward.

'We will remember them,' the crowd repeated.

'We will remember them,' Roger said quickly. In his rush to catch up with the words they came out a little louder than he'd anticipated but nobody seemed to notice.

A bugler played The Last Post, so haunting and clear that the minute's silence which followed became an unscripted symphony of muffled sniffs and coughing. Bob Summers turned and caught his eye, shaking his head ruefully as if to convey in one gesture every one of life's clichés that required no repeating. Bob Fucking Summers, of all people; smooth as butter: The Bag Man. The minute's silence was followed by The Reveille and the mood was broken.

'Never fails, mate ...' Bob Summers boomed, grabbing his arm and squeezing it hard as the ceremony broke up. There were lots of hands to be shaken. '... Not a dry eye in the place.'

He looked around as if challenging to be refuted.

'Premier wants to say hello. Leave it to another time if you want.'

'I wanted to have a word with you on your own, Bob.'

There was so much milling around and pressing of flesh it was like being on the floor of a political convention.

'Aren't we meeting tonight?'

'Yes, but there'll be some guests there that I thought I should warn you about. They may have some questions about Whiteman's Creek.'

'And you want me to give the right answers?'

Roger lent back and exposed his upper teeth, touching Summers lightly on his grey sleeve.

'We all want the right answers, Bob. You know my concerns. We don't want any unwelcome surprises when you announce the Windsor Road funding scheme. As much as I support the Government I would hope to have your support in return. It's a very important issue for us.'

'Of course it is, Roger; I know that. It's a very important issue for us, too. I don't mind admitting that we're struggling with it. Public-Private funding is under a spotlight. We have to tread very carefully.'

Shit! He knew something. Don't bend down; they're getting ready to fuck us up the arse.

'The worst thing would be an announcement without prior warning, Bob; a decision without a chance to negotiate it.'

Was that clear enough? Would The Bag Man see the offer he was already making?

'Relax, mate, relax. Whatever your fears, I'm sure they're unfounded. You can rely on me for my full support.'

There were all sorts of connections being made around them and political opportunities being missed. The Premier was about to depart. He couldn't hold Summers' attention any longer.

Relax! Who did he think he was: *Frankie Goes To Hollywood*? Fucking politicians; they were as slippery as wet soap. The Astor deal couldn't come soon enough. Looking around in vain, Roger tried to catch sight of Samantha and Albert in the dense crowds that were making their way out of the park. He started to move towards Whitlam Square so that he could cross over to his apartment at The Connaught. Before he reached the traffic lights his cell phone beeped, signalling the arrival of a new text message.

At that moment, as he removed the phone from his pocket, his worst thought was of the embarrassment he would have felt if it had gone off during the Memorial Service. Thank God for small mercies, as his father used to say.

23.

Saville Corp's Office

Not for the first time that day, Lawrence concluded that knowing was not enough. Or was it that knowing, in this case, was too much? It might be an interesting point to debate. The presence of knowledge might assist in confirming guilt, but the absence of knowledge was not available as a defence of innocence. Here was one of the pivotal points on which corporate law was so precariously balanced.

How would he put it if he were ever to accept that university post? There had to be a benefit from his years of practical experience. Law was like anything else; theory and practice. Standing before a group of students at the University of New South Wales (the sun streaming through the fly-stained windows and the audience shifting their buttocks on the hard wooden pews of the lecture theatre as they waited for him to say something that would short circuit the drudgery of learning), how would he explain it? What could he say so they would forever understand and remember him for it?

'I want you to concentrate on one word,' he might begin. 'When you come to consider the application of law remember that there are no moral absolutes and when actions or inactions come to be judged you, as practitioners, and the Courts before whom you must prosecute or defend your case, can only be concerned with interpretation of the facts. The legislation has been handed to you and you cannot, except in rare instances, change it to suit your circumstances. But I digress ...'

The word, Lawrence, the word: what is the word? Is it really, *'Knowing'*?

No need to answer too quickly; there was time enough to savour this recurring fantasy of his, of being transported to the halls of academe and being recognised as the font of wisdom and good humour; him, Professor Beck, middle-aged but trim, not tall, but agreeably short in stature; the eyes showing the warmth and depth of the man into whose knowledge and beliefs the young would be so tempted to plunge. Heavens above, he allowed himself few enough pleasures these days; there was no harm in a little fantasising around a proximate truth. But where others might be allowing the imagined light to be falling upon their genitalia - the region that governed most men's thinking, it seemed - his pleasure lay in the opportunity to expose the quality of his mind to an audience which he felt sure could not be short changed. He didn't need children to know that the young were no longer born with innocence and belief; that their ignorance was only of facts. Get on with it, their eyes would be saying.

Try this, he thought, looking up in his imagination to the top window in search of the sunlight's source, closing his eyelids to protect himself against the particles of dust that whirled like asteroids in the deep space of the lecture theatre. It is the responsibility of a company director not to continue trading *knowing* that the company is insolvent. It is the responsibility of a board not to approve any resolution *knowing* that it will not be in the interests of all shareholders equally. To act *knowingly* in breach of legislation may result in criminal charges.

For effect, perhaps, he could try expressing it in the negative. Thus, an investor not knowing the risks inherent in an investment in shares after having read the prospectus, may be entitled to sue for consequential loss. Conversely, an investor knowing information that affects the value of shares that is not known equally to all other shareholders, is breaking the law if he acts upon it for gain.

'In every transaction there is a tipping point. The consequences at law can be found in close proximity to that one word. Go searching for it. The word is, *'Knowing'.'*

Would that do it for them, he wondered? Would that give them the assurance for which they were looking; that the high marks they'd sacrificed their teenage years upon in order to gain admission to Law School, years when they could have been surfing the waves of their rising libidos instead, were not all wasted?

Most unlikely, Lawrence thought. Someone in the front row - a girl most probably - would put up her hand in protest, wait until she had an audience, and then, oblivious to his intent (which was, after all, to draw them into a broad-based philosophical debate), pick up only on his last reference and ask him why it was that the Securities and Investment Commission had never successfully prosecuted anyone for insider trading.

Ah! Not true, not true, he would bluster: there has been one successful prosecution. Hahn, I think, is his name.

One? Just One? Well, hello, Mr Beck!

Yes, quite so. Maybe there were other words he should be teaching them; or maybe they knew the words already. It wasn't *Knowing* that was essential to insider trading or breach of fiduciary duty; not to these young hard-heads in a hurry. His daydreaming was outdated. If he was really speaking to a young, contemporary audience he would find them far more cynical. He was describing a law founded on the outmoded concept of ethics, as if he hadn't heard that the whole field of moral science had been expunged from text books and tutorials as being redundant. *Knowing* indeed! It wasn't *Knowing* that mattered any longer in law.

He was sure Roger knew the word that mattered. There were two words. He had spoken them.

'You can't withhold the valuations from the market just to suit yourself, knowing that the share price is likely to rise the minute they're released,' Lawrence had protested to Roger sometime earlier as he listened to the outline of the Astor proposal: 'that's a clear breach of the regulations.'

'I don't *know* that the share price will rise, Lawrence. Maybe the market expects the valuations to be even higher and they'll mark us down accordingly. You're making a dangerous assumption. It's all very well to preach on about my responsibility to inform, but it seems to me I'd be bloody irresponsible if I presumed to know in advance how the market would react. The shares might go up, they might go down or they might not move at all.'

'That isn't the point. The point is that you are relying upon giving the new valuations to Astor in order to persuade them to invest and, in doing that, it means that all shareholders will not be informed equally.'

'That's crap. I'm a shareholder and I know what the valuations are. You're a shareholder. There's hardly ever a time when shareholders are informed equally.'

'Yes, but we're officers of the company, Roger. We may be better informed but we are forbidden to profit from that. We can't trade our shares. That's why we have a Compliance Committee.'

This was absolutely fundamental stuff, thought Lawrence, and the fact that he'd had to explain it was very worrying.

'For God's sake, Lawrence, don't be so fucking naive.'

Roger had unwound himself from the freestanding electronic whiteboard on which he'd been leaning for the last ten minutes since completing his dissection of the Astor deal. The whiteboard was his territory alone; no-one else dared approach it. He reminded Lawrence of the pelicans on the terrace of Catalina Restaurant in Rose Bay where he and Marjorie ate every Friday night. This was his preening and feeding ground, his stage, and he left it with reluctance.

'Look, I'm not going to debate it with you. That's the deal and that's the way I want it drafted.'

But the way in which he'd crossed to the window and waited with his back turned to the room was a sure sign that he knew the debate was not ended, even if he wished it to be so.

Lawrence had reviewed his handwritten notes.

'Let me go through this once again,' he said testily.

Anyone examining the whiteboard as it then stood would have taken it for a work by Jackson Pollock: colourful, energetic, but indecipherable. On the way to arriving at this state it might have revealed hints of an Edward De Bono Lateral Thinking class; sub-texts and commentaries fired off into orbit from the core calculations on the back of aggressive red arrows, ringed for emphasis in blue and green, violently expunged in messy black. Saville had no other way of thinking. Except with a marker pen in his hand, it was possible he was dyslexic, Lawrence thought.

'First of all, they are to contract to buy the Western residential sub-division for a hundred and sixty five million dollars. That's leasehold?'

'Leasehold!'

'Which you say is supported by the new valuations which I haven't yet seen.'

'I told you, they're in my briefcase and you'll have them later in the day.'

They'd already gone through this two or three times but it was Lawrence's way to continue repeating the facts, like running an engine until the loose parts fell out.

'Hmm,' he'd mused, as if for the first time. 'That's certainly a good price if we can get it, particularly if we can joint venture on their developments. And their incentive for paying this price is that we can issue new equity to them at eighty percent of today's price knowing that it will inevitably increase once we've announced the new valuations and the land sale?'

Perhaps Roger was now used to his method, or perhaps he didn't care. Where earlier he had been swooping and diving about the room like a pelican about to be fed, he now buried his head in the crook of an arm that rested against the glass of the picture window with its iconic, vulgar view of the harbour all the way to Sydney Heads; a view which cost them far too much money.

'Well,' Roger said eventually, returning back to his seat at the head of the board table as if exhausted by his hour of explanation, defeated and deflated by Lawrence's questioning of him (not looking Lawrence in the eye), and drained of energy, 'it's the best deal I can do. If you can do better, please tell me.'

'No, no, that isn't my problem. The issue I'm struggling with is the value. If they are to pay that amount for the leasehold interest in the sub-division, then across the board we need a twenty percent lift in values to satisfy the Banks.'

'Forget the valuations, Lawrence. In case you've forgotten, the only value that matters is what someone is willing to pay. Astor is willing to pay.'

'Yes, but on the basis of valuations you are showing to them alone and with the added carrot of some cheap shares. By my calculation we have to give the Banks a hundred and thirty five million of that sale price to maintain our sixty percent debt to total assets. But that's assuming they accept the value as being real.'

Lawrence's notes were very precise. There was no argument.

Saville had leaned back in his chair, legs out, hands behind his head, eyes to the ceiling in a familiar pose. He'd said everything he needed to say, in his opinion, and this was now just a process of acceptance. That's the inference his attitude made; an inference that both annoyed and alarmed Lawrence.

'You didn't hear me, Lawrence. What I said is they can have the lot, all fucking one hundred and sixty five million of it, on one condition: they release my shares from escrow. This sale will tell the market what it wants to hear; that we are grossly under-valued. The shares will rise and the Banks will be happy. It's as simple as that.'

This was said slowly and evenly through teeth that were exposed in the expression common to primates caught somewhere between aggression and conciliation. How often did he have to repeat himself?

Lawrence, too, wondered how many ways he needed to make his point. If these were really the values that Roger claimed them to be then they had to be released to the market immediately. It was price-sensitive information. As if the issue of new equity wasn't enough, on top of that they were contemplating asset sales that exceeded the threshold of shareholder funds without shareholder or stock exchange consent. That was something else that seemed to be glossed over.

But Saville had had enough. He looked at his watch and stood up.

'I've got you out of jail, Lawrence. You should be kissing my fucking feet. We put a hundred and sixty five million dollars in the bank and Alison Pyke gets to know what it's like to take it up the arse. I don't give a toss about your hypothetical theories as to who knows what and when. Your job is to draft it and, if they think there's something wrong, their job is to prove it. My job, as always, is to pull this fucking thing off, and I expect your support every inch of the way.'

This was his moment for leaving; leaving on large strides that brooked no objection, leaving as a form of theatre, man-of-action, man-of-destiny, man-alone-carrying-the world-upon-his-shoulders: Lawrence couldn't tell which one it was. There was more. Roger needed to be at the Commemorative Service and he'd be talking to Bob Summers about that Windsor Road funding while he was at it, letting him know exactly what was the meaning of political contributions, because he wasn't going to take any bullshit from mid-level bankers who spoke through their cunts; which was a lesson that Lawrence might like to learn if he wanted to be *really* useful. Or words to that effect.

Thus Lawrence sat alone at the large table, his notebook open in front of him with its neat handwritten draft which was already free of any anomalies or discrepancies as it had been from the moment he'd begun to transcribe Roger's whiteboard briefing. No-one captured and ordered the facts better than Lawrence Beck - it was well known - and facts were, of course, incontrovertible.

For a moment he was tempted to return to his daydream lecture to make that point before the angled sunlight through the top window of the lecture theatre moved off him and started to climb slowly up the wall behind (assuming that his imaginary young audience didn't lose patience and start fidgeting for escape); but first he needed to confront the fact that *Knowing* was not what mattered at law at all, never had been, never would be. What a ridiculous academic conceit that was.

No, he'd allowed himself to sink into the daydream like sinking into a warm bath. He wasn't a Professor of Law, never would be now; he was a commercial lawyer at the hard end of business. Pull the plug and step out of the bath, Lawrence.

Saville knew the words. He'd spoken them.

'Their job is to prove it,' he'd said. 'Your job is to draft it; their job is to prove it.'

Ipsissima verba. In the end, wasn't that all that law was about?

It was going to be a long and arduous afternoon if he was to prepare a Heads of Agreement capable of being signed the next morning. He needed to think carefully about references to valuations, and dates were important, too. It was now clear that Roger had taken these negotiations well down the track without telling him. In hindsight that could be used to advantage. Perhaps the Agreement could be back-dated, thus removing it from the proximity to the undisclosed valuations. Yes, that could be an option.

Feeling better, he decided to phone Marjorie and remind her what time they needed to be at the RSL dinner.

'I may be late,' he warned. 'Don't be surprised if I have to dash in and change, then run straight out again. You will be ready, won't you?'

'Oh, I should think so; having had the whole morning to consider what to wear. Joanne and I have debated it for hours.'

'Nothing too colourful, I hope.'

'I was thinking of my red dress and purple hat. Soldiers love hats.'

'Marjorie, for heaven's sake; this is a dinner for the War Widows Fund, not a comical party.'

'I was joking.'

'Oh!'

He wasn't in a mood for jokes. There was too much to be done.

'Would you mind watering the azaleas for me?' he asked. 'I may not have time.'

'I always water the azaleas; every day.'

'I water them on the weekends.'

'It isn't a weekend, it's Anzac Day.'

Somehow, what should have been a straight forward call felt unsatisfactory, almost as he knew it would.

24.

The Apartment

When Roger's secretary, Linda, had first been commissioned to find a suitable company apartment close to the office she'd suffered such a personality change that Saville had thought he'd be forced to fire her.

'All I want is a place to crash when I've been working late or entertaining,' he'd said. 'I don't want to drive home at one in the morning and then have to drive all the way back again at seven a.m. in order to beat the traffic; particularly if I've been drinking.'

This was so sensible - responsible even - that if she chose to repeat it to Joanne and Lawrence in those terms they might well have agreed that the apartment purchase was an absolute necessity, long overdue.

In his opinion his relationship with Linda was a model for others to follow. Having observed his father extracting twenty years of dedicated loyalty from Rita Hartman without once having uttered a personal word to her, Saville had concluded that he could achieve the same with his own secretary. It helped that Linda was in her late forties and plain, just as Rita must have been when she first started working for his father. Her family was from Malta. Her husband's family had been from Lebanon. Enough said. She needed the job and had long ceased being preoccupied with the need for a husband. Somewhere there was a grown-up daughter whose travails formed a safe and unobtrusive conversational continuum, like the weather. Roger would pay her well, he determined, so long as he didn't need to know anything about her beyond the boundaries of their working environment. Only once, at the very outset, had he felt the need to emphasise that he didn't issue requests to staff, he only issued instructions, and they then quickly settled into a perfectly impersonal working relationship.

But the mere mention of the apartment had brought on the weirdest and most unexpected change. It was as though his secretary had been replaced without his knowledge by an actress from Theatre Sports. What role she thought she was playing, he never did fathom. It didn't bear thinking about.

Walking through her office, he'd heard her on the phone talking in a voice two octaves higher than normal and considerably faster. Alerted by her tone he paused while she completed her sentence.

'We want the deepest and most comfortable armchairs,' she said.

His blood had frozen.

'I want soft pastels and lots of cushions. The fabric samples you sent me are too cold and severe.'

What fabric samples? Who the fuck is 'we'? Why was she impersonating Ruby Wax?

He went into his office and sat at his desk fighting to keep down a plume of anger that rose like vomit in his windpipe. It was disgusting. He felt violated. Why didn't she just take down his pants and give him an enema if she wanted to invade him so completely? What was it with women? No, he didn't want to think about it.

Later that day he called her in and told her he wanted her to talk with their IT Manager and set up a system that automatically captured a copy of every incoming and outgoing email within the company which she was then to summarise on a daily basis in a log that was to be forwarded to him weekly.

'You may find it time consuming,' he said sympathetically, 'but I'm worried by our potential exposure to unscrupulous competition and I can't rely on anyone else to ensure we are not leaking commercial secrets.'

He smiled. It was actually a very good idea.

'I don't want you wasting time on the company apartment,' he added casually. 'Hand it over to one of the Property Managers and tell him to report direct to me. It should be practical and plain; a place to hold meetings and a place to sleep. Tell him to keep it simple.'

He hadn't attempted to interpret the expression on her face. That was it; he would never make that mistake again nor, if she learned the lesson, would she.

'What about the Privacy Act?' was all she said; a question which he took to be rhetorical.

Now, some two years later, he looked at the apartment and its furnishings without enthusiasm. Whatever vision Linda had held in mind had clearly been avoided. No-one was going to detect the hand of a woman here. The sofa and chairs were Italian leather and chrome which, like the Bang and Olufsen TV and sound system, were so aesthetically anal in composition that they could only have been designed for people passing through. The sofa was so uncomfortable that when he watched television he slid off and ended up sitting on the floor. There were no cushions, no books or magazines, and the kitchen appliances had never been used, not even to make a cup of coffee. In the bedroom wardrobe there were two navy blue suits and three laundered shirts on hangers. The bed was unmade and there were bathroom towels lying on the bedroom floor.

Since entering the apartment over an hour ago he'd made at least three inspections of every room. He'd got down on his knees and looked under the furniture, opened every cupboard and pulled the curtains away from the windows. He'd searched diligently but without hope, knowing that the only thing worse than the situation he appeared to be facing was the possibility that it was a hoax. Then, while standing on one of the kitchen bar stools in order to peer into the storage space above the hot water cylinder, he came across a back copy of *The Wentworth Courier*.

As he carefully eased himself down from the bar stool his thoughts flew immediately to Linda. Perhaps he'd miscalculated when he abruptly removed her from responsibility for the apartment. Her silent response to his order may not have been acceptance, but, rather, shock and embarrassment. He'd entered into that part of a woman's being that describes the essence of her; which gives her almost as much purpose as child bearing; and he'd shattered it with a single unthinking blow. A woman's compulsion for home making was as strong as a man's compulsion for sex. Now, somewhere on the kitchen wall of her unit in Concorde, there must be a faded real estate cutting from *The Wentworth Courier* circled in red. Was it Malta she came from or was it Haiti? Did she insert fresh pins in that cutting every day? Had she taken a copy of the apartment key in order to come secretly when she knew he was away and inhabit its shadows with her spirits; spirits of shame and resentment? Christ, how close was Malta to Sicily? It was only a boat ride away. *Omerta*, silence and revenge, had been sitting in his outer office all this time; watching as he walked across the park in the late evening; watching as he came into the office the following morning. The only thing he'd asked her to do for the apartment was to arrange the cleaning. It had been a peace offering, but now he realized he had never met a cleaner and had no idea who it was. Maltese or Sicilian, Linda's own daughter even, he had left himself naked to their gaze.

And now this: his briefcase had been stolen.

He picked up the magazine from the kitchen floor and took it into the living room. The heavy glossy which was the free weekly bible for Eastern Suburbs women, crammed with two hundred pages of real estate advertising, fell with a thud upon the Milano coffee table. Dejectedly he perched himself on the edge of the sofa and began to turn the pages, glossy houses passing through his fingers as he flicked them over like a teller counting bank notes. Tennis courts and swimming pools sat smugly under azure skies and omnipresent sunlight; clipped box hedges lined white gravel paths and sandstone steps led between alabaster columns into cool dark unseen rooms where wealthy women planned dinner menus and waited while their husbands schemed over the next ascent of the ladder. Vaucluse, Double Bay, Point Piper, Bennelong; how high could you climb, the advertisements asked? The estate agents' names grew bolder, their borders stronger, their hyperbole straining to take the reader out of the slough of complacency into the stratosphere of envy. *'Seldom in a lifetime did opportunities present themselves, never to be repeated, defining lifestyle and rewarding that special person if only ...'* (If only they'd fall for it and allow the fucking real estate agent to earn more money, Roger thought.)

Full page frontals of waterside palaces briefly gave way to double-page spreads of Bellevue Hill mansions before, as if by some invisible command, modesty decreed a diminution in size and a change of language in favour of family values, a code for diminishing monetary values, the down rungs of the ladder that led south from the giddy heights of the inner harbour through the brick and tile suburbs of Waverley, Queens Park, Maroubra and beyond.

'Apartments ... City ... Executive ...'

He searched without finding the ad he'd expected. What was the cover date? Last November - barely six months ago - and he'd owned the apartment for nearly two years: so this wasn't the issue that had advertised it. He sat up straight and frowned, pursing his lips and drawing his knees together. It was as if he was sitting on a rock surrounded by water, uncertain as to whether the tide was coming in or going out.

The thing was he'd always known there was a moment like this waiting for him, from the minute he'd announced his intention to buy the place. Perhaps Linda had known as well; her embedded Catholicism visualising a body marked with shame, clear as the stigmata on the wax effigy of Christ on the altar of the Cathedral at Gozo, or wherever the fuck she came from. Were the soft pastels and the deep cushions that he'd heard her describing a pietistic attempt on her part to purify the unregenerate masculinity of his actions? For why else had he bought this fucking apartment, if not to place himself in the ante room of fate; bait for temptation? He could just as easily have hired himself a permanent driver if his need was to avoid driving at night, back to his conjugal bed within twenty minutes at the outside, sober or not, his actions approved; clean shirts on their hangers, breakfast at the table and the same driver waiting to return him to his labours at seven the next morning. No doubt Lawrence had already made the calculation. For the same cost of capital he could have afforded to have two drivers on permanent standby. As if he didn't know.

The pages started to turn again, knowing where they were going. *To Buy* became *To Let*. The allure of property hunting led to the burden of ownership. *Personal* and *Beauty* services led to *Trade Services* and *Plumbing*. The pages turned faster. The tide was coming in. He drew up his knees and briefly closed his eyes as he came finally to the back of the book.

ADULT SERVICES ...

The back of the book: this was where the Japanese started, reading from right to left. Was that why the adult section was placed there, or was it out of shame? How different would the Eastern Suburbs be if that section was moved to the front; if the eight pages of services for the genitalia were put where they belonged? Let Lisa and Cindy and Busty Delilah get their offerings on the table where they could be more easily found by generous gentlemen in need of tender loving care because their wives had their balls in a vice. Let the matrons, skipping through to the property pages in search of new levels of envy and desire at least have the subliminal reminder of the repetitive urge to ejaculate from which their worker husbands suffered. Give the honest whores priority of space and let the real estate whores know their place.

He closed his eyes, knowing what was coming, three lines that he could see with absolute clarity because right from the beginning they'd leapt from the page at him. *'Maxine will make you have pleasure. Private and discreet. Your place only.'*

He had no memory of throwing the magazine into the top cupboard. Perhaps he'd feared that if those three lines had leapt from the page at him they would leap from the page at anyone else who found the magazine lying in his apartment, too.

And now the bitch had his briefcase. The towels on the bedroom floor told him that no cleaner had been since last night. There was only one person who could possibly have taken it.

Alright, the tide was coming in but that was no reason for sitting down to drown. He stood up and flexed his arms, shaking his hands loose and stretching the sinews of his neck while checking his reflection in the glass patio doors. This thing didn't have to end badly. He smiled. Keep your charm and wits about you, he thought.

His cell phone lay on the kitchen counter in the place where his briefcase had lain the night before. He had a clear vision of it. That was where he always placed his possessions on entering the apartment. He'd come straight from a meeting with the valuer, Tom Higham, which is why he had the briefcase with him. He'd walked out of the Park Street building feeling dangerously light headed and turned towards Elizabeth Street with the intention of picking up his car from the office and heading home. If he had forgotten momentarily that Jo wanted him back early because Albert was staying the night then that was excusable in the circumstances. What he had just achieved with Tom Higham over the previous two hours had been far more significant than a family dinner. It wasn't a feeling of elation that filled him because the result of their negotiations didn't represent a great victory so much as the avoidance of a defeat. He had fought and prevailed. Nobody else would understand the relevance of that. He'd got down and got dirty because none of his over-paid fellow directors had the balls for it or even understood that their business swung by the thread of this single vital issue. While Lawrence wrung his hands and accepted the fate that the valuations would deal to them he, Roger Saville, had been out there making fucking sure nothing was left to chance.

Maybe it was anger that he'd been feeling. Maybe it was the sweet aftertaste of fear. He arrived at the junction of Elizabeth and Park, where he should have turned left towards Martin Place, but instead he crossed over into Hyde Park and headed towards The Connaught, making the same call on his cell phone as he did now and, just as he was now, he was greeted with the usual message asking him to leave his number so that Maxine could call back immediately. Which she'd done. He waited for her for forty minutes and when she arrived they did what they always did, now that she understood him. He only remembered Jo's plea for him to be on time for dinner when he was in the shower. It was already eight thirty by then. That's why he'd rushed out. That's why he'd forgotten his briefcase. He'd looked around at everything else in the apartment and not noticed the one thing that didn't belong there, thinking only that there was no risk in letting Maxine get dressed in her own time and closing the door behind her. They were regulars, he remembered thinking; they knew each other inside out.

This time his call was not returned immediately. He went back through the Menu to Messages and scrolled through to his Text

Inbox where he'd left the message which he'd received as he was leaving the ceremony in the park. Through Options he went to Call Back. No Number Found. He returned to Options and scrolled down to Reply. This was ridiculous. How could he find out whether the text message had come from her number? What if he'd got this all wrong and he was dealing with a different person, someone who knew the relevance of what was contained in the briefcase? The sender's number must be there somewhere in his phone. Samantha would know how to retrieve it.

The cursor flashed on an otherwise empty screen waiting for him to make up his mind. There were only three words in the message he'd received. *'I HAVE IT'*. Bald, brutal, direct; devoid of preamble and gratuitous niceties, just the way she'd approached his sexual requirements. You are missing your briefcase, is what she was saying: I have it. No need to spell it out more fully; the meaning was clear.

But, hold on. Had she looked at its contents before she decided to take it? Did she realise there was no money or credit cards inside, only a valueless plastic folder with a schedule of valuations and a covering letter that would mean nothing to her; a folder which she would have no means of knowing that he needed that day? Be calm, he thought. Do nothing to reveal concern. Documents can be replaced. Briefcases have no value. It was possible that she was just trying to be helpful.

First he needed to establish that it *was* Maxine who had it. The screen remained blank. He pressed Options. At the top of the list was Send. Send nothing. Say nothing. He pressed OK and, sure enough, there was her number.

25.

A Street in Newtown

'Let's go to Kilimanjaro,' Ari suggested in his sing-song voice.

'No.'

'It's very nice.'

'Fuckin' stupid,' Luke muttered.

Luke's head was buried in the newspaper as he walked, even as he walked across the intersection at King Street with traffic pouring at them because he'd ignored the fact that the lights had changed, probably deliberately, and reading the newspaper was like saying fuck you, run me down fucker and count the cost, and part of that deal was to actually be reading the paper, not just using it as a prop, so his cursing had to sound distracted and Ari was forced to keep up with him and search his features for further clues as to his wishes.

'You don't like it?' he asked.

Willie watched and waited, staying out of it. He hadn't said much since Luke had flung open his bedroom door and commanded him to stop wanking. Not that he had been wanking, but the crudity had unsettled him, causing him to flush and once Luke had withdrawn and he'd been able to pull on his clothes and gather himself he'd determined that he wouldn't reward Luke with friendliness as if everything was alright and he could treat him any way he liked: to hell with that. So he didn't speak. He followed along a pace or two behind and when they'd made up their minds where to go then maybe he'd decide whether to join them or not. It made no difference to him what café they went to. Besides, Luke seemed more interested in the paper.

'Do you like it there, Willie?'

Willie shrugged. He had no gripe with Ari.

'Kilimanjaro,' Ari added, in case Willie hadn't heard.

This was where Luke decided to raise the temperature, stopping in the middle of the intersection as if he'd only just realised what had been said.

'Kilimanjaro?' he shouted. 'You want to go to Kilimanjaro? You fuckin' mad? Where do you think Kilimanjaro is? It's in fucking Africa. You ever heard of people going to Africa to eat? You go to Africa to starve; you go to Africa to munch on stinking platefuls of gastroenteritis: you don't go there for breakfast.'

'It's a nice café. I like it.'

Ari smiled and shrugged, looking to Willie for support. Cars started honking. The scene had a familiar ring to it and Willie wondered whether the honking might not be the Lebanese taxi driver from the night before come to find them with a hand gun. He kept walking.

The pavements were crowded, just like a Saturday morning; no-one at work, stomachs rumbling, side walk odours luring people from their Newtown squats like the musk aromas of deer at rutting time. Willie walked and watched, wishing that he'd washed. His smell was unfamiliar, like he was wearing someone else's clothes. The smell threw him. Everything threw him. The light was harsh, stinging his eyelids and creating shimmering auroras that obscured his vision. His hands and feet tingled. Noises rushed at him like dogs at a passing bicycle and there was something electrical prodding at his bowels. He was thinking that he might be getting the flu, but he was also thinking there was a good chance that stuff from last night had not only wiped his memory, it had blown some fuses in his system, and the middle of a busy intersection was no place to deal with it. He concentrated on getting to the other side of the road and lifted his foot from the roadway to place it on the pavement, only to find that he'd lifted it too high, causing him to stumble. In the background he could hear Luke shouting.

It would be better, he felt, if he were on his own. He just needed space, that was all. Things would settle down. Luke was like a white-out. He drowned everything in static. He needed to get ahead of them, out of earshot, so he hurried past the Town Hall and looked for a shop where he could pause for awhile. There was one he knew, near the corner of King and Enmore, where he could just stand and look. He'd done it many times before. It was a shop filled with crap, a shop for people with no money and nothing to do; a jumble of wicker baskets and wooden photo frames, joss sticks and artificial flowers: crap like you get in Bali. But when he reached it he was confused. It was closed. It was never closed. Someone must have died. Further along there was a book shop. He paused to take stock. The window was filled with Lonely Planet guides to Thailand and Mongolia, Kenya and China. He peered closer. Maybe he should go in. He could find a book on Tibet. He pulled back, suddenly surprised by his own reflection. He not only smelled different, he looked different. No, fuck, he wouldn't go in. He didn't want to talk to anyone. A tuft of hair above his left ear sat out at an angle making him feel like a dork and the hair on his unshaven chin, being new to the task, had grown unevenly. He wanted a dump and he wanted it urgently. That's all he wanted. That's all he needed. Behind his reflection, and oblivious to him, Luke and Ari walked past, still arguing, and he turned and followed them leaving a sticky palm print on the shop window where he'd steadied himself while looking in.

Maybe it wasn't his smell he was carrying around. Maybe it was hers. It was fleshy but not muscular; not forced by exertion from straining pores or spent glands. It was almost sweet, not floral, more like fruits left too long to ripen and he'd accidentally picked them up so now their flavour was on his hands and on his cock where his hands had touched himself, and on his breath, too. She'd poked out her tongue when he swallowed the pills that Luke had given him and it had been startlingly plump and dark. Sitting in the middle of it had been two white pills of her own and when she withdrew her tongue again and swallowed the pills he'd felt an overwhelming desire to follow them into her mouth and be swallowed as well. It was an unrequited yearning, incapable of fulfilment because in that moment his desire was for her to masticate and digest him, absorbing his body into her own. It was weird. As he walked along the pavement, concentrating on avoiding bumping into people, he felt that desire again, only this time it was more like he had ingested *her* and she was dissolving in his intestines before passing through into his bowels. That was the smell.

'Who's got money?' Luke demanded.

He'd stopped at an Italian café to his liking, probably having had it in mind from the outset, undeterred by the fact that there appeared to be no vacant tables. Willie plunged his hands into his pockets without thinking. He had no cash, only a credit card. It didn't matter because Luke had already turned and gone in. There was a menu on a stand on the pavement which Ari read with great concentration. Through the window Willie could see Luke gesticulating to them to come inside.

'Nothing vegetarian,' Ari said.

There was something in his smile that Willie couldn't fathom.

'*Gianni's Home Cured Prosciutto with Sliced Parmesan on Italian Bread*, or *Ham and Mozzarella Baked Croissants*.' Ari read. 'It is not good to be a pig in Italy, I think. Have you ever been to Italy? Well, actually, there is no need because Italy has already come here and so has every other country in the world. But it is very hard to find a goat.'

Across the road the Kilimanjaro didn't appear to be open. There was bugger all open. It wasn't like a Saturday after all, more like a Sunday. Ari giggled. What was all the stuff about Kilimanjaro, Willie wanted to ask? And what sort of goat did he have in mind, a mountain goat? What the fuck was he talking about? Maybe Willie was the goat; was that the explanation for his smile? Perhaps they'd been talking about him, maybe even said something to him that he hadn't heard. It could have been something they'd seen or heard last night that Willie couldn't remember. So now they were laughing at him. By the time Willie had processed these thoughts a table had come free and Luke had claimed it, waving them in to join him.

Driven by the contraction of his bowels, Willie manoeuvred himself past the tables and chairs towards the back of the café in search of a loo, sure that all eyes were on him and feeling, when he emerged five minutes later, as if he'd dropped his trousers and dumped his excrement in public. Water from the hand basin had failed to control the errant tuft of hair but the strong smell of liquid soap on his hands and face lent him the allusion of being clean. He felt better.

'If you don't eat pork,' he said to Ari as he sat down, 'then you must be Muslim. But you eat goat.'

Ari smiled.

'Not Muslim.'

'Hindu, then?'

No.

'Hang on, I know; you're vegetarian, so you must be Buddhist. You like goat but you shouldn't because all life is sacred and has a soul, even a fly or an ant, and if you kill an animal or an insect you may be destroying the soul of your own grandmother.'

'What the fuck you talking about?' Luke demanded.

'I'm really interested in Buddhism,' Willie continued, ignoring him. 'If everybody respected life that way there'd be no wars or killing and people could make perfume without having to cut animals open to do it. There's nothing we need to survive that requires an animal to be killed. Look how many centuries Buddhists have been proving it.'

He was hungry now. He had the smell of soap on his hands and the hours that had gone missing overnight had not been noticed by Luke or Ari or they would have said something. He'd just needed a crap, that was all.

'I'd really like to go to Tibet,' he declared.

If that book shop was open he would go back and buy the Lonely Planet guide.

'I reckon that would be really great.'

He nodded silently to himself while studying the menu. It was disappointing that Ari didn't respond to his enthusiasm. Maybe Tibet was a bit difficult from a political point of view, what with the

Dalai Llama and everything. The Dalai Lama was a bit of a negative. His mother had met him and carried on like some gushy school girl about how great he was. That had nearly ruined it for him as far as Tibet went. Tibet was *his* deal. He didn't want to have to give it up because she wanted to make it her deal too; but what he was really talking about was walking in the mountains in really thin air that made you light headed and it being so cold that you got chilblains in full sunlight. He imagined that sunlight being almost blinding as it reflected off the gold leaf domes of the sacred temples, so bright that over thousands of years it had changed Tibetans' eyes until they'd become just narrow slits. Ever smiling, Tibetans knew the secret. They knew the secret so well that it drove the Chinese mad and made them want to kill them. But the secret was so simple that it could be placed for safe keeping in the mind of a four year old boy. Fuck, that must really get up the noses of the Chinese.

Yeah, he'd always wanted to go to Tibet. All his parents had ever wanted was to take them to flash hotels and resorts in places like Bali. What a waste. How hated they must be by people who live on nothing but thin air and faith. That's what he'd do. That's what everyone should do.

Luke spread the newspaper right across the whole table because he didn't give a fuck. He'd been out early to get it. Whatever there was to know, he would know it. The paper had dislodged the spoon from the sugar bowl and the bowl lay on its side dribbling sugar onto the café floor. He didn't give a fuck.

'Listen to this,' he said; '*The camera now pans over every angle and position, records every moan and groan. It shows exactly what cinemagoers do not expect to see during a sex scene on the screen: actual sex ...*' I've heard about this movie. These two sheilas get raped and they decide to get revenge by going on a wild fucking spree where they get blokes to shag them and then they shoot their fucking brains out. Someone's taking this fucking thing seriously: must be because it's French. Don't they know you can hire that sort of stuff in Paddo for ten bucks a night? Does that sound like our kind of movie, eh Willie: serious, intellectual, foreign? *Baise Moi.* Fuck me! You could learn a thing or two there.'

Willie was not yet ready to respond. Luke couldn't have his way on everything, setting the tone whenever he felt like it. To allow that would be to consent to his style. There were other styles, and better ones, that Willie was seeking. He'd know them when he found them; it was just a matter of looking.

'Says here that it starts today but they reckon they're going to close it down. I bet it isn't half as bad as they pretend. I reckon the people who made it are the one's who are causing all the fuss about it being too filthy to show, so that everyone gets a hard on and wants to see it. Jesus, people are stupid. People are just stupid fucking dumb cunts.'

Was it Tibet where they wore the saffron robes, or was Tibet where they wore all the woollen stuff, like multi-coloured socks outside their trouser pants and thick padded jackets with purple pockets and quilted collars, and caps with ear flaps that folded down? Maybe that was Nepal or one of those other places in the Himalayas, like Bhutan. He could do them all. They'd all be good. What he'd really like would be to stay and help them to build schools. That would be really, really cool. Fuck, that would be good.

'I don't know,' smiled Ari. 'That sounds like a snuff movie to me. Is it meant to be art?'

Ari smiled at everything, and it was always the same smile, but there was no message in it. Why didn't he tell Luke to get knotted?'

A waitress in a black dress with black woollen stockings came and stood beside them. The sugar on the floor crunched beneath her feet. She only looked at Luke. He had the newspaper. He knew everything.

I'm as hungry as a horse, Willie thought suddenly. The vibrating light around the edges of his vision had started to subside. His balance was fine now. He could feel his fingers. He smelt them. They were fine. He could pluck a guitar now if he had one. It must have been the diarrhoea that had thrown him. All he needed was a good feed. He smoothed down his errant hair and smiled at the waitress. Her tits were small and her hips were heavy but she was unaware of it. Luke leered at her while he folded up the newspaper.

'*Baise Moi?*' he asked, with a significant pause. 'Have you seen it?'

She shook her head. Her hair was dyed red, the colour of those ducks you see hanging in the windows of Chinatown restaurants. It had taken a lot of dye to get it that way because underneath she was naturally black and it wasn't the sort of job Pantene would be proud of because it hung down pretty stiff and lifeless. But maybe it looked better at night.

'Aren't you interested in art?' Luke continued. 'Shit, you've gotta keep up with things, girl.'

If she had any sex appeal, what did it for her, Willie thought, was the way she looked at you with her mouth open, just enough so her lips were parted but not wide enough so you could see in and that made it all the more interesting because it made you wonder. Then, while he was thinking all that, she unexpectedly poked her tongue out at Luke, showing a large silver stud drilled right through the middle of it, which explained why her mouth never closed.

'Fuck me,' Luke cried in mock horror.

It was just possible he'd found his match.

'You could earn good money with a tongue like that,' he said. 'You want me to show you how?'

The girl looked at him impassively and Ari smiled; but there was still no message in it.

26.

The Apartment

An hour had passed since Roger had received the first text message and still she refused to return his call. He was powerless and that was not something he liked. When this was over (and it bloody well better be over soon) he would give some thought to making her pay. There was bound to be some way he could arrange for life to be made uncomfortable; she was a prostitute, for Christ sake, a fucking whore; she'd have acted on impulse, unthinking and unplanned, just the way she would have turned her first trick, careless of the consequences because her myopic greed blinded her to them. That was their type, their faulty gene: stupidity and dishonesty fighting it out as to who would reign supreme and stupidity winning every time. Why didn't she open the damn thing before she took it and check whether there was anything of value? So now she'd have to offer some ridiculous explanation, realizing she'd fucked up. What was she going to say: that she rushed out of the apartment trying to catch up with him because she realized he'd left it behind? Oh, sure, very plausible from someone who happened to be naked in bed at the time. That she took it for safe keeping because she thought the cleaner might steal it? No, he'd be nice and relaxed until he had it in his hand and then he'd let her know she'd just lost a regular meal ticket that no girl like her could afford to lose. She'd opted for the short term gain and copped the long term pain.

He wanted those valuations now. Giving them to Butch Astor to read overnight was critical to building the momentum of their negotiations. By the time he came to their formal discussions in the morning he wanted Astor to be absolutely convinced of the price formula he was proposing. Being able to see the new values before anyone else was the edge that Astor would be looking for, but calling Tom Higham at home and asking him to go into the office to print out a replacement copy was simply not an option. How would he explain it: that he'd lost them? They were privileged information for God's sake. Why would he need them so urgently on the night of Anzac Day? Shit, Higham was already flighty enough as it was. It didn't bear thinking about.

He could just hear him.

'I'm really uncomfortable about this, Roger. I've been thinking about it all day. My professional integrity is at stake. I'm not sure I've done the right thing and now...well, I've really bent over backwards for you *against my better judgment* and I'm not sure...if you've now lost them ...'

Not sure he should give him a replacement copy? Take the opportunity to back down on the position they'd negotiated? Fuck, he wouldn't put it past him. What did 'better judgment' mean for a Property Valuer? It meant, 'Have I looked in every known direction and searched every known crevice to ensure that I've covered my arse? Have I checked what every other Valuer thinks so we're all covering our arses together, and then, just because I have no faith at all in my own judgment, have I checked what the actual punters have shown themselves willing to pay?' That's what 'better judgement' meant for Valuers.

'Only trouble is, Tom, there haven't been any sales at Whiteman's Creek because we haven't started selling yet. So that's both good and bad: bad because you can't point to evidence and good because no-one else can either. What you have to rely on is my statement to you that we won't be selling for anything less. I'll give you that in writing. You needn't put it in your report but you can keep it on the side for whenever you feel wobbly. Is that reasonable?'

That's what he'd said to him. He could have put it more crudely but he'd restrained himself. Fortunately Tom hadn't taken him up on the offer, knowing full well it wouldn't be worth the paper it was printed on. It proved to be the germ of an idea though.

When you're pushing shit up hill it pays to have taken a deep breath before you started. Roger had come to the meeting with Tom Higham knowing that he wouldn't find much air.

'I'm being heavily leaned on,' he said as they sat down. 'The Board and Banks are pressing me to rotate our Valuers or set up a Peer Group Panel.'

That's how he'd started.

'What have we paid you to-date for the Whiteman's Creek valuations: half a mill or more? I don't think that's a lot. It's money well spent, in fact. If we appoint a panel it'll be double that. With the developments we've got planned in the next two years the valuation fees will double anyway. I'm fighting to stay with one firm, Tom; I just thought you should know that. It doesn't make sense to me to reject all the knowledge you've built up on this project in favour of someone being brought in to it new.'

One more and I'm out, was what he was really thinking. Give me one last full fat valuation and I'll be gone.

'It's the leasehold that's the problem, as you know, Roger. It simply isn't usual in a situation like this not to be offering freehold title and we don't know how that would affect your ability to sell, particularly the residential housing component.'

'It makes no difference. I've given you the ground lease terms. All you have to do is capitalize their values and subtract them from the assumed values of the freehold. Is that difficult?'

Of course it wasn't difficult.

Tom Higham looked at the valuation schedules in front of him, reluctant to hand them across. What did they contain, Roger was desperate to know? Was he reluctant to hand them over because he knew Roger was going to blow up when he saw them? Did he want to keep earning those fees or didn't he?

'That's our usual treatment for leasehold land, Roger, but as I explained, in this instance we can't quite get our heads around ...'

Roger stood up.

'Well, I can't fuck about. I've got a billion dollar company to run and shareholders who expect me to get on with it.'

He'd gone in with an empty briefcase and it looked like he'd be leaving with it empty also. Higham wasn't going to hand over the valuations because he knew Roger wouldn't like them. Too bad; the little creep had just lost a million dollars in future fees.

'I was going to say, that we can't sign them off without a disclaimer.'

Roger sat down again.

'You always have a disclaimer.'

'I really meant ... a caveat'

'What sort of caveat?'

'That we don't think the leasehold terms are 'normal commercial".

'What's 'normal commercial'? The terms are the terms. We can make them anything we like.'

'But being set as low as they are they reduce the level of adjustment we would normally make in our formula for assessing the value of the leasehold component. Frankly, we can't see why you wouldn't just sell freehold title outright. It doesn't seem commercial.'

'That isn't your call, but let me clarify.'

He went on to explain, just as he'd done with the bankers, that the vision of Saville Corp was to add value through control and integration. The mistake that all developers made was in selling down parcels to other parties for piecemeal development, laying off their short term risk at the expense of losing control over the design and quality of the whole. Whiteman's Creek wasn't just a land bank, it was a total environment, a future suburb, a model urban landscape that would turn around the prejudice that existed against Western Sydney and set new benchmarks for middle income property values. The mechanism for control was the ground leases that they intended to retain. The ground leases were not a grab for more money.

'I'm going to tell you something in confidence, Tom. Right now

I'm negotiating a sale of the Western residential sub-division leasehold at a price that will silence all your fears. I don't know what value you've put on it, but that value will be academic when this sale is announced. The only value that counts, as you know, is what the buyer is willing to pay. We've all underestimated the shortage of land in Sydney and been way too conservative in our estimates for Whiteman's Creek. I'm lifting all our asking prices by twenty percent because that's what I now know we can get. If you're going to be way off the mark, Tom, it isn't going to look good.'

Nobody could better Roger when he was in full flight and he spoke uninterrupted in this way for a full ten minutes. When he'd finished he reached across and took the draft valuations from in front of Tom Higham and quietly read them. To his surprise the figures were as close as buggery to where he wanted them, but put together with the weasel words designed to protect Higham's arse they were as good as useless. No-one would take them seriously.

No doubt what Tom Higham was thinking while he watched him read was how he could protect his 'professional integrity' while still protecting his future income. He gazed at his graduation certificates hanging on the wall; the pompous heraldic shields and curlicues that such people rely upon as if letting some failed lecturer in grubby corduroy pants tell them how to think for four years somehow made them worthy of respect when what it should have done is make them hide the fucking evidence somewhere it could never be found. He fiddled with a duplicate copy of the report as if he'd forgotten what he'd actually written and he gazed at the photo of his wife and kids on his desk and wondered how he could buy them that lovely little colonial shack at Bluey's Beach he'd been promising them if his biggest client sacked him. And then he remembered something Roger had said.

'I suppose one way around it would be for us to put the caveat in a side letter.'

Roger closed up the draft valuation report and handed it back. He didn't say a word. When Higham left the office to have the changes made and returned with the revised document ten minutes later Roger didn't say a word then either. He took the new letter and read it without comment, then put it together with the revised valuation report in his briefcase and stood up.

'We'll see,' was his only comment as he shook hands and left the office.

No, he hadn't been over-whelmed with any sense of triumph as he rode down in the lift and made his way up Park Street with the intention of returning to his office. He'd felt flat, if anything; that edgy kind of flatness that signifies a sudden drop in adrenalin, like going off a high, that makes you want to pick it up again. That's why he'd called Maxine. We'll see, he was thinking: don't be too fucking sure you've covered your arse, mother fucker; and his mind had been racing. It was still going to be hard. What the side letter said, among other things, was that the valuation report was 'not to be read without the caveat contained herein'. The caveat itself, now moved out of the report and into the letter, remained unchanged and unacceptable. Well, thought Roger, we'll see. That would depend on who was reading it.

27.

The Kitchen at Mosman

'Earl Grey or Darjeeling?' Joanne asked, the words hanging in the air more clearly and brightly than she'd intended.

They were standing in the conservatory which she'd had built at the northern end of the kitchen so they could look down through the garden towards the swimming pool and out to the Inner Harbour. The room was bathed in sunlight and there was an additional aura that her father and daughter had brought into the room that she'd first sensed when she saw them walking towards her from the ferry holding hands.

'I can do either,' she added.

'Either would be fine.'

Albert smiled at Samantha as if acknowledging that this was a harmless ritual but not necessarily a useless one. They'd formed a bond during the day which had not been apparent before and Joanne felt excluded.

'Actually, a cup of tea is exactly what I feel like,' he said.

This time he smiled at Joanne, too. Though he looked tired, she thought, it appeared that the morning had gone well.

'Good. Then we'll sit out in the garden and I want you both to tell me all about it.'

Sophia, as it happened, had already laid out the tea tray, having an antenna for such things which slightly irritated Joanne who wanted the pleasure of busying herself at that domestic level and felt ambivalent about any demonstration of reliance on staff.

'You must both be starving. How about I whisk up some scones; they'd only take a minute? Lovely hot scones with freshly made strawberry jam, just like mother used to make?'

Damn! She meant the generic mother, the fictional mother, everybody's mother; not *her* mother. Too quick for an answer, she spun on her heels and plunged into the kitchen cupboards to pull out the flour and baking soda, letting the clash of the oven trays and mixing bowl do the talking. Sophia, having the good sense to realize that the kitchen bench space was being taken over by a superior force, left the room to continue with her cleaning. Samantha followed, having found a cold coke in the fridge and a Tim Tam in the pantry cupboard. All this happening - cupboards opening and closing, people coming and going - only served to emphasize to Joanne the aching silence which pervaded the house.

'Was the march a success?' she asked over her shoulder.

Perhaps if she turned the radio on it would be better. Her voice sounded too clear, scrubbed of the usual impurities of casual conversation, as if projected across an empty hall at an amateur dress rehearsal. Why did everything she had to say sound as if it had been written down and read out loud? If only she could be natural. If only she could stop being the person she'd created over the years since her mother died and start again, knowing what she knew now.

'I think Sam enjoyed it.'

He was so still, like a tree, anchored, barely moving in the breeze of her activity, the sunlight finding more silver in his hair than she was used to; his unaccustomed suit seeming to hold him like a binding. He had no small talk, she'd always known that, and her own talk always seemed smaller as a consequence. It was a trap. Two people couldn't be silent, for what sort of message was that? But unless both were willing to talk then one was doomed to be the fool. Why couldn't she just tell him who she was and make him tell her in return? The ferocity with which she sieved the flour into the stainless steel mixing bowl came closer to expressing her inner feelings than any words she'd yet uttered; the clatter of the sieve as she threw it into the sink defining her frustration; and yet she smiled apologetically and continued as if they were strangers.

'She'd been so looking forward to it. It was something she really wanted to do.'

The scone mix went into the oven. At least she knew how to cook.

'Were there many other young people marching ...?'

'Goodness, yes; there were lots. I was quite surprised.'

In turning to face him she'd picked up a tea towel to wipe her hands. It wasn't that her hands were either wet or dirty; the towel was a prop to emphasise the completion of a task that was meant to give her worth but which now only made her feel worthless. She threw it down on the bench in distaste, aware that he was already set on going out into the garden. Surely there was a conversation which could engage him?

'They learn about it at school,' she said brightly. 'It seems to have captured their interest and they want to know more, whereas my generation tended to want to forget about it. 'Oh God', I can hear people saying; 'he's going to talk about the War again'. I don't mean you; you've never talked about it really. I mean, it was a kind of joke to protect people from being ear-bashed by Dad's Army types. You know, there was a skit that Peter Cook and Dudley Moore used to do sitting on a park bench - or was it The Two Ronnies?'

She followed him to the conservatory door.

'You must be tired. Why don't you sit at the table in the herb garden? I want you to tell me what you think of my purple basil; it seems to have become perennial.'

He looked lost as if the layout of the garden confused him; pausing on the gravel path with his palms upturned waiting for directions.

'Around to the right, outside your bedroom ...'

The slow crunch of the gravel beneath his feet as he resumed walking was in stark contrast to the speed of her breathing. Standing at the kitchen sink, massaging her breast plate and waiting for the scones to rise, she felt utterly alone. This was meant to be the purpose of it all. Why have a house and garden, a kitchen that filled with sunlight, an oven that was fan-assisted for baking, a housekeeper who laid out the tea tray, a spare bedroom with fresh towels and gravel paths raked by Frank the gardener - if not for moments like these? He wasn't meant to keep walking slowly away around the corner of the house as if nothing she could say made it worth staying to listen and to talk; as if what she had to say was better not heard. Why did he keep that photo in his diary if it didn't matter?

She'd opened the folder which she'd taken from her father's suitcase only after agonizing over it. If there was a sin involved it was not a mortal one. She wanted only to know him better, she told herself. Yet it was hard not to admit the sense of shame that was mixed with her anticipation. If it had contained embarrassing secrets she would have been disgusted with herself, but if it had contained nothing personal at all she would have felt deflated; as if the only chance to advance her knowledge of him had passed and there would never be another.

There had been a time, when they were all newly married, when Prue and Tom used to hold *Murder Mystery* dinners on the weekends. They would each be given a character to play and an envelope containing clues. Not until they opened the envelope and learned a little about the other people sitting around the table could they begin to speculate on their own roles and whether or not they were the murderer, the victim or merely an observer. It was that kind of feeling that she brought to the opening of her father's private papers. Every little detail was a potential clue, starting with the folder itself.

If Roger had a leather file holder it would have been made of black calf skin - slim with gilded initials - given to him probably by a merchant bank soliciting his goodwill, and the minute it became slightly worn he'd discard it. So what did it say about Albert that he'd kept the cheap vinyl folder given to him at a conference six years ago? Apart from the fact that he would never be the target of merchant Banks it was most unlikely that he could feel comfortable, as Roger was, with something that displayed his own initials. It's probable that he had never considered the need for a personal organizer until that day when he'd been handed his conference papers. For a man of his generation who lived on his own without the stimulus of domestic ownership which women brought to a household, possessions would be decided solely by need. He wouldn't have needed a file holder in order to survive, yet the minute he saw it he must have decided to assign it a permanent use. Perhaps it was his reluctance to indulge in waste.

As she unclipped the tab that held it closed she had a sense that he'd progressed beyond merely finding a use for it to the point where it struggled to contain all that he'd found cause to store there. For a man of the bush it was the perfect portable office; the vinyl cover immune from dirt and water, the small calculator mounted in the inside cover powered by light cells, the ball point pen recycled from the local bank. She laid its contents out with great care. If they mattered enough to him to warrant keeping then they must be able to reveal his interests at least.

The reason the folder was bulging was because it held three bound books. The first was an A4 Note Book with spiral binding, two-thirds of its 240 pages filled with hand written notes and figures. The pages were dated and headed with *Plot Number* and *Block Number* references. The figures were in columns headed *DBH, DOS and SPH*. At the bottom of each page a space had been left under *Comments* where, in his neat tutored hand, he'd written the occasional note revealing that these were recordings of tree stands; some affected by wind damage or fire, and some by disease. Even where there were no comments, still the heading inviting commentary was included, like a pre-printed form. As she contemplated the volume of information represented by these recordings she had no sense of the physical environment in which they were gathered or the human functions performed to obtain them. She was a city girl; the bush, she knew, held its finger to the trigger of her father but it had never held meaning for her. Disappointed, she put the note book aside and opened the Collins Desk Diary that lay beneath.

It would have been foolish to suppose that an old man's diary would be a lens to his soul or a transmitter of his inner thoughts. It had no entries other than shopping lists; prosaic recitals of household rations, baked beans, potatoes, soap powder and batteries. Here and there an underlined instruction to himself to

'Call the Garage' or 'Pay Rates'. Mechanical and chemical needs gave the only hint of the priorities governing each day. The lists were crammed eight to ten to a page and the last one still only reached July 12th, 1988. 'Waste not, want not,' she could hear him say. How far removed was this parsimony from the Saville family household where regular spending was treated like a social obligation and where, as a result, there was no immunity to the infection of material gratification.

Joanne was not unwilling to be discomforted by what she saw in her father. It was quite possible that the disquiet she felt in her own life was caused by a seed he'd planted in her DNA; that the longing she felt for simplicity was because simplicity was not just the antidote to the dissatisfaction of wealth, it was what she saw in her father who was so painfully beyond her reach.

In the back of the diary was an address book that had started life in an even earlier edition and was tied into the spine with a piece of string. The names and numbers had been recorded in many different pens and pencils over a long time. Her own number had been changed three times as she'd moved with Roger across town from the Eastern Suburbs to Mosman, having children along the way. There was no other name she recognized.

None of this was destined to help her that morning. She'd risked shame in order to provoke a revelation and found that the provocation was too timid. When it came to real risk she was unwilling, as she'd shown once again in the kitchen, to go beyond twittering pleasantries and stammered evasions. Was she scared of knowing him or scared of him knowing her? More likely the latter, she now thought.

The third book was a printed copy of the Proceedings of a Plant Industry Forum held in January. She'd leafed through it without much interest until she came across a reference to him in the introduction as one of the keynote speakers, together with a photo. She was used to seeing someone close to her being described in print because Roger was regularly in the news, but coming across her father like that had shocked her. It had never occurred to her that he might exist other than anonymously. To find him being described in unrestrained terms ('the prophet for a promised land of sustainable farming') was like stumbling across a bigamist with a secret life. Was this hyperbole or mistaken identity? Her father was not a prophet, he was Godless. He had no visions; he worked alone with trees and barely spoke. He had no care even for a wife and family, let alone a promised land.

'His is a message of hope, based on good science and pragmatism ...'

What message, she wanted to cry, and who is he sharing it with?

'... fuelled with a passion that has sustained him through a lifetime's work.'

All this could be said about him by other people, apparently without fear of contradiction, while she, his own daughter, knew nothing. She knew little of his lifetime's work and nothing at all about passion: she knew him only as an absent figure, a deserter. What were they trying to say; that other qualities could override that and, God forbid, excuse it? But there was worse to come as she arrived at the transcript of the paper he delivered to the forum.

It was easy to put a face to the words that he must have spoken to the room full of agricultural scientists that day; it was the face portrayed in the introduction, unsmiling, lean and high boned, the straight grey hair cut short and firmly brushed into a parting: the eyes and face of someone who watched but was not watched in return. So she could see him as he stepped up to the lectern, cleared his throat and began to speak but then, when she read the words, it was not him at all. She felt betrayed and frightened. This was not her father. Her father could not utter words like this, especially to strangers. She would have heard these words first; would have known they were inside him. These were strangers: she was his only child.

'Our country is dying,' were the first words of the transcript. 'We began killing it over a century ago. As the country dies of salinity, it will kill people, too. It caused my father to take his own life. This is not a complex issue, it is very simple.'

She could feel the warmth of the morning sun on her skin but within she felt cold. All the sounds of the garden ceased.

'We are doing to Australia what we accuse subsistence tribes of doing to Central Africa. We are turning it into a desert of salt.'

Why had he never told her – his own daughter? Yes, suicide is a sin – a dreadful, sad and wasteful sin - but what about abandonment? What about silence?

28.

The Garden at Mosman

Sam came out into the herb garden carrying her school project for Albert to see. It ran to twenty pages and was copiously illustrated. When she'd mentioned it to Albert on the ferry he'd imagined something very different: hand drawn maps, flags and medals; evidence of tracing and laborious hand copying, stylistically earnest if juvenile. For Albert the word 'Project' summoned up images of flour mixed with water to form a poor man's paste. Most of his images, he realised, were a poor man's.

'You did this yourself?' he asked.

The text was immaculately printed: headlines in colour, quotations in italic script, pages numbered, reference sources listed in neatly tabulated footnotes. The illustrations were mostly in black and white, the iconic images which Albert had seen so many times in his life that they no longer held meaning for him; of multi-funnelled steamers loaded to the rails with departing troops and wharves filled with women in hats waving at the men for all their might. Then there were the landing boats and trenches; soldiers digging latrines, comrades in arms beaming for the folks back home, bodies arched backwards over bomb craters, their bellies exposed to the heavens. What meaning did these old photos have for the generations who hadn't experienced them? Did they gaze into them with any sense of the emotions of those times - the fear, the pride, the excitement and foreboding - or did they bring their own new and different emotions to the images: sentimentality and admiration coached into them by a manufactured, hyper-inflated mythology?

'I used Publisher,' Sam announced proudly.

'Oh!'

'It's really cool. You can manipulate text really easily. I find Adobe a bit too complicated. I mean, we're like learning Adobe and stuff at school but if I want to do a project quickly I find it a lot easier to use Publisher.'

'It's very … impressive.'

More than that actually: it was in some respects intimidating. She spoke a language with which he struggled, having only a rudimentary sense of what she was saying, and she spoke it with such fluency that he recognised it must be her native tongue. It wasn't just a modern dialect, it was a new vocabulary born out of interests and lifestyles that he would never experience. His own language by comparison was a dying one. Perhaps that was as it should be, but why did he feel disturbed?

She leaned across him and turned the pages until she came to the inside back cover.

'There!' she said. 'My heroes!'

The headline read, *'Our Family of Anzacs'*. There were two black and white photographs framed by an inverted triangle of red poppies. The caption read, *'William John Strange, Gallipoli, 1915'* and *'Albert John Strange, New Guinea, 1942'*

Albert looked at the page silently, stricken with an unexpected despondency. Death, age, regrets had long ago been purged from his system. He was, he believed, immune from the sorrow of life's impermanence, but seeing his father like that, such a solitary, plain and mortal figure in his ill-fitting uniform naively posing for the camera stopped him in his tracks. Had he deceived himself about his immunity; could grief, like pneumonia, catch you unexpectedly and knock you to the ground, or was it a sickening disappointment he was feeling?

'Not heroes, Sam,' he muttered. 'Not heroes.'

On the ferry coming back from town he'd feigned sleep, not wanting to deal with these issues, tilting back his head and closing his eyes, savouring the light sea breeze that blew up the harbour, a soft veil of exhaustion settling gently over him: remembering …

Some time after having been de-mobbed, Albert had stood at the sink in the kitchen of his mother's house in Cessnock one early morning, watching the red dawn spreading west from Maitland across the Lower Hunter Valley; watching but not thinking. It was summer and the locust chorus had risen with the sun until the volume, exaggerated by the imbalance of his senses, reached such a pitch that he was impelled to press his fingers to his ears and listen instead to the coursing of his own blood. While he stood there, the saltpetre in the Capstan cigarette he'd newly lit burned it to the end, or at least until it singed his fingers, and he threw it with a curse into the sink. With his hands to his ears he hadn't heard his step-father enter the room until he heard the sound of a striking match and knew he must be sitting behind him at the kitchen table.

'We think the day is long,' his step-father said, 'but when you see how quickly the sun races up from the horizon you realize how fast time is slipping away.'

In the kitchen sink Albert's cigarette stub sizzled like a dying fly. When he'd left for the War he hadn't smoked. Time had passed but it hadn't yet slipped away. He frowned and continued to look out the window, making a point of seeing things. The lawn was brown, the earth was red. In the summer heat no flowers survived. All the roads were dirt and destined to remain so for many years and a motor car would be watched from its first sound until it was out of sight.

Haymaking had finished as the last remaining pastures had withered under the summer heat and he'd been paid off, staying a day or two with his mother before heading south in search of other work. Prime Minister Chifley had introduced unemployment and sickness benefits two years earlier but they were not ever collected by anyone Albert knew. Self-sufficiency was an obligatory social test and no attempt would be made to persuade him to take food and board longer than two days, even from his own mother. His mother, after all, lived in the house of his step-father. No-one wished or even thought to debate this, let alone Albert.

His step-father worked for the Post Office, which was considered an essential utility. He'd been too old to go to war and been forced instead to watch it guiltily from behind the grilled counter of the Maitland sorting office. On the evening two days prior when Albert had arrived to stay, the three of them had talked briefly. The War still hung over the country and would for many years. Now people talked about the Peace. The Peace somehow seemed like part of the War as well: the after part. His mother said she hoped he'd be able to find a good job and something he could make into a career. His step-father said the Post Office was vital to the running of the nation, like trains and electricity. Then they listened to the radio before going to bed.

On this morning though his step-father had something to say and he'd come into the kitchen early in order to be able to say it before Albert departed.

'What General Blamey said was wrong. 'Remember, it's the rabbit who runs who gets shot'. That's what he said. The man's obviously never been hunting.'

Albert held on to the side of the concrete sink and continued staring out the window, no longer seeing but waiting; waiting for more words to come.

'Was he suggesting that if you sat nice and still the Japs wouldn't have noticed you? What then? Were they meant to march on past to Port Moresby, next stop Cooktown, Cairns, Townsville and Mackay? I don't blame you for running. Look what they did to your friend Jim Percy. He was told to sit still and they chopped his head off. Sometimes it pays to run. Anyway, turned out alright in the end; the Japs got what they deserved. We're here and that's all that matters.'

Of all the conversations they might have had about the War, of all the things he might have chosen to say, this was the least expected. God knows, maybe it was a protective instinct that had caused him to get up out of bed early in order to say this. More likely it was shame. General Blamey, from a distance of many miles, had accused his own soldiers on the Kokoda Track of being beaten by an inferior enemy. Yes, Albert had heard that. Those of his mates who'd survived had heard it too, and with so much egregious excrement floating around they'd all spontaneously decided to keep their mouths closed. It would be years before those who knew the reality would talk about the War properly and by then it would have acquired a totally new reality, one that Albert wouldn't recognize.

He turned to his step-father.

'We were kids, eighteen years old,' he said before leaving, 'just doing what we were told.'

'Did you know any heroes?' Sam asked, barely disguising her disappointment.

'Oh, yes. Jim Percy, for one. He died, but that wasn't what made him a hero. It's a hard thing to explain, and harder still for me.'

29.

The Mosman Garden

They hadn't run, like his step-father suggested; they'd retreated and re-grouped. Of course, he'd been talking about himself when he said they were just kids, but at the time he forgot that. He had in mind only those who died. One way or another war gave everyone an opportunity to feel shame: Blamey for his reputation as a general, his step-father for staying at home and Albert, perhaps, for still being alive when people like Jim Percy weren't. There were men who sat in RSL clubs through the years drinking and talking but the more one talked, Albert felt, the more surely the story was bound to change. It wasn't so much that as the words spilled out the truth drained away; the truth was like a dog that took on the characteristics of its master. In this case the master was the collective desire of all to find a telling that shamed none but the damned.

'Why is it hard to explain?' Sam asked. 'Was it horrible ...?'

No, that wasn't it. He couldn't talk about it because it was too keenly felt and no words or explanations could express it. Words, in fact, would dissipate the feeling. Only the feeling was pure and untainted. People would say, 'Try and forget it', missing the point altogether. There was an obligation not to forget it. Words would only change it and that was worse than forgetting.

Take the Kokoda Track as an example.

In the chocolate brown mud of New Guinea, on that one ridge, more Australian boys died than in any other place throughout the War. Untrained and massively outnumbered they found themselves in monsoon rains in a place that mountaineers would hesitate to climb in fine weather with local guides. Move and the ground beneath their feet turned liquid.

The liquid ground rose in front of them a thousand feet and slid behind them a thousand more. What was the relevance of why they were there? They were never told. Somewhere, in a dry room in a safe town in front of a pin board and maps they were judged to be delaying the Japanese advance, according to the Generals; but that was someone else's reality. 'What are we doing here?' you whispered to your mate. 'We're making mud,' he whispered back; 'pass it on.' But when you turned to pass it on, your other mate was gone.

The mud was filled with leeches. Rain ran down the tree trunks like they were copper spouting. Trees, mud, rain and leeches; and between the trees there were spaces where bullets sought out flesh in a manner far more telling than the leeches.

Stepping out from behind a tree, Albert had been unexpectedly confronted by a Japanese soldier. Whenever he remembered this moment in later life he had to remind himself about how the senses worked. There was the heavy feeling of total saturation and the pungent smell of mud; there was the sound of unremitting rain; and then there was the blinding rush of fear in the face of approaching death. He couldn't recover the memory of that fear now but it had been captured there on the face of the man before him. The Jap must have been hiding on the other side of the same tree. They were so close that Albert had to step back to have room to raise his rifle. When he fired he started to slide backwards. Though slow at first, there was no way of stopping. Instinct told him to stay erect at all costs for if he fell face down there would still be no way of stopping and he'd be trapped in the mud. It happened a thousand times a day. So he slid, away from the gap between the trees and the startled Jap whose face exploded with blood and who he never saw again, down the hillside with flailing arms but without a cry, holding on to his rifle with an iron grip lest it be knocked from his hands, coming to rest eventually against a kauri tree and clutching it in relief. All there was to say about it in hindsight was that no skill could have been exercised, either in killing or surviving; no more than it could be in riding a skateboard down an avalanche.

'But what I want to know,' he asked Sam now, 'is where did you find these photos?'

'In Grandma's photo albums. Mum's kept them all. There are heaps of photos there. I just scanned them in.'

Albert stood up and removed his jacket. That part of the garden where Joanne had chosen to plant her herbs was a sun trap. The white gravel reflected the sun's heat back into the rosemary borders and the thyme edging. No wonder the purple basil chose to become perennial. He placed the jacket over the back of his chair and sat down again feeling stiff from the morning's march and wondering whether Joanne might be able to find an anti-inflammatory for him.

'Why did you leave Grandma?' Sam asked suddenly.

Albert quickly sat down again. The question had finally come. Was this the reason he'd approached the day with such feelings of dread; not because he didn't want to be reminded of the War, but because he wanted to avoid being asked that question? Hadn't he known that one day it would be asked, that the price of surrendering his seclusion and allowing himself to be claimed as a grandparent would inevitably expose him to the risk of this moment? Yet the question, when it came, was something of a relief, like the bullet in the jungle that you knew was there, somewhere, and couldn't be avoided forever. Though you didn't willingly place yourself in its path, when it hit you the tension and fear of the state of avoidance passed and a new state was entered. Perhaps you did put yourself willingly in its path. Perhaps the state of avoidance became too hard to maintain.

'I don't know, Sam. She was a lovely woman.'

That was something he always said. It was easy to say.

'She was a city person. She needed people. The city gave me a kind of sickness I couldn't describe as though I was being weighed down.'

Just as he'd felt that morning on the march, so it had been for him then every day, as though he were being slowly poisoned with heavy metals, mercury or lead, slipped into his food. So oppressive was the weight that he'd become completely preoccupied with it until there was no other aspect to his life. Everything in the city had been poisoning him so that had to include his wife.

'I needed space and solitude. She didn't like that. The bush was as bad for her as the city was for me. When we married we hadn't known that.'

'Couldn't you have compromised? I thought that's what relationships are all about. That's what they keep telling us, anyway. It's not like there aren't beaches and parks and things in Sydney. You could have lived at Pittwater or the Blue Mountains or something. I'm sure Grandma would have been happy with that. Like, did you ever try and work it out or did you just leave?'

Albert looked at her sharply. He felt a sudden squeeze of anger at his throat. No-one had ever questioned him like that. He'd always been prepared to take blame unequivocally. That's what he'd always done with Joanne: take full blame and end the matter, no questions asked.

'It's not something you do lightly or that you ever want to do, Samantha. There are some things that you know you have to do. You'll find that out. I never imagined when I married your grandmother that I would need to leave her.'

He wasn't sure what he'd imagined. When he tried to remember the person he'd been he failed to recall anything of himself that explained motivation or purpose. It was like he was adrift, semi-conscious, floating in the currents, and when he banged up against something he instinctively pushed himself away in case it was a net or an encircling boom. Discuss it? 'Work it out?' She'd known how he felt. Going to the beach or the Blue Mountains wasn't going to fix it. It was just one of those things.

'The thing is Grandpa; I could never leave my only child, no matter what.'

Luckily for both of them at that moment Joanne arrived with the tea tray.

30.

At the Garden Table

'How are you two getting along?'

Joanne put the tea tray down on the garden table with an exaggerated sigh of relief.

'I didn't realize you were out here, Sam. I was looking for you to lend me a hand. Would you mind going and getting the scones and side plates? I couldn't manage everything on my own.'

'I was showing Grandpa my Anzac project.'

'That's lovely, darling.'

But for the moment the Anzac project was in the way.

'What did you think of it?' she asked her father as soon as Samantha had gone off to fetch the scones and she was able to move the folder aside and begin laying out the cups and saucers. 'She put an awful lot of work into it.'

Feeling as if he, too, might be in the way, Albert stood up to make room.

'It's very good.'

'She did it without any help, you know.'

'So she said - except for the photos.'

Which ones were those? She hoped the scones wouldn't be cold by the time they got there. Should she pour the tea or wait? Perhaps she should have brought a tea cosy. Even on a warm day the water could go cold by the time you brought it out to the garden.

'It might have been better if we'd had this in the conservatory,' she thought out loud. 'But still, it's such a lovely day and this area is a real sun trap. Did you notice my purple basil; isn't it absurd?'

Well, it must have been warm enough because he'd taken off his jacket. How strange, she thought; seeing him dressed like that he could so easily be someone else: a retired business man or lawyer, rather than the rural labourer that he'd insisted on being all his life. In a business shirt and tie with his steel grey hair he conveyed a sense of dignified seniority that seemed to her to be perfectly at home in this setting. Only his hands gave him away, but even those, now that she knew something of the purpose to which they'd been put, were not undignified.

'Can an annual suddenly decide to become a perennial just because it likes the conditions?'

She felt driven to insist on his attention like a competitive child. Jealous of the easy relationship Samantha seemed to have formed, it was as if she were now asking him to look at her project, too. The fact that they were only plants in a garden, tended by a gardener, made matters worse for her. What else could she think of about herself that was worthy of a conversation?

Albert walked slowly along the border of the herb garden as if judging a pastoral exhibit at a country school. They don't deserve that attention, she wanted to say, they're only herbs; she was only looking for something to talk about. Following his gaze she had a sudden fear that she was making a fool of herself. Perhaps the 'Dark Opal' basil wasn't an annual. She'd always assumed it was, but perhaps it wasn't, in which case he would be searching for an explanation for her question.

'I've always assumed it's an annual,' she rushed to explain. 'Perhaps it's not.'

'Some plants that we call annuals are just short-lived perennials,' he replied thoughtfully. 'The climate can affect their life but usually it's a cool climate that makes them live longer, not a warm one. I don't know about purple basil; I've never encountered it. Parsley and mint are pretty much my limits: mint for potatoes and parsley for carrots.'

He paused.

'You've got quite a collection here. You know ...'

He turned back towards her, frowning, as if puzzled by it all.

'...You've created a home you can be proud of.'

Oh, she hadn't expected that! She stopped fiddling with the tea tray. Yes! Yes, she *was* proud. It wasn't without thought and care that it had been made this way. It was true that she may have had help in creating the garden but that was incidental to the vision and drive which she'd brought to it; the passion which she'd felt to create a home that they would all love and never want to leave. Of course, she had the money to do it, she must never forget that; it would always have to temper any claim she made for recognition. She was sure he was only too aware of that.

'We're very lucky,' she explained. 'I know how fortunate we are compared to some.'

She wished Samantha would hurry up with the scones before they got cold. Now she was left facing him with a new topic hanging in the air for which she wasn't prepared and which he, it seemed, wanted to pursue because he hadn't turned away again and buried himself in the safety of the herb garden but continued to face her, still with that puzzled frown.

'I wanted to say also ... about Sam ... that you have reason to be proud of her, too.'

At that point Samantha arrived with the scones, thereby excusing Joanne from having to reply.

She knew that the young generation got on better with old people than did the generation in-between, so she shouldn't have been surprised that Samantha's relationship with her father was closer than her own. At one step's remove it was easier for them; there were no expectations unfulfilled, no performance judgments so critical that when they reflected on the one party they reflected on the other party, too: 'If I am what I am, it is because you are what you are'; the unending sentence that was parenthood. She mustn't be resentful of it, she must be happy that it was happening.

'Now, we're all going to have scones with strawberry jam,' she said forcefully, 'because I'm not going to make them for nothing and, Dad, I'm going to pour you a cup of Darjeeling because I know you like your tea strong and the Earl Grey can be a little wishy-washy, so tell me if it's too strong for you and I'll add more water, then we should all have a proper look at Sam's project because I haven't had a chance to go through it, darling; you whipped it off to school so quickly, and Daddy hasn't seen it either.'

But her hand shook. The empty cup rattled in the saucer as she picked it up and the stream of tea that poured from the spout waved in the air like a little boy finding a target for his pee, so she dared not fully fill her father's cup in case it spilled and then she put it down in front of him where it sat conspicuously half empty. What was she going to say if he asked about Willie? How could she hide the fact that she'd been through his private papers? Barely able to breathe she desperately sought a diversion.

'I told Grandpa that you didn't have any help' she told Sam. 'It's all your own work.'

'Except for the photos; you went through Grandma's albums for me. They're the best part.'

'Oh, yes, they were a lucky find, but you did all the rest.'

Albert seemed keen to look at them again.

'I never knew they existed,' he said, 'let alone that your mother had kept them.'

'That's what women do,' Joanne said brightly. 'Women are the keepers of family treasure. They hold on to the history and mementoes because they are important for the younger generations who want to know who they are and where they came from. There's nothing as precious as that.'

She didn't mind if this sounded accusatory: that's what she wanted.

'When a woman flees a burning house she'll snatch up the family photograph album in preference to her jewel box. You see that in the bush fires. You can always buy another broach but you can never replace treasured memories. Once they're lost they can never be recovered.'

Had he never wondered what memories her mother had retained

of him; never been curious about who was the keeper of their family history? Surely he didn't think that his leaving had been like the removal of an ornament from a shelf leaving an empty space? He couldn't hide his actions in the pretence that there was no evidence of his prior existence.

'Mummy had lots of photos,' she emphasized, driving home the point. 'We look at them often, don't we Sam? The sad thing is that I couldn't tell her much about her great grandfather because you'd never talked about him yourself. All we had was this one photo. Perhaps you could tell her now?'

Albert looked at the photo of his father with an expression bordering on suspicion. Perhaps he, too, had little he could tell. There were bare facts that he probably thought didn't need repeating and beyond that he would be struggling to think of what to say. Men were so reliant on facts for their construction of reality that in their absence they were content to leave a void. He could survive without needing to construct a father just as he'd survived without needing a wife and child.

'He died when I was seven,' Albert said suddenly, 'so I'd have been a bit young.'

He smiled ironically. Maybe he knew what Joanne was thinking.

'A man I met at Maitland told me he was a lucky man.'

'Was he a gambler?'

'No, no: he was a farmer. He got a ballot farm.'

'So, why was he lucky?'

'Not many soldiers went to that war and came back alive - let alone to land up with a farm. In those days they didn't even have the dole.'

'So there you are,' Joanne said: 'now you know something about your great grandfather.'

Something she'd never known, she might have added, feeling as though this information had somehow undermined her claim that it was only women who preserved the links between the generations.

'So he became a farmer. Then what? Always a farmer?'

She chose her words carefully, aware that she was getting dangerously close to the point where she might inadvertently reveal that she'd been spying on him. She was sure she knew that he'd been a farmer because she'd seen it somewhere, on her mother's marriage certificate perhaps. You couldn't get married in those days without declaring who your parents were and what were their occupations, so it must have been in the family folklore.

'Then what?' she repeated.

'When he first came back from the War he'd entered the ballot for a settlement block and been given one of the new pieces of land being opened up by the Murrumbidgee irrigation schemes. There was a great belief in those days that Australia could be turned into a green and fertile land, as lush as the green pastures of England: *'the green, green grass of Home'*. All it needed was water. The problem was that the water was in the wrong place. That was the belief then and it still is today – that water will solve everything.'

'Did he not get the water?'

'Oh, he got the water alright, as much as he wanted, and for a time things went pretty well, but what he didn't know – because nobody knew – was that some land simply can't be watered; that water actually poisons it.'

'How?' Samantha wanted to know.

'It seeps down into the sub-soils where it dissolves the salt pans. As the water table gradually rises it brings the salts to the surface where they poison the top soil and everything that grows in it. He wasn't as lucky as his mate from Maitland thought: his land proved to be too shallow and after eight years he had to walk off it with nothing to show.'

'Was it traumatic for you?'

'I was only two and I have no memory of the farm. My father's job by then was to sell motor vehicles and tractors. It was a hard time. When the Depression struck nobody wanted to buy motor cars or tractors. In the cities one in three men was unemployed and in rural areas it was even worse. It's hard to imagine it today. Then the War came and we all forgot about the Depression.'

'Is that why you signed-up, Grandpa: because of the Depression?'

'Goodness, no; I joined up to save Australia from invasion.'

What was missing was the explanation for those words she'd read that morning. Had he been speaking metaphorically? Was he speaking about the death of energy and spirit that must afflict a man driven by the elements into financial ruin? God knows, it was happening in the bush every day at this very moment. They prayed for them regularly at St. Agnes and raised collections, but it was a problem that was intractable: no-one wanted food, they only wanted computers and Play Stations.

'So how did Grandpa die?' she asked, smiling gently at Samantha to let her know that it was on her behalf that she was asking.

'He drowned.'

Albert reached out and dropped a scone onto Samantha's plate. He wasn't going to be the only one eating and he'd clearly developed a taste for the strawberry jam. This was a moment that Joanne recognized should have been as close to her ideal of family life as it was possible to describe, yet she was unable to let it continue undisturbed. It was a beautiful day, warm and clear without a cloud in the sky and she was sitting in her picture-perfect garden reminiscing with her father and daughter while fighting the urge to escape to the kitchen. This wasn't, as Prue would say, a case of Joanne being antsy, 'a social insect celebrated for industry'; this was driven by a fear of her own potential for disintegration. It had no rational cause, it was not even as though she was menopausal, and yet she couldn't stay and continue.

She stood up abruptly.

'You *are* going to come to the RSL dinner tonight, aren't you?'

'Well, I ...'

'It's just that I noticed you'd packed your suitcase and I wondered if you'd forgotten. You're both coming - Samantha, too. It's for charity. We've booked your places.'

She began to back away.

'Does that sound like your cup of tea, Sam?' Albert teased.

'I'll phone Roger and find out when we need to leave. There should be time for you to have a lie down if you want it.'

She didn't wait for a proper answer but headed back to the house knowing there was no way she could continue without revealing that she'd searched through his private possessions. She couldn't even acknowledge to him the surge of sadness that had accompanied her finding of the black and white photograph tucked in the back of his vinyl folder, carefully wrapped in grease-proof sandwich paper, softened and smoothed by years of careful handling: the photograph of her, Joanne, standing on the porch with her mother about to go off to her first day at school forty-three years ago.

31.

The Newtown Café

'We're going to the movies,' Luke announced. 'Eat up and pay the bill. It starts in half an hour.'

'What are we seeing?' Ari asked.

'The fuckin' French flick; what d'ya think? Get ourselves an education. Who's got money?'

'I'm skint,' Willie murmured, taking out his credit card.

'Let me see that.'

Luke reached across and grabbed the card from Willie's hand.

'What's this: *St George Everyday Student Savings*? Since when did students have savings? Does Daddy give you a little allowance, does he? Does Granny send you Postal Orders for Christmas? Look at this, Ari; we're in luck here.'

Willie lunged forward to retrieve it, knocking his plate in the process. The knife fell to the floor with a loud clatter and the customers at the adjacent tables turned around to see. He was bigger than Luke and could handle him easily if he got a grip. He pushed back his chair to stand up but his knee was caught behind the table leg and the jolt spilled the hot chocolate which he'd been saving to drink last. His fork followed the knife to the floor.

'Don't be a prick, man,' he hissed. 'Give it to me.'

'Who's the prick, *man*? I'm just looking at it, *man*. I didn't see you paying for any of that dope last night. I think you owe us. What do you say, Ari; do you think he owes us? Shit, I wouldn't want to think we were hanging out with a bludger, would you? You know what we think of bludgers. Daddy wouldn't want you to get a reputation like that, man; that's why he puts money in your account, to help educate you and to encourage you to pay your way like a real man. Shit, he doesn't want you to be just an *Everyday Student*, he wants you to be generous and open-handed, unlike those many mean-spirited little arseholes that hang around people like leeches and parasites, smoking their dope and fondling their chicks. We all know arseholes like that, man. Thank God you're not one of them.'

The waitress with the red hair and the tongue stud, hearing the sound of falling cutlery, arrived at the table like a tow truck at a crash scene, arms akimbo and eyes glaring. She'd spotted Luke as being trouble and she was determined to stay right on him. There was hot chocolate running down Willie's leg from his crutch and his thin paper napkin was going to do little for the stain.

'What say you get this one,' Luke said sweetly, 'and I'll get the next?'

He held the credit card aloft and handed it to the waitress with his eyebrows arched and a dimpled smile on his face which was all the more insulting for being so false. It was all a game. Everything was just a huge big fucking game.

'Want to come to the movies?' he asked the waitress.

'No.'

'Don't know what you're missing.'

She went away with Willie's card.

What Willie didn't know – what nobody knew – was whether the card would be accepted. Whenever he took it out now it felt like an unexploded hand grenade. He would put it on the counter with a feeling of dread. If he could, he'd go to the cashier when there was no-one else there. 'Credit or Eftpos?' they'd ask. Credit, always credit: they never decline small amounts, he'd found. But now? Now it would be just his luck that the bird with the small tits and the heavy hips would phone for a credit check. Who wouldn't when a smart-arsed punk like Luke was paying? Then she'd come back to the table with a sneer on her face. 'Declined!' she'd say. She'd say it loud, too, so everyone could hear. He could see her expression, the hand on the hip, the amateur theatrical drama queen doing her big disdainful bit. 'Declined! Your card's no good. Got any better ideas?'

Goddamn, shit and fuck! The need for money was like a malarial fever, always hanging over him, causing his teeth to chatter just when he thought everything was fine. He should have known. It's the insidious disease you can't escape. You let it into your bloodstream and it infects you forever no matter how hard you fight to purge it. You can flush out your veins so there's no remaining trace; start again with brand new purified blood that's never been near the source of infection before and it'll make no difference; you're a carrier; you're doomed.

He rubbed the stain on his trousers. How the hell do you get chocolate out? If he went to the loo and rinsed it with water it would look like he'd pissed himself. It was going to look like he'd pissed himself anyway.

'Who's signing?' the girl asked cynically, returning to the table.

'Not me,' Luke replied, quickly handing the plate on. 'That would be dishonest.'

So it hadn't been rejected after all, and now Willie was actually pleased to pay because all he could feel was relief. But it made no sense. Something weird was happening with the card. On three occasions now when he'd been to an ATM to get cash, he'd found there was five hundred dollars in his account. Every time he went it was the same. He'd count up what he spent and then go back again. There must have been something wrong with their computer and they were fucking up big time. It hadn't just happened once. Was he going to tell them? Yeah, likely! Maybe he'd read the statements wrong. Maybe there'd been more in there than he thought. But it couldn't last. He'd have to find a way of making some real dough before they found out.

He signed the credit card slip with a flourish, like he really loved paying for them all.

'No tip?' the girl said belligerently.

'Yeah,' Luke replied. 'Put one of those things through your clitoris and get some fun into your life.'

Ari thought this was so witty that he had to get out of the café before he exploded.

They walked back to Newtown Station and caught a train to Central. Willie still had his student season ticket but he wasn't sure whether it had run out so he walked very fast through the side gate avoiding the swipe machines while Luke leap-frogged the turnstiles and ran down the stairs laughing. At Central they realised they were still a long way from Paddington Town Hall where the movie was showing and it was too far to walk so Ari shouted them a cab fare.

Willie and Ari sat in the back seat, not speaking because they didn't know each other and were only there because of Luke who was clearly in a hurry, not wanting to miss the opening scene of the movie. Coming up Wentworth Avenue they got stuck at the traffic lights trying to turn into Oxford Street. There seemed to be an awful lot of people around and they were wandering about in the road like it was meant to be a car-free day; old buggers who seemed to have no idea where they were going.

'What is this?' Luke wanted to know. 'Have they emptied the old people's homes?'

He wound down the window and started shouting at them while Willie was thinking what a strange mix it was for the small Indian and the tall Polish girl to be flatting together, and he wondered how it had happened. He'd been thinking, too, that he'd like to talk about her because he needed to remember the previous night. He wanted to know what the others thought had happened; what they'd seen and heard and what they thought of him as a result. Maybe he was looking for a little flash of admiration in Ari's eyes, or even envy; but he didn't want to sound too keen in case the bits missing from his own memory of events were best left forgotten. It wasn't like he'd shown any particular interest in her; he'd just been lying down on the floor chilling out and she'd chosen to sit down beside him. It was no big deal.

But he couldn't get her out of his mind. He'd lain beside her naked body and pored over her skin, watching the blood coursing through her veins. He'd listened to her breathe as she slept and seen the hairs growing between her legs. Oh, Jesus, he wished she'd been there when he'd woken up. He wished she were there now. Had she realised he'd pissed all over the blanket on the floor? Had she been angry and disgusted when she found him next to her and told the others before she left the house?

'I need to get some money,' he remembered. 'Can we stop at an ATM?'

She couldn't have said anything because Luke would have been all over it like a rash. He wouldn't have been able to let it alone. Anyway, he'd been on the floor alone when he woke up with the wet blanket; she'd been in the bed. Everything was sweet. He must have fallen out of bed after fucking her and gone into the other room. Whatever those pills were, he was never going to take them again. It was scary having no memory.

The cabbie pulled up just past Taylor Square opposite the bank and he dived out of the cab and crossed the road. His balance was still shot and he had to concentrate as he threaded his way through the passing cars, but thinking about Nicole had made him feel high. He wanted to be friends with Ari. Shit, he was a nice guy. It was great that Indian people could come to Australia and just fit in. He took everything in his stride. No wonder that bird wanted to flat with him. She was such a great bird she must have had any number of offers, but he could see why she'd ended up with Ari. Asian people were just so *un-aggressive*. It was cool.

He took two hundred dollars from the machine and buried the notes deep down in his hipster pocket so there'd be no chance of them accidentally slipping out. Then he took the printed receipt which showed he now had three hundred and two dollars in his account. He couldn't figure that out and he wasn't going to waste time trying. It was the Bank's problem: let them figure it out. He'd make the two hundred last as long as possible while he decided what he was going to do. One thing was for sure; he wasn't going to be forking out for Luke's ticket when they got to The Chauvel. He could fucking pay for himself.

When they got out of the cab the driver leaned across and wound down the window so he could talk to them. He seemed to be singling out Luke.

'You little shits want to pay some respect to old people,' he said, 'particularly on Anzac Day.'

That was the first time Willie realised what day it was.

32.

The Apartment

Roger had grown increasingly angry. He'd waited another hour and she still hadn't returned his call. That fucking girl had no idea how seriously she'd pissed him off, but there was no point in hanging around the apartment any longer. He frowned. There was a strange noise. Then he realized that his cell phone, which he'd left on the kitchen counter, was vibrating because he'd forgotten to switch the bell tone back on. He grabbed it and checked the Caller ID. It was Joanne.

'What is it?'

'Have I caught you at a bad time?'

'It's always a bad time, Jo.'

'I wanted to check what time we're expected at the dinner and should I bring my car into town?'

'Yes. I mean, no, get a cab. I'll meet you there. I think it's seven. Check the invite.'

'Are you alright?'

'Of course! How did Sam go on the march? I looked out for her but didn't see them.'

'It went well. She seemed excited. I picked the two of them up from the ferry.'

'Good. That's good.'

'Well, I'll let you get on with your work.'

That's exactly what he needed to do. Christ, he'd nearly forgotten that he'd arranged to meet Greg Cummings at 3.30. Then he needed to get back to the office and make sure Lawrence was keeping those contract documents on track. There was too much at risk to allow Lawrence to start having second thoughts now.

This other little matter would have to wait. He couldn't afford to be distracted. Fuck her; why wouldn't she call back? She'd already acknowledged she had the damn briefcase and it was obvious it contained nothing worth stealing. She wouldn't have admitted she had it unless she was anxious to keep him as a customer. Maybe that was the problem: there was no hurry because it contained nothing important.

Alright; he'd give her a little nudge - not another voice message because that would sound too anxious - just a simple text so that she knew he wasn't taking it lightly.

I WANT IT

33.

Saville Corp's Office

Lawrence stood up and stretched his legs. Thank heavens for Bill Gates, he thought. Once it would have taken him days of drafting and re-drafting to get those agreements into an acceptable state. It seemed incredible now, but lined foolscap paper, wrist cramps and illegible transcripts by illiterate legal secretaries used to be the norm. How distant those memories had become.

It was such a freedom to only have to rely upon oneself. He may not have been the earliest adopter of technology (he'd hesitated until it proved itself) but he doubted if any of the major law firms could teach him anything about it now. The great advantage that he had over partners in large practices was that his system didn't need to take account of other people. When he saved a document to his H-drive it was stored there for his retrieval alone. He knew that it would sit there safely, uncorrupted by unauthorized amendments. There was nothing more reassuring than that.

How long had it taken him? He looked at his desk clock. It was 3.40. He'd been at it for three hours solid, but in that time he'd pulled together the draft of the Sale and Purchase Agreement for the residential sub-division as well as the Memorandum of Sale covering the issue of new shares. Apart from the settlement dates and final prices, only the details of the purchasing entity remained outstanding. It had taken him a lot less time than he'd anticipated and he enjoyed a mild sense of satisfaction.

Now, he realised, he was hungry. Breakfast was the most important meal of the day but it counted for nothing if one then proceeded to miss lunch. Metabolism was like a spoiled child: no matter how well you'd treated it four hours previously, it would still demand attention again four hours later. Eat in moderation but eat regularly, that was his rule, for digestion needed to be regularly stimulated or it would grow lazy and lay down fat. If women would only realise that, the dietary industry could be abolished. It was just a pity that there were times, like this, when the pressure of work caused him to break that simple rule.

The city's lunch bars and cafes would be closed on Anzac Day, he figured, so he would have to resort to the boardroom kitchen. Luckily he could rely on their corporate chef's frugality. A long time ago he'd noticed her aversion to waste and learned that she had a tendency to recycle unused food over the following two days. Wednesday lunch had included smoked salmon and a creamy potato salad with onion and mayonnaise, the thought of which now caused his stomach to rumble. He might accompany that with a crisp apple juice or a sparkling mineral water, and then he'd give some thought to the Stock Exchange notices he'd have to draft.

Roger Saville, of course, would not be giving any of this a moment's thought. It was doubtful that he even understood the process. The extraordinary thing for someone who prided himself on being such a deal-maker, and who'd inherited from a father with such a reputation for astuteness, was that he should have remained so ignorant of the detail of business for so long. How did he think all this was going to happen? How could he possibly progress this great deal (which only he could be trusted to negotiate, apparently!) without Lawrence there to guide him through the minefield of legalities? Did he truly not realise the implications of what he was proposing, or was he a lot smarter than that? Was he smart enough, actually, to realise that Lawrence would sort it out?

Yes, there probably was a bit of that. After all, he would only be responding to the lessons of the last ten years. Even Pavlov's dog would have learned in that time that Lawrence was bound to come along and tidy everything up. So maybe this time he should hold back a little. Instead of rushing to anticipate the damage and then repairing it in advance, maybe he should sit back in the safety of the trenches and watch the action. When the soldiers on the field were hurt and bloodied they would turn to him for his magic sponge knowing they wouldn't be allowed back into action until he had tended them. Maybe then Roger would appreciate how dependent he was.

It wasn't a bad idea. In fact, it was rather tempting. The thought of the bloodied nose and the plaintive eyes as Roger trudged from the field of battle unable to continue without Lawrence's ministrations was very appealing. The risk, of course, was that Roger would not just receive a bloodied nose; the risk was that he would receive a broken neck, in which case it would be game over for all of them. No, there needed to be a middle way. He could still map the minefield, because that was just as much in his interests as Roger's, but he could make his point quite adequately by being less ... available.

The smoked salmon in the kitchen fridge was still fresh and moist because the caterer had wrapped it in cling foil. Lawrence liked that: he liked her values. So many of their chefs in the past had seemed driven to dispose of perfectly good food so that one could have been forgiven for thinking they were running a pig farm on the side. The potato salad was not quite as fresh but that was because she'd used a white potato variety which tended to go grey once cooked. He only took one spoonful on that account and doubled up on the salmon to make up for it, passing on the rocket salad remains which failed to tempt him.

Back in his office he spread a napkin neatly on his desk top, arranged his knife and fork as he would if laying the table for guests, centred the plate with the salmon to the left side and then poured himself a glass of ice-cold San Pellegrino. This was almost as good as anything he would be offered at Catalina's. He enjoyed eating on his own, undisturbed. It brought great clarity to his thinking.

Having absorbed the detail of the transaction, he was now ready to approach the deductive stage with confidence. Out of the detail emerged one or two key issues. He considered the implications of the new share issue first. The company was entitled to issue up to three percent of new equity in any one year under the special 'Working Capital' provision contained in the prospectus. That provision had been Roger's idea. He'd seen it as a potential way of acquiring shares for himself at a discount, ignoring Lawrence's advice that he would never be able to benefit from it. The Astor deal, however, was exactly what it should have been designed for. Providing the issue was made within three years of the prospectus date and provided it was done at fair market value, no shareholder consents were required. Market value was easy to determine if they applied the prospectus formula. What mattered there was the test of fair value. He would come back to that.

Next he considered the sale and purchase of the leasehold interest in the sub-division. On the surface, and in the absence of any other factor, this was a straightforward case of 'willing buyer and willing seller'. Yes, it required shareholder approval due to the size of the asset being sold, but essentially they were in business for that very purpose: to sell assets at a profit. Shareholders would be delighted.

Where, then, were the problems? In the first case it was the test of fair value. Could the share value be judged unfair if the market was unaware of the new property valuations? Answer: very likely. Putting the valuations to one side, could the purchaser of the shares be deemed to have an unfair advantage if the shares subsequently rose because of the separate transaction in which he was involved as a buyer of the land? Surely *not*. It must be presumed that he believed he was buying the land at fair value. He was quite entitled to purchase shares in the belief that they would go up (wasn't that why everyone bought shares?), but if he believed he was paying the right price for the land then that was hardly a given.

Was he paying the right price for the land? The right price was what a willing buyer was prepared to pay. Perhaps it was a coincidence that the offer price was exactly in line with the new valuations that only Roger had seen. On the one hand Roger wanted those valuations in order to give Astor comfort. On the other hand the existence of the valuations undermined the fairness of the new equity pricing. There was, thought Lawrence, only one solution. It was simple and its logic was without flaws. Having arrived so confidently at it, he felt flushed with pride and pleasure. That pleasure would grow sweeter the longer he made Roger sweat on it.

34.

The Lobby of the Westin Hotel

'I think you can assume,' Greg Cummings confided, 'that the Companies and Securities Advisory Committee will recommend that a prohibition should be introduced on short swing profits.'

He leaned forward so far in his chair that anybody watching would have thought he was about to give Roger a blow job. What was it with merchant bankers?

'They've made it clear that there should be no statutory exemption to permit persons to trade before publishing price-sensitive information, but at the moment they're relying on the Continuous Disclosure Regime. I think they'll toughen up. That's what ASIC wants and eventually the Treasurer will give it to them. That's the message we're getting.'

Roger sat back in his chair and tried to hide his disdain. Alright, he'd play the game.

'I know what a profit is,' he said pleasantly, 'but what's a short swing?'

He'd resist making a joke about golf; jokes only puzzled merchant bankers. He'd pretend instead that what Greg was saying was clever and important. Being clever and important was the juice that kept them going. This was their way of giving themselves an air of authority, like they had a direct line to ASIC, the Attorney General and God; which is why you paid them such outrageous commissions to complicate the shit out of some simple deal, wrapping it up in arcane jargon so it all sounded like science. Without all this bullshit they were just jumped-up car salesmen.

'Six months under the Canadian rules,' Greg replied with authority.

He looked around furtively in case someone else could hear. Maybe he wanted someone else to hear. Between them was a low glass table on which stood a three-tiered cake stand now almost empty. Roger had ordered tea and sandwiches because he hadn't had anything for lunch and the acid was eating a hole in his stomach, but they brought out half the contents of a patisserie shop as well which somehow, he didn't know how, they'd managed to eat between them and now he felt bloated.

'Are you going to explain to Butch that we're trying to protect him from being an insider? If we issue these shares at a discount I don't want him trading them as soon as he sees a profit.'

'He knows that. He's there for the long haul. Let's get him on board and then look to how we hook him into Plan B. I've been working on some ideas but first we need to sign him up to Plan A.'

There was one more item left on the cake stand that Roger hadn't seen and Greg couldn't resist. Maybe that's why he was leaning so far forward; the sweet aroma of the strawberry custard tart had drawn him like a bear to honey.

'Does he know how fucking good this deal is? He gets in at forty-eight cents: that's a gift of fifty two cents a share. It's insane.'

'He knows that. He knows that. He recognizes that that's the sweetener and he appreciates it, but, hey, he's hard nosed: he also knows he's paying full valuation for the land. He wants to see that. He wants to be comfortable before he signs. He's no pushover.'

'What are you saying?'

'Nothing. Don't get alarmed. You've spoken to the guy; you know what he sounds like, all laid back and Yankee Doodle. He might have gone to Stamford and talk like a regular guy but this is a Singapore company and they don't get big without being smart. They're Asian, after all; they drive hard bargains and they like to have control. We'll get there. We're only just into the race so let's concentrate on our rhythm.'

Greg had been an Olympic rower. No doubt that's how he got the job. Now he was a financial genius and a philosopher.

A young woman with lots of hair and bare legs walked across

the marble tiled floor of the hotel lobby holding the hand of a little boy, coaching him in a loud voice as to how he could make an elevator appear at the touch of a button just like a magician; just like Harry Potter, in fact. Everyone watched her. She didn't look like she'd ever have to pay for anything in her life. Roger looked at her and wondered why he didn't have a woman like that. He was rich. How rich did you have to be? Maybe it was just a question of resetting his sights.

'I need to know whether we have a deal,' he insisted, dragging his eyes away. 'If Astor's going to play silly buggers at the last minute then I want to know now.'

'I can't guarantee anything, Roger. We've given them all they wanted short of due diligence. What he's told me is that he only needs to settle on the price. If you've got valuations that back you up then he'll be happy to pay. It's all about face with the Asians. They hate anyone to think they've paid too much. You're giving him a big win on the equity price but he doesn't want to lose on the land value.'

'For fuck sake, how can he possibly lose on the land value? Doesn't anyone understand that land of this nature can only go up? It doesn't matter what he pays: the day after he's paid, it will be worth more.'

'He knows that. He knows that. This is all about face. You hand him the valuations and he knows his face is protected. Believe me, it's that simple. He's flown a long way to do this deal. You'll see for yourself this evening: he's excited and ready to go. We've put a lot of work into getting him this far. It's too good to fall over now.'

The problem was that Greg was like an estate agent: both parties laboured under the illusion that he was working for them when in fact he was working for himself. All he wanted was a deal. He'd say anything to keep the two parties together, but could he be trusted to look after Roger's interest? Could anyone be trusted to look after Roger's interests, for that matter? Wherever he looked all he could see were pilot fish. *'Naucratus ductor'*, his father used to warn: 'they're not there to guide you; they're there to feed off your scraps'.

'Look,' Roger said suddenly, 'I'm going cold on Plan B. There'll never be an opportunity as good as Whiteman's Creek. I'd be crazy to sell Astor any part of my shareholding at this stage. Let's just concentrate on the deal we've got. I don't know why I even allowed you to think it was a possibility. I must have been having a bad day. He can acquire the three percent allocation we've promised but if he wants to go further he'll have to stand in the market.'

Strawberry and custard were caught in mid bite and oozed colourfully from between Greg's top teeth. He sat back smartly and wiped his mouth.

'Besides,' Roger added casually, 'there's no way round the Takeovers Code that will allow me to extract a premium for control. Maybe I'd be better off driving the share price down and then privatizing. I could do a Lang Walker and go and live in the sun; not have to put up with fucking shareholders and analysts sucking me dry. That's got a much better ring. We should look at it.'

A shower cloud of disappointment swept across Greg's face.

'Don't be hasty,' he protested. 'We think we may have a solution to Section 698. There are ways around everything.'

He leaned forward again, unaware of the strawberry seed that was still lodged between his front incisors.

'We've been looking at your private company; the one that holds your assets. It's true that Section Six doesn't allow the purchase of a company where that company holds a relevant interest in a listed entity which is greater than nineteen percent; however, there are exceptions allowed under Section Six Eleven, including where the acquisition results from *another* acquisition of relevant interests in the voting shares of *another* listed company ...'

Why was he so anxious, Roger wondered? Why the urgency?

'I don't understand,' he interrupted, putting up his hand to slow the traffic of words; 'who is this 'we' you're talking about? There are only two people in the whole world that have ever put my shareholding and the Takeovers Code into the same conversation *even hypothetically*. Who have you been discussing this with?'

I'll have his fucking guts for garters, Roger thought. The minute the Astor land sale goes through I'll cut his tongue out and feed it to the fish. There's absolutely no-one you can trust but yourself.

'Not a soul, Roger, I swear.'

The shower cloud of disappointment had suddenly turned into a thunder storm and Greg was reaching for his umbrella.

'Absolutely not a dickey bird,' he insisted. 'Your name has never been mentioned. I only ever talk generalities. It occurred to me - *me*, not *we* - that we could usefully look at what the Packers have done; bring in fifteen percent of the public and list your investment company; slip some hard assets in there while we're at it and then invite a takeover of that vehicle. Instead of dealing with sixty percent of minorities, the buyer would only have to look after fifteen. I'm just trying to show that there are ways; there are always ways.'

He smiled reassuringly. Thank God the strawberry seed had now gone. Roger pulled his own top lip firmly down over his own front teeth determined that no glimpse of friendly white would be visible, at the same time leaning back in his chair to give himself distance.

'I want to give a clear instruction, Greg.' His voice was low but firm. 'This subject has never even been raised. If I should ever, by whatever means, hear that Lawrence Beck or Butch Astor or anyone else suspected that I was even willing to contemplate a sale of my stake in Saville Corp I would regard it as a serious breach of trust. I let you talk about this idea because everyone likes to know their options and what they're worth, but it was only ever an idea of yours, never of mine. It's like my house. How much do you like it? How much would you pay? You want to make an offer? That's great, but it's not for sale. Do you understand? It's not for sale.'

The bastard! Who the hell had he blabbered to: Lawrence, Butch, half of Sydney? If the Banks got a sniff of this they'd run screaming for the exits. Alison Pyke would be reserving her seat at the front row of the guillotine, practising her secret smile in the hope that it would be the last thing he saw as the blade dropped.

'Absolutely understood, Roger; you can rest assured.'

35.

The Offices of Saville Corp

Lawrence's plate was clean and his glass was empty. He placed his knife and fork neatly together and contemplated his next task. The hands on his silver-plated desk clock were at odds with the hands on his watch. Preferring to trust his watch (a Patek Phillipe that had never been a second out in twelve years) he picked up the clock and adjusted it, realising that Roger's ceremony in the park must have ended hours ago and surprised that he hadn't already returned to the office demanding attention. No wonder he'd managed to get through his work so quickly.

There were now three hours to fill before they were due at dinner. The sensible thing was to leave the office before Roger got back and remain out of contact until they all met later that evening, taking a lesson from his own book and making himself less ... *available*. But three hours was an awkward time to fill. The thought of returning home diminished the glow of pleasure. He was not in the mood to change his clothes and potter in the garden, nor was there anything to which he could settle in his study. Marjorie would be doing the crossword or working on a tapestry. She would offer him tea and hover in the kitchen in case there was something he wanted to say. There wouldn't be anything he wanted to say and eventually she'd go outside for a cigarette and then return to her tapestry. He'd turn on the television to find it dominated by football and repetitious news clips of Anzac Day marches in Wagga Wagga and Dubbo. Roger would phone and complain that he was getting no support. Where were the contracts? Why did he have to do everything on his own? Little by little Lawrence would be drawn to the point of no return. He would tell him the solution. He would hand it to him, as he did so often, on a plate; and Roger would snatch it as if it was his own.

No, he didn't want to go home. It wasn't as if he had no other image of life than the one he lived, it was rather that the images were incompatible with the one he lived. Take Jeffrey Smart as an example. It was no coincidence that Roger had chosen to give him that painting. It was as if Jeffrey Smart had painted it with only one person in mind: everyone who saw it said that. They meant that the painting was incredibly precise. He didn't mind that. They meant that it was, somehow, so prosaic – white lines and traffic bollards on a bitumen highway – yet so intensely rendered that it imbued the prosaic with an almost surreal quality. In fact, what Lawrence would say was that this style of painting made the telling point that fidelity of representation was startling precisely because most people's vision obscured reality. When he looked at it he felt admonished for his own willingness to take appearance for granted but also, conversely, comforted by his insistence on detail. A Jeffrey Smart painting was a metaphor for Lawrence Beck, if only others understood all that that meant.

How was this incompatible with the way he lived? Perhaps because he was also, in his heart of hearts, merely a vision obscured, lacking that fidelity of representation that only people who were willing to be absolutely true to their nature possessed. Too often, he believed, he compromised his own standards. It was his responsibility to live by them absolutely, but he failed. It was like putting the onus back on the object rather than the viewer. That was what Jeffrey Smart did in his paintings. The objects made the viewer see them because they represented themselves so intensely that even people lacking in vision couldn't help but notice them.

He'd read that Smart was a homosexual and lived in Tuscany. There was a stone house with garden steps that led to a rose garden. Darkened doorways with Etruscan lintels opened into a cool interior beneath a clay tiled roof. A middle aged man sat in the garden at an easel in bare feet. When the sun grew hot he went inside and stood on the cool flagstone floor waiting for coffee to brew. Once a week, or less, friends would call with wine and vegetables and they would eat pasta and talk. On the easel a brief section of an on-ramp of the N-7 would be taking shape, the sun penetrating into the bare concrete buttressed columns that held it up in the air and casting long shadows behind the orange steel drums that protected the pile of grey and white road grit waiting to be spread.

It wasn't that Lawrence fancied he was homosexual or that he had a yearning to live in Tuscany that made him see these images; it was the growth of life out of detail. The painting, he felt, grew as surely as an embryo; not suffocated by the painstaking minutia but, on the contrary, entirely reliant upon it.

Suddenly he knew what he wanted to do. He took his plate and utensils to the kitchen and placed them in the dishwasher, returned to his office and gathered up his briefcase and car keys, then turned out the light and headed for the lifts. There was a gallery in Paddington that had a Jeffrey Smart that he had been thinking about for weeks, ever since he first saw it. Better than the one in his office, it featured a petrol tanker in the process of filling up a storage tank at a service station: two men in overalls and a long hose like a snake. The gallery would be open he was sure, for the owner couldn't bear the thought of missing a sale.

If the Astor deal went well and their share price rose, this would be his present to himself.

36.

The Lobby of the Westin Hotel

Roger had no appetite for further discussion. His mind was elsewhere. He was trying to remember the locations and brandings of the cash machines in Martin Place. There was the ANZ on the corner of Pitt Street and the Commonwealth Bank opposite. Did the NAB on George Street have an ATM or was that now behind the temporary hoardings they'd thrown up around Landmark House? If he used one and there was a limit on the daily withdrawal permitted, would that machine alert the other machines that he was making further withdrawals and bar them? He had three cards: a Qantas Visa Gold Card linked to his private account, a Gold Corporate Mastercard and an American Express Platinum Card. What were their daily limits: one thousand, two thousand? He'd never tested them. Maybe he should go straight to the American Express office - assuming the damn thing was open on fucking Anzac Day. He was sure he could draw five thousand at a time from them; he'd done it before, in Europe and the States. But then, they'd want to see his passport. Where the hell was it? Oh fuck! Not in his briefcase?

'… so I suggest we leave the valuations with Butch overnight so he can get comfortable,' Greg was saying, 'and then we go out to the site in the morning and get down to the agreements in the afternoon. I presume Lawrence will be handling that side of things?'

'What? Oh, sure.'

Roger took his cell phone from his pocket and opened his saved text messages. His problem was that he didn't know how much he'd need, let alone how he'd got himself into this position. Maybe he had it all wrong. There was still a chance she realised she'd made a mistake and was looking for a way out of it. If it wasn't for the urgency associated with the valuations he'd have left her to stew, but now he'd conveyed that urgency to her and he felt certain it was going to cost him. All that he'd said was that he wanted it. Of course he bloody wanted it; that wasn't giving anything away. And she had shot back, 'HOW MUCH'. It was obvious where that question was heading so he'd made sure she realised his patience was at an end. 'URGENTLY', he had curtly replied barely a second later, to which the bitch had merely repeated, 'HOW MUCH'.

She was trying to push him to make an offer, he could see that. Well, he was damned if he was going to. There was nothing in the briefcase that warranted payment; she must know that. The only cost to him was inconvenience. That's all he was prepared to negotiate.

'I NEED IT 2NITE,' he texted.

'He's an invaluable man, old Lawrence,' Greg added enthusiastically as they parted. 'It must be comforting to have him on the team.'

37.

The Chauvel Cinema

In the dark, where he couldn't see or be seen, Willie knew exactly who he was. He knew his body, most importantly, better in the dark than when he could see it under light. His arms and legs and feet and hands felt comfortably his own. It was as if a tight bandage had encased him, hiding him from view; so tight that it had numbed all feeling and as the cinema lights went down the bandage was removed allowing his skin to expand and release tiny little tremors of feeling that ran out across the surface of his body like millions of playful ants.

He stretched his legs under the seat in front. The cinema was full. Before the lights went down he'd felt surrounded by potential threat, avoiding people's faces, embarrassed because he was a dirty young pervert who had come to see a porno film while everyone else was an intellectual art critic; he had frequent and uncontrollable erections while they had middle-aged superiority. For all he knew, one of them could have been a friend of his mother.

He'd been anxious, too. If there was such a stink about the movie's rating, maybe you had to be twenty one to get in. He didn't know if he could lie when challenged. He didn't want people looking at him if he was. He'd stared intently at the cinema carpet instead, and at the back of the seat in front. Then the lights went down.

In the dark Willie could feel the warmth being given off by other bodies, like night storage heaters, and hear the sniffs and snuffles of movement as intimate as a crowded dormitory. The people who'd felt so threatening under the lights morphed into black anonymous silhouettes. He couldn't see their faces and they couldn't see his. Up above them in the glaring light of the projector, a world more certain than any that Willie had ever experienced began to play out. This was why he gave himself so willingly to movies: it was the certainty they offered. The actors could be confident in all their actions because they knew they couldn't be undone. Unlike life, the story already had a course and an ending that was guaranteed.

He missed the opening rape scene even though it went on for quite awhile. Well, he didn't miss it; he just failed to take it in. He was still arriving even though he was there; still getting out of the cab back on Oxford Street, still coming up the staircase of the Paddington Town Hall wondering what the fuck they were doing in this old ladies' building, standing bemused at the top of the stairs where there were all these dykes with cropped hair and corny leather jackets, and geeky geography teachers in knitted sweaters, all whispering and looking furtive and severe. Okay, some people could take it all in, rapid assimilation and all that stuff, but he ran his reel more slowly, maybe; he liked to rewind. There was so much going on that he couldn't be rushed.

Actually, he'd been pretty convinced they were in the wrong place at first and he'd started to turn and go down the stairs again. There wasn't anywhere you could buy tickets, just a whole lot of people standing around like they'd turned up for a meeting to complain about council rates and been kept waiting outside. It really didn't look like this was the right place to be seeing a French movie, let alone a porno flick, so he started off down the stairs and coming up them was this bird in black fishnet stockings and very, very high stiletto shoes which made him think again. He turned back and looked for Luke who'd gone to this poor excuse for a refreshment counter and bailed up some dork who was standing there frozen in fear as if no-one had told him what to do, and it turned out that this was where you got tickets and the angry people all thought they were in some sort of queue, but Luke didn't give a fuck about that.

So, when the rape scene started, Willie was still settling in. There was a girl with brown eyes who was grabbed by some yobbos in a car park and punched around a lot. Actually, there were two girls and one of them took a hammering on the concrete floor of the car park and the other one took a hammering on the bonnet of a car. The brown eyes of the girl on the bonnet of the car were dead flat and they looked out at the audience and beyond into the far distance saying over and over again, 'Well, fuck you', only silently. The guy doing the fucking had a hairy white arse with pink pimples and every time he rammed it into her, her head jolted like she'd been banged up the arse at the traffic lights. The guy looked such a fucking dork, Willie thought, with his grubby blue jeans down around his ankles and trying to be so tough with his fake hostility and the crunching knuckles in the face routine. That's about all Willie took out of it. The sub-titles didn't help. If it had been a video, maybe, he would have rewound it. That was the good thing about videos.

The other issue was Luke. He wouldn't fucking sit still. Willie hated people who jiggled around in cinemas like they were the only ones there. It made his skin hive and he couldn't concentrate. It was even worse when it was apparent that you were with that person. It made you want to shrink into a protective shell where you couldn't hear them.

It seemed, at least at first, that Luke was going to give a public commentary. Shit, that was all they needed. But when all the shouting on screen gave way to this metronomic meaty thud and they could stop reading the sub-titles and start thinking about what silent, eerie places car parks were, the only other sound in the cinema was the crinkling of paper as Luke concentrated on unwrapping his refreshments.

After the rape scene the girl with the brown eyes wandered around for what seemed like a day or two, into and out of French cafes that didn't seem to have a lot to offer, and into and out of desultory conversations that didn't seem worth having, and the streets belonged to Arab guys who didn't like anyone and the only purpose to life seemed to be the faint hope presented by each street corner that things might be better when you rounded it, which of course they were not. For this girl, in particular, every time she rounded it things were worse until she got fed up and shot the next mother-fucker who would stand still long enough for her to point the gun. It was only mildly surprising that the mother fucker she shot happened to be her brother and he was the only one that had spoken to her with any other purpose than hatred in mind. Maybe that was the point. Up until then Willie had been thinking he wouldn't mind looking after her. Her name was Manu. She was small and he was big: he could protect her. It wouldn't be too bad. She might like to lick him like a kitten and jerk him off while they watched TV. Compared to what had happened in the movie thus far she'd probably love to do just that.

He only started to go along with it all when the scene shifted to this tall bird, Nadine, who was hanging out in a flat somewhere and getting pissed off because she'd been smoking dope and badly needed a beer. He knew how that felt. Fuck, he really liked the way she flopped around with only her panties on and he was bloody sure that what she'd been doing, lying on the bed, was playing with herself, and once she'd found the beer she'd go right back to doing it again, so he gave her all his attention. This girl, actually, was exactly what he had been looking for. Her long leggy thigh leading up to the panties was just about the only thing in the world he knew he craved; above flattery, above fortune, above sleep, he wanted it pressed against his cheek. He got a thumping great hard-on just watching her laziness and the full-on, dopey way she flopped herself all over everything like she knew she could come any time she liked. Even when she grabbed her flatmate by the hair and slammed her head into the wall until it was like a crushed tomato Willie still wanted to stick his head between her thighs. Every time the camera decided to have another close look at her Willie was right there having a close look too. He was sure she was going to turn around and look at him and poke out her tongue with two white pills on it which no-one else would see and he would stand up and leave the cinema to find her waiting for him outside ready to put her tongue in his mouth, just like Nicole.

At the end of the flatmate scene Luke sniffed loudly and coughed, then slipped his hand onto Willie's thigh and squeezed it firmly, just missing his erection. The light in the cinema had grown brighter, or his eyes had adjusted, and he could see the look on Luke's face, his brow furrowed and his lips puckered in a teasing smirk that directed Willie to look down at what he was holding cupped in his free hand. The light wasn't quite that good. Willie took what he thought was a pencil but which he quickly recognised from its feel was a shortened drinking straw. He leaned forward until his face was down in Luke's hand and put the straw to his right nostril, sniffing as quickly and silently as possible. Then he did the same with his left nostril, shuddering slightly at the sweetness before straightening up and waiting.

The girls, Nadine and Manu, meanwhile had become bosom buddies, nicked a car and headed out of Paris. It was pretty obvious they were headed for oblivion; the only interest was in how they got there. Now that they had each other it was becoming a different movie. Nobody minded the ride to hell so much if they were holding hands with a friend. Would it be the same, burying his head against Nicole's thigh if she had someone else with whom she laughed and committed murder? No, what he wanted was for him alone: it was an exclusive pool to drown in.

It didn't take long for the ice man to call. He sneaked up silently and ran a frozen cube around Willie's temples and down his cheeks before blowing a cold blast of air down his back, causing him to shiver and cross his legs. Then a thrilling explosion took place inside him, a chain of miniature blasts that rippled through him like a rope of nitro glycerine tearing across the rock face of a canyon, each explosion releasing a flash of heat that flooded his body. He put his fist in his mouth because there was a bubbling sound like a pent-up geyser rising inside him and he didn't know whether it was a voice or vomit that was rushing to get out.

Nadine, who had ceased being Nicole in his mind on account of her disloyalty and detachment from all actions except the felicitous stroking of Manu's hair, arbitrarily decided to put her gun into their latest victim's mouth. He didn't know why, but Willie immediately started to laugh. Maybe it was the fact that the victim was so obviously meant to be one. He was the sort of sleaze ball who could never get a fuck unless the woman was already dead, or he found himself in a bad porno movie. The gun was just impossibly big, the way cocks are in the same movies, and she needed two hands to hold it so of course it was obvious she was going to make him suck it like a dick before she blew his head off and Willie couldn't help himself because he saw it all so clearly. 'Yeah, suck on that, Sleaze Ball', Willie wanted to say the minute he saw the gun and then, long before she pulled the trigger he was calling out something like 'Ketchup', because that was what he reckoned they were about to see and he dug his elbow into Luke's arm to make sure he didn't miss it.

It was such a great feeling, knowing what was going to happen, almost like he was directing it; the light and sound were so clear and there was a rhythm to the popping of their guns like a hidden sound track that only the ultra-sensitive could hear. It was like, *'slap, slap'*, the beating of a hand upon his thigh and the exquisite tickling of his scrotum. At that moment Willie thought this might be the best movie he would ever see. Shit, they just went straight to it, the way life really was if you knew how to find the sub-text; none of that bullshit about giving in to it all and being a tame little victim. This was the honest way. Live life briefly but brightly.

But then sadly, or so it seemed to Willie, they suddenly began to lose the plot. Time seemed to drag and he had the feeling something important was happening elsewhere that he shouldn't be missing. Maybe it was because there was just too much more energy than sense as they drove around the countryside killing people to a written commentary of banalities that were hardly worth the translation. Maybe it was because he'd inhaled more air than coke and was coming down fast. Anyway, Willie lost his erection and started to get restless. The girls on screen didn't know any of the people they were killing and neither did the audience, so how could anyone stay interested? It was like watching someone else playing a video game. Fuck, it was just stupid.

Was it his imagination or did it seem like the projector light had started to fade? The picture altered. What had been clear and blue became dull and orange, like someone had run out of money. The sub-titles didn't stay up long enough for him to read and the girls on screen started laughing with each other at private jokes which no-one else shared. Willie couldn't sit still. He wanted to scratch but most of the itchiness was coming from inside. Worse still was that feeling that something was going on that he'd completely missed. Manu half reminded him of his sister, Sam. Was that why he'd felt protective towards her? But this was a girl who let men fuck her up the arse and chewed gum while they did it. Then she pumped them full of bullets. This was a movie made by women. Could Sam ever do that? Would he ever know what she was capable of doing? How could any woman be trusted?

190

38.

The Kitchen at Mosman

There was no way of predicting when the chemicals would suddenly be released, or why if they'd been gradually building up in the body they should suddenly overwhelm that part of the brain that moderated social behaviour turning a loving and sensitive daughter on the flick of a switch into a screaming monster filled with hate. It was the suddenness that frightened Joanne.

She'd returned to the kitchen with the tea tray and made her call to Roger when Samantha came in seemingly perfectly normal and cheerful. She wanted to know what she should wear that night and they'd talked about how older men liked women to be dressed simply but formally; how they were uncomfortable with glamour which they saw as either frivolous or flirtatious, neither of which was appropriate in the circumstances.

It was a good conversation, Joanne thought, which had given her an opportunity to transfer some advice in the context of an equal and mature dialogue. Samantha went off to her room to work on some ideas. She was fourteen. She was experimenting. Joanne was happy to let her exercise her own judgment in the matter, for it was an age, all the mothers agreed, where it was important to cut them some slack.

So she was unprepared for Samantha's aggressive and accusatory re-entry to the kitchen ten minutes later. What on earth had Joanne done wrong? Well, it seemed that everything was wrong. Her daughter's life was in ruins. She'd decided that none of her tops were suitable for the skirt she wanted to wear. She knew the top she wanted and she needed Joanne to drop everything and take her out to buy it. Of course, this was unreasonable, not to say absurd. She had a wardrobe full of tops that were more than suitable and to have suddenly become fixated on something she'd seen while trawling the malls with her friends after school was precisely the warning sign that Joanne had come to fear. She knew that Samantha would not accept being thwarted and yet giving in to such a demand would only encourage and perpetuate her behaviour.

So she did the only thing available to her: she tried to be reasonable. She offered to come and help Samantha go through her wardrobe. She'd check and see what was in the ironing basket. She was sure there would be something that would look absolutely stunning.

'Shall we do that together?' she asked.

She kept her calm but she felt only dread.

'Mum, you simply don't understand.'

Samantha's voice rose steadily, reaching towards a volume that was going to be difficult to restrain.

'I do understand, darling, but you have a number of perfectly good tops that go with that skirt and it isn't reasonable for you to ask to go shopping now. Besides, it's Anzac Day and I doubt that anything will be open.'

'Chatswood Centre is open 'til 5.30.'

'Well, there simply isn't time. You'll just have to make do.'

'There's heaps of time. We've got two hours.'

'I just don't think it's reasonable for you to expect me to drop everything and drive you to Chatswood because you want a new blouse when you've got perfectly good ones in your wardrobe.'

'They're not perfectly good: they're hideous. I'm not going to wear them. I'll go to Chatswood on my own if you're going to be so selfish. I hate you.'

Joanne gripped the edge of the kitchen sink and took a deep breath. It was all very well for them to tell you not to over-react. Avoid confrontation, they said; remember that all parents of Year Nine girls have to put up with the same thing. Put yourself outside your situation and think of the solution you'd offer if you were advising someone else.

'How about I let you go through my wardrobe and you can find something you like there?'

She turned around from the sink and faced her daughter with the sunniest smile she could muster. Surely that was a reasonable compromise?

'I don't want to wear your crappy clothes. I know what I want and you won't let me have it because you never do because you're just a loser and a control freak.'

'Samantha! I'm not going to accept that behaviour. I will not allow bad language in this house.'

'Crap! I learn it from you. Crap, crap, crap, that's all you speak. You and Dad use far worse. You're just a bloody hypocrite.'

'Alright, young lady, that's enough. I've tried to be flexible and give you another option but now you've gone too far. I want you to take time out in your room. Well talk about this later when you've calmed down.'

'I'm not taking time out, I'm going to Chatswood and you're going to take me. You can't treat me like this. You never do anything for me. All I do is boring work and I never get to go shopping. You go shopping all the time. You get everything you want. I get nothing. It isn't fair.'

'How's this, then? We'll go together on Saturday when we've got more time, just the two of us. We'll make sure we find just the top you want.'

Was that the incentive for good behaviour that she intended it to be, or was it just a bribe: a reward for bad behaviour? It was impossible to get it right. What all the advice seemed to be admitting was that there was no way to control these mood swings or moderate the foul language; it was just a matter of surviving them. Surely she'd never behaved like this when she was fourteen? Hormones didn't flow any more; they crashed like tidal waves on the shore so the whole house shook.

'Besides, I don't want to leave Grandpa alone in the house when we so seldom get the chance to see him.'

She turned back to the sink, looking for something she could wash.

'I was proud of you today when you showed us your project, Sam. I could tell that Grandpa was very impressed. He said so.'

Give praise; they all respond to that. Who didn't? Give praise often and don't spoil it by adding criticism.

'I don't care. You'll just say what you want; you always do. Grandpa's asleep and he wouldn't even know if we went out for half an hour. You don't talk to him anyway. You don't even know what he thinks. All you think about is yourself. You're a selfish cow and I hate you. I'm going to leave home and never come back, like Willie. You can live alone in your own selfish little world and I hope you'll be happy. You're a loser, Mum, a loser!'

Oh, no, she wasn't going to take this. She'd tried to compromise and avoid confrontation, but she had to show she wasn't going to allow foul tantrums, let alone be bullied into accepting criticism of herself. This had to stop.

'That's enough!' she shouted. It would do Samantha good to see how angry she was. 'You're going to your room and you're grounded. I'm taking your cell phone back and I'm going to tell Daddy that I want your internet connection removed until you're old enough to know how privileged you are. You've become a spoiled little brat and I blame myself for giving in to you all the time. Well, that's now finished. Now go to your room and stay there.'

She'd been aware that she was shouting but she couldn't prevent it. Her heart was pounding and she wanted to smash something on the floor. Let her see my rage, she thought; let her be frightened by it. This can't go on. Why doesn't she see that? Why isn't Roger here to help me?

The sound as Samantha slammed the kitchen door behind her was like a bomb exploding and Joanne clutched her ears in an attempt to shut out the vibrations. The noise would have woken her father and alarmed him. Sophia, working upstairs in their bathroom, would have heard it clearly, too, and set her face in disapproval. The day, which had been progressing so reasonably until then, had abruptly turned on its heel and run off in another direction. Nothing was safe anymore, no happiness was sure. She sat down at the table in the conservatory and held her head in her hands. What she asked for was so simple, yet clearly she was being punished. It seemed as though some deliberate malice had infected their lives which must have been brought upon themselves. If she could just know what it was she would do anything to put it right, anything.

For the second time that day, she realised, she was sobbing. Perhaps it would be better if Samantha left home, too. She'd rather lose her physically than lose her by degrees through rage and loathing. Her face as she left the room had been just like Roger's, the top lip sliding up in disdain and the eyes so hard and uncaring. She was so frightened of that look. It had always said to her that she had something to fear, something over which she had no control no matter how hard she tried; that some day of his own choosing Roger would elect to leave her. That was the look she'd seen in her daughter's eyes.

Nothing she'd done in life had worked. She'd taken it for granted that the purpose of life was to create a family; that she'd find a partner to whom she would be grafted to form a new whole; that she would grow and nurture children to become her lifelong friends and confidantes; that the ripples of their lives would spread out and encompass other families, sons and daughters-in-law, grandchildren, homes, holidays and possessions that they'd treasure together. She'd lived her life with that belief, thankful to God for such good fortune, not realizing that it was a total lie. Couldn't God have found a way of warning her that she was totally alone? Was this His way of telling her that she had only Him to rely on; that this was the lesson that had to be learned by those who took life for granted?

She was so unprepared: first Willie and now soon Samantha. She had to prepare herself. She had to face the truth that she and Roger were not grafted. My God, as Prue might say, they weren't even in the same orchard. Would she say that? Had she been saying that privately and never bothering to tell her best friend, Joanne?

39.

The Spare Bedroom

The fatigue that Albert felt couldn't be blamed on the morning's march for he was well used to walking long distances, yet his feet ached, his arms were weak and when he bent to take off his shoes he could barely reach them. The damn things had cut into his ankle, too, and he couldn't undo the knot in the laces. How had this happened since yesterday? How, in one day, could his leg muscles shorten, his gut expand and his energy drain away: was it a return of the malaria or just the city that was doing it to him?

He lay down on the bed with a sigh, leaving his shoes hanging over the end in case they marked the bedspread. So much had happened, he felt: more people, talk and emotions than he was used to handling in a decade. He was not made for it. But he'd always known that and he was at peace with it. He only hoped that Joanne understood that. He didn't regret being here now, but that didn't mean it had ever been a realistic option for him to come to the city.

He closed his eyes, convinced that he would fall asleep instantly; closed his eyes and waited, feeling his body surrender its tensions, searching the darkness of his closed eyelids for signs of the dense mist that rolls in and engulfs the mind, blotting out the world.

God, but his feet were sore.

Then, as he'd done on the ferry, Albert slipped suddenly into a light sleep, and out of the mist he began to see a small boy swinging on a wooden gate that creaked at his irritating persistence and towards him, grim faced and resolute, a woman came bustling along the unpaved road gathering dust in her wake. The woman stopped and the boy swung open the gate without dismounting, his mouth open like a calf, waiting as boys do to be spoken to or not, watching as the woman scurried up the path to the unpainted house holding in her hand a piece of paper. He thought it must be rubbish that he'd dropped somewhere and she'd come to complain.

Albert shifted his feet on the bed. This was too real. The woman came out of the house with his mother, who was crying, and took him firmly by the hand. The gate stopped creaking. There was silence.

Sam had asked him how his father died. Was it Sam or Joanne? He knew the answer to that question but instead of giving it he had chosen to repeat the historical version. He'd pieced the truth together for himself; maybe he thought they should do the same, though they didn't have possession of the same evidence. The small boy, evidently himself, kneeled on the ledge of the bay window in the parlour of the stern woman's house with his cheek pressed flat to the pane craning to watch as a bus passed by bearing his mother. Catching a glimpse of her hat, he wondered why there was no wave of her gloved hand if it was true, as she'd said, that it was the thought of missing him that had caused her to cry. It was not without sound, this memory; he could hear the bus changing gear as it laboured down the country road. He'd heard that sound all his life. He could smell the muslin curtains, too, and the dry odour of the old wooden house that seemed suspended in time.

He was not fully asleep but his eyes were firmly shut searching the screen of his eyelids for more images. The reason he'd never wanted to speak of all this was now abundantly clear. From the distance of seventy odd years most of it was inexplicable. He could explain how people had behaved but it was impossible to explain why they'd behaved that way. Where would he begin with Sam? If it was so hard for Albert to credit that he'd lived in such a different world and was now living in this one, then how could he explain about his father so that it was not merely a piece of text? It was impossible. Why was the boy left in the house with the stern woman without any explanation until one day his mother called, without the hat and gloves, to collect him? Why did he have to say thank you to the woman, and why had she hardly ever spoken to him during that time?

The piece of rubbish she'd come bearing in her hand that day, he soon worked out, was a telegram. That's how it was done back then.

There were few phones. Everyone's world stood ready to be stopped by a telegram and that one, his mother eventually told him, said that his father had drowned and they were moving to Maitland (though the news about Maitland must have arrived in a separate telegram, or perhaps it was only a statement of intent at that stage). She'd been particularly stern, too. He was quite convinced that he'd done something wrong.

'But he can swim really well,' he'd blurted. 'He could swim to Africa and back.'

That wasn't a lie; he'd seen him.

'We'll be alright,' his mother said, and he supposed she hugged him, but he had the feeling she was annoyed with him.

It might have been that he went straight outside, or it could have been a week, a month or a whole year later that he was swinging on the gate when a girl he knew vaguely from school crossed over the road and stood and watched him as if expecting him to do some trick. He was just swinging on the gate. Eventually she realised this and walked away, disappointed, like she'd paid and got nothing in return.

'Your father drowned himself,' she said over her shoulder. 'That's a crime.'

The gate kept creaking until tea time when he was called indoors.

Albert woke with a start. Perhaps this was the real reason he'd come to the city and broken his vow never to march, Albert thought: because he had a secret to reveal. Sam wanted to learn everything and she seemed quite capable of objectivising tragedy. She'd find a place for her great grandfather, regardless of how his life had ended. She might even relish the drama of it all, but Joanne wouldn't take it nearly so well. She'd realise that she hadn't been made privy to this most telling of family secrets. Worse still, she'd know she'd been lied to. It would confirm everything she'd ever felt about Albert. She'd be angry with good cause.

With a sigh of relief he eased his shoes off and let them drop to the floor. There was no chance now that he would sleep properly.

He could see how it had happened. They were such different times that nobody now would understand. In those days suicide was a crime. Being a widow was a crime. Poverty was a crime. They were all things that could never be talked about. There was no shame as deep as the shame of his mother, for being widowed in that way and being a burden on the world. In India they threw them on bonfires. In rural Australia in the 1930s they threw them under a veil of silence and into domestic service in Maitland. Perhaps his mother had believed she was protecting him by never talking. In his turn, he protected her by never talking either. They all did it: it was the unspoken rule, not speaking.

Then it became too late to speak. The next generation turned the world into a communal psychiatrist's couch with everyone confronting their demons, real and imagined, but for his generation it was a matter of pride not to engage in such acts of self-indulgence. They maintained their silence, but now it had an added quality: this was the silence of the disapproving critic. For God's sake, his generation wanted to say; stop encouraging everyone to feel so sorry for themselves. If you want to know what it's really like to have it tough, we'll tell you about the War and the Depression, about shame and poverty and bare survival. But, of course, they didn't tell them because that would have meant they were equally guilty. It would have tainted the hardship they felt they'd endured, reducing it to comparison with the imagined hardships of the spoiled and lazy new generation of which they complained.

Perhaps he'd fancied himself as a stoic without acknowledging the self-righteousness that accompanied that. Was it really necessary to be so staunch? He hadn't been responsible for his father - of course not - or for the circumstances they'd found themselves in; nor had his mother: his mother had merely been a victim of the social times. Was there any harm in explaining how it would have been for a solo mum living in the Depression; the desperation of a young woman in a dry continent looking in the mirror each day and watching her youth drain away like water in a tub? Did it demean him in any way to explain that the silence of that generation was a way of protecting youth from knowing the harsh truth; that sternness with boys was deemed to be character building; and that all this sprang from a climate of ever-present poverty and the imminence of ruin?

Yet, for some reason, he'd chosen never to speak of it. Only now could he feel this reticence melting. With Sam he'd felt almost tempted to talk. He could give her the facts and she could deal with them as she wished, he thought. There was no need to explain or excuse them: they were what they were. So, why not with Joanne? Was the immediate generation too close to trust? Would they be too eager to see things that were not there? Is that why, on the march today, it seemed to him there were only the very old or the very young, and very few in-between? Then he must find a way to talk to her before it was too late.

40.

The Kitchen at Mosman

Joanne started to get up in search of a tissue when she suddenly felt a hand on her shoulder. Preoccupied with her own self-pity, she'd been deaf to the footsteps.

'Dad?'

She sat down again and put on her brave face.

'I'm sorry if we woke you. We've been having a little contretemps, I'm afraid. These teenage years are more difficult than I'd believed. It can be like a rollercoaster at times. One minute everything's calm and the next minute it's turned upside down. Hormones! It must be what they eat. I read that the chickens and the hamburgers now are filled with oestrogen. That's why there's so much obesity. Even the boys are growing breasts and for the girls it's like a double dose. So we're the ones that cop it.'

She sniffed. Her nose was running. She must have looked a mess.

'At this age they can't bear to be thwarted,' she blundered on. 'They get an idea in their minds and nothing will put them off, no matter how you reason. I know you'll say that we spoil them, but I really don't know how to do it differently. I hate being the one who has to say no all the time and compared to her friends she's not over-indulged. It's just the way the modern world has gone. Everybody has to have everything and they want it now. It's my fault; it's my generation that let it get this way, but I don't know how we're going to stop it.'

Oh well, to hell, she thought; what was the point of pretence; he probably thought this anyway? He didn't seem particularly shocked. He reached out and took her hand. His was dry and cool. Hers was moist and hot.

'Sounds just like a teenage girl to me,' he smiled.

'Oh, Dad, what would you know about teenage girls?'

'Only what your mother told me. 'Joanne is being difficult', she used to write. She seemed to write it quite a lot.'

'When? When did she write to you? I was never difficult.'

'Your mother and I wrote to each other once a month. She'd write to me on the last Sunday in the month and I'd write to her on the first Sunday. I remember your teenage years rather well. 'Joanne is still being difficult'. She said it was hormones then as well, I seem to recall. I don't remember anything about the hamburgers and chicken.'

He was making fun of her. This couldn't be true. She'd adored her mother. She'd never been difficult. He was making it up.

'You used to write to each other every month?'

He nodded.

'Until she died.'

The veins on the back of his hand were inscribed in midnight blue and his skin was brick red with burnt Umbrian sun spots that bordered on melanoma. His touch was rough as well as dry, yet his nails were shaped and clean. His fingers, she realized, were not unlike her own.

'I didn't know that,' she murmured.

He handed her his handkerchief and she took her hand away to unfold it, jolted by the thought that this man, living all his life on his own, had washed and ironed it himself, preserving it intact for decades, never surrendering his habits or his standards.

'Did you keep them?' she asked.

'Yes, I did.'

'Why?'

He did, but *she* didn't, apparently.

'Well ...'

He seemed undecided. Perhaps he didn't know why he'd kept

them; there was very little that he threw away, after all. Did he really mean once a month for all those years?

'Dad, Willie has dropped out of university. We don't know where he is.'

She quickly refolded the faded cotton square with its new wet stain and handed it back to him, avoiding his eyes. There, she'd admitted it and the world hadn't ended.

'I seem to have failed at parenting on all fronts,' she laughed bitterly. 'Sometimes you think you have everything and then you find out that you have nothing. It comes as quite a shock.'

He didn't answer. Apparently she hadn't folded the handkerchief correctly and it was more important that he laid it out and started again. So they sat in silence until he'd finished and then he put it in his pocket and took her hand again, which she really didn't mind.

'I've always understood about vines that they are seekers of light,' he said. 'It's best to plant their roots in the shade and let the shoots go in search of sunlight. If you plant the whole vine in full sun then it believes it has no reason for growing. I wonder if children aren't the same.'

She looked up to find him looking at her intently, seeking a reaction, but there was something in his eyes she hadn't noticed before. She laughed. He was mocking her. He was gently taking the piss.

'My, God,' she said, 'you sound exactly like Chance the Gardener.'

'Chancey who ....?'

'Peter Sellers in *'Being There'*.'

'Peter Sellers is my favourite actor.'

'Really? I never knew that.'

'What was it he said? *'Life is a state of mind'*?''

41.

Roger Saville's Office

The sun had done its business for the day and was making a quick exit, scurrying off across the Blue Mountains with a sudden haste as if it had only just realised the length of the journey ahead. Forty degrees and four thousand kilometres west to Perth, it seemed to be saying, I'm outta here; leaving in a blaze of glory so it would be all the more welcome when it returned, or maybe just making the point that night had less appeal by comparison. This was the sun that played such a central role in the life of the nation: the prodigal sun.

High above the surrounding roof tops, like an eagle in his eyrie, Roger leaned back in his desk chair and watched it do its thing, turning the wall of mountains that constrained the city to the west from deep indigo to midnight blue before daubing the high crests with splashes of crimson and gold, thick as molten lava, a departing Helios laying down a ring of fire that warned all but the intrepid not to follow. The city sat contritely and allowed itself to be washed in the resultant colours.

It was Roger's father who said, 'Never own anything you can't keep your eye on', and who, living by that maxim, had never bought anything outside York and Kent Streets. He could walk around all his properties in his lunch hour, and he'd done so, every day. He knew every nook and cranny of every building within five blocks; which shops were failing, which tenants were expanding, how the wash of demand was ebbing and flowing and how he could profit from it. Come sundown he was reluctant to go home. Who knew what hungry dingos might be out there? The world was full of scum bags. In the morning he couldn't wait to leave the house and get back to his office to check that everything was still alright.

It hadn't been the most salubrious part of the city in those days. The western ridge of the CBD was one of the older parts and the buildings showed it. That's why he'd started buying there in the first place, because it had fallen out of favour and become affordable. But it had character. The City wasn't going to let people tear those old buildings down (well, they did for awhile, but luckily there wasn't much profit in pulling small buildings down to put up new ones and eventually people realised that cheap old buildings were better to look at than cheap new buildings, anyway), and one day, he knew, they would come right. With careful nurturing he would prove they could occupy a profitable space in the rental market.

If Roger had ever been going to feel at peace on this day it was now as he looked across the tiled turret of the old GPO clock tower, past the new glass office towers at Number One Martin Place and 363 George Street reflecting the orange and violet colours of the Pro Hart sky, and down into the familiar and timeless brick and sandstone facades of his father's old stamping grounds. His father had been right, of course: they *had* come right. He'd not just sat back and waited; he'd worked at it like only an émigré knows how, with a simple and effective formula to which he'd held resolutely until the day he died, offering a cheaper rent and a shorter lease in return for fitout clauses that saw the quality of his buildings being progressively improved at the tenants' expense. By the time Roger inherited the portfolio and put Lawrence to work dividing it up into strata titles for sale, there was hardly any refurbishment needing to be done.

It would be wrong to say that Roger was at peace, however: he was merely at rest. He'd returned from his meeting with Greg Cummings at the Westin Hotel feeling that everything was getting out of control. He'd developed a nagging fear of the consequences of the deal falling through, and he wondered if that was because the attention demanded from the transaction had drained the business (meaning himself) leaving it weaker and more vulnerable. Fuck, he had no idea what was going on elsewhere, this was all he'd thought about for weeks, yet when Astor United Holdings had first been introduced as a potential punter for the Western sub-division it had just been another prospective buyer of real estate, only one of many. Every agent and broker in the southern hemisphere was bringing tyre kickers to their door. Saville Corp was land banking and it was the nature of the game that they could expect to be engaged in similar discussions for the next decade. But other pressures had conspired to elevate the importance of this particular discussion and now he wasn't sure that it hadn't developed a momentum that was uncontrollable.

It had to be said that it was Lawrence's fault. He hadn't managed the Banks properly. He'd been too honest with the institutions and they'd lost their nerves as a result and failed to support the share price. That was it in a nutshell and now they were being stampeded into delivering quick results just to satisfy the insecurities and aspirations of middle managers. He should have handled this himself, offered Alison Pyke a job on two hundred thousand a year looking after the analysts and sent Lawrence and the whole damn Compliance Committee on extended leave. The whole thing had got out of hand. They'd become a bureaucracy living by a rule book. Sometimes he doubted whether anyone remembered they were property developers. *Property developers*, for fuck sake: dreaming, scheming, risk taking pioneers: the John Batmans of the twenty first century, not pension fund managers.

Cummings had smelled that vulnerability. He'd held out his hand with a sugar-coated pill in it and seen the look in Roger's eye. Astor wasn't just a buyer of real estate looking for a sweet deal, he was saying; he was an escape route and that was what he, Cummings, was offering. Roger had looked at the hand for a fraction of a second too long, giving away too much of himself and instantly regretting it. He'd come back to the office and poured himself a stiff drink. That was unlike him. (It was very stiff: three fingers of vodka and one of lime.) He looked out west towards the sun-dazzled ramparts of the Blue Mountains and tried to figure why he had given himself away like that. To the east and the west, Sydney had pushed as far as it could go. To the north and south it was ringed by National Parks and it was never going to cross the Nepean River and climb into the mountains. There was nowhere for it to go, yet every day thousands more people wanted to pour in. All your life you could dream of sitting on a land bank like

Whiteman's Creek, so why was he feeling this way? Was he too far removed from it? Was he ignoring what his father had said: 'Never own anything you can't keep your eye on'? He'd had his eye on other things and if he wasn't careful he could lose it. That was what he was feeling.

He felt like another drink, but remembering his father's maxims reminded him of his duty to call his mother, something he'd omitted to do for over a week.

'How are you, Rose?' he asked solicitously as soon as she answered, knowing he was going to be punished.

'How should I be? No better than last week when you didn't come and see me.'

'Samantha went on the Anzac march today,' he announced, immediately changing the subject, 'with her grandfather; with Albert.'

'He can march at his age?'

'He's not so old. He's seventy eight.'

'A chicken! How are his hips? Wait until his hips go; he'll find out about marching then.'

'How are yours?'

'Terrible. Why do you ask? You know how they are. I can't even make it to the delicatessen now. I'm a prisoner. They've changed the traffic lights on New South Head Road so you have to run to cross over. How can I run with my hips? Luckily they still deliver the groceries. I had to tell the new caretaker to bring the box up to my apartment and not to leave it outside the door where people can steal from it. Our nice Mr Bezzami has left and now we have a new one. He hardly speaks the language. I had to tell him that we paid for that service in our management fees. Can you imagine, an Arab: how can an Arab be managing an apartment building? I thought I lived in Australia, not Beirut.'

'Mr Bezzami was an Arab.'

'Not a proper Arab. He'd been here a long time – almost as long as us. Why don't you buy this building? Can we not afford to buy a simple block of apartments where people live nice quiet lives and pay the rent? Do we have to go buying swamp land out in the bush? Is that what we've come to?'

'It isn't swamp land, Rose. We don't need to buy apartment buildings just because you don't like the new caretaker. It's not a good investment.'

'It isn't good to own the roof over your own mother's head? Are you telling me that because you think your father can't hear? He can hear alright, it's you who can't hear. Do you think he's happy knowing you've put all our money into that company where other people can see it? Do you think he's happy that you borrow all these millions? I hope you know what you're doing. Every time I open the newspaper I worry about you. Are you going to be another Rodney Adler, another Jodee Rich? Why does everything have to be so grand? Your father would only ever use his own money. If he couldn't afford it, he wouldn't do it. The minute you use other people's money you become beholden to them. When you make a mistake they come for you like wild dogs. Listen to what I say. It's what your father would say.'

'I'm not a Rodney Adler or a Jodee Rich. Allow me some credit, Rose. I'm not my father, either. Things are different now. It's a different world.'

'It looks the same world to me; same greed, same lies. Even Mr Packer fell for it. Your father wouldn't have fallen for it. He'd have paid for his own cup of coffee and wished them goodbye. Now I see them all blaming each other. How could Mr Packer and Mr Murdoch let those boys do it? They inherited the greed but they didn't inherit the brains; that's the problem. I hope you've got the brains, Roger, because I worry every time I think about you.'

'I inherited the brains, Rose. You've nothing to worry about.'

Such a good conversation, he thought; just exactly what he needed at that moment.

'I have plenty to worry about,' she persisted. 'There are people who gave my son their money so he could get rich and now their money is worth half as much as it used to be. What should I tell them; everything's alright, you inherited the brains? I don't want to go to my own club anymore in case someone wants to ask me things they think I should know. I don't know a thing, I tell them. He is my son; I hardly know him. Once we were happy to make a living, now everyone has to make a fortune. What happened to cause it to change?'

'You need a holiday. You're not getting out enough. Why don't you go and spend a week at the Golden Door in the Hunter Valley? Take a friend and indulge yourself. Let me arrange it.'

'I haven't got the energy. The country tires me. It's for animals and peasants. You know I don't like the country. Besides, in case I hadn't told you, I can't walk. What would you like I should do in the country if I can't walk?'

'Then stop putting it off and go and have the hip replacement.'

She went silent. He didn't know whether she was afraid of operations or afraid of the thought of no longer having anything to complain about, but he wasn't in a mood to press her.

'Come and stay with us, then. You need to get out of your flat.'

'I have to come to you? You are too busy to visit me so I have to come to you? Am I so bad?'

'Rose, Rose ... you know how busy we are. I promise we'll come this weekend.'

'And bring Willie.'

'I'll try, Rose.'

Christ, what else?

'And don't call me Rose.'

'Why ..?'

'I'm your mother.'

For forty six years she'd insisted on being called Rose. Now she wanted to be called mother. Had she noticed he was now a forty six year old man, he wondered? How simple it must seem to her. All she worried about was what her friends at the club might say if they lost their money. He could have told her why they invested the money in the first place, but it wasn't worth it. They were gambling on his ability to pull off a big win. That was it in toto. They didn't know him, and they knew nothing about his chances, so why didn't they go to the casino instead? At the casino they'd walk away from their losses and they wouldn't blame anybody but themselves, but if they didn't win at Saville Corp they'd howl to the heavens like wounded wolves.

It was true his father never invested money that he couldn't afford to lose but it had taken him fifty years to create assets that weren't worth a tenth of their assets now. She never gave him credit for that. Times were different but he was still his father's son. Nothing he was doing was complicated. It all made simple sense. He'd got the valuation he wanted by fudging the ground lease terms in favour of the lessee. Astor would have the third party assurance that he needed in order to protect his face and the special issue of discounted equity (which Roger had never been able to take advantage of for himself) would sweeten the deal and provide much needed cash. Once the sale was completed there was no need for the valuations to ever see the light of day. The sale price could be announced to the market and that would become the new reality. Tom Higham's side letter could be shredded and the leasehold terms re-written in line with normal commercial rates. The Banks would be happy, the markets would be happy and he could demand the release of his shares from escrow.

Simple! That was all he had to concentrate on. He didn't need another drink now; he wanted to keep his mind clear. His immediate priority was to retrieve his briefcase as quickly as possible. The cost was not relevant, nor was thought of revenge. Maxine was waiting for him to make an offer, probably because she didn't want to pitch her demands too low. Well, she was a working girl and she'd put in some effort. He'd pay her the equivalent of two tricks: a thousand dollars for an empty briefcase. She could count herself lucky.

42.

The Beck House in Rose Bay

The garage door closed behind him and Lawrence switched off the engine and lights, leaving the radio on. There were five minutes left until the next news bulletin and he tilted back the head rest, removed the seat belt and nestled down into the comfort of the lumbar supports to wait. After two minutes the garage door closure light went out and he was left in darkness, secure and content in his leather cocoon, savouring the clean masculine aromas of leather soap and silicone wax which were still fresh from the weekly grooming.

The news, when it came, was predictably not worth the wait. Like an induced coma, Anzac Day had rendered the nation lifeless. He turned off the radio and reluctantly got out, fumbling in the dark for the handle of the laundry door.

The laundry led to the kitchen and the kitchen led to the front hall. Opposite the front entrance door was a small alcove containing a reproduction French table and an ormolu clock. Behind the clock was a large gilt mirror that had the effect of expanding the otherwise limited space into which visitors entered and at the same time exciting them with the distraction of their own images. It was here that he'd imagined the Jeffrey Smart should hang, but now that he looked at it he realized he was wrong. The confined space wouldn't do it justice and its effect upon entry would be too fleeting. This was disappointing. It would have to be the lounge, then, which was off to the right as people entered and was the first room into which guests were ushered. He didn't like this room. It was filled with furniture inherited from Marjorie's family; furniture that seemed to know it had been handed on rather than willingly sought; too fraught with sentimental implications to lightly discard.

It was also a room about which he felt inhibited from expressing an opinion and consequently one with which he had never engaged. He couldn't see the Smart hanging there, either.

The excitement which had been nibbling at him on the way home turned to irritation. It was one thing to be accommodating of someone else's needs, but quite another to be left feeling uncomfortable in your own home. Perhaps the dining room was the answer? It had the merit of being without other distractions, at least; just the dark oak table, matching sideboard with silver tray and decanter, six oak ladder-back chairs with two matching carvers and plain primrose walls adorned with a single print of bathers at Watson's Bay, circa 1929. The print could well afford to go. God knows where it had come from anyway: another of Marjorie's hand-me-downs, perhaps?

Yes, it would be perfect above the sideboard, he thought; an engaging topic of conversation as everyone sat down and a subtle stimulus, as the evening wore on, for the pursuit of topics other than the usual real estate prices. He could see it. It was perfect. The one drawback was that guests on one side of the table would have their backs to it and the room wasn't wide enough to turn the table sideways, unless of course … (he drew in his breath, astonished at the ease with which the idea had come to him) … unless he brought home the painting from his office to hang on the opposite wall. Of course, of course; *two* Jeffrey Smarts in one room - Smarts to the power of two - a setting, finally, worth the fuss and formality of invited guests, the sheer bother of preparation and polite conversation to which Marjorie had always aspired and for which he, to-date, had held so little enthusiasm. With two Jeffrey Smarts on the wall, all that could now change. Perhaps he and Marjorie could start using that room even when they were on their own. They could get into the habit of laying the table at night, flowers on the sideboard, candles even; a routine of structured informality out of which an interchange of conversation might grow. The kitchen bar top had caused such deterioration in their eating habits that they now fed themselves in their own home as if it was a takeaway bar. Most nights he took his plate into his study and ate alone. The Smarts could be the impetus to change all that.

His own enthusiasm surprised him. Taking down the bathing

print from the wall only confirmed his belief that the room was perfect. If he had any doubts about the wisdom of parting with that ten percent deposit an hour ago they had now evaporated. For the first time in years he began to think of other changes they might be inspired to make to their home, but, as he climbed the stairs in search of Marjorie, he knew that his enthusiasm needed to be tempered with caution. There was no evidence that his regard for Jeffrey Smart's work, which he'd developed in isolation, was even known to his wife, let alone shared by her, and it was not an inconsiderable sum of money that he was spending. She would need to see that he'd given this purchase a lot of thought and that it meant a good deal to him.

At the top of the stairs he called for her and she answered from the spare bedroom, which she'd converted to her workroom. He took off his jacket and tie and hung them in his wardrobe. The morning's walk from the Domain car park up the hill to the office had left him sweating and he'd need to have a shower and change his shirt before they went out for dinner. Perhaps now was not a sensible time to discuss the painting with Marjorie. They'd be distracted by the need to get ready, and the last thing he wanted was for the topic to be raised later in front of the Savilles. But, as he made his way to her room, he realised it was going to be difficult to keep the secret to himself.

Marjorie's workroom was not a space that he often visited. Despite initially having good intentions, she'd succumbed to smoking while she worked and Lawrence found it difficult to credit that she was not conscious of the odour creeping into her tapestries and yarns. It was a sunny room with a large casement window opening out over their courtyard through which, in the manner typical of self-deceiving addicts, she imagined she blew her smoke.

'How was your day?' he asked.

Surprisingly the smell was not bad and the window was closed as the temperature outside had started to drop.

'Good. Very quiet. And how was yours? Did you sort out all the world's problems?'

'As a matter of fact ...'

He hesitated. She might as well know.

'Roger's conduct is becoming more and more reckless. I'm not sure that I can continue to hold the line.'

'What's he done now?'

She didn't seem to be either interested or concerned.

'It's not what he's done; it's what he's threatening to do. Ignoring the Disclosure Rules for a start, and leaving me to sort it out if things go wrong.'

'Isn't that usual?'

'This time I may just surprise him by not providing the solution.'

'So the company gets into trouble?'

'Not necessarily …'

'I can't imagine you letting that happen.'

She looked at him with a half smile that seemed disengaged from the conversation, whether because she didn't take him seriously, or because she was concentrating on her tapestry work, he couldn't tell.

'Precisely!' he emphasised. And wasn't that the nub of the problem? But this wasn't what he wanted to talk about.

'What are you working on?' he asked.

He walked around behind her and examined the focus of her concentration. It was difficult to interpret the images with any certainty but he suspected they were Aboriginal.

'A commission?' he asked, in his most neutral voice.

'It's part of a panel for a series we're doing on Dreamtime.'

'Who's 'we'?'

'Oh, a friend and I. Dreamtime is a reflection of the duality of indigenous people which they take completely for granted and which we have no knowledge of; the temporal and the spiritual living side-by-side in all they do.'

'As when, for instance, they're beating their women and abusing their children: is that part of their Dreamtime, or is that their *Bad Dream time?*'

'It may well be. Very clever! They take it for granted that the spirits are always present, like constant companions. I wasn't sure how to depict this because I didn't want them to look like ghosts. Ghosts are a European concept. Then I realized that the Cubists, like Picasso, had found a device for showing the other dimensions of a personality in their portraits, called orthogonal projection. It's really just placing side views of the subject at right angles to each other. What do you think?'

'Well, I can see what you mean now that you've explained it.'

'But you don't like it.'

'I wouldn't say that.'

Because that would be foolish.

'I must say that until you told me I wasn't sure what I was looking at. Do you think other people will know? Perhaps it needs to be finished. I'm sure when it's all put together it will be very interesting.'

He wanted her goodwill and it wouldn't hurt him to work for it.

'I struggle with abstraction, as I'm sure you know, but I do admire your willingness to lay down the challenge, let alone the skill and patience to execute it.'

'You prefer realism.'

'Not the chocolate box variety, no. I like hyper-realism, if there is such a thing. I can't see the point of an artist deliberately obscuring a vision and then passing it off as a personal interpretation if it doesn't add to the viewer's understanding of what they're looking at. Surely the more useful contribution an artist can make is to clarify the vision.'

'Well, the visual arts can be about story telling as well. What you see is not necessarily all that's there.'

'I think it's very good,' he attested in an attempt to allay any doubt. 'I'm sure it will be very good indeed.'

She was not without her admirers, he knew, and her technical proficiency couldn't be doubted. Maybe the choice of subject and its treatment was a tapestry thing and he was not an appropriate person to judge. From what he'd observed, tapestry was a peculiarly female pastime, like the making of quilts, and he was sure that it contained a sisterhood dynamic that excluded men. He would be safer on more familiar ground.

'I saw a rather interesting painting today which I think you might like,' he said casually: 'a Jeffrey Smart.'

'Like the one in your office?'

'Similar, only better.'

'And where did you see that?'

'At a gallery in Paddington that I just happened to pop into on the way home.'

'I thought you were working all day.'

'I was. Actually, I'd seen the painting before and I just thought I'd have a closer look at it, seeing I had a few minutes to spare.'

'So you're thinking of buying it?'

'Well, I'm not sure. I was going to tell you. His work fetches a lot of money now. It's in great demand.'

Should he offer to show it to her before he confirmed he'd bought it, or would he run the risk that she would come out against it?

'Can you afford it?' she asked, frowning as she threaded a new needle.

'Yes, I think so. There's a good chance the company shares may go up shortly and I thought we might cash a few in.'

His voice was deliberately casual as if trying an idea out for size.

'They won't go up if you let Roger break the rules. You obviously know something, then.'

She turned and looked at him curiously, interested at last.

'I don't know anything that needs to be disclosed to the market,' he protested, 'but I do think we'll soon start announcing some positive results, yes, and I would expect our shares to recover some of their lost value when that happens. It's not something I'd shout from the roof tops though. I wouldn't want you talking about it.'

'That's alright. I'm glad to hear it,' she said, 'because I was going to tell you that I needed to withdraw some money myself. I'm planning on going to Europe.'

43.

A Bar in Paddington

Willie put his hand in his pocket, deep down where he'd buried the two hundred, and slid one of the twenties carefully out. It slipped from his fingers and into the bartender's hand like it had been specially lubricated, and there was no change. It was dark in the bar. The only illumination came from the poker machines lining the walls. Red, green and yellow fruit shone like party lights, reflected in the mirrors and bottles and murky depths of patrons' eyes. Willie wasn't going there – into patrons' eyes, that is – because this was a fags' pub. He wasn't even going to the barman's eyes because he'd accidentally touched his fingers in the money exchange and he didn't want to run the risk of misunderstandings. So he mumbled 'Ta' and concentrated on picking up the three schooners without spilling them, back across the carpet on feet he could hardly see to the table where Luke and Ari were waiting.

Luke had chosen a table by the toilet door because he needed light to read the newspaper, without which he became nervy and agitated as Willie now knew, because life in all its ridiculous forms was assembled there for his dissection each day and if he wasn't given access to it he'd start dissecting Willie and Ari instead. So, Okay, they'd sit by the dunny door so Luke could read his friggin' paper and here was their beer to help pass the time. Willie was in no hurry. He had no view of where the stream was flowing. They were sitting in an eddy and when the current picked them up he'd float along.

'Here's one for you, Ari,' Luke announced, slapping the newspaper. 'This arsehole has been drugging little kids and doing the dirty with them. So what does he say when he gets done? *I've been battling good and evil. There's a side of me that's very, very good. But there's a side that's very, very bad.'* Can you believe that? These are six and seven year olds he's fucking. Gives one of them too much Normison and, oops, she dies. We'd better be careful with that Ari. Presumably that wasn't his good side that got the dosage wrong. Fuck, I hate paedophiles. They should cut out their balls and stuff them in their mouths, the bastards. At least let the kids grow up before you start messing with them.'

He reached for the beer without a thankyou and drank greedily as if trying to drown his moral outrage.

'Perhaps those girls in the movie had been molested when they were young,' Ari suggested. 'That wouldn't surprise me. They had that look.'

'The tall bird looked a bit like Nicole,' Willie commented, 'and the little one looked just like my sister. I really freaked, man. It was like stumbling into a sicko home movie. All it needed was for my Mum to be grossing out in the background and I'd have known I was having one real bad trip.'

Luke snorted derisively.

'Your Mum was there, dick head, you just didn't recognize her. That's the whole fucking point. Everyone's sister and mum was there 'cause that's what women want to do to men. They want to be arseholed by them so they can blow their fucking brains out, which is all any of 'em want to do and would do if they didn't need our bloody sperm. You just wait; one day they'll figure out how to divide their own cells in a petri dish and then it's goodnight nurse.'

'That girl was lazy,' Ari said. 'Nicole is always doing something, I think. She is very ambitious. I don't agree that they looked alike.'

'Well ...'

Truth was that Willie couldn't remember exactly what Nicole did look like. The only recall he had was from the distorted perspective of his position on the floor, looking up at her suddenly standing above him in her boots and black dress in the doorway of the living room. He remembered the white under-soles of her feet which were the nearest thing to him when she came back into the room and sat down against the wall, and her toes that he'd believed at the time were able to transmit wordless messages from his hand back to her brain, like the wires fixed to cans that Scientologists used to pick up inner thoughts and fears and by-pass the conscious lies people told to protect themselves from clarity. But, try as he might, he couldn't remember her face so maybe it was true that the tall girl in the movie didn't look like her at all; maybe the only similarity was the feeling he had that he'd like to be wanted by her.

'Well, I saw something that looked familiar,' he insisted. 'Maybe it was her tits.'

And he looked to Ari for some sort of confirmation; a nod or a wink, or even one of those little trade mark giggles that he gave away so easily.

'What do you know about her tits?' Luke asked sarcastically.

There was already a game developing and Luke's attention was not properly focused on what was being said. He leaned into the light spilling from the doorway of the toilets so he could read his newspaper and every person who wanted to go in or out was being forced to wait while Luke finished reading his sentence. Ari was already getting nervous about where this might lead and unable to give attention to the conversation either. Willie had got nowhere with his attempts to steer the subject towards Nicole and the missing pieces in his memory bank. If he couldn't even remember her face then what could he remember? He remembered clearly bits and pieces of her body lying on the bed but her head had been curved back so it almost touched the floor and what he'd been looking at when he lay down beside her that morning was the underside of her chin, which was a hard thing to remember people by if you couldn't recall their faces.

'I reckon Nicole's tits are firmer than that bird's in the movie,' he muttered.

That may have been because she was arched backwards when he saw them. What would they be like if she was kneeling over him and they were hanging down; he must have seen that, too, so how come he couldn't remember?

'You think so, do you?' Luke snorted, smacking the open newspaper for emphasis. 'I don't think you know a fucking thing.

Anyway, it was a load of crap. Anyone who could get a hard on over those slags must be into bestiality. We paid good money to subject ourselves to serious brain damage. Here's what we should have gone to see: *'Monsters and mayhem in a teenage search for identity. Facing adulthood is a tough, furious and confusing ride ... Sparkleshark ponders the fractious speedway to maturity and the facades we use to get there.'* I told you it's all here, kiddies, if only you'd care to read the paper. Wee Willie thinks he's an expert on Nicole's tits and we know he's just caught up in the *'fractious speedway to maturity'* 'cause Nicole doesn't show her fucking tits to anyone for free and Willie Boy is a tight arse who doesn't even pay for his own nose candy, and what do we think of that, eh Ari: not a fucking lot?'

Willie flushed with anger. He could handle Luke's agro most of the time but this one seemed better targeted. Was it the inference that he was making it up about Nicole or the accusation that he was a tight arse that had got to him? How could he be making it up about Nicole: they knew he'd stayed with her and slept in her bed? There was definitely something going on. Ari wouldn't look at him and Luke now pretended to read the newspaper like if he stopped for a moment he'd be overcome with hilarity and the secret joke, whatever it was, would be out. He was a fucking dick head.

'I didn't ask for the coke,' Willie protested; 'you offered it. If you don't want to share it, then don't offer.'

He could take Luke and Luke knew it. He could take him in one hand if he wanted to.

''If you don't want to share it, then don't offer'', Luke mimicked half-heartedly. He knew it alright. 'Did you hear that, Ari? I always thought that sharing was Rule Number One. Apparently not.'

Ari was nodding his head like one of those stuffed dogs people put in the back of their cars, grinning and taking small, frequent sips from his beer. There was no way he was getting involved. Even if he wasn't Buddhist, there must have been something in his blood that steered him clear of conflict. Behind Ari were two guys in their thirties wearing muscle shirts and leather hipsters, holding hands and grinning at each other. They were into the music which was so outright gay it was laughable, and while Willie watched them they poked out their tongues at each other and wiggled them, then plunged them into each other's mouths and played tonsil hockey, which was so bizarre that Willie was shocked out of his anger and rendered speechless. The music was the sort of stuff Samantha played: *'Kelly can you handle this? Michelle can you handle this? I don't think you're ready for this jelly ... my body is too bootylicious for you baby'*; and they were using it like child pornography to turn themselves on; like baby oil to grease themselves up.

Rule Number One, Willie thought, had to be something more meaningful than a school house motto. He'd been listening to all that sharing, caring, giving crap all his life and couldn't see anyone who spouted it that he'd want to emulate. It was the sort of stuff his mother's church group spouted: The Friends of St Agnes brigade, making themselves feel good. Only people who had nothing at all could possibly know what Rule Number One was. Sharing, caring and giving were for people who had plenty; it was their insurance policy to make sure it wasn't snatched away from them. Maybe he'd only find out what the real Rule Number One was when he put his hand in his pocket and there was nothing there. He had a feeling that was the only place he'd ever find out what really mattered. You didn't have to be a monk on a mountain top to escape the material world, but you had to be prepared to cut yourself free and be entirely alone. He wasn't afraid to try it. Fuck, he was so sick of all this shit.

The music switched to *Ja Rule*, which was more of the sort of stuff that Samantha played, and the boys at the next table smiled and nodded to each other in time while they figured where else they could stick their tongues. Willie stood up and reached down deep into his pocket for the notes he'd stashed there. He'd paid for the beer and he'd paid for his cinema ticket so he had a hundred and sixty dollars left which he slapped down on the table. There it was, as simple as that. He felt elated. He felt less elated when he remembered he still had a credit card in the other pocket but he'd deal with that later. This was a big step.

'There!' he proclaimed. 'Fuck you.'

He sat down and grabbed his drink. Luke turned the pages of his newspaper noisily and pointedly refused to look at the money. Ari giggled. In the background the two muscle-shirters took it in turn to stick their tongues in each others ears. Ari's cell phone rang like there was someone back stage who'd been watching and was now trying to get through with instructions. Yes, Willie determined, he'd live on thin air and faith, alone on a hill, far, far away. He'd find it. It would be pure and simple, silent and uncomplicated and his body and mind would be so light they would float. He just didn't need any of this shit.

They say that up in the mountains one puff of ganga is enough to make you float. In the rarefied air the lungs are so desperate for oxygen that the absorption surface doubles and triples in size like a yoni hungry for cock. One little mini-micro speck of THC landing on that swollen tissue is like a mortar bomb that sends waves of expanding light through the body, causing it to levitate, free from gravity and weight, floating above the unbearable heaviness. That's the rush he wanted. That was the place he wanted to be, in a light zone of absolute clarity where the only sound was the whistling of the mountain winds and the reassuring beat of his own heart.

'So, what's that for, mate?' Luke asked casually. He wasn't going to look at Willie but he couldn't hide his smirk of triumph. All day he'd been trying without success to get a decent strike and at last Willie had gone for the bait. Alright, let him have his little moment.

'Don't say I don't pay my way,' Willie commanded, 'because it isn't fucking true.'

He stared into the dregs of his beer as he tipped it to his mouth, swallowing the last of the green and orange reflections from the fruit machines. Now that he'd handed over his money he couldn't even choose to buy another. The music was pumped up loud and the bar was starting to fill. Luke had given up on his game with the newspaper and was no longer blocking the entrance to the toilets which were now enjoying heavy patronage. Each time the door opened there was a smell in the air that reminded Willie of a hairdressing salon. There was nowhere animate within the room where he could allow his eyes to settle.

'I have a good idea,' Ari said, closing up his phone. 'That was Nicole. Why don't we go and meet her at *Louee's*? It's a club down the road and she can get us in. What do you say to that?'

Willie felt a sudden contraction in his abdomen like the diarrhoea had returned. He hadn't thought of Ari and Nicole as being friends, calling each other on their cell phones. Maybe he'd been making a complete dick of himself talking about her during the day. Maybe she was Ari's woman and, if he couldn't even remember clearly what she looked like, maybe he'd passed out and pissed himself, never even getting to be alone with her, except in the morning when he'd crept into her bed while she was asleep. Maybe, if anybody had fucked her, it was Luke or Ari and now they were laughing at him like he was some stupid little kid who persisted in bragging when everyone knew it was an obvious lie. But, if that was the case, why were his clothes in her room and where did Luke and Ari sleep?

'Did you tell her who you were with?' he asked.

'We can all get in. There's no problem.'

What Willie really wanted to know was whether she'd called on the cell phone because she wanted to see him and figured he might be with Ari. In the black hole of his apparent amnesia any light at all would do but he wasn't going to make the mistake of appearing eager. Let Luke make the decision.

The music had grown even louder to the point where they were having to shout and the horny faggots at the next table were singing along in unison like it was Karaoke Night, their eyes so hungry that Willie daren't look up.

'.... *you never thought I'd make you smile while I was backing you fast and fucking you all t' while ...*'

Luke stood up and picked up the money that Willie had slapped on the table.

'Let's go then.'

Willie shrugged as if he didn't care one way or the other and stood up, too, then turned and made his way to the door. He'd be glad when he was out of there; it was like being in a room full of live electric cables. The air outside was clear and fresh and the night had plenty of time left to run.

44.

The Taxi

'Try as I might,' Joanne whispered, 'I couldn't persuade her to change into something more appropriate.'

She shook her head in exasperation. Perhaps she could have – *should* have – insisted that Samantha wore a dress, but she had been too wary of the consequences of another outburst to risk taking a firm line. Her brain felt bruised and she nestled back into the dark comfort of the taxi's rear seat, happy for traffic on Military Road to slow them down and for the journey into the city to last forever. The tensions of the day had fallen away so unexpectedly that she felt mildly intoxicated; a feeling of dizzy contentment which she wasn't conscious of having tried to manufacture but which, now that she recognised it, she wanted to savour.

Samantha had marched to the front passenger door of the taxi, determined to isolate herself in her own independent zone so, whether it was appropriate or not, Joanne and Albert had found themselves together in the back seat sharing not only the intimacy of each other's body space but the opportunity for whispered judgments on Samantha's behaviour. Perhaps this was why she felt so light headed. Samantha's pre-emption of the front seat, prompted by her pique at having to defend her clothes, had avoided the requirement for a decision as to who would share the back. Now, cocooned together in conspiracy, Joanne and Albert could focus on a source of amusement that they viewed with equal affection, a safe and neutralising bond so far removed from the feelings of disconnection she'd experienced during the day that she felt they'd already been on a long journey together.

'She looks very pretty,' Albert assured her.

'Yes, but ...'

They weren't going to a teenage disco at the Surf Life Saving Club; they were going to a formal dinner in aid of the War Widows Fund. Would Britney Spears have dressed that way, knowing the age of the people who would be present? Perhaps she would. Oh relax, Jo, she told herself: what does it matter? You've dressed your daughter all her life so far and now that she's searching for her own identity you have to allow her to develop the image that makes her feel most secure and confident. If that's a blouson blouse that exposes her midriff and a hipster skirt from *Roxy* that barely covers half her thighs it's because what she is seeing in the mirror is the front cover of *Dolly* magazine and *Girlfriend* where she and all her friends would love to be. Image! Should I tell her, Jo wondered, that there are two curses destined to afflict her as a girl: the monthly flush of her breeding sac (to which she was finally adjusting after a year) and the nagging fear about her appearance that would never disappear?

'... I'm constantly amazed at how she fails to feel the cold, that's all.'

Bare flesh, when young, was as warm and elastic as a tight-fitting wet suit. Let her enjoy it while she could. In any case, she did look pretty, very pretty, and it was important that she knew it, for the tyranny of the mirror would always be lurking, waiting for its chance. And that tyranny, thought Jo with perverse delight, bound all women together. It was the sisal that created the bonds of sisterhood and once these years of teenage alienation had passed it would bind the two of them together, too. She could afford to smile and be patient: for mothers and daughters there were years of mutual reassurances yet to come.

'I was lucky enough to avoid mini skirts,' she confided to Albert. 'By the time Mummy let me start choosing clothes everyone was wearing caftans. We never dreamed the mini skirt would return, let alone that girls would want their belly buttons to be seen. I suppose it's all quite harmless, but I do draw the line at sticking pieces of metal through their skin. I'm holding my breath that that particular fashion will have died a natural before Sam's old enough to try it.'

She'd struggled to know what to wear that evening herself.

226

Sitting at her mirror brushing her hair, she'd tried to savour again the rush of excitement that she'd felt moments earlier when Albert had revealed that he and her mother had written to each other every month for all those years. The joy had lain in the realisation that their relationship had not been as bitter as she'd imagined. The sadness was that they weren't able to bridge the gap and manage to stay together. She'd been tempted to challenge him to explain why they couldn't do that; to force him to say outright what was more important than giving a child a father, but she'd been frightened of scaring him away. She had a vague picture of a wary animal that had been gently coaxed in from the wild with food and warmth but that would always stay close to the door and look for escape the minute it felt threatened. The animal could have been him or it could have been her.

'What it would be like to be young!' she sighed aloud.

Samantha, in the front seat, turned around and smiled mischievously.

'Were you ever young, Grandpa?'

'Ah!' Albert stirred. 'I suppose I must have been. I'm trying to remember. It was a very different world.'

Far from the contemplation of his youth, he'd actually been thinking about the cellular structure of trees, having suddenly remembered a series of coloured photos he'd taken for a conference. Why the images should come to him at that moment he couldn't imagine. Perhaps they were in some way relevant to his present circumstance. It had started with a cross-section of a newly cut stump: something like *Acacia Melanoxylon* with its black heart of dense lignin and compressed resins ringed with yellow sapwood and fibrous bark. He guessed the tree was about seventy eight years old, which was a lot for a Blackwood: his age. The last ring of xylem – the seventy eighth – had struggled to carry water and nutrients up the tree, perhaps because the lignin, which was meant to strengthen its tubular walls, had merely thickened them instead, blocking the capillary action that drew life upwards from the soil, ending mitosis.

It was a metaphor. That was why he was remembering it. The

tree had died when it failed to take up further nutrients. Yes, that was the point: the tree had died. The leaves and branches had fallen and the bark had dried out and gradually peeled off.

He let his head fall back against the seat and allowed himself to sigh. So, that was the feeling he'd been struggling with all day. The *anima mundi* of the physical world, that spirit of time and place that soaked into the hungry repository of human experience to be digested into nutrients for life, was dead to him. He looked and saw but the images instantly died. He listened and spoke but the sounds failed to record. Yesterday, today and tomorrow had become written in invisible ink for he'd ceased to absorb the nutrient of memories. He was here but he was not a part of it. The cross-cut image of the tree had flickered in front of him for the good reason that the process of mitosis, the division of cytoplasm to form new cells, had ended in both of them; him and the tree. The repair and growth of tissue had ceased and the outer rings of his life were no longer capable of transporting experiences that would form part of his core.

Were there no more rings to be added? Was this it, then? Was the study of the end grain of his life all that was now left to him as he waited for the decomposers?

As they came up the off ramp at Palmer Street, leading to the lights at William, Joanne leaned forward and took command.

'We're going to the National Art School in the Old Darlinghurst Gaol on Forbes Street,' she told the driver.

'I know where the jail is, lady; it's on Oxford Street.'

'Yes, but I want the Forbes Street entrance. Get onto Bourke Street until it crosses Liverpool and I'll show you from there.'

There was enough in her tone to suggest that any other options the driver might have favoured were best forgotten.

'If you don't take control,' she assured Albert, 'you can end up in Campbelltown. Not one of them speaks English.'

Albert was sure that the driver, who seemed like a dyed-in-the-wool Aussie to him, could speak English perfectly well and was unlikely to have missed the whispered aside, either; but perhaps this was all part of the running commentary of the city; part of the urban patois, like farmers discussing weather. He had no desire to usurp her role on account of age or gender. It was her city, not his. He was a traveller through time, peering into a future that he knew had arrived without him. This was a future that had come too late for him to join; nor, on balance, did he want to.

Albert peered through the front window of the cab as it quickly turned into William Street before the lights changed again. Up ahead was the familiar red and white Coca Cola sign that was a marker for Kings Cross. Left and right were the illuminated windows of the car rental companies. The traffic was fast and confident and the side streets were busy. Joanne was talking and Samantha was animated, joining in, but Albert was trying desperately to squeeze his brain and force it to give out the thought that was deposited there. Of course, like old spark plugs and distributor points, his mental synapses had become corroded and this was not an unfamiliar position to find himself in, to be trying to jump start his brain. Or, alternatively, perhaps there was a spark but it had difficulty in traversing what was meant to be a soft grey mass of nerve cells because they'd become hardened with time, a repository not for lignin but for aged memories.

'It's an absolutely super venue,' Jo enthused. 'The Old Cell Block – well, there are actually quite a few old cell blocks at the Gaol but this is the one that was used for women and it's been converted into a theatre and a hall for venues – anyway, this is where we hold our National Art School exhibitions every year, and people hire it for banquets and functions because it's such a wonderful building and also because it's so atmospheric and *spooky*.'

'What do you mean 'spooky'?' Sam wanted to know.

'Well, darling, although it's been a college for many years, it was built as a prison for the convicts and lots of people died there and were very unhappy. You can see their scratch marks on the sandstone walls and the tiny windows of their cells where they were incarcerated; plus, of course, there are ghosts and people love the thrill of ghosts.'

'What ghosts?'

'The ghosts of dead prisoners and those that were hanged there. People swear they can feel them.'

'Mum! You *are* making this up, aren't you? Tell me you're pulling my leg, because I'm *not* going to dinner if there are ghosts.'

'They used to hang 'em outside the gates,' the cabbie announced, 'and big crowds would turn up to watch. It was just like going to the footie.'

He seemed sorry to have missed it.

'We get people asking us to take them up there to see the gallows. There's one bloke I know takes people on special tours in a black hearse, hunting for ghosts. The Ghost Hunter, he calls himself.'

'We don't want to go into all that,' Jo protested good-naturedly. 'We'll never get Sam out of the car. No more talk of ghosts now, do you hear?'

Suddenly everything she said reminded Albert of her mother; the tone, the phrase, the inflection and the toss of the head that brooked no contradiction. The familiarity was so intense he felt driven to retreat hard up against the door of the cab. Ghosts were disembodied spirits of the dead manifesting themselves to the living, but the Gwen he saw in Joanne was not disembodied at all. Was this an hallucinatory effect brought on by his memories, or was Gwen genetically planted so firmly in her daughter that Joanne was beginning to replicate her? How much was down to his own mind playing tricks on him, for he had never felt this before?

No; this was wrong. Joanne was not Gwen. Gwen was the memory imprinted in his heart and mind, the unique markings of his end grain and when he died he took that end grain with him. She would exist in the end grain of Joanne but those markings would be different.

And where would he exist, then; for how could you exist except in other people?

Women are the keepers of family treasure, Joanne had said earlier in the day. Treasures and secrets had seemed to him to be the same thing. Secrets were personal. Exposing oneself personally placed an unnecessary burden of embarrassment upon others; it was a form of bad manners. So, he'd always kept things to himself; that had become his way.

'We're here,' Joanne announced as they drew up outside the black panelled gates in the stone wall of the old jail, 'and there, if I'm not mistaken, is Roger waiting for us.'

Albert was not ready. He was close, but he wasn't quite there. Once more around the block would be perfect. One more long wait at another set of traffic lights and he would have it all sorted.

'Ready, Dad?'

Joanne held out her hand to encourage him to follow her out on her side of the cab. There were a number of taxis arriving at the same time and the roadway was jammed.

'There's something I needed to tell you,' he said. 'Your grandfather committed suicide.'

'I know.'

She smiled and stepped out, just as Gwen would have done. He could have chosen to tell her in that instant that there had never been any doubt about his loving her mother or that they always felt they shared a child, even if they didn't share the same values about raising a child. He knew now that he ought to tell her that. More importantly, he knew that he *would* tell her that. He'd tell her everything. He'd tell her that women in particular presumed that love was paramount to all other feelings and that all actions could be tested against it; but that fear and self-loathing could be stronger than love and any hatred carried deep in the soul would eventually destroy it.

He'd try and explain that to her, but it wouldn't be easy.

45.

The RSL Dinner

'Let's not stand on formality,' Roger urged his guests. 'Why don't I call out your names as we get seated and then all you have to worry about is the name of the person next to you.'

'Bloody good idea,' agreed Bob Summers.

'Let's start with you, Butch. You've come the furthest so that makes you our guest of honour and I'd like you to sit next to me here on my right. Butch is the head of Astor United Holdings from Singapore and his company is looking at property opportunities here in the burgeoning State of New South Wales, including our own Whiteman's Creek.'

'In which the New South Wales Government has a considerable interest, Butch,' Bob enthused.

'And why wouldn't you when you take a five percent cut of everything we sell? ... But moving on ... next to you, Butch, I'll put my wife, Joanne, who can tell you all about the arts, if you're so inclined, 'cause that's her specialty, making sure none of the country's artists die of starvation, which doesn't leave much time for looking after her husband, but we'll survive that I'm sure, and Bob, how about you sit on Jo's right hand ...?'

'To keep it warm ...?'

'Ha, ha, to stop her writing out cheques, Bob. No, no, just kidding ... and Bob Summers, for those of you who don't know, is a senior cabinet member in our State Government and Minister of ... I can never remember your title, Bob, because you seem to be Minister for everything ...?'

'No, not everything ... My job's to keep the wheels turning so the

State can continue to grow, that's all.'

'What you'll find here in Australia, Butch,' Greg Cummings chimed in, 'is that the state governments are very heavily involved in infrastructure development and job creation. The catch cry here is Public-Private Partnership and there's a lot of that involved at Whiteman's Creek.'

'In Singapore we're well used to Government wanting to take the lead,' Butch noted politely.

'I don't think we're saying that Government takes the lead,' Roger cautioned, 'it's more a question of their ability to obstruct. Bob is a remover of obstructions. Now, I've just realised that the boys outnumber the girls tonight so I'm going to put Marjorie on your right, Bob, and split you up from Sheryl which will probably mean that Sheryl can actually get a word in edgeways for a change. Sheryl is Bob's lovely wife of … How many months is it, Bob?'

'Four months of romantic bliss, mate.'

'And Marjorie is married to Lawrence Beck, my Director of Corporate Governance who keeps us all on the straight and narrow and makes sure we don't spend too much. Lawrence, why don't you take the chair to Sheryl's right and Greg can sit between her and Marjorie? Greg Cummings of Marrick Vaughan and Samuels, our financial advisers, requires no introduction to you, Butch … and how about you, Bob …? No? Good! Now, here's someone you won't know who I'd like to introduce as a special guest tonight: my father-in-law, Albert Strange. Let's not forget that this is Anzac Day and if anyone should be occupying a seat of honour it is Albert, who not only fought in the Second World War but is also the son of one of the veterans of the Gallipoli Campaign, so it's a very special privilege having Albert join us tonight.'

'How wonderful,' Sheryl exclaimed.

'A true dinkum digger! You bloody beaut,' echoed Bob, making his way around the table to pump Albert's hand vigorously.

'One of the people who made it possible for us all to be here today,' Marjorie added solemnly.

'Precisely! We don't see Albert very often because he prefers the bush to the city but he came down today to take our daughter on the Anzac Day March. So, Albert, if you wouldn't mind sitting next to Lawrence, then between us we'll put Ms Britney Spears, here. It is Britney Spears, isn't it, or is it my young daughter, Samantha, pretending to be Britney Spears? Perhaps we'll find out when she sings.'

'Dad!'

'You look lovely, dear,' Marjorie offered.

'Don't tease her,' Joanne instructed. 'I'd far rather she was Britney Spears than Kylie Minogue. You're out of date with young fashion, that's all.'

'You know the difference between Britney Spears and Kylie Minogue?' Bob asked.

'Twenty years?' Greg suggested.

'Britney's determined to be chaste and Kylie's determined to be chased. You get it? It's better when you see it written down.'

'Well, why don't we all sit down,' Roger suggested, 'now that we've finished with the introductions.'

The scraping of chairs on the flagstone floor echoed against the high stone walls of the ancient cell block as diners took their places at the tables that filled the hall. Regimental banners and Allied flags hung from the beams where once there were walkways patrolled by prison guards. There was something mediaeval about the setting, the crannied walls hinting at a turbulent past heroically survived.

'This is very atmospheric,' their Asian guest commented, gazing around in puzzlement.

What on earth could he be thinking, Roger wondered? And what could *they* have been thinking to have invited him here without knowing what he was like and what sort of venue they were going to? Someone's bollocks were going to be cut out for this. Who the fuck had been responsible? He was trying to remember whose bright idea it had been. Was it Bob Summers who had twisted his arm to purchase the table tonight, or was it something that Joanne had come up with? He seemed to recall that it was a bit of both. Hadn't he received the sales pitch one night at home from someone in Bob Summers' office, and hadn't Jo gushed about the venue and the chance to get her old man down from the sticks to celebrate Anzac Day with Samantha? He never liked committing to things in advance and here was a good reason why. Given a choice this was not where he would be at this moment.

'Greg told me that your schedule was tight over the next twenty four hours,' he explained to Butch apologetically. 'Unfortunately this dinner was a long standing commitment of ours, but I thought it might give us the chance to get to know each other before tomorrow. Anzac Day in Australia is a bit like Independence Day in the States. There'll be speeches about sacrifice and national pride and all that nonsense, and the older generation will tell the younger generation they're a spoiled bunch of shirkers. You know how it goes. I'm sure it's the same the world over. You must have experienced a similar thing if you lived in the States?'

'I can't really say,' Butch answered. 'There's so much flag waving in America that it's difficult to tell the occasion. I remember Thanksgiving and Halloween. Halloween could be very scary.'

Roger laughed.

'Then look on this as a combination of Thanksgiving and Halloween. That's why we're having it in a jailhouse.'

This was Greg's fault. He was the one who should have known better. Roger had realised as soon as he saw Butch walking across the lobby of the hotel that this was not the right way for them to be meeting. First off, he was Asian. Forget the American accent and the Western name, an Asian is an Asian. If you wanted to do business with them over a meal, then make sure to order a whole steamed fish with ginger and shallots and see that they're offered a seat facing the door. Fuck, who knew what might be served up for a bunch of drunken old soldiers in a colonial jailhouse? This had all the makings of a very bad idea.

'He means that the jail is supposed to be haunted,' Joanne explained from the other side. 'So that would make it the perfect place for a Halloween party, though we don't encourage Halloween in our house because I never liked the idea of children being out on the streets knocking on strangers' doors asking for sweets. Still, if you're going to be investing in Australia it's just as well to find out what makes Australians tick and this is a very Aussie occasion.'

'Then I feel honoured,' Butch replied graciously, though you couldn't tell what he really thought because he wore dark glasses over his inscrutable eyes and the way he gently brushed down the collar of his navy blue reefer jacket and tweaked his striped silk tie suggested that he was thinking something else. But how could you tell?

'It's the perfect introduction to Australia, Mr Astor,' Marjorie observed dryly from the other side of the table, 'having your first dinner in a jail. We are incredibly proud of our convict roots and do our level best to behave like crooks at all times.'

'That's a bit rich,' Bob protested. 'You didn't need to be a crook to be a convict.'

'Quite so,' Lawrence agreed.

'In England you could be hanged for stealing a rabbit,' Sheryl observed brightly.

'No, you were hanged for stealing anything worth five shillings or more,' Lawrence corrected her.

'Are we sure we want to know?' Roger asked quietly, sensing Lawrence was on the verge of a lecture.

But his hint was ignored.

'It was the British way of keeping the lower classes under control. Up until the American War of Independence they'd been sending them there, but once they lost those colonies they had to look further afield; so, when Captain Cook arrived in Australia and claimed it for Britain, that became the next best option: *Terra Nullius*.'

'Terror what …?'

'Empty land,' Marjorie explained.

'Lawrence is our expert on all matters relating to the Law,' Roger added.

'The British considered Australia to be an empty continent,'

Marjorie continued. 'Aboriginals were not judged to be human beings, you see, therefore the land was declared *Terra Nullius,* which basically translates as *up for grabs.*'

'Oh ..!'

'No, no, no,' Bob protested. 'That's all ancient history. We've got legislation now that protects Aboriginals.'

'Now that all the best land has gone ...'

Roger was frowning. This was all getting a bit touchy.

'Anyway,' Bob groaned, obviously feeling the same way; 'let's not go down this dead end road. History is the past. The people who've made Australia the great country it is today don't paint their faces with mud and eat witchetty grubs. Not that there's anything wrong with that, but you wouldn't be describing Australia as a great modern nation if the whole place was one big Aboriginal reservation. This Government is very culturally sensitive – unlike the Howard Government, I might add – and we pride ourselves on that, but let's move on.'

Marjorie could be like that, Roger remembered. He seemed to recall she'd been on a march for Reconciliation.

'So, how was the land at Whiteman's Creek obtained?' Butch asked Roger.

'That was Crown land put up for tender by the State Government.'

'And before the Crown owned it?'

'The Crown has always owned it.'

'I see'

What was he getting at? He seemed confused.

'Not all the vacant land around Sydney is owned by the Crown,' Bob explained; 'a lot of it's freehold title. But the Government controls its use through zoning. We have to plan expansion carefully, as I'm sure you'd recognise, and that means roads and electricity, sewerage and schooling. You can't have developers throwing up thousands of little brick boxes and leaving the mums stranded in the back of nowhere with no transport or shops and no medical centres for their kiddies. Everyone in the world wants to come and live in Godzone and we've gotta be bloody careful we don't let 'em flop down anywhere without the proper planning and services. One day the land's gonna run out and we'll find ourselves up shit creek without a paddle unless we've got our infrastructure right so it can support greater density.'

'But there seems to be so much land in this country. There is more than enough for everyone, so why is it so expensive?'

'Because everyone wants to live in the big city, mate: bright lights and big bucks, that's what people want. Sydney real estate goes up in value every year. There isn't enough of it.'

'And that's what makes Whiteman's Creek such a good investment,' Butch concluded, not without a trace of humour.

'Bloody oath!' Bob proclaimed.

Roger took a short, sharp breath and then let out a gentle sigh of relief. It was beginning to sound like he could sit back and let others do the work. No-one was going to sell the merits of Whiteman's Creek as strenuously as Bob Summers. The sales tax on property was what filled the State Government's coffers to over-flowing and gave them the slush funds to persuade voters to keep them in power. No politician, let alone Bag Man Bob, was going to say anything to undermine a property developer. Besides, who could deny the growth rate of the city and the unique position which Saville Corp now occupied in it? Yes, perhaps he could relax, after all. Butch was urbane enough to keep up with the banter and didn't seem to need protection so this event could actually turn out to be a good ice breaker.

'Let's see what they've got for us to eat,' he said, picking up the gold embossed menu.

'Have the barramundi,' Joanne suggested. 'It's such a lovely delicate fish. I'm sure you'll enjoy it.'

Yes, everything was going fine. Albert was helping Samantha with her choice, and Greg was helping Sheryl with hers while feasting on the depths of her ample bosom, a fact which was probably not lost on Bob but was something he would have to get used to as the price of acquiring a substantially younger new wife. Marjorie was showing signs of wanting a cigarette already, and Joanne was playing the perfect hostess and wife, protecting Butch from any unwelcome culinary surprises. A couple more minutes of this, Roger thought, and he should be able to excuse himself while he went and got heavy with Maxine. He'd agreed to pay her double time. The cash was in his trouser pocket and now it was up to her to deliver.

'One thing that I meant to ask,' Butch said while there was a lull in the conversation, 'about the name, Whiteman's Creek. Is that an acceptable name for this development, do you think?'

'How do you mean?' Roger asked.

'Perhaps I should ask Mr Summers, as his Government is concerned to be culturally sensitive. Do you think Whiteman's Creek is the best name?'

There was a momentary hesitation from Bob Summers before he answered. The question appeared to bewilder him, just as it bewildered Roger. Only Marjorie seemed ready to express an opinion.

'It's what the area was called,' Bob stated. 'That's always been its name.'

'Ever since the arrival of the white man,' Marjorie added dryly.

'Oh, look,' Bob blustered, beginning to get the point, 'that's the beauty of Australia: we say it the way it is. *Blackman's Bay, Chinaman's Gully, Nigger's Reef, Coonawarra Wines* ... names are like stories, stories are history, history is what makes us ... like the ... like the ...'

'Rings on a tree,' Albert said quietly.

'Exactly!'

46.

The Dinner Table

Lawrence was furious. He wasn't showing it, of course, because he knew how to keep his emotions in check, but he wasn't going to allow Marjorie's behaviour to pass without comment; that would be tantamount to giving his approval. The poverty of judgement she displayed must be evident to everyone, tarring him by association. What on earth possessed her to make such a ludicrous comment at such a delicate time? 'We do our level best to behave like crooks,' she'd announced facetiously. Did she think she was being funny? It wasn't bad enough that the greed and feckless behaviour of the country's corporate leaders was the subject of banner headlines in all the daily papers; no, she had to champion criminality as though it were a national sport.

He'd tried often enough to warn her that irony and sarcasm were not clearly recognised as such by the majority of people. Now she was trying out the subtle arts of facetiousness on a stranger from another culture. The fact that the stranger was also on the verge of investing millions of dollars with them might, on its own, have sent out a cautionary signal you would think. Oh, no, not to Marjorie. Perhaps she did it on purpose. Perhaps this was her way of underlining just how little respect she had for business in general and his endeavours in particular.

So, of course, he'd been obliged to put the record straight. People didn't understand the damage they were doing by maintaining the myth of Australia's lawlessness. They misunderstood the history because they were too lazy to learn the true facts. The facts were as he had explained them. People were transported to the Colonies because they were a nuisance to the British ruling classes. They came, therefore, with the highest recommendation. Continually boasting of their criminality, no matter how jocular the tone, ran the risk of being believed. Worse than that, it gave legitimacy to the belief that criminality was a national trait, unavoidable because it was in the blood. Hence the spectacle of people like Ray Williams, Brad Cooper and Rodney Adler performing for the media like three startled monkeys; surprised that they should be so despised; indignant that those whose savings they squandered should not have sympathy for their own losses. It was a legitimacy that Roger might well be tempted to claim whenever the situation suited him, too. Hadn't he explained all of this often enough to Marjorie to at least cause her to think before she opened her mouth?

Then, to compound it, she had got on her Aboriginal bandwagon, suggesting that Whiteman's Creek had been stolen from them (well, that might as well have been the inference), and Astor had picked up on the connection, you could be sure. Even now she wouldn't leave it alone.

'When it comes to property,' she said to Bob Summers, 'you might say that the Crown has a history of double standards, don't you think?'

'At least we've got standards,' Bob laughed.

'This sounds to me,' Lawrence quickly interjected, 'like a family airing its dirty linen. No-one denies, Marjorie, that the early treatment of the Aboriginals was extremely harsh. Perhaps that is not surprising when one considers how the first white settlers had themselves been treated by the British Crown ...'

'Here, here!' someone said.

'We don't have children,' Marjorie informed the table, 'but I think my husband is saying that the abused child becomes the abuser in turn. Either way it pays to be careful.'

She was attempting to conduct the table like some sort of choirmaster. What had got into her? He must presume that she'd been drinking.

'You are not allowing me to finish,' Lawrence objected. 'It is too easy to make sweeping statements. Conversely, it is too hard, apparently, for people to look at all the facts. In most cases it is quite clear that the Aboriginals did not own the land in the first place.'

'Give us a history lesson, Lawrence,' Roger encouraged him. 'Tell us the legal interpretation.'

'I can do that for you,' Summers chimed in. 'The Abos don't even know what the word ownership means. Even after two hundred years of coaching by people like Marjorie, they still don't understand. Forget it.'

There wasn't much point in Lawrence continuing.

'I think I'd better rest my case,' he said to Albert next to him.

A prudent man would have stopped there, but prudence was in short supply, as Lawrence well knew.

'We don't bother with bullshit,' Summers explained to Butch, 'and the average Australian doesn't give much thought to false sensitivities, either. Mate, there's no confusion over who Australians are and what they want. It's very simple. They want a government that gives them decent roads and a chance to own their own house. They want bludgers off the dole but no-one left stranded who can't look after himself. They want to enjoy a beer and a night on the pokies if they feel like it and they don't want to be told what to do by do-gooders and lefties. If other people want to come and enjoy the same lifestyle that's fine, so long as they blend in and, above all else, don't jump the queue.'

It was fairly difficult to argue with that and Lawrence decided he would definitely leave the subject alone. He wasn't the host so he had no responsibility if the conversation went off the rails. Roger was the host and Roger, as usual, gave every appearance of not giving a damn. Had Lawrence been the host he would have considered it the height of rudeness to discuss racial issues in front of a guest from a different culture. Why not throw the White Australia Policy out on the table while they were at it? The fact that Astor was Asian should not hold them back. After all, we don't bother with bullshit, according to Summers. This is the country that sent a representative of The Humbug Society to parliament in 1860. If you want to do business here, you better get used to it, Mr Astor. (Strange that he should have an English surname. Perhaps he was Eurasian.)

'This duck lasagne looks mighty light on duck,' Roger announced as the food was served. 'Is the dinner tax-deductible, Lawrence?'

Really, was it worth answering? If Roger was so intent on belittling him he was better to be ignored. Lawrence could, of course, show him up quite easily. Did he really want a history lesson and a lecture on law as he'd so fatuously suggested? Well, he could have given him one, and a right fool Roger would have looked when he was finished. People who poked fun at scholarship were invariably seeking to divert attention from their own lack of it. They weren't smart enough to realise how it redounded back upon them.

The history of land sequestration by the Crown was actually a very interesting subject, if only people were prepared to listen. How could anyone express opinions on Aboriginal rights, property law, taxation and social equity without having the faintest idea of the background issues? Bob Summers was quite happy to support legislation without any knowledge of the facts, motivated solely by the rhetoric of Government press releases. Revenue and re-election were his priorities. Oh, by all account the Premier knew his history, from Plato and Plotinus to the founders of the American Constitution; but he wasn't going to be silly enough to represent himself to electors as some sort of modern day St Augustine of Hippo. No-one wanted to discuss the foundations of society. All they were interested in were guttural expressions of prejudice. Shock Jock radio announcers were the closest they wanted to get to philosophers. Bob Summers was their perfect representative.

What was so galling was the idea that these people might presume that Saville, being the Chief Executive of the company, represented beliefs to which Lawrence was prepared to subscribe. It had to be assumed that his boorish indifference to intellectual debate, his constant rendering of all human endeavour into the lard of personal profit and his cynical disregard for regulatory compliance in any form were values that Lawrence supported. How could people think otherwise? Roger was the boss, after all; Lawrence was merely the Company Secretary. That was the injustice of the situation: he was essentially stymied. If he promoted his own erudition it would only serve to show up Roger's lack of it, undermining his own situation even further.

'So,' Butch enquired quietly, 'what is the Government's attitude to Whiteman's Creek? Is it supportive?'

'Why wouldn't it be?' Summers demanded.

'From what I have heard,' Butch answered, looking to Greg Cummings for assistance, 'the Government is wanting the land developers to fund roading infrastructure.'

'I think Butch is referring to the speculation over the Windsor Road funding, Bob. There's some concern about how the Government is going to handle that issue.'

Roger leaned back in his chair and looked down his nose at Cummings as if he had just released a nasty smell. He wouldn't have been happy that this subject had been raised and he would have been even less happy at the inference that Greg had been discussing it with Butch outside of Roger's presence. Lawrence suddenly felt a tingle of exhilaration. He'd warned Roger that this issue could blow up, now let's see how he dealt with it.

47.

Oxford Street

For Willie, the man-child, the world was a street that had no end and every engagement was like a side street leading to another world that had no end. How could anyone know what lay down all those random side streets where chance could lead you? And if no-one could know all the infinite twists and turns that could take you down new and never ending streets that hadn't been imagined, how could anyone know the end and why would they try and predict it? What the fuck did anyone know? But if Willie was half thinking this then maybe he was thinking, too, that he could choose to pass along these streets in company or he could do it alone. Alone was scary, but maybe, if he was ever going to know why he was alive and what was the nature of the world that was intended just for him, he should do it on his own.

That could have been why he was walking along Oxford Street ten paces behind Luke and Ari; a street where any pause for engagement could lead to events that would be written in psychedelic neon, or, equally, into dark alleys where blunt instruments waited to bludgeon him without warning, leaving no more memory of him than his muffled cry. Alert to the possibilities, Willie's walk was imbued with the acuteness of sense that enables the night stalker to stalk, sure of his ability to see in the dark. He'd fallen ten paces behind because he'd paused for an instant at a travel shop window, having a sudden premonition that it provided a glimpse of one of those side streets of which he may have been thinking; sure as he looked into it that he could see a long way down it towards another turning.

'Shift your arse,' Luke shouted.

They'd reached Taylor Square which was, theoretically, the gay heart of bohemian Darlinghurst but had been turned by the Road Transport Authority into a pedestrian obstacle course. Orange and white traffic barriers blocked access to the pavements on two sides and green mesh safety curtains shrouded islands of debris where normally refuge could be taken from the relentless flow of traffic pouring down Flinders Street towards the Airport. It was enough to cause even Luke to stop and scratch his head.

'How the fuck we meant to get across there?' he complained.

He danced a jig of impatience, slapping his thigh with the ubiquitous newspaper, finally confronted with an obstacle he couldn't bully.

'Where we going?' Willie asked.

'Across the road and up past Kinselas,' Ari explained.

'If we ever get across the fucking road,' Luke moaned.

Taking the money out of his pocket and putting it on the table in the pub had been one of those turning moments for Willie. In that instant he'd felt himself head down a side street where he'd never previously ventured. Like so many impulsive acts it had been more daring than anything he could have consciously conceived. He'd been without money in his pockets before, of course, but he'd never volunteered to be penniless. It was the act of allowing himself to be destitute that changed things. He'd put the cash down and looked away wanting it to be gone, knowing that he had simultaneously surrendered his power of choice, placing himself in the hands of others.

There was a spot buried deep within the brain that scientists had identified as being like the control centre for good moods and positive emotions and somehow they'd found that this control centre lit up brightest among practising Buddhists. Who knows how they showed these things – with electrodes and x-rays and what-have-you – but Willie could believe it and sometimes even sense it in himself, and maybe that is what had caused him to reach into his pocket and pull out the money and slap it on the table. Didn't Buddhists turn their backs on the material world and enter a vow of poverty? Maybe money was like a faulty wire that short-circuited the control centre to that part of the brain. That was quite fucking possible because he felt good now. He felt better than he'd felt all day; in fact he clapped Luke on the shoulder as he joined them at the kerbside with such enthusiasm that it caused Luke to look startled, which made him feel even better still.

The night air felt good, too. It was a perfect night and everyone on the street looked cool and interesting and Willie had the feeling that if he stopped someone at random they would turn out to be, not just a side street, but a broad sweeping avenue that could lead him to great places that he'd never been. It was as if having no money had suddenly left him with so many choices. All the decisions that relied upon what he could afford had now been removed from him, and all the options that had nothing to do with money had opened to him as a result.

The traffic flowed on and on and there were no lights anywhere that seemed even capable of saying WALK and Luke's agitation grew extreme so he turned and started walking down Flinders Street. Maybe he was looking for somewhere safer to cross so Willie and Ari followed. There was an Italian place on the corner and next to it was a sex shop. Next to the sex shop was an ATM and that made Willie hesitate for a moment for, of course, he still had his credit card in his pocket despite the purity of his belief that he was now cleansed of money.

Luke stopped in the sex shop doorway and glowered at the interior. There was something about it that he appeared to disbelieve. The blue neon sign said *Tool Shed*. Maybe it wasn't a sex shop. Maybe they sold screwdrivers and spanners. He scratched his head and disappeared inside and Willie and Ari looked at each other and shrugged, then walked back to the corner just as the lights changed and the blind man's buzzer told them it was safe to cross. They loped across the intersection to the Courthouse Hotel and waited in the doorway of the Judgment Bar to see if Luke was following but he'd disappeared.

Further down the pavement people were eating at tables set up on the sidewalk, sheltered bizarrely by a fence of tall cactus fronds. There was a strong smell of fish frying in oil. Although Willie was hungry there was nothing he could do. The weight of self-determination had been lifted from him leaving him feeling strangely light-headed. He might waste away or he may, like a dog, chance to be fed. This was the essence of Buddhism.

'We won't wait,' Ari concluded. '*Louee's* is just around the corner. He knows the way.'

Willie nodded but hesitated to follow. There was something missing. How would he get in?

'Luke's got my money,' he explained, returning to reality.

48.

Outside the Cell Block Hall

Roger was not going to allow Maxine an opportunity to interrupt.

'There's nothing of value in it, Maxine; I keep telling you – apart from my passport. Are you into stealing passports, Maxine? I can get a new one in twenty four hours. You'd be lucky to get a hundred dollars for it. I have to say, Maxine, I'm very disappointed. I thought you were smart. I liked you. I have to suppose you just made a mistake. I think you realise that so let's put it behind us. I need those business papers tonight. They don't have value to anyone else but me. It's purely a matter of inconvenience, that's the only reason they can have any value to me. Tomorrow they'll be worth nothing. So, I'm willing to accept that you're a working girl and time means money to you but you've got to bring them to me tonight. Get them to me in the next hour and you'll get your money. A thousand dollars is what we agreed but I'm willing to double that if you get here on time. That's the deal! Do you know where Taylor Square is in Oxford Street? Do you know where Forbes Street is? There's a Technical College. Do you know where the Technical College is? It's in Forbes Street off the Square. Can you be there? Call me. Call me when you get to the gate. Don't come in. Or text me, yeah, better that you text me. I'll come outside and meet you with the money then we'll forget this ever happened. Maxine, I want those fucking papers tonight so don't piss me around.'

He didn't raise his voice or attempt to threaten. His whole tone was very reasonable. They each knew what they wanted and the main concern now was to avoid misunderstanding. He smiled while he was talking because that way it was easy to sound pleasant no matter what he was saying. This was something that Roger had learned long ago. Smiling came easily to him anyway because of the shape of his mouth. He continued smiling as he closed up his cell phone and returned it to his top pocket. Now that was done he could concentrate on Butch Astor.

As he walked back into the long hall he felt assured at last. The problem had not lain with the girl, it had lain with himself. He'd been disconnected from events all day, observing them like a ghost at a wake, curious but invisible, unable to engage. Now, he realised, it was because he'd been unsure about his own motives and direction. What had he thought he was doing? Was he solving a liquidity problem for his Banks, or was he trying to bail out and escape? Was he setting Astor up with a sweetheart deal because he'd lost his nerve and wanted to take the money and run, or was he being coldly practical and shoring up his position ready for the big play that lay ahead? It hadn't helped that he'd given confusing signals to Greg Cummings; that had been a mistake. All he could say was that he'd been distracted by the negativity of others: something he hadn't expected because, certainly in the case of Lawrence, it was something he should have been used to. There were some people who would never understand the moral superiority of the borrower over the lender because the Banks had the hex on them. Lawrence was a prime example. He anticipated the stench of failure so keenly that he never risked it. But the one that had unsettled him the most was his own mother, Rose. Could she smell failure, too? Was the smell coming from him because he'd momentarily lost his nerve, or was it a smell of her own making because she saw in him a willingness to push boundaries that would have been anathema to his father? Well, how many times did he have to say it? He wasn't his father, he was better; she would see.

Yes, he felt a lot more assured. He was confident that within the hour he would have the valuations back and everything would then go to plan. The money he'd agreed to pay was of no consequence and he wasn't going to waste anger on the girl; she was an opportunist, after all, and wasn't everyone an opportunist in their own way? They were all, as his father used to like saying, fish that swam at different depths, all waiting for the opportunity to feed on the food that filtered down to them. She'd get her scraps and that would be the end of it. He had bigger fish to concentrate on.

He paused in the doorway and took stock of the room. It was not big. There might have been only twenty or thirty tables, but each table had two uniformed waiting staff assigned to it and the confident clamour of conversation spoke volumes about the nature of the guests. This was no ordinary gathering of old diggers bussed in from the Western Suburbs. Well, the menu and the table linen should have told him that. They were paying a thousand dollars a head, for fuck's sake; that was enough of a clue in itself. Like the VIP enclosure at the War Memorial that afternoon, this was less to do with soldiery than it was with politics. Politics and Big Business swam together. They were the top of the food chain. He'd forgotten, but now he understood why they'd booked this table.

Crossing the room, carrying his smile ready to share with any familiar face that swam into focus, his train of thought returned to its more customary track. It was up to him to pull this deal off, just as it had always been, and he wasn't going to be distracted again. Just look around. They were dining in good company, anyone could see that, and it was his efforts that had got them there. This was the top echelon, the place where everyone wanted to be, and Saville Corp bore his name now, not his father's. It would do no harm for Astor to see this and realise the level at which he was dealing. Perhaps his mother should see it as well. You didn't just arrive in Sydney and step off the plane into this sort of gathering unless you had a talent for being at the top.

'I've asked for a copy of the latest valuations to be brought over for you,' Roger explained quietly to Butch as he returned to the table. 'I thought you might like to have a look at them before tomorrow.'

In his absence the dinner party had launched into animated conversation. Summers was telling Greg Cummings about the efficacy of Viagra and Margaret was lecturing Butch and Joanne on the difference between tapestry and embroidery. Lawrence was bending Albert's ear on the follies of the housing boom and only Sam, looking like she'd been sentenced to community service in a home for the intellectually disabled, was in need of being rescued.

'Tell me about the march,' he prompted her. 'I looked out for you but couldn't find you in the crowd.'

'It was Okay.'

'Only Okay ...?'

'No, it was good, but like it was sad, too. I mean ...'

'That's war, Sam. People go to war and get killed. It's been happening forever and always will. It's a sad fact of life.'

'I didn't mean that. I mean, like what's going to happen to Anzac Day when people like Grandpa are all dead? Who's going to march then?'

Roger suddenly remembered why he'd conspired to put this guest list together. He'd been so damn distracted by the loss of his briefcase and the constant nagging by Lawrence over the banking covenants that he'd forgotten the purpose of inviting Albert.

'Hey, Bob,' he interrupted, 'my daughter here wants to know what's going to happen to Anzac Day. I suspect that our table is unique in having a survivor of the New Guinea Campaign whose father was also a survivor of the Gallipoli Campaign. Not that we anticipate losing Albert any day soon, but what's going to become of Anzac Day when all the survivors have gone?'

He could see that every table had its trophy returned servicemen and he didn't want people to overlook the status that Albert's presence conferred on the Saville Corp table. It would have helped, however, if Albert had worn his medals.

'It's a smart question, young lady,' Bob acknowledged. 'A lot of people regard Anzac Day as our National Day. It would be a bloody disaster if it lost its importance. It's up to your generation to keep it going. What do you think, Albert?'

Albert didn't appear to know what to think. He looked at Sam as if trying to remember who she was and then smiled in recognition and took hold of her hand. They'd obviously had some sort of bonding session during the day, encouraged no doubt by Joanne. Women weren't happy unless they could wring some emotion out of events.

'I'm sure there'll always be an Anzac Day,' Albert said eventually, 'as long as there are still politicians.'

Marjorie laughed loudly and, to his credit, so did Bob. For his part, Roger found his smile caught awkwardly between humour and confusion as, in the background behind Albert's head, and apparently advancing towards their table, he suddenly caught sight of Alison Pyke.

'To keep sending young men to war, you mean ...?'

He sat up straight and adjusted his smile to one befitting the charming and confident host. To his surprise he felt a surge of excitement and found himself preening. She looked more glamorous than he remembered, dressed again in black but showing bare shoulders and arms and with her hair longer and less severe. Even more surprising was that her advance towards their table was not focused on him but on Greg Cummings, and as she came up behind him and slid her hands over his eyes, laughing with delight at his startled reaction, it was apparent that her intimacy with him ran deep. Greg leaped to his feet and they spoke animatedly out of earshot while Roger steered the table conversation towards an affable critique of the meal thus far, all the while alert to Alison's eyes and their direction. The waiting staff had begun running out the main course plates with an urgency that revealed they were under instructions to meet a deadline, and on the high stage at the far end of the room people had begun to play with microphones, which suggested that the evening was soon going to be taken over with speeches.

Joanne, having found a topic of conversation that had taken Butch's interest, returned to it with enthusiasm leaving Roger concerned that, once the speeches started, there wouldn't be an opportunity for him to talk with Butch as he'd planned. Maybe it didn't matter now. His fear that Butch would feel out of place was unwarranted. On the contrary, he seemed comfortable and relaxed and, apart from his misplaced concern over the racial implications of the naming of Whiteman's Creek, there were no warning signs of disquiet. Summers had smoothly defused the roading issue by waffling on about Public-Private Partnerships and everything was turning out well.

If he'd been anticipating that half smile of Alison's to be shone in his direction, that smile that somehow managed to be directed knowingly at him alone and which had so effectively drawn him into their Hayman Island bedroom tryst, he was destined to be disappointed. As their conversation ended Alison smiled vaguely in the direction of his table, showing no sign of recognition before departing, and Greg returned to his seat wearing a boyish grin.

'I didn't know you and Alison Pyke were good friends,' Roger chided pointedly.

Was he screwing her, he wondered? It sure as hell looked like it. And how much pillow talk had they engaged in? Why had she avoided coming and saying hello to him and Lawrence like that? Was she embarrassed? Lawrence was dealing with her all the time, for Christ's sake. It didn't stack up.

'We met at The Property Council Ball,' Greg explained sheepishly. 'I gave her a lift home in my taxi.'

'Must have been a long taxi ride,' Bob Summers suggested.

'No, no, not that far ...' Greg didn't mind what was being implied at all.

'Go on, darl,' Sheryl Summers teased her husband; 'you're only jealous. His imagination works overtime,' she explained to everyone. 'There's only one thought on his mind.'

'Well, I can't depend on testosterone any more. These days my libido relies solely on creative imagination. It's alright for Greg, here; he's a young jumbuck compared to me.'

'You're not suggesting the fire's gone out, are you, Bob?' Roger chimed in.

'It's more like a controlled burn, mate. What was once a raging bush fire has now been brought under control; that's how I'd describe it.'

They all laughed sympathetically, including Roger, despite the fact that he was not at all pleased at the discovery that his Investment Adviser was fucking a member of his Banking Syndicate's Credit Committee. It was a safe bet that wasn't covered in Lawrence's Compliance Handbook.

49.

The Dinner Table

Roger's view that they were all fish swimming at different depths would not have been known to Albert who was, instead, feeling like a fish out of water, unable to follow the currents of conversation that swept around the table. The things that people chose to say in social situations had always bemused him, even when he was younger. He knew that intrinsic to their choice was a sub-text of things unsaid and that subtext was so foreign as to be unknown to him. When Lawrence chose to complain to him about the true consequences of the housing boom he sensed that he really wanted to say something about Bob Summers; and perhaps Roger, too. When Marjorie pilloried the Colonial treatment of Aboriginals she seemed to be searching for a way of pillorying her husband. He was guessing at this. He himself used language sparingly. It was a dangerous and volatile substance to be treated with care. It was better and safer to be known as a man of few words.

As a naturalist, Albert's interpretation of life inclined towards botanical and zoological explanations, which was why he felt like he was a silent observer watching a pack of feral animals, trying to understand their behaviour. Yet, just as, in the taxi, he'd sensed that the moment and his part in it were no longer capable of adding lignin to the rings of his life so, too, now he was sure that this moment and his presence in it added nothing to life in general. When it came to this type of society - this city environment of monetary ambitions - he had never sought to belong; but where once it had made him feel awkward and tense, now he felt released. It no longer mattered to him. At some point during the day he'd surrendered. If life had been wrestling with him, pushing him towards a predetermined position on the mat, then maybe this was where he was meant to be: the son of his father, the father of his daughter, life lived, no more and no less.

He watched Joanne in animated conversation with the man from Singapore and saw in her vibrancy the striking confirmation that his purpose in life had been fulfilled, a purpose that he'd been afraid to acknowledge for so long. He looked closely where once he'd been afraid to. His fear had been that he would only see her mother there and if she caught him looking she would find guilt in his eyes and throw that guilt back at him. She wasn't her mother, of course; she was a new person, busily laying down the rings of her own life, rings that made her unique and which he now felt for the first time he could regard with warmth.

'I know,' she'd said as they got out of the taxi, and it had been like a time switch hidden inside his DNA, waiting all his life to be triggered. How simple it had finally become.

Behind him on the stage the speeches began. Albert tilted his head politely as if listening but his mind wandered back to his earlier thoughts about the tree. The tree had become analogous to his life; but if he was to die, he couldn't allow himself to merely lie rotting in the earth, he needed to create another outcome. Was it his will that had drawn those words out of Joanne? The old sought to make peace with the young, the dying with the living. They secretly craved the opportunity to edit their obituaries before they were published. Was that what he was doing? Please God he was doing something better. Please God he was adding something to the rings of his daughter's life, and his granddaughter's, too, that would not otherwise have been there; rings of support that countered the rings of neglect.

When Bob Summers stood and headed for the stage, summoned by the MC to make his contribution, and they all turned their chairs towards the rostrum to give him their attention, Albert turned his chair around as well. He patted Sam on the knee and shared a knowing look with Joanne but his mind was drifting towards an image of a tree that was still standing, fully grown but no longer increasing in size, its future annual rings barely divisible from those past. How long would it be allowed to stand, he wondered?

50.

Louee's Club in Paddington

Willie was feeling stupid.

He couldn't see properly in the half light and he couldn't hear clearly either because the base control on the sub-woofer that was positioned just behind his chair made his ear drums vibrate. He didn't know what anyone was saying and he didn't know how to join in because he knew he'd end up saying pardon so many times that he'd feel like a retard. The chairs were low, too. His arse was practically on the ground and his knees felt like they were up above his head. That wasn't why he felt stupid though. He felt stupid because Nicole hadn't even spoken to him. Shit, she'd acted like she didn't even know him, giving him a look like, *'Is this person with my friend?'* The friend was clearly Ari. She had any amount to say to *him*. He was her fucking soul mate. Not that he could hear what they were saying 'cause the music was so fucking loud. Why was it so loud, for fuck's sake?

And what were they doing here?

They hadn't had to pay to get into *Louee's*. All they had to do was mention Nicole's name on the entry phone then open a door at street level and close it behind them and walk up a flight of stairs to the first floor where they found themselves standing in what appeared to be someone's flat. There was techno music playing and all the light bulbs were red. No-one greeted them.

Willie had said something stupid. He said, 'It feels like someone's place.'

Perhaps, as he got close to her, he was getting nervous; half wanting an excuse to escape. Of course it was someone's place: it was Louee's place. Even then Ari wasn't bothering to take much notice of him. It was beginning to feel like they were only together because he was Luke's friend. Oh, well, so what, Willie had thought. It was no deal. He was just hanging.

Ari acted like he knew his way around. He went into the first room at the top of the stairs. If this was meant to be a flat, as Willie supposed, then it might have been a dining room except that it was filled with these low chairs that looked like office furniture bought in a liquidation sale. Apart from being filled with chairs the room was otherwise empty. There was a door to the right that led into another room which might have been a kitchen and in the middle of this room was an island bar with high stools around it and sitting on the high stools blowing pinkish-white puffs of smoke into the air were people that turned to look at them, concluding quickly that they didn't know them. That smoke had the sweet familiar aroma of a rich and well-dried herb. Yeah, Okay, Willie thought.

Ari had raised his hand in salute and then headed back out into the passageway towards the rooms at the front of the house. These were similar to the first room except that the walls had been partially knocked through so that there were archways linking them and the liquidation furniture had been arranged in groups around glass coffee tables that must have been picked up at the same sale so the effect was of a series of waiting rooms and there through the first alcove they'd found Nicole. But she hadn't recognised him - hadn't acknowledged him, anyway. That's why he felt stupid.

Well, it might have been the light. In the red light everything was brown that should have been black and Ari, who should have been brown, was a strange shade of orange. If this was the way dogs saw the world it was no wonder they barked at coloured people. With the noise and the strange light everything felt uncertain and then when Ari perched himself on the chair beside her Willie had no choice but to take a chair opposite and watch them. It was inevitable that she wouldn't have spoken to him, he consoled himself, because there was no way he would have heard; but she might at least have acknowledged him with her eyes. So for five minutes that seemed like an eternity he sat there feeling resentful and endeavouring to look like he had no interest either in being there or in seeing her. There were other people in the room that he could pretend to look at. The red light was like a protective cloak.

See, the thing is, Willie thought, none of it really matters, so I don't give a fuck. Where he was going there wouldn't be any of this shit. He was going to a different place. He was going to another place altogether. Any time he wanted he could turn towards it. Nobody could follow. Turn down the road and follow the light; see where it led. Where he was going the light would be different, and the music, too. This place was so like everything he'd fought against all his life. This was so like his life; just so fucking obscure.

Anyway, why shouldn't he look at her? Nobody was looking at him and the room was in blackout, like a news clip from CNN of a mountain pass in Afghanistan viewed through the night scope of a fascist GI looking for someone who wasn't even there. (See, they hadn't caught Bin Laden, had they? They didn't even know where he was.) She could put her big boots on the table with their Caterpillar treads and her black ankle socks showing out the top but a sniper could ping her and she wouldn't even know it. The sniper could be him. Who would ever know it?

In the red light her long legs were pinkish-grey instead of white. They were long like his. He remembered that. Her skirt was so short he could practically see her fanny. Maybe that was the idea. Her whole body was so indolent and questioning that he wondered what answer she was looking for. Just as she'd done the night before, leaning against the wall and allowing his hands upon her feet as if they were asking a serious question, so now her body seemed to be laying down a challenge. Sure as hell it wouldn't be little Ari she wanted inside her. No, she was pointing her legs at him. This is what she'd done last night. She'd given him her feet. Her feet were the furthest point from her head and her head was where her mouth was. Her mouth was where she hid her tongue; the tongue that she'd laid out before him, so dark and plump with the two white pills that he'd chased down inside her until they disappeared along with his memory.

In the dead zone in his brain where his memory had disappeared there must be images stored that she would be recalling now seeing him sitting opposite her. Maybe if he could be alone with her he'd be able to retrieve those images, too. Was she stretching out her long legs to him because she wanted him to start again? Was she secretly urging him to reach out and remove her heavy boots, exposing the white soles of her feet and the slippery skin between her toes?

51.

The Stage of the Cell Block Hall

'Ladies and gentlemen! Thank you, thank you!'

Bob Summers held up his hand to still the applause and then, leaning into the microphone, adopted his sly, conspiratorial face; the face that made him one with his audience.

'I'm not going to make a political speech,' he lied. 'Yes, you can all rest easy. This is no time for politics. I hope the Prime Minister is remembering that wherever he is tonight. I know, I know, that's being political and I withdraw that remark. These are difficult times and it doesn't hurt me to say that I support John Howard and his decision to send Australian troops to Afghanistan one thousand percent.'

He waited for the light ripple of approval.

'So we all agree?' Applause was so easy to buy. It was just a matter of waiting.

'But does it surprise you that in this country there are people that disagree? Where have these bloody people been? What have they learned? Have we given shelter to our enemies? The freedom that we fought to protect in two World Wars and the prosperity that we and other western nations have struggled to provide out of the ruins of those horrendous conflicts are once more under attack. Make no bones about it, September 11 was a declaration of war from people who hate democracy, who cannot abide freedom of speech, who abhor the emancipation of women and who despise pleasure in any form.'

Now the level of applause gave him the permission he sought. They were with him.

'What the hell did we fight for? Do those towel heads in their caves really think we're going to roll over and give it all up? I suggest they read the history of Anzac Cove, El Alamein and the Kokoda Track. And to those people who say it's America's fight, not ours, I suggest they read the history of The Battle of the Pacific and work out how far Australia is from the Coral Sea. If it wasn't for America we'd all be eating sushi tonight.'

A titter of half-nervous laughter. Say it, they were begging. So he did.

'I've only got one thing to say to those people,' he intoned severely: 'Your turban's too tight and the blood's not getting to your brain.'

Ah, that was better. How they loved it when you were politically incorrect. Now all the tension was gone and they were his for the taking.

'But I didn't envy John Howard because none of us want to send young people to war,' he confided solemnly. 'There's a good reason, right there, why I will never be Prime Minister. Yes, alright, there's *another* good reason. I keep wondering what I'd do in the same position. My mother used to bake Afghans, you know – those hard biscuits with chocolate in them - and she was damn good at it, too. Maybe I'd send her to sort it out; she's frightening enough and she won't take crap from any man but she might have trouble getting the hang of a bazooka.'

He'd have expected more of a belly laugh for that one. Maybe they weren't quite as relaxed as he thought.

'What I mean is that I'd do anything not to send our country to war and who amongst us isn't the same? But history tells us that that's a luxury we'll never have. It's a sad but true fact that wars are here to stay.'

Maybe tonight was a night for a bit of statesmanship.

'Forty years ago one of our greatest generals, Field-Marshall Sir William Slim, gave a speech to my school. The virtues of the Aussie soldier, he told us, were resourcefulness and the ability to make the best of the most bloody awful conditions imaginable. I remember him sticking out his jaw and looking at us like we were rotten little buggers with our hands down our pants. The easier and more gadget-filled our lives become, was his message, the harder it would be for us to defend ourselves.

'Well, I wonder what he would think if he was alive today. For the modern Aussie kid hardship is when his Game Boy batteries go flat. Resourcefulness is when he borrows his mate's cell phone. The most bloody awful conditions imaginable are being stuck at home without a video to watch. Don't we all know it to be true? Times have changed and yet, I'll tell you something - you know what I'm going to say because deep down we all believe it - this generation will be no different to the last. The next generation will be no different again. Push an Aussie and you'll get a fight and don't expect to go home early or in one piece.

'Thank you, thank you.' (It was pretty obvious they were going to love that.)

'I speak from my heart because that's where I do my thinking and that's where my words have to come from. When you have a heart it doesn't matter about a brain, it only matters that your heart belongs to your country and your fellow countrymen. That's what makes us who we are. That's what makes us invincible.

'But times change. I hear people being outraged at the concept of Australian soldiers' wives being paid compensation for the death of their husbands on active service in Afghanistan. Do you know what these people say? They say, 'If you join the Army those are the risks'.

'If you join the Army those are the risks? What's the risk to those of us sitting comfortably at home if they don't join the Army? What's the risk of people like that, who resent the ninety thousand dollars, ever giving *their* lives to protect their country? Saddam Hussein offers a bounty of twenty five thousand US dollars to the families of suicide bombers who attack Israel. Is the life of an Australian soldier worth less than the life of an Arab terrorist? Work it out. Work it out. If you need the exchange rate I can give it to you.'

Oh, they could work it out alright. Look at all the heads that were nodding.

'No, we haven't paid compensation to our war dead before. There were so many and their sacrifice was so great that it would have overwhelmed us. But our debt to them and to their widows is none the less because of that. We know that in our hearts. That's why we're here tonight. Every individual and company sponsoring a table owes their freedom and prosperity to those that sacrificed their lives for their country. The very least we can do - as my host, Roger Saville, would tell you - is to aid and support their widows.

'Please give a generous hand for the generosity of our sponsors.

'Thank you.'

It was always good to garner applause for others.

'You know, as I was climbing up on the stage tonight I felt my knees creak and I was reminded of that story of the old man who goes into the ice cream store and slowly and gingerly eases himself into the seat and asks for a banana split. 'Crushed nuts?' the young waitress asks, oblivious to his pain. 'No', he answers sadly: 'arthritis'.

'Oh, yes, we laugh at old age because we have no other defence against it, but a young lady at our table tonight reminded me that time is as ruthless as any bullet and one day soon we'll look around and find that those to whom we owe our freedoms are no longer here. Then we'll wonder why we didn't treasure them as we should.

'I feel ashamed to be standing here talking about sacrifice. What do I know about it when sitting opposite me tonight is a man who fought to defend us in the jungles of New Guinea and whose father before him fought and survived on the beaches of Gallipoli? Wouldn't we all rather hear from him? Even if he chooses not to say a word – because I haven't asked him and I have no right to make presumptions on his part – wouldn't we all prefer that he stood here, at least for a moment, so we could pay homage to him and to all of his generation to whom we owe so much?

'His name is Albert, Ladies and Gentlemen, and, Albert, I am going to stand here until you come and join me on stage so we can honour you as you deserve and only then will the audience stop clapping. So join me everyone to persuade on stage a true hero and a proper Anzac.

'Albert ...?'

52.

Louee's Club

'Have we scored?' Luke's voice suddenly shouted from behind.

Willie sat up, startled. The music stopped and he turned to find that Luke had killed the switch on the woofer, something that Willie could easily have done if he'd known about it. Now he really felt stupid.

'Not even a drink?' Luke complained.

'We were waiting for you,' Ari giggled.

'Willie ...?'

'I have no money.'

'What a useless bunch of pricks. Well, I've spent all mine at *The Tool Shed*, so don't look at me. Looks like it's on you, Nicole, seeing you're the only one with gainful employment. Besides, it's against the rules for guests to pay in someone else's club.'

He sniggered like a whinnying horse, as if it was the funniest thing, kicking Willie's legs out of the way so he could grab the chair next to him and flashing a shopping bag for them all to see in case they missed it. Maybe the snigger was related to the shopping bag. Look at me, look at me, his actions shouted; I am the coolest, cleverest person you will ever know. Trouble was, with his knees up above his head and his bum dragging on the ground (already convinced of his own stupidity) it was unlikely that Willie was going to challenge him on that. Nicole watched him without any interest.

Willie knew intuitively that inside that shopping bag there would be an item of entertainment that would demand their attention and his hopes of retrieving the intensity of awareness that he'd felt with Nicole the previous evening were about to be dashed. Still, if he couldn't reach her through the glow of energy generated by his stillness, and she continued to refuse to turn her eyes towards his, then he was going to have to participate in the game that Luke was about to thrust upon them as he plunged his hand inside the bag.

'I have here a little catalogue of useful tools that every boy and girl should keep in his bedside drawer,' Luke announced with a flourish.

Ari stood up and patted his pockets as if suddenly realising that he might have brought some money after all. Nicole removed her boots from the table and allowed him to pass.

'Stuff in here that would come in handy for you, Nicole. They've got dongs with balls, dongs without balls, double enders – all you could wish for. Don't suppose you need it though. How about some lube? Strawberry flavoured or banana? What do people prefer? Fuck, it's all here, man.'

The girl in the movie had those eyes. They were like windows to a darkened room at night and deep in the shadows of the room, unseen, someone was looking out. There was no way to bring her to the window and no way to persuade her to turn on the light. To see into those eyes he would have to find a way of entering the room. Even then he wasn't sure that he'd be able to see into them.

'Do we have to ...?' Willie asked disdainfully.

If he could match her disinterest, that might get him closer to the door of her room, at least.

'I mean, we get the picture.'

'Hey, don't be so shy, Willie Boy; we know you modelled for some of these. How else could you have so much pocket money? It's not like you ever worked for it. Not like Nicole Baby. But that's alright: be proud. Now, which one is you? Maybe yours is the 'Powercock'. Yeah, this is you: twenty centimetres of cock and balls. Look at that! Does that look like you? Whaddya say, Nicole, does that look like Willie Boy? No? Not big enough? Nah, twenty centimetres isn't very big; twenty centimetres is a weeny. You could easily miss it in the dark.'

'It must be yours then,' Nicole said, not caring whether she was heard or not.

She squinted at her finger nails as if she'd only just noticed them, and then began to chew at a piece of cuticle on her index finger. Willie laughed aloud and immediately regretted it. He needed to match her boredom; to show her they were in the same place, so he laid his head back and looked at the ceiling, then closed his eyes and feigned sleep, just as he'd done the night before when he'd wanted to say interesting things but feared his tongue was travelling at the wrong pace. Oh, I could have said that, he thought. I could have put the little creep down. But he hadn't.

'Penis envy, Nicole,' Luke replied. 'We all know that women secretly envy men. You resent not having penises so you carry vibrators in your hand bags instead: 'vibrating, pulsating, surging, escalating pleasure tools'. Maybe you don't. You probably hate penises. You're probably content with your vibrating cell phone. Hey, Ari, I've found something for you here.'

Ari returned to the table with a giant bottle of Coke and four empty glasses. This was hardly worth sitting up for. Coke for God's sake; Coke and flicking through sex catalogues: was this for real? But both Luke and Nicole sat up with interest. Then Ari took an envelope out of his pocket and sprinkled a pile of small tablets onto the glass-topped coffee table. He did it like they were diamonds and he was a jewel thief, with a smug conceit that was clearly anticipating their praise and admiration.

'Ya-Ba Da-Ba Doo!' Luke exclaimed.

They looked like aspirin pills except they were pink. Everything was pink.

'Are we popping or we gonna do a line?'

Luke looked quizzically at Ari but, before he could answer, Nicole leaned forward, took two tablets off the pile and popped them in her mouth. Then she poured herself a glass of Coke.

'Okay, we're popping.'

Luke and Ari did the same. Now there were two pills left on the table. Nicole's eyes were everywhere but they weren't on Willie. He wanted to be his own man. He wanted to take them in his own time. He wanted her to watch him.

'What are they?' he asked casually.

'Ya Ba, man. Thai louees. Real mad medicine. Cheaper than beer. You gonna pop them, or what?'

Of course he was, but fuck he'd not seen them before, that's all. He'd go where they went. So he popped them, poured a glass of Coke and sat back and waited. Luke went back to his catalogue like he'd just had a sip of coffee and they were sitting around reading the newspapers. Nicole started tapping her booted feet in time to the music and looked at her watch. Willie lent forward as best he could and put his elbows on his knees so he could cup his head in his hands. He hoped like hell that this time he would see it coming because he didn't want another night like the last one.

'So listen to this one, Ari,' Luke enthused, 'and tell me what you think. It's the *Julie Ashton Anal Beginner's Kit'*. What do you think it contains?'

'I don't know, perhaps a special lubricant?'

'Lubricant? Yes. What else? Come on.'

'I really don't know. You tell me.'

'You're not playing the game, Ari. What's the matter with you? Fuck, everyone's so anal. This kit must have been designed for you bastards. Do you want to know what it contains or don't you?'

'You're going to tell me.'

'I'm not going to fucking tell you. You're all a pack of fucking wankers and you bore the shit out of me.'

He threw the catalogue down and plunged his hand back into the shopping bag which lay on the floor at his feet.

'I was going to share my big surprise with you but none of you deserve it. Fuck, doesn't anyone around here know how to have a bit of fun?'

He took out a bulky packet and tore aggressively at the plastic wrapping.

'This is for you, too, Nicole. It's something we can all share: 'Construction Man'. He goes nicely with your boots.'

Luke's demented laugh had returned, the one that had cut through Willie's haze the night before, asking the question as to what he was doing hanging around with someone he didn't really like. The laugh got up Nicole's nose as well, it seemed, because now she was paying attention.

'You're a pervert,' she said, very flat and well directed. She didn't like Luke either.

'Not a pervert,' he replied. 'A pervert is someone who fucks little children. A pervert is a paedophile. I only fuck grown up people and rubber dolls. I am not a pervert.'

He was delighted with the attention and keen to start the show. Ari giggled.

For the first time since he'd arrived at the club, Nicole looked directly at Willie. She wore a mask of alabaster skin and painted lips. There were dark holes for her eyes, devoid of light, and deep within those holes, somewhere, Nicole was looking at him. His chest tightened and his heart beat rapidly. A cold flush swept over his skin. Everything in the room disappeared except the hollow eyes in the mask of her face. He waited and waited but she didn't speak. His mouth was so dry he felt unable to release his tongue.

'Those pills,' he stammered; 'the ones we took last night...'

Where was she? He quickly searched her eyes. She was coming to the window, he could feel it. She would suddenly appear. The blood was rushing through him in a torrent that roared in his ears.

'Because,' he stammered again, 'I don't remember ...'

'Normison.'

'Normison?'

'They help me to sleep.'

Luke giggled. Willie's blood was moving so fast that his heart couldn't keep up with it. A sweet and sour flush, part pleasure and part pain, raced up his legs and into his groin and he began to rock, keeping the channels open, afraid of the potential rupture if he interrupted the flow.

'What's your name?' she asked.

'Willie.'

'Your other name.'

'Saville.' He couldn't breath.

'I hate that name. If your name is Saville,' he heard her say; 'don't ever come into my room when I'm asleep or I will cut you. I sleep alone.'

The amphetamine rush took him over the rapids and into the foaming turbulence below, smashing him against the rocks and tossing him into the air like a weightless doll. When it had subsided he realised that she'd left the room and Ari had gone with her.

53.

The Grounds of the Darlinghurst Gaol

Roger didn't hear the end of Bob Summers' speech because the beeper on his cell phone told him he had a text message. Whispering to Sam that he had a call of nature, he left the table and went outside.

The perfect spring day had delivered a perfect spring night, cool but clear and without any hint in the air of the rain forecast for tomorrow. The sky above the city had absorbed the glow of street lamps and headlights but within the walled courtyards of the old penitentiary the shadows were deep and shapes were unclear. Roger paused briefly outside the door of the Cell Block Hall, checked the brief text message on his cell phone confirming that Maxine would be waiting at the gate, and allowed his eyes to adjust to the gloom.

The jail had been designed as a coach wheel. The hub was the circular building holding the bathhouse and chapel and the cell blocks were the spokes. The wheel's rim was the stone wall and watch tower that formed a high barrier against the outside world. Though now converted to provide class rooms and offices for a busy technical college, the jail buildings this night were mostly in darkness and the students absent. Sounds of laughter and applause flowed out through the Cell Block door behind him into the dark night, echoing across the worn flagstone paths and dissolving against the round walls of the chapel.

While dealing earlier with the greeting of guests at the Forbes Street gate, urging Greg to go on ahead with Butch while he waited for his wife and daughter, then following Joanne's lead because she knew her way, he hadn't taken notice of directions and now he was confused as to where they'd come in. Beyond the perimeter walls the steady roar of city traffic offered him some clues. To his right the roar was heaviest and he could picture the stream of traffic pouring up Oxford Street into Taylor Square and turning off towards Randwick and the Eastern Distributor. Further away, beyond the chapel in front of him, the noise was muted, lighter and less urgent. That would be where the taxis were turning into Darlinghurst Road heading for the Cross, slowing to allow the cabbies to express their prurient disdain for the rent boys leaning against the outer wall of the Gaol before speeding away in disgust. They definitely hadn't come in that way, and he was pretty sure they hadn't come past the chapel, so he turned around and headed in the opposite direction. There were signs to the Administration Office that he didn't recognise and then he saw the large black painted steel gates that opened onto Forbes Street and he immediately slowed down.

It was colder than he'd first thought. A light breeze ruffled his trouser legs and he shivered. He hadn't touched his wine at the table but that vodka he'd taken at the office had made him feel queasy; that and the shock of seeing Alison Pyke and then being ignored by her. He needed to know what that was about because there'd been something deliberate in her actions which he hadn't liked.

But now he had a more pressing issue to face. The light outside the gates was bright and there were people on the pavement and cars passing. He hadn't considered the possibility of being observed when he retrieved the briefcase from Maxine, had only presumed that the exchange would be swift and terse, inscrutable to passers-by, as enigmatic as all the casual exchanges made upon the streets of a large city at night. Then the reality of what he was doing and the proximity of the hall and his dinner guests made him pause. A quick exchange in open view would be easy to explain but if Maxine harboured further ambitions and an argument developed then it might prove more difficult. His own intentions were quite clear: pay the money and be done with it. He was past anger. But what if her instincts were to press for more? Could he trust himself not to react in anger then? Fuck, it was one thing to admire her gall but quite another to allow her to keep upping the ante; yet the cold wind that seemed so at odds with the mild night was like a poltergeist seeking his attention. Wake up, it was whispering. The cash in your pocket isn't about to be paid out as a reward for the recovery of stolen goods; this transaction is all about your inability to make it public. This is blackmail, and blackmailers rely on fear of discovery to keep their victims' payments coming.

No, there was no way he was going to stand openly under the street lights and exchange money with a prostitute; he'd do the business under cover of the trees that overhung the internal gardens of the jail, blending with the complex shadows of the tall palms and the thick shrubs. He didn't need light to know what he was doing, only resolve.

Thus resolved, he tilted his head back, adjusted his jacket and in less than twenty purposeful strides he passed through the open gate and reached the edge of the pavement. The traffic came from his right and he looked that way as if expecting a vehicle with which he had a rendezvous. The people who'd been standing outside the gates were now walking away from him, unaware of the act he was performing. Maxine, he guessed, must be behind him and to the left. He made a show of examining his watch and then turned to look to his left as well, as if frustrated that his rendezvous had failed. She was leaning against the steel standard of a parking sign, the briefcase at her feet, waiting for his acknowledgment, but he continued his act without looking at her, sighed audibly in exasperation and then returned back through the gates.

He uttered only one word, 'Follow', and continued on without looking back.

54.

The Stage of the Cell Block Hall

What could Albert say or do? When confronted with complex issues that have defied the best attempts at explanation, a sensible person is well advised to hold his tongue. Men of few words understood that gratuitous verbiage only obscured the issues further and Albert, of all men, was the one with the fewest words of all. He'd avoided all this. His memories and his feelings had survived very well, locked away in silent darkness, protected against the deterioration brought on by constant examination. They were preserved in formaldehyde. Opening the lid would only expose them to contamination.

But as he reluctantly climbed the stairs onto the stage, urged on by the rhythmic clapping of the audience, his legs creaking in a cruel echo of Bob Summers' parody of old age, Albert realised that he was now sixty years older than the events he'd sought to preserve. What if the formaldehyde was no longer working? Would it hurt to take the jar out into the light and examine it? Summers was blatantly milking the audience for applause, applause that reflected upon himself and swelled the hearts of his audience with false sentiment and self admiration and he, Albert, was being press-ganged into performing in a populist's promotion, he knew that, and yet there was no escaping it. He couldn't sit obstinately in his chair shaking his head when he'd already been threatened that they wouldn't stop clapping until he came on stage; and he couldn't stand mutely once he'd got there, believing that the power of silence out-muscled rhetoric.

Now Summers' hands were all over him, turning him around to face the audience, patting him down like a bullying quizmaster with a bag full of sponsors' prizes and a gormless contestant who needed to be guided through the process of winning them; his florid face glowing with the pleasurable knowledge that the audience had given him permission to behave as he thought fit.

'And what I failed to tell you, Ladies and Gentlemen, is that Albert's granddaughter is also with us here tonight and today they marched together in memory of those long dead and that's what Anzac Day is all about and that's why it will never cease to be the most important day in our nation's calendar, because each generation recognises the debt we owe to those who sacrificed their lives. Without them there would have been no freedom, democracy and prosperity as we know it.'

The words spilled from his poker machine mouth like they'd all struck the jackpot; brightly packaged coins of propaganda falling in a torrent before the gullible spectators. He had no right to sequester the moral capital of others in this way, Albert thought, but, God knows, they were all guilty of complicity. The words slid out so easily, and hadn't he, Albert, allowed Samantha to talk this very same way that afternoon? Hadn't he fallen into the trap of accepting platitudes and clichés from someone he loved because he could find nothing better with which to rebut them?

'But I'm not going to tell you what Anzac Day means to me. I only want the opportunity to say thank you, on everyone's behalf; thank you to all those who answered the call and were prepared to lay down their lives in defence of our country: to Albert, to Albert's father before him and to all the young men of their generations who offered themselves so unselfishly. Let us say thank you while we still can.'

Summers had his arm around Albert's shoulder and he squeezed him, trying to force some words out of him and into the hand-held microphone which he waved between their two mouths; something safe, something banal to prove what a great old digger Albert was - Bob Summers' very own pet Anzac. His breath was extraordinarily ripe, like fresh mangoes grown in the rich soil of his own performance, mangoes that could so easily turn and go rotten, and Albert held himself stiffly, his head partially turned away from that breath, his lips thin and straight. But the awful thing was that Albert couldn't think of anything to say and what was squeezed out of him was just a grunt, a sort of semi-compressed burp that sounded vaguely like 'thank you', at which he immediately shook his head for obviously that wasn't what he meant. The stage lights shining up into their faces made him blink and Summers' arm around his shoulder might be suggesting to the audience that he needed holding up. Let us say thank you while we still can. The old codger's not long for this world, as you can see.

'Tell us, Albert,' the quizmaster prompted, 'was the sacrifice worth making or, now that you see how we've all turned out, do you have second thoughts?'

Oh, he was good. The money or the bag? Come on, you've got to answer and you can't say, 'neither', because that's not part of the game. The audience understood the game and they all laughed, but Albert shook himself free. He wasn't a small man. Though he knew his bones were no longer as thick as they used to be and his skin was a trifle looser, he still stood tall with a full head of hair and he was damned if he'd let the old codger tag rest comfortably on him - let alone that of the performing monkey - so he took the microphone out of Summers' hand and cleared his throat.

'To be honest, Mr Summers,' Albert said quietly, 'we didn't do it for you. I don't think we had any idea at all why we were doing it. We were just doing what we were told.'

He smiled, because he knew that Summers had been making a joke and he didn't want to appear unpleasant, but a portion of the audience laughed. Was what he had said funny also? Then he needed to correct that.

'I apologise if that sounds rude. My discomfort with what you say about Anzac Day, you see, is this notion that young men were somehow in possession of the facts and knew the consequences of what they were doing yet deliberately marched off to sacrifice their lives for others. It simply wasn't like that. We were completely ignorant of everything.

'Well,' he looked around for Summers who seemed to have stepped back beyond the arc of the footlights, 'if you want to send young men to war that is the best way to keep them, I suppose – completely ignorant.'

He lowered the microphone. That was as much as he felt inclined to say and yet the sudden silence in the hall seemed to confirm that it was incomplete as it stood. Either he was being rude or he was being foolish. God, this was the last thing he'd wanted, but now that he'd started it needed a fuller explanation.

'Please don't think I'm belittling the sacrifices made. That ignorance probably made the sacrifices even more admirable. I'm just saying that nobody going off to war can ever have the faintest idea of the reality until they experience it.

'There was a time, you know, when ex-servicemen didn't want the public to take part in Anzac Day for this very reason. They didn't think people who hadn't been there and fought would ever understand the reality and the day would turn into something else; a festival of death or a rallying cry for patriotism. And they were right, that's exactly how it's turned out, but I suppose we'd have to ask what would be the alternative. Should we let the whole thing fade away and be forgotten?'

How could he say this without showing his contempt? Grief was personal. It didn't belong to the State, and certainly not to someone like Bob Summers. It was something that resided privately inside, never to be forgotten. Most importantly it was not something to be dressed up gaudily in playmaking robes and performed year after year like a Santa parade. That's what he'd wanted to tell Sam.

'I can see that it's important for each new generation to be confronted by the story of war, but who among us knows what the true story is? My granddaughter showed me her school project today and it's clear that she knows more facts about Gallipoli and the war dead than I'll ever know, but I can't decide whether those facts should make her proud or angry. I don't know what to tell her. My dead mates wouldn't know what to tell her either. The sad truth is that war soon becomes history and history is doomed to repeat itself. People will still keep going to war whenever politicians make a reasonable excuse for one. Only the weapons and the enemies change.

'But perhaps I've said enough. That isn't why you're here.'

He held out the microphone in Summers' general direction,

expecting him to take it from him, but unable to see above the glare exactly where he was standing. The room seemed unusually quiet as if it had retreated from him. Perhaps Summers was refraining from coming forward, he thought suddenly, because he wanted to distance himself from what Albert was saying. He'd expected him to play the game and stick to the tried and true vocabulary but instead he'd broken from the rules. Whatever he was, he wasn't sounding like Summers' pet old digger was meant to sound.

'And I don't mean to attack politicians,' he apologised, forgetting at first to hold the microphone to his mouth so he was forced to repeat himself.

Still there was no movement from Summers. Perhaps he'd taken it personally.

Albert cleared his throat and looked up beyond the lights to where he knew the audience to be.

'The thing is ... It makes me uncomfortable when people attribute freedom and prosperity to war.'

He raised his voice because he didn't want to sound uncertain about this. It was important that, if he was going to say anything, at least he got the facts right.

'I don't believe that's what war delivers and I don't want my grandchildren to believe it either. If we have freedom and prosperity in this country it's because social equity and welfare was demanded by people as a reaction to the Great Depression and they were willing to vote for anyone who gave it to them. 'Never again', people said, meaning starvation and ruin, not war. Do you see how easily that's forgotten?'

This was what he'd meant to say to Sam that afternoon. It was something he needed to explain to Joanne, too. Their family had spilled blood on account of poverty and shame. Was that less meaningful than a casualty of war? When would they ever have a chance to talk about all of that? Who else was there to explain it to them, if not him?

55.

The Grounds of the Darlinghurst Gaol

Roger didn't like any of this. He didn't like the position he was in and he didn't like being in the dark, but he was damned if he was going to allow the two of them to be seen.

Ironically, all he could think of was his wife because Joanne had said over dinner that prisoners made the best gardeners. She'd been putting a proprietorial stamp on the venue, showing how much she knew about the place and he'd only half listened. The prison Governor would have had the finest residence, she said, and that was the building facing him as he returned in through the gates, and he would have had the finest garden, too, and that was where Roger headed, walking quietly on the stone pathway because he didn't want to turn and see if Maxine was following, listening for her footsteps instead.

'And if you believe it,' Joanne had also told her audience, 'the ghosts of prisoners still tend their gardens, and if you pick certain flowers the ghosts will follow you home. Isn't that lovely?'

'No,' Sam had protested, 'ghosts are not lovely, they're scary.'

'But a great way to stop students from damaging the gardens,' Joanne had explained, and everyone had laughed.

There was laughter and applause now, drifting through the night air from the Cell Block Hall, and Roger guessed that Bob Summers must be winding up his speech. Did that mean the evening would be coming to an end or were they slated for more gripping outpourings of jingoism and patriotism? He didn't know. He hadn't paid attention. Surely to God they wouldn't be finishing this early? He stopped. There was no sound of footsteps behind him. Bugger! She hadn't followed. He turned around in alarm and nearly tripped over.

'Christ!' he swore.

She almost trod on him. Her shoes must have had rubber soles. He was jumpy. His heart was racing.

'What the fuck are you doing?' He hissed angrily.

He hadn't planned on being angry. He was tense, one ear on the sounds from the hall. He wanted it finished quickly. The briefcase was in her hand and he lent forward and grabbed it firmly. He didn't want her to fight him, to cause his anger to explode, and she let him have it without resistance.

'I'm so sorry it didn't contain anything valuable,' he said sarcastically. 'You've been to so much trouble for nothing.'

Her face was a mask. He'd forgotten how tall she was, how still and deep; a mute, expressionless vessel into which he'd poured his own dark oils without giving or being asked for an explanation.

'Did you hate me for what I asked you to do?' he demanded. 'Is that why you stole from me – looking for revenge? You sell sex you know. If you didn't like it you could have objected.'

Part of him wanted to swing the briefcase through the air in a broad arc up and over the horizon of the prison walls and back down hard into her face, shattering the impassive calm of her ceramic mask. Why the fuck was he the one feeling guilty? He had nothing to be ashamed of.

'Do you realise you've just lost a good customer?' he asked.

'The world is full of customers,' she replied flatly.

It was extraordinary; she continued to behave like she was in control. All the time this had really been a power game. The money he'd paid her, and the money he would pay her now, was her demonstration to him that she retained command over him. No matter what she permitted him to do with her body it was at her consent and his cost, she was saying. His deeds reduced him, not her, because she had never participated in them. She could permit anything.

He fumbled with the catch on the briefcase and opened the lid. Even in the dark he could see that his documents were there. He felt in the pocket of the lid for his passport and then took out the manila folder containing the valuations, awkwardly pinning the briefcase under one arm while opening the folder and squinting at its contents. Of course it was all there. Why wouldn't it be all there? It had no value except to him.

He closed the case again and put it on the ground and then he took the wad of notes out of his pocket that he'd accumulated from the Martin Place ATMs that afternoon. He didn't attempt to count them. His anger evaporated as suddenly as it had come and he couldn't think of anything to say so he bent down and picked up the briefcase again.

'Just a minute,' a male voice said suddenly.

Roger stepped back, startled. There was someone else in the shadows behind Maxine who he hadn't noticed.

'Won't you count it Maxine?' the man said. His voice was vaguely solicitous, almost gentle.

'I don't need,' she replied disdainfully. Then she turned on her heels and walked away, casually stuffing the notes into her hand bag as if they were no more than loose change.

As his alarm subsided, Roger allowed himself to smile at her retreating figure. So, she'd brought her pimp for protection. He should have realised she'd have to share her winnings. But what neither of them had understood was that money meant nothing to him compared to inconvenience. She probably believed she'd scalped him. How little she knew. It wouldn't have mattered to him if she'd wanted ten times that amount. She wasn't in control, he was. Whatever she felt about the power of consent was meaningless compared to the power of money. Well, she was just another body for sale, the bitch, and he could buy a dozen like her.

Their dark silhouettes briefly appeared in the light of the open gate onto Forbes Street, turned left and disappeared from sight, like creatures of the demi-monde silently returning to it. Roger sniffed the night air and shivered. He didn't like the dark. He had a fear of fruit bats and there were big old trees in the prison grounds that were certain to harbour them. He turned and headed back towards the lights of the Cell Block Hall.

56.

The Stage

'To be honest,' Albert admitted to the silent hall out beyond the foot lights, 'I don't like Anzac Day. I'm unable to find a proper explanation to justify the deaths that others were unable to avoid. It always feels to me like the day has been purloined by the living from those who are dead; that we are using it for our own purposes and not paying close enough attention to what those purposes are.

'To be honest … There, I've said it again and I swore I never would!'

He shook his head ironically. That's something he hadn't been. If he was honest he would stop being oblique and say what he really thought instead of prevaricating. It might not change anyone else's view but at least it would allow him to salvage something from the day. Could he tell them about Jim Percy? How would they handle that? How would he handle it? He'd never talked to anyone about Jim, yet it is probable that he'd been silently rehearsing, unbeknown to himself, for a long time, and that is how Albert felt as he began. This was a story that he knew well even though he'd not told it before. It was not a story about himself and yet it was one that he realised he felt a need to tell. Perhaps it was the presence of Joanne and Sam that suddenly made this seem the right occasion.

'I once had a mate who used to criticise me for using that phrase – 'to be honest'.'

He looked at the microphone that he'd tried to hand back to Bob Summers and then lowered it. He wasn't giving a speech, he was sharing a memory. Those who wanted to hear would have no trouble doing so.

"Are you saying that you're not normally honest?' he'd ask.'

Those damn lights were so bright that his eyes were watering. It was easier to half close them.

'He had a point, I suppose. We don't listen enough to what we're saying. I suppose that's my point now. The more you say something the less meaning it has. If you repeat 'Lest we forget' often enough you'll soon forget what it is you're not meant to be forgetting.'

He shifted his feet and bent his knees a little. It wouldn't do to suddenly lock up and find himself losing his balance.

'My mate's name was Jim Percy. He and I enrolled on the same day in 1942 and went into training camp together. He came from Dungog, not far from Stroud. He was a good bloke but he was one of those people who used to question everything. Being his mate could be a bit tricky at times as he was always in trouble with authority. He had no truck with knee-jerk appeals to patriotism, you see. 'How hard do politicians and generals have to think about sending people off to their deaths,' he used to demand, 'if no-one ever objects?' They reckoned this made him a conscientious objector, but then, if that was the case, he wouldn't have enlisted, would he? He wasn't so much a conscientious objector as a *conscious* objector: a pain in the backside some would say.'

He might as well admit that. It was no good trying to sanitise the story because that would make him just as guilty as everyone else. Tell it as it was. He was your friend but he made you feel uncomfortable.

'Just before we shipped out, Jim was transferred out of our unit and I never saw him again. The word went around that he'd questioned one order too many, because one of the things about discipline and punishment in closed societies like the Army is that it can develop a momentum and be hard to stop. Jim's questioning had become dangerous to be around. It provoked increasingly hostile reactions. We didn't know what they'd done with him and we didn't ask. It was safer not to know.'

They didn't want to know because they were powerless to do anything about it. They'd bought into the system and had to live by it. That was the reason for his shame and his silence. That was the thing he needed now to confess.

'If we ever talked about him we said he was a lucky bastard, saved from death by an over-active tongue; a traitor to his mates. There were many in my platoon, including myself, who were happy to see him gone because it can be quite a strain that constant questioning. I think we all accepted that unquestioning obedience was necessary in war and Jim would have been a hindrance. Most of us happily took orders and never asked. If I'm honest, it was a relief to have Jim gone. We weren't to know the truth – there was so much happening, so much urgency and chaos – until after the War had ended and we returned home. It turned out that he'd put his hand up to become a wireless operator and was sent up to the Gilbert Islands to monitor Japanese ship movements as they sailed south from the Marshall Islands.'

There, he'd said it. When Jim had disappeared from the regiment he'd felt relief. Proximity to constant dissidence had not just made him uncomfortable, it had actually frightened him.

'There were seventeen wireless operators in the Gilberts apparently, and they were all captured by the Japanese. It seems that none of them were armed. I'm not sure but I think that was a convention, not to be armed; if so, it explains why Jim volunteered, because he was never comfortable about the thought of killing people even though he accepted the need to go to war.

'Anyway, having captured these unarmed coastguards the Japanese tied them up and left them out to burn for three days in the full sun. This was the equator and their skin would have fried and begun to blister on the first day. On the second day their eyes would have swollen and closed and their lips would have sealed shut. On the third day they were dragged into a clearing, forced to kneel in a circle and one by one they were beheaded with a Samurai sword. I'm sure Jim would have questioned that if his lips were capable of forming the words, not that it was ever going to save his life, and I think now that Jim was the only one among us who had it right.

'You could ask what sort of human beings would do that to others, I suppose. We did ask that question. Shinto was the national religion of Japan. It called for unquestioning obedience to the Emperor, who was seen as divine, and they obeyed ideals of military chivalry which we regarded as cruel and bizarre, yet we believed in unquestioning obedience, too.

'The enemy is always discredited on moral grounds but your own side never is. Why was there no protest against the systematic campaign of civilian slaughter by the Allies; the deliberate targeting of non-combatants on such an enormous scale in Germany and Japan? I'm talking about Dresden and Frankfurt and Hiroshima and Nagasaki. Even to this day, is the killing of civilians still seen as just retribution? When we started to realise after the War what had happened on both sides we thought it was all so obvious that everyone must have understood and all we had to do was ensure that nobody forgot. We saw no harm in allowing the United States to demonise communism because Stalin was the devil, just as Hitler had been. We saw no problem in confusing Judaism with Zionism because one was a victim and the other was a solution. In fact, as it turns out, no-one understood. The Japanese went to war to extend the realm of their divine Emperor's imperium. Now, today, America is a religion and the test of your Americanism is how much you believe in America and how much you demonise Muslims.

'I'm sure that if Jim were alive he would ask the questions and I'm ashamed of my own silence. Venerating Anzac Day in the way we do only adds to that silence. As Jim so rightly knew, patriotism must be questioned every inch of the way if it's not to be used against us. When that happens we probably can claim to have true freedom. But I don't know about prosperity. It seems to me that everyone is in debt because they've been persuaded that their lives will be so much better if they have everything. Is that what we mean by prosperity?

'I didn't mean to say any of this and I certainly don't question the sincerity of those who want to show their respect for all who've died. I now accept that there'll always be war and whatever it is in mankind that threatens our safety and freedom is never fully beaten but merely licks its wounds and retires to await another day. But I hope, when the young are called to war again, they will, like Jim, not go without questioning.

'There was a song we used to sing in the Fifties and Sixties which ended with the line, *'When will they ever learn?'* You must know the one. No-one seems to sing it anymore. I suppose we know the answer.

'Now, Mr Summers, if you don't mind, I want to hand back this microphone and ask you to help me find the steps so I can get off this stage, because I've said more than I ever intended and a lot more than I should ...'

57.

Outside the Cell Block Hall

Well, Roger thought, he'd handled that fairly well, all things considered. Okay, he'd slipped up by leaving her alone in the apartment, but that was only because he'd wanted to perform for Joanne. If he hadn't realised he was running late he never would have allowed Maxine to remain there on her own. And being so intent on getting home for dinner with Albert had caused him to forget his briefcase. But he'd handled it. He always handled it. No need to beat himself up over it. He'd flown close to the flame but he hadn't been burned by it. It might be a good idea, though, if he gave up that apartment. He'd lost his enthusiasm for it a long time ago.

He took a long, deep breath of the night air. It didn't seem so cold now. The applause inside the hall had died away but the fainter sound of a voice over a microphone suggested that a new speech was in progress. If they went on too long he would suggest to Butch Astor that he took him back to his hotel early. He could run through the valuations with him and get a feel for where he was at. It might be a good idea to separate him from Greg Cummings, as well, and make sure he hadn't been given any false ideas. There was only one way to run negotiations like this and that was one-on-one.

He lengthened his stride. The sooner they were away from this place the better. He couldn't understand why people could like the idea of entertaining in an old prison, let alone building a school there. Not that he believed for one moment in ghosts or the concept of places being haunted – that was just the product of imagination – but it stood to reason that if you built a place for incarceration and hanging it was always going to have that atmosphere about it. They should have pulled the damn thing down.

Enjoying the feeling of relief that flowed from the briefcase now held so comfortingly in his hand, and intent on getting back to Butch, Roger had failed to notice the glow of a cigarette in the darkness against the Gaol House wall, so when he heard his name called out softly he stopped abruptly. Locating the cigarette but being unable to make out its owner, and not immediately recognising the voice, he made an assumption.

'Marjorie?'

She laughed.

'No.'

He stepped closer. His heart was thumping, the feeling of relief instantly replaced with anxiety. He'd been observed. He'd need an explanation.

'Who's Marjorie?' she asked.

She moved forward out of the shadows and her smile was unmistakable.

'Alison ...?'

The smile that always seemed to be sharing a secret; the eyes of the silent witness. Had she observed him?

'I didn't know you were a smoker,' he said in mock disapproval, trying to be casual.

She ground out her cigarette stub with her foot. His earlier impression, that she was looking more glamorous than he remembered, was reinforced. It wasn't just the extra flesh exposed; it was the bloom on her skin and the tilt of her chin. Was this what happened to women when they were being fucked and wanted everyone to know it?

'You didn't say hello when you came to see Greg at our table. I was hurt. I wondered what I'd done.'

He let her see that he was calm and relaxed and deliberately intent on being charming. There was no safer distraction, after all, than flirtation.

'I didn't want to interrupt you,' she replied unconvincingly.

He had the impression that she was feeling awkward. There

were any number of reasons why that might be. He remembered her distant expression as she'd lain on her back beneath him in Hayman Island and wondered if that was what she was remembering, too. Did Greg manage to get more out of her than an enigmatic smile when he was rooting? The truth was that seeing them together he'd been jealous. Of course, Greg was an eligible bachelor. Women didn't screw for orgasm; they screwed for property and security. She probably screamed her head off for good old Greg.

'Well, this is a happy coincidence as I've been meaning to call you.' He reached out and squeezed her arm, making the gesture more fraternal than intimate. 'I have a proposition I want to discuss. It's a job offer. I've hesitated to call because I didn't know how the Bank would react if they knew I was trying to poach you but I'd like, at least, to have the chance to talk to you about it because I think you might be interested.'

He was going to add that it would, of course, be strictly business, but something cautioned him against it. He was already talking too quickly and saying too much. If she was surprised by his unexpected statement she didn't show it. Maybe that was the reason for his caution. She had an air of knowing, as if she was always a step ahead; but she can't have known he was going to offer her a job because he hadn't known himself.

'It would be a hell of a challenge but I have the feeling you'd be ideal for it. Why don't we meet early next week?'

She waited for him to say more but, in the circumstances, he felt he'd said enough. He'd need time to think through the details because this was a girl, he knew, who would catch him on the detail if he got it wrong.

'You want me to call and make a time?' she asked.

'Please do that.'

He reached forward and touched her arm again. She must have been flattered, or at least curious, but she wasn't going to display it. He suspected it wasn't her style.

'You keep strange company,' she said, changing the subject.

She looked off into the distance towards the Forbes Street gate and then back towards him with the smile he recognised from the bedroom on the island. It could have been mistaken for a knowing smile but it was actually only a technique; a smile used by a girl in a men's world to confuse people into thinking she knew.

'The courier ...? Yes, they get weirder and weirder.'

'She looked more like a prostitute.'

'Is that what you call the look? Whatever it is, it seems to be fashionable. So, next week then ...?'

He smiled warmly and then walked confidently away towards the door of the theatre where once again he could hear enthusiastic applause, thinking as he walked that he might have replied that all women were prostitutes and the least dangerous were those who stated their price. But, of course, he knew better than to say that to a woman.

58.

The Dinner Table

Joanne's heart had been in her mouth. It was so unfair of Bob Summers. Surely he would have known how mortified her father would feel being dragged up on the stage in front of so many strangers, being placed in the spotlight and having a microphone shoved in his face? You simply didn't do that to people of his generation; it was rude and thoughtless. And that awful flattery – so obviously insincere and over the top – would have horrified him. He was such a private man and he didn't deserve to be exposed to cheap city politics. Summers opened his mouth and out it all poured, cheap, cheap, insincere and thoughtless; so typical of politicians, so typical of all that her father would despise.

But why hadn't she gone forward and protected him? Hearing his name suddenly being called out she'd risen from her seat in shock and held out a hand to him, but his back had been turned to her and with the whole room applauding like it was some sort of game show of course he'd had no option but to respond, because he wouldn't have wanted to offend and that was what Summers would have calculated. He was using him. It was so cynical and blatant and they'd allowed it to happen. And where was Roger through all this? Why did he keep neglecting his guests?

She'd put her hands to her cheeks as soon as she'd heard the sound of Albert's name, for they'd flushed with shame. How was she going to convince him that they'd never intended this? Why should he believe her when it was so obvious that everyone at the table was using someone to promote their own cause? They were all as bad as each other. This was how they led their lives in Sydney; they were hucksters and arrivistes, endlessly self-promoting. It never ceased. And the whole room knew it. They all laughed when Summers asked his question (*'now that you see how we all turned out, do you have second thoughts?'*); laughed cynically and without embarrassment. Oh yes, we're all as bad as each other, they thought. Ha, ha!

She could have spat at him.

But oh, how dignified her father had been. How erect and calm, refusing to be pushed around; so much his own man, and then quietly showing that he had no intention of being treated as a puppet in Summers' game. Suddenly you could have heard a pin drop. Clearly the whole room had been expecting something different. They were relaxed and off-guard, comfortably full of food and wine, ready to be patronised. Only good things could be spoken of the dead and everyone felt a little better hearing them spoken. It was not entirely unexpected that an old man with a stiff back and steel grey hair should be invited to speak, for it was Anzac Day, after all. But what he said, and the way he said it; that's what silenced them. A few had laughed at first, but only because they were in the mood to do so, and then immediately they realised they'd made a mistake. His courtesy shone like a beacon in a sea of vulgarity. What powerful things good manners were, she had thought.

When they began to realise that he was not going to say what they expected, the audience froze; almost as if everyone were steeling themselves against being noticed. No-one touched their wine or moved their chair. The waiting staff seemed to disappear. Joanne had wanted to get up and sit beside Sam, to hold her hand, but just as she was about to push back her chair and move around the table Albert had decided to hand the microphone back to Summers. In doing so he must have switched the thing off and not realised it. Her heart went out to him and she didn't dare breathe for he brought the microphone back to his mouth and repeated what he'd just said but failed to notice that his voice was no longer being amplified through the speakers. The bright lights and the shock of being on stage must have disoriented him, and yet he appeared to have been quite unfazed. No-one called out, not even Summers moved to put the problem right, and yet, if anything, the failure of the microphone seemed to increase the impact of what he had to say. Perhaps it was because they were forced to concentrate. It wasn't a big hall. He didn't have a weak voice. He spoke as he thought, slowly and clearly.

Sam, who might ordinarily have been expected to suffer from a teenage cringe attack on seeing a member of her family being put under the public spotlight, had seemed transfixed. And then, of course, he'd made a point of mentioning her and she'd turned briefly to Joanne with a look of horror mixed with delight before turning back to him and proceeding to hang on his every word right to the end.

When all was said and done, and her father had made his way carefully down the steps and back to the table, her initial anxiety had proven to be misplaced. The applause was generous and the mood respectful. What he'd chosen to say was probably a timely antidote to the usual paean to patriotism that most speakers seemed to resort to on these occasions. God knows, everywhere you looked there were people at war, but they were people who'd been expressing their tribal and religious hatreds for hundreds of years. Surely Australia was immune from those sorts of problems? Never for a moment had she ever felt any fear that her own children would be involved in horrors like her father had experienced. But it was easy to forget the world that he and his generation had known and appalling to think of the thousands who'd been sent away to their deaths.

'It was a lovely speech, Dad,' she enthused, getting her breath back. 'I hope you don't think we knew that was going to happen. I truly had no idea.'

'It was wonderful,' Marjorie stated emphatically. 'Thank goodness you said what you did.'

Joanne's pride and relief, however, were overshadowed by a deep sense of loss. It was the feeling she had sometimes upon awakening, of a dull ache in her breast plate and a bruising of the muscles in her throat. Once, recovering the elusive images of the dream she'd experienced prior to awakening, she'd clearly remembered a small child falling into a swimming pool and slowly sinking to the bottom. She saw herself reaching out impotently, her legs unable to move her towards the pool. The child's eyes were closed and it sank gently, in slow motion, as if suddenly revealing it was not a child after all, but a water baby; a creature of another world that could never be loved with the sense of ownership accorded to a child of one's own flesh. The feeling of grief, then, was compounded by the realisation that the person being lost was never going to be able to be possessed. That was how she felt now.

She'd been driven to insist on her father's attention during the day like a competitive child, angry that he should tell that story of his own father; such an important story, yet being told to her for the first time almost incidentally. Why hadn't he told her before, she complained to herself? Not knowing had undermined her. Then there had been her surge of excitement upon learning that throughout all those years he and her mother had written to each other every month; the excitement tinged with ineluctable sadness, first for the tantalising failure of a relationship that might so easily have been all that she'd longed for it to be, and second, that she'd lived her entire life not knowing; believing herself to be the product of an utterly failed relationship when in reality it hadn't been that way at all. Her lifetime of loss was plucked from her. The child that was her closely held grief proved to be an altogether different creature: a water baby.

'Do you hate the Japanese?' Butch asked quietly once Albert had sat down.

He'd removed his dark glasses, which must have previously lulled Joanne into forgetting he was Asian for now she felt mildly panicked, scrambling frantically through everything that had been said in search of anything that might have been offensive.

'Gracious, no!' she blurted out on her father's behalf.

'It's often forgotten that Japan was our ally in the First World War,' Lawrence added helpfully.

'Quite right,' someone else chimed in.

So it wasn't necessary for Albert to reply; yet, once again, she felt that need to rush to protect him. Well, there was absolutely no doubt, now she looked at him properly, that Butch was one hundred percent Asian, despite his name and accent. Why on earth had he been invited, therefore, to an Anzac Day function? What had

Roger been thinking?

'Many Australians do, I think,' Butch continued pleasantly, 'and not only Australians.'

Around the table everyone leaned forward, looking silently at their plates, waiting for the next word. Joanne could see that it hadn't dawned on any of them until that moment just how inappropriate it had been to invite Butch to this event. They had collectively forgotten the significance of the Anzac gathering, treating it like all their other excuses for wining and dining, as just another opportunity to do business. What on earth had they been thinking? Where was Roger? Why was she having to deal with this on her own?

'That might have been the case once, Butch,' Greg answered on their behalf, 'but not anymore. Not this generation.'

Everyone nodded.

Joanne drew in her breath and held it tightly, not daring to catch her father's eye. No, their generation couldn't be held guilty of hating the Japanese, they were saying. Blame that on the old buggers. Blame that on Albert. Their generation got on well with everyone, particularly when money was to be made. Albert was on his way out, anyway; an obsolete curiosity from the past. This whole Anzac thing was just a quaint, meaningless custom. Drink up. None of that stuff mattered anymore.

Bob Summers returned to the table.

'Good speech, mate!' he boomed. 'Put me in my place, alright. Here's to Albert.'

They raised their glasses. Not Albert and not Joanne. The child floating in the pool, unreachable, could have been either of them.

Butch put his dark glasses back on and turned to her, smiling politely.

'My family name was Itagaki,' he said, as if making small talk. 'My father changed it after the War by deed poll. He liked the name Astor because John Jacob Astor was the richest man in America. He was known as 'The Landlord of New York'. General Itagaki, on the other hand, was 'The Butcher of Singapore'. As far as I know, he was no relation. What your father said was very interesting though.'

'Yes?'

'Is it a sign of prosperity if everyone is in debt? It is an interesting question. Of course, in the property business you cannot succeed without debt. That is the first thing you have to learn.'

'Yes. I think it was very different in my father's day. His generation never bought anything unless they could pay for it.'

No mention of the friend who was beheaded, then. What marked out her father was his questioning of prosperity. Perhaps she should explain that he was actually questioning her with that remark; criticising her spoiled lifestyle which was clearly anathema to him. Who else could he have been referring to? She'd always known that was how he felt, but the world had changed from the one he'd known, and it would never be the same again. There was no point trying to explain it to him.

'That was mean of you to call him up on stage,' she whispered to Bob Summers on her right. 'You might at least have given us warning.'

She felt compelled to whisper, as if they were gathered at her father's death bed. It would have helped if Greg hadn't spoken of this generation as if the other one (her father's presumably) no longer existed. That had been his inference. The world belonged to this generation now. The War had nothing to do with them, he was saying, and nobody at the table had objected. It was as if Albert and all that he had to say no longer mattered. Perhaps they were right. Perhaps that was why her legs were unable to move her towards the pool no matter how desperately she reached out.

At this point, Roger returned to the table as if nothing had happened. He wore that vague, infuriating expression that she'd learned not to bother to protest; the expression which, on this occasion, suggested there was nothing abnormal in deserting his dinner guests without explanation; and he was carrying, of all things, his briefcase, as if to make the point that there was no time when it was inappropriate to do business.

'Daddy,' Sam greeted him excitedly, 'you missed Grandpa's

speech.'

'What a shame! I didn't know he was going to give one.'

Joanne smiled at her daughter's enthusiasm but she couldn't help thinking that nothing was safe; no happiness was sure. Then the coffee arrived and the conversation became lively again.

59.

Outside the Cell Block Hall

Alison Pyke dropped her cigarette butt on the stone path and ground it out with the sole of one foot, swivelling her leg slowly and thoughtfully while peering into the darkness towards the Administration Office and the gardens that masked the exit to Forbes Street. She'd deliberately not eaten all day and felt edgy as a result. Two cigarettes in quick succession had killed her hunger but left her slightly light headed as if on the verge of a migraine. The lightness may have had something to do with her conversation with Roger Saville, or perhaps it was the anticipation of going home with Greg Cummings. Then again, she was due to get her period and that always filled her with static. All she knew was that the harder she looked into the shadows of the garden shrubbery where earlier she'd watched the silhouettes of Saville and the girl with the briefcase, the more the shadows played tricks with her eyes. She was sure she'd seen something white flutter to the ground before the girl and her companion walked away – so sure that she'd waited for one of them to stoop and retrieve it - but now she couldn't make it out. Perhaps she was mistaken.

In a minute she would go back in and quietly rejoin the Bank's table. There was no hurry; she'd served her purpose already by diluting the obvious ageist and sexist bias of commercial banking. They'd had their money's worth from her. It was ironic that a night which she'd dreaded in prospect had turned out to be such a bonus in reality. She smiled at the thought of Greg's pleasure in seeing her and his willingness to openly display it. She'd enjoyed standing there with him for the whole room to see. Being wanted made her body change shape. Her toes turned out, her belly moved forward and her neck tightened. It made her blood quicken and her breath freshen. Being wanted could sometimes trick her into feeling that it was the whole damn point of everything. It made the night air on her bare shoulders cause her to shiver as if caressed. But it wasn't everything. There was something far more satisfying and enduring and she'd caught a glimpse of it a moment ago.

She knew that Saville didn't want her, despite his charm and his finger tips deliberately laid on her arm. Oh, he was willing to be wanted himself, she suspected, but deep down she doubted that he cared. He worked on the basis of need. What she'd glimpsed, however fleetingly, was that he needed her. Why else would he offer her a job? He didn't even like her. (She'd seen that in his eyes as he had so ponderously screwed her to the Hayman Island bedhead.) Well, that was fine; she could walk away from being wanted whenever it suited her, but being needed was where she sought to be.

Alison adjusted the straps of her high heeled shoes and stepped lightly across the uneven paving stones towards the gardens of the Administration Block. Sure enough, she hadn't been mistaken. There was the piece of paper she'd seen flutter to the ground as Saville had apparently opened the briefcase that the courier girl had brought him. She bent down and picked it up, saw enough in the gloom to recognise that it was a letter and then tiptoed back to the window of the Cell Block Hall where it was light enough to read.

The letter was from Coleraines, the Valuers, and it was addressed to Saville Corp. She read the opening paragraphs quickly, conscious that the buzz of conversation coming from the hall signified that the speeches had ended.

Re: Whiteman's Creek Valuations (Attached)

She knew the firm and the writer well. Valuations were the Bank's prophylactic; the first line of defence against being deceived by clients.

> *We have supplied these valuations based on information provided by you and subject to the following comments and qualifications which must be read together ... etc, etc ... You have asked us to value the leasehold interest on the basis of ground lease terms that are, in our opinion, not commercial ...*

She stopped reading, folded it up neatly and put it in her clutch purse; then she swept her hair back over her shoulders and headed for the entrance door. Greg had said that he would come and join her at her table for coffee and she didn't want to miss him. She could read the letter in full at some later time when she would reflect properly on its significance.

60.

The Dinner Table

Lawrence stood and stretched his legs, picking up his chair and deliberately moving it back a pace or two to give himself room to clear Sheryl Summers' handbag and shoes which had spread across the floor to his left as she'd become progressively intoxicated. He refrained from excusing himself as he doubted that anyone would have been interested or even noticed. The fact was that he'd had little to say in the last two hours since Marjorie had chosen to announce to the world that she was off to France to show the good people of Bayeux how to make tapestries - as if they didn't know - and Bob Summers had countered by letting everyone know the mechanical details of his sex life. His silence had not only been intended as a demonstration of dignity, it had also been a clear signal to the whole table that he had been insulted in the most unforgivable way.

To give himself his due, it should have been apparent to everyone that this embarrassment was as much for others as it was for himself. Vulgarity, after all, had no place in mixed company, let alone among strangers, let alone on an occasion such as this which was, presumably, intended to be sombre and reflective. They were honouring the dead, for heaven's sake, not having a knees-up, but Marjorie (who he suspected had already had a drink or two before he got home) had insisted on regaling the table with her grand plans for an artistic sojourn in Europe while Summers wanted everyone to know about the modern marvels of medical clinics for men. Bad enough that the time and place were inappropriate, somehow the two subjects had become linked; that is, Marjorie's pronounced intention to travel and, *ipso facto*, desert her husband, and Summers' new found faith in male medicines.

'So, you're abandoning the marital bed in order to thread your weaves with a bunch of Froggies,' Summers had announced, in case anyone had misunderstood what Marjorie was trying to say. 'And what does the Master of the House have to say about that?'

'We don't have a Master in our house,' Marjorie corrected him, 'and I gave up the marital bed a long time ago. I couldn't stand the noise.'

What on earth had prompted her to say such a thing? Was she trying to be funny?

'Ah-ha, so he's a farter! You're not the only woman to complain about the involuntary night time flatulence of men, you know; we've all been guilty at some time. But the answer to the problem is quite easy. Tighten his bloody scrotum. Get the old Viagra working and he'll be as tight as a drum. Fixed me -- right, darl? Send him off to the Men's Clinic. You'll be back in the marital cot before you know it.'

'Perish the thought,' Marjorie had replied. 'Anyway, that isn't his problem. The problem is that Lawrence snores. You have to hear it to believe it.'

It was hard to imagine how mature adults at a formal dinner could suddenly go from farting to snoring in one easy bound, clearing the scrotum on the way, but it had happened. Lawrence, of course, was speechless. If it hadn't occurred to him before that his wife had no loyalty to him, then he certainly had no illusions at that moment. He'd been aware for a long time that she took him for granted, ignoring the premise on which equitable marital partnerships were based, *ipso jure*, that the benefits of his work and income required some compensatory input on her part. Try as he might, he could not think of one contribution that she made to his life. On the other hand, who did she think was going to pay for this fancy trip to Europe, and might it not have been politic to discuss it with him first before announcing it to the world? How would she feel if she went to the piggy bank that he so generously filled with her monthly allowance only to find it bare? How would her grand plans look then?

But discussion of one's sleeping habits and bodily functions went beyond disloyalty. It may have been amusing to others, but to Lawrence it revealed a vindictiveness that he would not readily forget. So why, of all people, had Joanne felt compelled to join the sport?

'Isn't it just the worst thing?' she added gratuitously. 'Why do men do it? It must have something to do with their Adam's apples.'

'Which only men have,' observed Cummings, 'because Adam felt guilty at eating the forbidden fruit, which caused it to stick in his throat; whereas Eve, being a woman, felt no guilt at all and swallowed it without any problem. The proof of this is evident in the total lack of guilt felt by women when they embark on extra-marital affairs compared to men who are racked by it. Am I right, Bob?'

'You're the expert, mate.'

'Women snore, too,' Roger Saville quite rightly noted. 'That fucks that theory.'

Lawrence was appalled that this conversation was taking place in front of Butch Astor, let alone the young girl, Samantha, so he had reluctantly moved to put them right.

'It is actually a perfectly natural phenomenon. Air is drawn down the Eustachian tube causing the soft palate to flutter against the back wall of the pharynx like the reed of an oboe. It can affect us all.'

'Some more than others,' Marjorie insisted.

'It doesn't bother me,' Sheryl said brightly.

But Marjorie had to have the last word.

'It's the most disgusting thing in the world,' she shot back.

She couldn't help herself; she'd always have to have the last word. Lawrence had seethed. Let her damn well go to France, he thought. Let her carry her own bags and order her own taxis and find her own accommodation and worry about when her money was going to run out: it would do her good. He'd made a mistake telling her about the painting. Now she'd be convinced they had money growing on trees. Well, he'd soon disabuse her of that belief.

For the time being he would keep his own counsel, but he was unlikely to forget this moment.

The conversation had then rambled off in different directions, leaving him to stew in silence. Joanne locked Butch into an esoteric discussion about Japanese art and culture, which was hardly the purpose of inviting him, but there was no way of breaking into that conversation and Roger was, as usual, so disinterested in the proceedings that he spent half the evening wandering off outside. The speeches, when they came, had been a welcome distraction.

What all this had meant for the prospects of their vital negotiations with Astor United Holdings seemed to have been completely forgotten. If he'd been the host he'd have made damn sure that he paid close attention to Butch and used every opportunity to feel out his attitudes. But, of course, he wasn't the host. It wasn't down to him, so the critical questions to which Bob Summers could have been called upon to give reassurances were destined to remain unanswered. It was an opportunity wasted; a further example, if one was needed, of Roger's laissez faire attitude to business. Well, one thing was for sure; Lawrence wasn't going to stand accused by association. It was time Roger – and Marjorie – received a lesson on the dangers of taking him for granted.

61.

Louee's Club

A different room, this time at the back of the house, smaller; just space enough for the four of them and one other. The one other was Luke's inflatable doll, *Construction Man.* Four crappy chairs positioned around a crappy glass-topped table. When they leaned forward to sniff through the straws their knees were up around their ears. This did not make Willie feel very cool. What the hell; it wasn't exactly a rave scene. Luke insisted on kneeling on the floor so *Construction Man* could occupy his chair. The inflating of the doll had seemingly exhausted him. At least that shut him up. The doll's legs stuck out straight into Luke's back like two giant pink sausage casings and it wore a stupid lolling grin like a retard in a wheel chair on a day's outing at Darling Harbour. Its other parts were, thankfully, obscured. Willie didn't want to go there. That was his main thought actually. Don't fucking go there.

The remains of two lines of speed smudged the table top like tyre marks on an open road. Shit, officer, someone's been speeding. Wasn't me. Must have been him. We didn't see the red light. The red light fills the whole fucking room.

Nicole had paid for it. This wasn't candy for kids like those little pink louees they'd had earlier. This was crystal meth. He didn't ask why. He had no money of his own so he could only go along with what was offered. Nobody asked why. She and Ari just appeared with it and he and Luke got up and followed them to the back room. Nursing anger and pain, Willie hadn't spoken since they left. He wasn't speaking now either.

He watched the others go first, feeling distant and left out, except that when they each sat back in turn there was still a half line lying on the table top and that was his, so he wasn't being left out after all. It took him a while to get it up the straw as he worked down the last of the line because he wasn't used to it but, aw shit, when it came on it was so fast it nearly knocked him off his chair. Now Willie could feel it racing through him, going like the clappers out along his arteries, looking for a gangbang. He could feel the Tibetan wind blowing through the snow capped mountains cold as ice and he felt absolutely pure. He was Lennon, he was Krishna, he was the cold hard truth and the purifying fire fuelled by pain in the crucible of destiny. He was an electron fleeing through weightless space at the speed of light, holding tight within himself all the powers of Teutonic fusion which, if once released, would explode into the universe with the radiant force of a thousand suns. He was God. He was life. He was gone. There was no stopping now. Out he went in the great elliptical arc that carries the blinding light on its powerful journey. His body became a supernova, one hundred million times brighter than the brightest star.

Oh, fuck. Oh, fuck.

Oh, how he longed to fly, Mother of Jesus, Mother of Mine, to be free, fleeing across the roof of the world, the mountains and valleys, spires and streams, silent and swift like a whistling glider with the speed of a jet, high, high and all alone. Down he zoomed, rushing at the earth's floor with the fury of an alpine eagle, talons bared, then up, up, pulling against the g-forces, climbing high towards the sun with his cheeks flattened and his eyes pinned shut, through the blue azure into the heart of the orange orb, melting into infinity, radiating forever deep waves of love and hurt for those, like him, who had loved and been hurt by the cold hard realities of living. So strong were his arms that they could crush giant boulders and render them to dust. His hands could throttle the life out of snarling dogs and snap the backs of rapists and muggers. His chest was an impenetrable cushion of muscle that could absorb all the weapons of hatred that the world chose to hurl at him, and nothing could hurt him.

Oh, fuck. Oh, fuck.

Wait. Slow down. Giant crabs crawled across the landscape beneath him in search of prey, out of the animation computer and the imagination of nightmares, towards the pleading eyes of their trussed-up prey. Willie watched and waited. How good was this? How long had he waited to be so sure of his inner strength? Bring it on, he breathed; bring it on. Nothing in all the world could harm him now. There was absolute certainty in this. The eagle became an albatross. The albatross wheeled in the wind and swept down upon the crabs now beached in fear beneath. Two flaps of his giant wings and he was away again, splinters of smashed crustaceans left dashed upon the rocks. The ocean heaved in envy at his freedom.

'Put the fucking accelerator down,' Ari shouted. 'I'm a Monaro.'

'Sshh! Sshh!'

The girl was talking. Nicole was talking. He'd saved her – saved her from the crabs – and she was talking. What was she saying? Oh, man, he was going so fast he kept leaving her words behind. All he could see were her eyes; eyes like Manu and Sam, deep within the recesses of a darkened room, reflecting the red of his exploding sun. He could listen to her words now because they had no power to hurt him.

'Fucking Monaro's shit, man. Fucking Spider Porsche is what I'm in. Fucking Holden Rodeo tooling down Parramatta Road on a Friday night, that's what.'

'Shut up, Luke. Fucking shut up.'

She was talking alright – talking Polish. She was saying, 'the walls are falling down around the ghetto and the rats are running towards the light while people who have eaten coal are poking out their tongues at the enemy who turns away in fright'. He could see the children in their rags running in the rubble and the thin coal-black hands of the starving widows pushing up the wooden cellar trap doors towards the light, their faces wincing in pain. A black shadow swept across the landscape as he swooped down to protect them. He was Icarus, the winged Schindler whose talons were powerful and benign. There would be no more suffering now, no pain and sorrow, no darkness and despair. In the Tibetan hills they would drink milk and wear saffron robes. All would be forgotten.

'There's a fucking place I know man, and I'm going to go there.'

He could feel it. He knew for certain that it could happen.

Ari was giggling and clutching his sides, almost falling off his chair, and Luke was doubled up in false agony as well, his whole body vibrating like a jelly, the vibrations transmitting through his back to the pink plastic legs of *Construction Man* behind him so that he was wobbling, too; his fucking great eight inch dong dancing around in the red firelight like a crazy witch doctor on a pogo stick inches away from Luke's head; and Luke turned around to follow Ari's excited pointing finger while Willie closed his eyes and whirled back into the furthest reaches of space.

'You all think with your dicks,' Nicole said with disdain.

Now Willie could feel himself coming back. There were no straight lines in outer space, it was all parabolic. Face it, man; *'a star that explodes catastrophically'*, that's the definition of a supernova. He knew that. Shit, that's the stuff you learn in school. It was all over in minutes; brighter than the brightest sun and all fucking gone in minutes, that was him.

'You run around like big men pretending you know how to rule the world and all the time you just little boys with dicks in your pants,' she said. 'Ha, ha, look at me; see how big I am. Ooh, my dick is so big. It's bigger than yours. Don't you think I'm clever?'

'Oh, fuck off,' Luke told her.

That was the problem. See, Luke was the orbiting companion star. Now he could feel it clearly. Luke was causing his gravitational collapse. He was being dragged down by the accretion of Luke's shit. But he didn't have to let it happen. He could kill Luke with one swift whack. Holy fucking shit; it was frightening how strong he felt. His muscles were going to explode. His legs were going to burst and shatter the glass-topped table into a million shards. Unless he held on tight it would all happen right there and he wouldn't be able to stop it. He had to block the room out. It was too small. Don't listen to the girl. She was turning out just like the bitch in the movie. Don't go there. Think of something else.

There were tiny toothpicks in the saucer on the lazy Susan at the yum cha luncheon in The Golden Dragon on that Sunday in December when they waited for his father to turn up, and nobody was hungry except him, and Sam played on her Game Boy and never spoke. He ate the crab all alone while his mother watched him. The crab shell cracked and splintered in his mouth and punctured the lining of his cheek so the ginger and chilli sauce blended with his blood and ran around inside his head until it found the tear ducts in his eyes. Why else would he have cried? He couldn't put his hand inside his mouth and remove the sharp shell. His hand was powerless. His mother watched. He swallowed the shell and choked.

Don't go there either. Go somewhere else. Go back into the hills. Find clear air.

'Even the big man in the striped business suit with the black briefcase and the polished shoes is just a little boy hiding his little dick, waiting to take it out and show it like he thinks it is the Eighth Great Wonder of The World. None of you are any different.'

'What was in that black briefcase, Nicole? Come on, you can tell little Luke-y. You can't stop fucking smirking so it must have been something good.'

'There was nothing in the briefcase. There's never anything. You are all just little boys waiting for your next wank.'

Luke gripped *Construction Man's* cock and rubbed it violently giving off his insane hyena's laugh while Ari giggled out of control. The wind whistled past Willie's head as he tucked it in to his chest and headed for earth. He'd flown too close to the exploding galaxy. Serotonin, dopamine and adrenalin began to leak from the gaping holes in his damaged body like blood from a wounded albatross and it was all he could do to hold himself aloft on his outstretched wings. Why had she said that to him about going into her bed? He had the strength to save her. Couldn't she see that even wounded and dying, he would have the strength to save her? For that was his destiny. When the supernova explodes, the expanding shell of debris creates a nebula that radiates for hundreds and thousands of years. He was Lennon, he was Krishna. Look, for God's sake, look and ye shall see. If he didn't speak out she would never know. Or was she really Nadine? Was she only interested in sticking a giant revolver in his mouth and making him suck it before she blew his brains out? Was that her game?

'I don't understand,' he said to Nicole, 'why you have to be so aggressive. What's with this stuff anyway? Come on. Come to the window. All this hiding in the dark is gutless. Why do you want to trample on everyone? Is that what the big boots are for? You wear your mini-micro skirt so everyone can see your fanny and all you want to talk about is men's dicks.'

'She paid for our speed,' Ari pointed out. 'Don't bite the hand that feeds you.'

No. Not good enough. He would have paid if he hadn't given his money to Luke and Luke hadn't spent it on the rubber doll. It was only money. There were far more important things. If these people didn't know that then Willie shouldn't be with them. It was his destiny to meet someone who would know – one or many. He needed to turn down that street where he'd never walked before and there he'd find them, because his life needed it. He fucking needed it now.

'You want us to get down on our bended knees or something?' Luke wanted to know, joining in.

He *was* on his bended knees. He reached across the table and snatched Nicole's cell phone that she'd left lying beside her abandoned straw.

'How much did you just get paid for the briefcase? Tell me Ari; how much was it?'

Willie couldn't get enough breath into his lungs. The table was too close and his rib cage was squeezed between his legs so he had to breathe quickly to compensate. The old heart was banging away like a saucepan lid in his ear drums. Everything echoed. Nicole was definitely now Nadine. He could see it in her eyes.

'Let's have a look in your Inbox,' Luke sneered, 'and I don't mean your cunt.'

'What briefcase?' Willie wanted to know. He didn't remember seeing any briefcase, unless it was the thing she was carrying last night. What the hell had happened last night?

'Oh, yes, oh, yes.' Luke crooned with delight; 'there are messages in your Inbox. Listen to this. Listen to this everyone. *'I want it. I need it 2nite. Bring it to me.'* Fuck, this is great. What's your working name, darling? What did he pay?'

'Give it to me.'

'What do they call you?'

'Give it to me.'

'Tell me your name.'

'Maxine.'

'Fucking *Maxine*! Did you hear that? How dirty is that? I love it.'

For all the rapid breathing he was doing Willie still couldn't get enough air into his lungs. He needed to stand up. He needed to shout.

'What? You think there is something dirty in that, taking money from men? I'll tell you something dirty. It's you boys lying on the floor all night playing with each other's dicks. That's dirty.'

Willie's feet got trapped beneath him. His knees caught the hard edge of the glass-topped table as he struggled to stand up and he cried out in pain.

'Shut up! Fucking shut up!'

62.

The Dinner Table

The arrival of coffee at round table gatherings usually signalled an opportunity for guests to change places and converse with someone new. The first to vacate his chair was Greg Cummings, who'd apparently exhausted the intelligence of Sheryl Summers on one side and been exhausted in turn by Marjorie on his left. His eyes were elsewhere as if anxious to leave, but not without having a word with Lawrence first.

'Are we all set for tomorrow?' he wanted to know.

'I have draft agreements ready, if that's what you mean. Though I would have preferred more notice. These things aren't meant to be done in a day, you know.'

'Knowing you, I'm sure they'll be spot on. And what about the valuations?'

'Those are Roger's department. He assures me he has them.'

'Excellent! Well, the sooner we can get copies in front of everyone tomorrow morning the better our chances of getting agreements signed before Butch leaves. I know how much you desperately need this to happen. We're all banking on it.'

Greg's large hand squeezed Lawrence's arm reassuringly as he leaned down, lowering his voice like a Roman conspirator. Lawrence stiffened but refrained from replying, his instincts telling him that the judicious response was to present a deaf ear.

'They can be delivered any time,' he replied blandly, ignoring whatever inference Greg was trying to make.

The feeling was inescapable, despite Greg's assumption to the contrary, that Lawrence was not privy to all the facts, for there was nothing he'd ever heard spoken that would lead someone to suppose they desperately needed this deal to happen. It would certainly ease their position, yes, but not to the point of causing them to bank on it. Was that the impression Roger had been giving? When was he going to learn that he wasn't running a private company, answerable only to himself? He shouldn't be allowed to hold meetings on the company's behalf without another company member being present. He was putting them all at risk. It was quite inexcusable.

'Well, I have a prior and I mustn't keep her waiting, so I'm going to slip away quietly,' Greg whispered, 'and I'll catch you in the morning.'

Yes, well, presumably 'the prior' was Alison Pyke and that, thought Lawrence, was precisely what made Greg Cummings a lightweight, because any man who left business unfinished in order to *chasse la femme* was not to be taken seriously (not that Investment Advisers were ever creatures to be taken seriously). His departure, however, left one gap at the table which, unfortunately, was between Marjorie and Bob Summers; not, therefore, a gap that Lawrence felt inclined to fill. Then Roger got to his feet and moved around to the chair that Lawrence had vacated, leaving Butch Astor with an empty chair beside him. If there *were* agendas being run to which Lawrence was not privy then this was where he would likely discover them. He had an absolute duty to the Board, let alone to himself, to ensure that he could verify Astor United's intentions and, as charming as Joanne might be, he was sure that Butch would want the opportunity to talk to him also, so he took his coffee and moved to the other side of the table.

'Mr Astor -- Butch - Lawrence Beck,' he introduced himself. 'We'll be meeting tomorrow but I wondered if you had any thoughts on how you would like to handle the agreements. Presumably you would like your advisers to see my drafts as early as possible?'

'Yes, please.'

'And the terms are as you have negotiated with Roger Saville?'

'We have talked about the terms on the telephone and with Greg

Cummings. Of course, I have to see the valuations and also visit the site before the price is finalised. Roger kindly had the valuations brought here tonight so I can be prepared for the morning. You will have seen them, so presumably you are satisfied that I will be happy with them.'

'Of course! Yes, we all think it will be a very successful development.'

'And I understand from Greg the need for urgency as I believe it will not be possible to arrange the equity purchase after a certain date which does not give me very much time. Could you explain that to me, please?'

'Ah!'

How typical of Roger and Greg to have tried to impart urgency to the negotiations without explaining fully the reasons for that urgency.

'The ability to issue up to three percent new equity per annum was a special provision of the prospectus issued in June '99 and requires only Board approval. The provision expires at the end of three years, which is, of course, just two months away.'

Which is very convenient, Lawrence thought, but it might have been better if they'd explained the legitimate reason for urgency rather than letting Astor form the impression that they were merely trying to put pressure on him. It was a good thing Lawrence was able to explain it.

'It was a provision that allowed us to raise new working capital during the early stages of the development without making a general offer,' he went on, 'which, in this case, provides us with an excellent opportunity to invite you onto our share register at a favourable price, seeing we are going to be partners anyway.'

'Yes, but that is the point I don't quite understand. If the new shares can be issued at eighty percent of the average market price, why wouldn't Roger Saville, for instance, take advantage of that?'

'Oh, that's simple. His investment company, Saville Holdings, can't go beyond forty percent without making a full takeover offer; hence the opportunity for you.'

Perhaps it was just his manner, but Astor appeared to be confused. He took off his dark glasses and looked quizzically at Lawrence with that rather red-rimmed myopia which was characteristic of Asians. He may have been tired from his flight, or he may have been less well briefed on Australian regulations than he should have been, but the last thing Lawrence wanted was for him to be worried about the validity of the proposed transaction.

'You see, under our code you can go to nineteen percent ownership of a company, at which stage the creep provisions come in, but you cannot go beyond forty percent without making a general offer for all shares. The Proportional Takeover provisions in our company constitution allowed Saville Investment Holdings to go to forty percent but no further, unless he was prepared to make a full takeover offer. That's where he sits now and he is, as you know, our majority shareholder.'

Astor replaced his dark glasses and nodded, apparently satisfied that he understood. It would have been a lot better if Lawrence had been brought into the discussions earlier because nothing, in his experience, put negotiations off track as readily as a failure to fully explain all the details. Where there was ignorance there was doubt, and where there was doubt there was the potential for proceedings to fail. How many times had he tried to explain that to Roger?

'This is not the ideal place for a first meeting,' Lawrence apologised, 'and some of the conversation has not been – how shall I put it – exactly business-like, but I hope I have explained that properly.'

For heaven's sake, what must he have thought about Summers' vulgarity and Marjorie's airing of the bedroom linen? It made Lawrence shudder to think.

'Oh, yes,' Astor assured him. 'Actually, I found the evening very interesting. I've learned a lot about Australia tonight and I've had a very good conversation with Joanne about art and so I think I have been very fortunate to be a guest here, which I was not expecting. But I am also looking forward to reading the valuations and seeing Whiteman's Creek for myself tomorrow.'

Good, Lawrence thought; he might just leave it there then and start making a move. He was glad he'd introduced himself and shown the professional face of the company but there was no need to overdo it so he smiled, shook hands and excused himself, noting that Roger was also beginning to make a move, having finished smarming up Sheryl Summers for whatever reason. He needed to talk to him before he was engaged in conversation by someone else. Not for the first time, Lawrence was quite sure that he had the key that would unlock the transaction and ensure that it won the necessary approvals. He was also sure that their share price would rise as a result and that the deposit he'd paid on the Jeffrey Smart that afternoon was not going to weigh on him for long. Would Saville thank him? Would Marjorie thank him, for that matter? Probably not, but at least he'd have his own satisfaction. Nobody could take that from him.

63.

Outside the Darlinghurst Gaol

At last it was over.

The woman, Marjorie, who had done so much of the talking, took them in hand and led them through the prison grounds to the gate which she said led out onto Burton Street, which was the right direction for them to take, she insisted, if they wanted a taxi. Albert and Samantha followed obediently, having accepted Joanne's instruction that they go home independently as she and Roger were likely to get caught up with his Japanese business guest, and heaven knew how long that might take. Remembering the earlier tales of ghosts, Sam took her grandfather's arm for comfort. It was dark and the prison buildings were a maze so they were happy to follow the mother duck who'd assigned herself to their care. Lawrence, her husband, followed behind like a somewhat disapproving drake but Marjorie knew where she was going and found her way quickly out onto the street.

'Our car is just over there,' she pointed. 'If you go down to the corner of Darlinghurst Road there should be masses of taxis at this time of night. Would you like us to come with you while you find one?'

'No, no,' Albert protested.

So the four of them made polite farewells and went their own ways.

'I really didn't like that place,' Sam shivered. 'Do you think it's true that there are ghosts?'

Albert squeezed her hand and chuckled.

'Absolutely not!' he proclaimed.

It had been a long day and the little strength that remained in him was carefully rationing itself for the task of getting home to bed. So much had happened that he had difficulty in remembering it. Sleep would sort the memories out and allow him to form conclusions. For the moment he was uncertain whether he felt happy or sad, proud or ashamed. His speech had melted in his mind leaving only a puddle of mixed emotions to recall. It was as if he were recovering from an intense fever, as if the long march and the foreign surroundings had weakened him, robbing him of judgement, allowing him to speak of personal things to which he had never previously given voice. Either that, or some form of transubstantiation had taken place, releasing the body and soul of Jim Percy into his consciousness out of the Eucharist of an Anzac feast. How, then, could he so confidently deny the existence of ghosts?

It was all so confusing. The only thing certain was that an irreversible change had occurred in his relationship with his daughter and his relationship with himself. He'd peeled the protective cover off the family chest of Shameful Secrets, lifted the lid and found it to be empty. 'I know', she'd said. 'I know'. Forty wasted years exposed in a single day. He should have been happy, but instead he felt drained. He wasn't ready for so much emotion, let alone the intimacy it threatened. Before he could be comfortable confronting it again he needed to retreat and recover himself. With luck, if they found a cab quickly, he'd be able to go to bed before Joanne and Roger got home.

Following Marjorie's instruction, Sam went ahead towards the traffic lights on Darlinghurst Road, skipping, half dancing in relief at being freed from the dinner table; the constrained energy of her youth unable to resist the freedom of the open footpath. During the day Albert had been buoyed by this youth, lifted up and carried along by the lightness of her being but now, feeling responsible, and neither knowing nor trusting the environment, it worried him. He would rather she stayed close by his side. Perhaps he would have preferred also, if he could have brought himself to say it, that she were dressed differently; for the mini skirt and bare midriff that had seemed no more than a teenage expression of free choice back home in Mosman now seemed less appropriate in the glare of the late night public street lights.

He hurried to catch up, hoping that his expression of disapproval would somehow blanket her exuberance but unable to suppress the feeling that she seemed more in control than he was. Prompted by a green light, the traffic was accelerating past them and the taxi that stopped when Sam stepped out quickly in the road to hail it had to back up from the intersection to where they were standing. Cars coming behind tooted angrily, swerving to avoid it and Albert was forced to shake off his distractions and step forward to take over.

'We want to go to Mosman,' he explained through the front passenger window. 'Is that alright?'

The driver looked at him as if the question were unintelligible then pulled away suddenly through the intersection light with a screech of burning rubber.

'The bastard!' Sam said rather surprisingly, and Albert turned and frowned at her.

He didn't like profanities and her confidence, which he'd admired earlier in the day, was beginning to make him uneasy. He needed to get his bearings and, above all else, he needed to assert control. Darlinghurst Road, he could see, was a one way street with the traffic coming from the Oxford Street end and heading towards Kings Cross. Albert wondered whether Marjorie's advice had been correct and they mightn't have been better heading the other way, so he took Sam's arm and they started walking against the flow of traffic.

'What you have to do,' Sam instructed him pertly, 'is actually get into the cab and then tell them where you're going. It's the only way you'll get them to take you to Mosman if you're in town. They're obliged to take you.'

'And if they don't?'

'You can report them. They can lose their licence.'

'Where did you learn that?'

'A friend told me. It's like the law.'

'Then perhaps we should try it and find out if your friend is right.'

The contrast between her obvious comfort with the city's lores and his own discomfort was not lost on him. Fortunately the only cabs passing as they walked beside the Darlinghurst Gaol walls in the direction of Oxford Street already had passengers and their roof lights were turned off. Albert needed some time to adjust to this idea of occupying the back seat and insisting on his rights in the face of an unwilling driver. He feared that at this moment he lacked the resolve, for confrontation unnerved him at the best of times being seldom, if ever, called for in the environment where he'd chosen to make his home. Unlike his daughter, whose city instincts had honed her into a constant state of alertness, he was quite likely to allow himself to be driven to Campbelltown by someone who didn't speak English. He was old and tired. He was rural. He just needed to go home.

When a taxi did appear with its orange roof light glowing it was Sam who saw it first and Albert had to react quickly to flag it down and beat her to the back door. He pulled the door open and started to get in before something stopped him. The cabby's face leered at him in a manner that he found distasteful. Whatever instinct it was that stopped him also caused him to retreat, cautiously moving his weight back off the leg that he had already started to insert into the open doorway. He hesitated to speak, aware that the driver was revving his engine provocatively, his lips drawn back over crooked teeth and the music from his radio drowning out the words that dribbled quietly from his mouth so that Albert could barely hear them.

'What?' he asked, and then he shouted it again. 'What?'

Was he losing his hearing? Was the cab not available for hire? What was the man saying? From behind he could feel Sam trying to grab him by the arm, causing him to lose his balance, and in the same instant the cab lurched forward, slamming the open door against Albert's elbow and sending him stumbling to the ground. The shoe on the foot that he'd inserted into the cab door caught on the sill and was pulled half off and he fell heavily back on the kerb, landing with one arm on the pavement and one in the gutter. The street became an echoing canyon of blaring horns and orange flashing lights and there was a relentless roaring sound like a waterfall in full flood as the blood surged from his rapidly beating heart building pressure in his middle ear. The pain from his coccyx ran up through his bowels like the electric rays of a cattle prod and he winced in agony, gingerly taking his weight off his thin buttocks and realising as he did so that he'd grazed his hands and they were bleeding. Briefly he closed his eyes and as he did so he caught a glimpse of himself sliding backwards down the hill that he had recalled earlier in the day, clutching his rifle and trying frantically to maintain his balance. He saw the smooth adolescent face of the Japanese soldier in front of him; saw his lips drawn back in fear over crooked teeth as silent words flew from his mouth, drowning in the torrent of the relentless jungle rain; then, just as he opened his eyes, he saw shards of bright crimson glass condense into a pattern of splintering rays like a kaleidoscope.

There were no bones broken, only dignity. He shook his head. The fate of old trees was to fall down. When he looked up the taxi was long gone and Sam was kneeling beside him with his shoe in her hand, her anxious face caught in the no-man's land between embarrassment and alarm. The kaleidoscope turned and the clear lights of the oncoming traffic replaced the startling red blood of his unexpected recollection.

'Oh, Grandpa, Grandpa, are you alright? Are you hurt? Can you move?'

'It's alright,' he assured her, 'I'm still alive.'

Although he allowed himself to be helped on with his shoe and to get back up on his feet, there was no tenderness in his surrender to her for he had been called away in that moment to deal with a rising surge of anger and disgust; at himself, at the city, at the weakness that had allowed him to be drawn against his instincts into a world he'd successfully protected himself from for so long. Everything that he detested coalesced into the sneer on the cab driver's face and the filth that had spilled from his mouth. His anger was the more intense for its impotency; his disgust more distasteful for his need to swallow it.

'Come,' he commanded. 'We'll get a cab on Oxford Street.'

64.

Roger Saville's Car

Like a wind change it had swept over him, subtly altering his mood. Now Roger was fully alert to it, ready to take advantage of the freshening strength of determination it was delivering to him. This was what he'd been waiting for all day. He'd felt becalmed as if drifting in the eddies of other people's currents, waiting for that invisible force that would provide him with forward momentum of his own. Now it had arrived, and with it came the one realisation which his father had never needed to coach into him: *Trust no-one but yourself, because in all the things that matter, you are alone.* It wasn't enough just to say it. It had to be felt. Whenever that feeling arrived, unexpectedly like a sudden stiffening breeze coming down the harbour, it exhilarated him.

The breeze had stiffened in the last half hour. It was building into a gale and that was just what he wanted. Fuck the lot of them. Did they really think he would lie down and surrender? He was his father's son. No, he was better.

What was the other maxim he liked? *When the going gets tough, the tough get going?* No, that was different. That didn't capture the heady certainty and the liberating sense of singleness, the surge of adrenalin that spilled through his whole body as he cast himself free from coercion. There might be a sailing analogy that was better: sailing was the perfect source of aphorisms. It had to do with relying solely on oneself. That's what none of them understood.

He could still remember when they'd tried to force him into playing rugby at The Scots College. He was tall and they'd made the automatic assumption that he would want to be part of a team, one of the jocks, a member of the blazer brigade. But he wasn't an Anglo; the very idea had made his skin hive. He couldn't bear to bind with others and feel his energy being diluted in the combined mass of an eight man scrum. What was wrong with people, he had wondered, that they had this urge to be part of the pack? No-one could explain it to him. Every experience seemed to be teaching him just one lesson: *Trust no-one but yourself, because in all the things that matter, you are alone.* His father was so right. It was like a marker in the Saville genetic code. (He had learned to sail lasers after school off the beach at Percival Park instead. He sailed so well that they quickly left him alone.)

What did all that say? *There's only room for one hand on the tiller?* Yes, that was true. That was part of it. But in the laser there was something else as well. There was only room for one man in the boat, and come hell or high water that was the way he liked it. *Answer only to oneself.* It was the only reliable maxim when he found himself in troubled waters, and that's where he found himself now.

Oh, yes, they were troubled waters alright, and he was certain that this was encouraging these fuckwits to miscalculate. Lawrence, Summers, Astor, his own fucking wife; this was what none of them understood. He could withstand any wind force that blew across his path. Let it howl from any direction, let it scream in his rigging and rip his mainsail to pieces; he'd go where it took him. Did that bloody tart, Maxine, really think she could put him off course? Did Alison Pyke harbour illusions that she could ever dismast him? While others dropped their sails and huddled below decks he'd grip the sheet tighter, change his tack and accept the challenge of the open water. The one thing he would not do is cravenly seek the safety of the lee shore. Fuck them all. They'd misread him, every one of them.

As he turned the car down Stanley Street towards Hyde Park, avoiding his wife's questioning eyes from the seat beside him while proffering his head in profile towards Butch Astor sitting in the back seat so that his friendly smiling teeth could be glimpsed, giving Butch the encouragement to believe that whatever he was saying mattered immensely to him, Roger allowed the mood change within him to build in intensity until it drowned out all doubts and hesitations. At some point he would tell them what they all needed to hear and it would give him the utmost pleasure. At some point he would calmly tell them the single fact that they'd all over-looked.

For the moment he could afford to wait because with every passing second he was sailing away from them, putting on so much distance that he would soon be out of reach.

Yes, he'd been becalmed alright, and he'd known it. He'd been unable to summon up a breeze all day even though he'd caught glimpses of it out across the water. Then, all of a sudden it had come in a rush. The sweetest irony was that all those who believed they had a place on board his boat had unwittingly, in the space of barely five minutes, combined to remind him that he was sailing alone.

It had started as Roger returned to the table after talking with Alison. What was she except a salaried minion working for a ponderous bureaucracy that had no other function than to lend other people's savings to those who were brave and imaginative enough to turn a profit on them? He didn't need the Banks the way they needed him. Without the likes of him they wouldn't even have their jobs. That was something he'd too easily forgotten, but then, in that single instinctive act of offering her a job himself, it had immediately become clear. He'd buy her for two hundred thousand dollars a year. It was peanuts. He'd put her between himself and the Banks and remove Lawrence in the process. Why the fuck hadn't he done it sooner?

He'd sat down and slipped the briefcase under the table while Samantha informed him that he'd missed Albert's speech. Then immediately she leaned into his ear with a furrowed brow, not unlike her mother's, and told him they'd made the most awful faux pas (her mother's expression, not his) and that Butch had turned out to be Japanese and Albert had spoken out about the Japanese atrocities during the War and what on earth were they going to do now because it was too embarrassing for words and obviously it was his problem to deal with.

Well, clearly he'd sensed that the breeze was already on the way because all he'd done was laugh. He'd laughed because it was funny. Perhaps he could have explained to his daughter that it really didn't make any damn difference in the world. He could have told her that the only thing that would upset their guest would be the possibility that he wouldn't make money out of their deal; that he wasn't there for the warm fuzzies of liberal hypocrisy, he was there for the loot. Of course, he didn't. What the hell use was there in telling her things like that? She was a child, and a female one at that. He said instead that he'd be sure their guest would understand the nature of the occasion and make allowances for the context of her grandfather's speech whatever form it had taken, and he said out loud to Albert that he was sorry he'd missed it.

The first hint of a breeze, then: for some it would be disquieting, but for him it had felt long overdue.

As the coffee had arrived and people had begun to stand up and move about he'd remained seated and watched Greg Cummings as he whispered to Lawrence while looking over his shoulder in the direction of Alison Pyke. Suddenly he distrusted him. How the hell had he ever allowed that prick to possess information about his private affairs? He was Maxine in drag. Saville Corp, and Roger Saville in particular, was a trick to be scored, a pocket to be picked, a wallet to be raided. He never should have let him into his confidence. At least Maxine had no concept of the value of what she'd found. Where was Greg counting on getting his cut? How quickly would his big goofy face collapse when he was told that his contract with Saville Corp was now void because of his conflict of interest with sweet Alison? He'd take pleasure in telling him that. All fucks came at a cost but some were more expensive than others, Greg. That's what he'd tell him.

The breeze had freshened. He went and talked to Sheryl in order to get a closer look at her breasts, only to find that she was drunk.

Then Lawrence had trapped him. The dark cloud of his disapproval had been hovering on the far horizon of the table all night and Roger had studiously ignored him. He wasn't going to guess at the cause of his disapproval this time. No doubt it was everything and nothing. Why bother to fathom it? So certain was Lawrence in his belief that he alone knew the hazards of every situation that it was best to leave him in the comfort of his certitude. By the time the hazards had proven themselves to be inconsequential, if not illusory, there would be new ones for him to worry about.

Roger had seen him coming and tried to escape by moving to sit next to Bob Summers but Lawrence had caught him by the arm before he could sit down.

'Roger, I need to warn you of something before you go too far,' he bleated.

'So?'

'The Board is unlikely to approve the equity sale to Astor at such a deeply discounted price if they are aware of the new valuations and their likely effect on our share price.'

'So?'

'Astor is unlikely to proceed unless he has those valuations.'

'So?'

'Tell Astor that the equity purchase has to be made first. Show him the valuations on condition that they are then destroyed. When the land sale goes through it will establish a new market value in any case. Our share price will rise and everyone will be happy.'

He looked so incredibly pleased with himself. The smugness made Roger wonder how he'd put up with him for so long.

'What the fuck did you think I was going to do?' he hissed. 'I never intended for one moment that those valuations would be seen by anyone else. They're a jack up. We all know what game we're playing, Lawrence.'

'You mean ...?'

'Leave the business to me.'

He freed his arm and sat down next to Marjorie, leaving Lawrence gasping for air. Maybe he should have suggested that he accompany his wife on her trip to Europe, he immediately thought. He could ease him out by degrees; give him the dignity of a soft departure and avoid having to deal any further with his obdurate resistance to anything that offended his false sense of morality. How could he have supposed they would ever allow the valuations to be released when they were based on phoney ground rentals? Oh well, at least he'd arrived at the right conclusion eventually.

The wind had picked up further. There was an edge to it. He

turned to Marjorie and told her in a low voice that Lawrence was due a long holiday with air fares at the company's expense and she was entitled to the air fares, too. Now was the right time to go. She could make Lawrence carry her bags to Europe and attend to the accommodation so she could concentrate on her tapestries. It was typical of Lawrence not to have mentioned it but he was going to insist that they took up the offer. It wasn't good for the company to allow Lawrence to bury himself in work without taking a break. What did she think?

If she'd been pleased by this news she didn't show it; but perhaps its implications would take a while to sink in, he'd thought. Marjorie never had been easy to fathom.

Then he'd turned his attention to Bob Summers.

65.

Louee's Club

When the glass tabletop shattered it exploded like a rifle shot. Willie, whose legs were trapped under the metal edge, teetered above it afraid to move, waiting for the pain that he felt certain would follow. Nicole and Ari, safe in their seats, turned their heads and shielded their faces. Luke, who'd been kneeling on the floor with his face above the glass, screamed out in alarm before swimming backstroke away from the source of danger, surfing over the top of *Construction Man* and sending his chair crashing backwards onto the floor. The frantic thrashing of his legs propelled *Construction Man* into the heart of the splintered table where the broken glass punctured him with a loud explosion that sounded like an amplified fart.

Ari and Nicole shrieked hysterically. Willie straightened.

'In case you missed it,' Ari spluttered, 'I think you broke the table.'

'Shit, man, shit,' Luke protested; 'take it easy!'

Willie's mouth hung open in preparation for the noise that welled inside him. There was a howl like the waul of a hungry wolf anticipating satiation; a scream like the sound of an Aztec priest ripping out the heart of a living sacrifice; and it came from deep within his own throat. The muscles in his chest which had been engorged with power as the crystal meth had first exploded in his brain now wrapped themselves around his lungs and squeezed them like a boa constrictor, forcing out the wind in a primeval cry of rage as he launched himself through the air, arms outstretched, knees bent to land with all his devastating weight, reaching for Luke's throat.

Perhaps if he'd landed on Luke's chest, as his flight path intended, he could have killed him and his rage would have quickly abated, but his knees clipped the upturned chair and he landed heavily on the floor instead which hurt him. Prostrate on the floor, unbalanced by the chair beneath his legs, he thrashed out in search of any part of Luke that he could hurt, straining to free his arms like a swimmer in a sea of molasses.

Any part would have done. He wanted to kill him. He wanted, at the very least, to hurt him. He wanted to kill himself and silence the fucking pain. He wanted to destroy the past and present and leave no trace of them for tomorrow. He wanted the supernova to explode into infinity because he couldn't bear the moment to continue. But it wouldn't happen. The molasses grew thicker and his arms grew heavier. Ari and Nicole clutched at his shirt and hair and he fought for his breath as if drowning. Then he found himself lying on his back with Luke sitting on his chest screeching in his face with the demented cackle of an enraged cockatoo.

'Shit, man! Hey, shit man, what the fuck you doing? Jesus fucking Christ, man, take it easy. You wanna fucking kill someone you pick someone else. I'm your fucking friend man. What the fuck you doing? Your brains fried? Your fucking valves popped? You gotta learn to handle the rush. Listen to me, fuck you. You gotta learn to handle the rush. You gotta learn control. You can't come out to play 'till you learn some fucking control, 'cause if you don't learn control you'll fucking kill someone, you fucking arsehole creep. Learn some fucking control, will you. Shit, we treat you like a friend and you do this to us. We cut the ice with you and let you in for free. We fucking share with you, man; we do the fucking sharing thing and you try and fucking kill us. You don't even pay your way. We let you in for free. We let you bunk on our floor and the next thing you're trying to fucking waste us. What are we to think, man? You gotta learn to handle it. Don't they teach you anything at those fucking tight-arse private schools? Don't they teach you how to handle the rush? Don't they teach you who your friends are? Who are your fucking friends, man? Where are all your big prick friends with their beamers and their yachts? Eh? Eh? Why don't you fucking bludge off *their* crystal, man?'

Hanging on to Willie's jaw with one hand and squeezing it hard, twisting his head from side to side while Ari knelt between Willie's legs and held down his feet so he couldn't kick them; giggling, always fucking giggling. And Nicole, where was Nicole? Back in the shadows behind her shuttered eyes.

'Fuck, you think you're so fucking superior with your poofy fucking voice and your wanky fucking mystic shit Tibetan jerk-off crap and you can't even handle a rush. You're a fucking psycho, man. You're a dangerous fucking dog, a fucking dingo that steals from people's tents and eats their babies. Someone ought to put you down, man. You're a menace to society, you know that? Eh, Ari, isn't that right: a fucking menace to society? We break bread with you and you try and bite our hand. We take you in under our roof and you can't wait to kill us. That's a psycho. That's a dog that needs to be put down. But I'm going to let you live. See, I don't think you've been brought up right. I don't think you've been taught values and respect. You gotta learn that, man; you gotta show it. See, Nicole's got values. She works for what she gets. She doesn't sit back and wait for it. Oh no, she gets down on her hands and takes it from filth 'cause that's what you need to do to survive. Nobody gave her a fucking Student's Savings Card. She fucking earns her money, man. You should respect that. Then she lets you share the shit, man. She offers it around. That's 'cause she's got values. Fuck, man, you've got so much to learn, you fucking arsehole creep.'

The grip on the jaw was hurting. The soft tissue of his inner cheek was pressed hard against his back molars drawing blood. His eyes watered. He struggled to free his arms but Luke had them pinioned by his knees.

'You abuse hospitality. You got no values and you got no respect. You get into her bed uninvited. She told you she doesn't want that and still she lets you cut the ice. What sort of poor, pathetic fucking bastard is that? Then you try and kill us. First you try and fuck us and then you try and kill us. You got no respect. You got no values. You get a hard-on 'cause Nicole's more of a man than you are. She's Max the Man compared to you. You're Willie the Wanker from the chocolate factory. Get a fucking life man.'

Now his face was only centimetres from Willie's and his breath was warm in his ear.

'You know what? I fucking hate that. No respect and no values. You should take that little soft prick of yours down The Wall and pay your way. You should peddle your arse the way Nicky Baby does and find out what life is really like. Call yourself Lefty. Yeah, tell all the punters about that big left bend you got. Do it for Krishna. Learn to share. What would you rather do, sweetheart? Cut the ice with your friends, or go home to mummy? Eh? Eh? You got a fucking lot to learn, man.'

Then it was over. The breath in his face was his own. Willie got to his feet slowly as the others started to leave the room. No-one spoke. He looked at the broken glass and the crumpled plastic doll with its hard-on. There was still air in its head. Its mouth flopped open, waiting. He looked at his hands expecting blood. There was nothing. Nothing was broken. His knees hurt, but it was nothing. Whatever had happened was so remote that it might not have happened at all. There was nothing to be said. There was, strangely, a kind of karmic calm in the room as if it had been emptied of all consequences. A determination had been made that nothing mattered. In the end that was what it all came to: nothing. That was what Willie was thinking, if he was thinking at all. It was all crap. It was all just bits of shit flying through space. Sometimes the bits collided. So what? It only mattered to the bits; made no fucking difference to the greater scheme. Who could pull back and see the pattern formed in the sky? Who could see beyond the bits of shit flying through space and see the shape of the universe? Not him, not Luke, not Nicole: nobody.

His friends clattered noisily down the stairs to the street and Willie followed them. Someone came out of the kitchen and tried to talk to him about some crashing and banging sounds they'd heard and Willie grunted and kept walking. Huh? What did he know? Out onto the street and turn left. The others were twenty meters ahead. Ari was telling a story about a drug dog. It sounded like he was singing in a very high voice, following the story up and up towards its ending. Luke, Ari and Nicole: they were a three. Willie stayed twenty paces behind.

He thought he now knew how he'd got it all wrong. He'd

presumed there were conclusions to be reached and decisions to be made. That's how life was to be led. From the smallest fucking kid that's how they'd trained his brain to think. Son, brother, pupil and friend, here's how it works: learn the consequences and make your decisions accordingly. There was an unspoken promise in this. The promise was that it gave you control. Yeah, sure! Look how well that worked. If the pathetic fucking lives of everyone he'd ever known were examples of control then he'd rather be out of it. Look at his mother, hanging from a thread of insecurity, afraid that one little twist of family instability would snap it; actually believing that God took notice of how well she arranged the flowers in church each week, so zonked out by the narcotic of good citizenship that she couldn't even see that her husband was screwing around on her. Some fucking control that was! And how about Dad, the biggest flying fish in the whole imperial galaxy? Was there any proof that fish had feelings? Did they consciously swim against the currents or were they just swept along like paper cups on a windy pavement? Control of what exactly?

No, he could see what was going on. They trained your minds this way because it gave *them* control. It was like having the whole class lined up in rows, sitting at their desks watching the blackboard. What was the biggest challenge? How were you going to get through forty minutes when you'd forgotten to take a pee? How were you going to sharpen your pencil when you'd lost your sharpener? Everyone was so fucking focused on consequences. That's how they kept the lid on. That's why everyone waited to die, no matter how long it took. It was all about control alright, but it sure as shit wasn't personal control.

He needed to milk that fucking cash card before the banks found out. He needed to fly high and fast to a place where all of this could be forgotten.

66.

Roger's Car

Roger stopped at College Street before turning right, glancing across at Joanne as he checked the traffic on his left, smiling inwardly at the careful composition of her face which was intended to convey disapproval and censorship for his eyes only, not realising that he'd long grown immune to it. She was furious that he'd used Albert's remarks about the Japanese as an excuse to insist that her father and Samantha caught a taxi home rather than come in his car. He'd wanted to be sure he could talk to Butch without distractions, he'd said. They might have to stop at The Westin and continue those talks if they were going well. That possibility wouldn't occur if they had a teenage daughter and her grandfather in tow, he'd explained.

Now, listening to Butch playing mah-jong with words from the back seat, drawing and discarding ideas as if there was some prospect that he might be the one player to end up with an entire hand of winning combinations, Roger wondered whether he mightn't just tell him that he was playing the game alone. Roger had stopped playing. He'd moved on. Oh yes, the wind was up alright. They were all contributing to it equally and he welcomed it.

Bob Summers' contribution had been consummate.

'The Treasurer asked me to prepare you for some bad news,' Bob had said.

'Windsor Road.'

'They're going to make the developers pay for it.'

'Why am I not surprised?'

'Is there anything I can do?'

'Apparently not, Bob.'

That was the great thing: when the wind came it was a mighty relief. He could lean into it and focus all his senses on his own survival. Of course they were going to make them pay for it, the bastards: they wrote the rules. The ballot box gave Government the power to rob and extort with impunity. He'd never expected anything else.

He drove around Hyde Park and into Macquarrie Street, letting Butch do the talking.

'I learned a lot about Australia tonight,' Butch announced.

His voice was a disguise. He was Asian to the core.

'You mustn't judge a country on the events of one evening,' Joanne insisted.

'But my judgement is not critical,' he protested. 'Australians say what they think.'

Not about the things that matter, Roger thought. We say things that good manners prevent others from saying only because we've realised they are things that don't matter, but when it comes to being honest about things that count we're as silent as everyone.

'I liked your father's honesty,' Butch assured Joanne.

'Please don't take his remarks personally.'

'And I liked the honesty of your fellow director, Mr Beck.'

'Lawrence?'

What the fuck had Lawrence said to him? He hadn't seen them talking.

He turned down Hunter Street so he could get onto Pitt which was the only way to reach the entrance of The Westin on the corner of Martin Place. He decided he wasn't going to stop in order to keep talking with Butch. He was going to drop him off and keep going. He could feel it strongly now. It was coursing in his veins like a wind-driven sea running before an incoming tide.

'He said that you have Proportional Takeover provisions that soon expire and theoretically it would be possible to acquire forty percent of the company while the shares are still at a deep discount.'

'He told you that?'

'And I was thinking that would be a good thing for me to do rather than buy the land which would make the share price go up. Clearly your company is undervalued.'

'What a good idea,' Roger answered sardonically. 'Why not make a hostile takeover?'

'You wouldn't mind?'

'I champion free enterprise Butch, but, now that you are in possession of the unpublished valuations, I would imagine you might be guilty of insider trading. We have strict rules on things like that I'm afraid. They can be a pain in the butt at times.'

All along Pitt Street Butch was silent. When they reached the door of the hotel he said how much he'd enjoyed talking to Joanne and how privileged he was to have shared a special occasion that meant so much to their country. He looked forward to tomorrow.

Roger asked Joanne to take over the driving, claiming that he believed he'd drunk too much. It was true he felt intoxicated but not from liquor.

What none of them understood was that he alone controlled Saville Corp. He'd created it and he would decide its destiny. He had the minority shareholders' money and the Banks' money, too. Nobody could ever defeat a forty percent shareholder who sat in the CEO's chair. No bank would ever dare call in its loans with an asset like Whiteman's Creek as security. The share price was low because they didn't pay a dividend and their assets weren't liquid. Let Butch make a Proportional Takeover bid and then see what happened to the price. Was he really that naïve?

His mother had it wrong. He was completely in control. They all had it wrong. Roger Saville answered only to himself.

67.

Darlinghurst Road

Albert's head swam and his body ached but he didn't want to dwell on it. He didn't want to give Samantha encouragement to speak. If she'd heard what had been said and commented on it he wouldn't be willing to acknowledge it. He started walking quickly, dragging her by the hand, ignoring her questions. There were youths lounging on the pavement and leaning indolently against the prison wall. Two cars were stopped by the kerbside with their drivers talking through the passenger windows to a group of languid louts who laughed too loudly, finger-combing their hair as they bent to their reflections in the glass of the rear doors.

He knew what they were. It was a swamp that Albert felt himself crossing. It was an ooze of mud and slime that clutched at his trouser legs, filling his boots and threatening to suck him down. He daren't slow in case he began to sink. All his energy was required to press on, dragging Sam by the hand, straining for safe ground, looking neither to left nor to right.

'*... She's young enough to be your fucking granddaughter,*' the taxi driver had sneered before he sped away. There were other words, too, but those were the ones that had got through to him. The swamp was filled with a putrid smell and he could barely breathe for his lungs refused to take it in. The Japanese soldier's exploding face danced like a wind-blown balloon before him, the only person he'd ever killed and, for all he knew, a child who may never have deserved it. One of the youths negotiating at the car window gave out a wolf whistle and turned to follow them with lupine eyes and a painted mouth.

'Grandpa, please!'

He ignored her complaints. His goal was the safety of the main thoroughfare and the security of shops and restaurants. If he hadn't fallen he would have taken the cab's number and reported him. If only he'd kept his balance he could have slammed the car door shut in protest and smashed his fist on the roof. She shouldn't have tried to restrain him like that. He'd have had his measure.

'Don't worry,' he called out; 'we'll find one. They need to be going in the right direction.'

They reached the corner of Oxford Street and only then did he let go of Sam's hand. As quickly as it had come his anger abated. There was blood on his hand and now it was bound to be on hers, too. He'd alarmed her.

'Your mother was right,' he admitted; 'some of these cabbies don't deserve a licence.'

He took his folded handkerchief from his pocket and offered it to her, seeking to restore calm. He hadn't meant to be so severe. Everything was alright, they had a bond, but she mustn't get blood on her blouse. He attempted a smile.

'What a day! Now, which direction are we headed?'

She pointed right.

'That way goes to the city. This way goes to Bondi. We need to cross over. Are you sure you're alright?'

She handed his handkerchief back. She was her mother, her grandmother, a woman, a child. This time it was her job to lead. Clearly she thought that would be better. The pavement was obstructed with construction netting and they picked their way past it with care. There were public toilets boarded up and hoardings promoting enrolment in the National Art School. Traffic poured in both directions in an uninterrupted stream that deafened him. They didn't speak. She led him briskly, still the young girl, but with a swing of self-confidence which, poisoned by the cabby's insinuation, he now found disturbing. Despite himself he felt as though he'd lost an innocence on her behalf, the importance of which he'd never previously been aware. He thought about Joanne's lament to him that her daughter was no longer her best friend and wondered whether that happened with all children. Was the purpose of giving birth solely to replace yourself, and as the child came to adulthood had you served your purpose? Was that the source of Joanne's sadness? Maybe there was no point in living on once that job was done. How else to explain the bewilderment of the old and the arrogance of the young?

They waited at the traffic lights on Oxford Street and then crossed to the corner outside the Courthouse Hotel. He was limping now, unable to disguise it; barely able to keep up. The blisters from his shoes didn't help. If his muscles and his bones took longer now to adjust, so too did his eyesight and his hearing. One side of the street was dark and abandoned like a war zone; the other was as bright and noisy as Luna Park, packed with young people out strolling the restaurants and bars. The fact that many were young men holding hands hardly impacted on Albert as he was distracted by the need to concentrate on himself. The shop windows promoted body piercing and contraceptives. There was a display of fetishist leatherwear on a plastic model with a *mons erectum*. All this was lost on him. He had to get Sam safely home. He needed to summon his energy to conquer one last act.

Without further ado he staggered out into the road, held up his arm and pointed it high into the orange sky above the city. His legs and arms ached and the pain from his bruised coccyx was like a cancer in his bones but he clenched his jaw firmly and stood rock solid. He'd be in Condobolin this time tomorrow night and he might never see this city again. He'd be looking at a black sky filled with diamond white stars, smelling the earth as it quietly absorbed the nutrients of all that had lived and died. He'd put his wife's letters in a clean carton and send them to his daughter, and he'd open a bottle of home-made beer and drink a toast to his good friend, Jim Percy, and if he had to stage a sit-in in the back of a cab to get there, so be it.

Then he felt a hand on his chest and another hand pulling at his outstretched arm and he looked down into the grinning face of his granddaughter.

'Come on, Granddad,' she said; 'you're useless at hailing cabs. Let me do it.'

68.

The Street

Left again, around the corner and heading for Taylor Square, Willie was still twenty paces behind. Nicole's Caterpillar boots trampled the sidewalk into submission. If she wrapped those long legs around someone's neck she'd snap it in an instant. She was a whore and a thief. Was Luke her pimp or Ari? Maybe both; who knows? Who knows anything? All he knew was that there had to be another way.

But what was so different about him? He was a whore, too. He was a whore to that fucking cash card. How could he ever be free while he knew there was money in the ATM? Someone was doing it to him on purpose; someone who wanted to control him and stop him turning down a different street that would lead him to a better end. It was impossible, therefore, to be truly free. Even if he purposefully chose to act without any regard to the supposed consequences, he was still not free. The money owned him like a parent. It would always be waiting for him to return to it. Only the dead were free.

There was a smoker's ashcan on the pavement outside Kinselas Bar and Willie stopped and dropped his credit card into it. Now his pockets were completely empty. He kept walking, half expecting to start floating like an untethered balloon. Perhaps that would come later.

At the corner of Oxford Street Ari reached the conclusion of his story, his high voice piercing the roar of the traffic and bouncing back along the pavement.

'... because he'd stuffed the drugs up the dog's arse, you see, and the dog kept trying to sniff them, going round and round and round until it got so giddy that it fell over.'

They stopped walking. Willie stopped as well. Round and round Ari went, too, with Luke and Nicole looking at him like they'd heard the story before, or they weren't in the mood for it, and when they looked behind them in his direction Willie found out that he was invisible. That bit of shit that was his body had apparently been left behind. It might be lying upstairs on the floor in *Louee's* next to *Construction Man*, gradually emptying itself of the stale air that had been used to inflate it. It might have dematerialised when he withdrew his energy from it, for, without will, what was there to keep all those molecules flying around in the shape of a human being? From here on he would create himself in imitation of the greater universe that no-one living could possibly see. Invisible was good. Hearing and seeing were good. Being unseen was the trick that God used. How could you know Him if you couldn't imagine Him? Imagine being invisible.

Unaware of Willie's epiphany, the world rushed on. That was Okay. Cars and taxis growled and screeched at each other to get to places where others had just been; bits of shit flying through space. Who could see the pattern? High in the Snowy Mountains water tumbled down a mile long shaft hitting a turbine and generating power that was delivered to a grid that was carried on giant steel pylons across thousands of miles of otherwise unscarred country, into a Sydney sub-station and out along the subterranean conduits beneath the pavements of Oxford Street to light up the neon and acrylic signs in the sex shop windows. An illuminated billboard next to a power pole right on the corner outside Emperor's Gourmet offered cheap calls to family and friends all weekend for subscribers to Telstra. There was no pattern to see. Take it all away and there would be nothing. Imagine that: nothing.

But the bits of shit still insisted on being seen and heard, even though he wasn't there. A voice cried out above the roar of traffic and he recognised it from the practised anger. Luke was framed momentarily against the bright white backdrop of the Telstra billboard, arm outstretched in mock indignation, mouth drawn back over bared teeth.

'I hate that,' he screamed. 'I hate fucking paedophiles! Old men with young girls.'

Just beyond Luke's outstretched arm Willie could see there was an old man standing in the road waving his arms, and at the pavement edge he caught a glimpse of a girl with a bare midriff and mini skirt who had her arms outstretched too, though Willie couldn't see clearly because Luke was bouncing up and down in a parody of uncontained rage, partly obscuring them. He shouted out again, vomiting up the accumulated hatred which he'd been practising through the day, and then his body exploded in mock fury and he leaped forward as if to punch the old man full in the face. Now Willie was able to see more clearly because Luke stepped back suddenly, the familiar asinine laugh dying on his frozen face as the air was filled with the high-pitched scream of brakes applied too late.

The scream hung forever in the air as the tall, grey-suited body slipped away from the young girl's outstretched hands and fell with a thud against the Telstra billboard and then down, head first upon the ground.

With casual grace Nicole swung her long leg back and down in a thoughtful, balanced arc. Her Caterpillar boot exploded against the side of the old man's head as if it were a football lying on the green grass of the Sydney Stadium. The young girl, who looked like Manu who looked like Sam, cried out in such fear and pain that the roar of the traffic on Oxford Street was momentarily silenced.

In the end that was what it all came to: nothing. That was what Willie was thinking, if he was thinking at all. It was all crap. It was all just bits of shit flying through space. Sometimes the bits collided. So what? It only mattered to the bits; made no fucking difference to the greater scheme. Who could pull back and see the pattern formed in the sky? Who could see beyond the bits of shit flying through space and see the shape of the universe? Not him, not Luke, not Nicole: nobody.

69.

Roger's Car

Joanne took the tunnel instead of the bridge. It was so New York the way the traffic poured through the white-tiled freeway beneath the harbour, the weight of all that water above and the massive extraction fans sucking out the carbon monoxide that could so easily kill them all if the power failed and terrorists blocked the entrance. It filled her with awe and a touch of trepidation, so when she emerged into the open air, with the skyscrapers of North Sydney looming above her like a mini Manhattan, she felt a surge of excitement and relief. What an amazing city they lived in.

There were two lanes of traffic on either side of her as they merged with the bridge exit onto the Warringah Freeway and she had to concentrate to stay within the lines. She was driving slightly faster than felt comfortable, urged on by the speed of those to the left and right of her but also partly by her own sense of urgency. It was only 10.30 and, providing they weren't held up along Military Road, it wouldn't be too late to ring Prue when they got home. She was desperate to talk. No, that wasn't quite right. It wasn't talking she needed. So much had happened that she wasn't sure she was ready to talk. What she needed to know was whether everything was now different; whether, for once in her life, she had no cause for sorrow, and Prue was the person she could count on to tell her.

She put her left indicator on and swept across into the Falcon Street exit lanes. The day had delivered so much that was unexpected. Perhaps she was greedy for more; perhaps that was why she was hurrying. She needed to be there when Sam and Albert arrived so she could confirm to herself everything that she felt had happened. She didn't need to talk; she just needed to be there.

'I have an admission to make,' she said as she turned onto Military Road.

She laughed at herself.

'I think I've made a dreadful mistake.'

'What's that?'

It was too ridiculous for words.

'I gave instructions to the bank to top up Willie's account whenever it falls below $500. That wasn't very clever of me, was it?'

Roger laughed.

'No wonder he never comes home; he has no reason to.'

'No.'

Perhaps she'd better do something about that in the morning. It *had* been rather silly of her but she couldn't be blamed for being a caring mother. When was the caring and agonising meant to end? If Roger had only given Willie the time and attention that a boy needed he might still be living at home.

The traffic on Military Road was heavy as usual. It didn't seem to matter what time of day, it always slowed you down. At least Albert and Sam would be slowed down too.

'You know what I was thinking,' she mused as they stopped at the lights at Wycombe Road. 'I was thinking how nice it would be if we all went away together on the boat in the May holidays; just the four of us, like we used to do when the children were young. We could spend a whole fortnight together exploring the Hawkesbury River, anchoring at Pittwater for dinner and rowing across to Scotland Island, fishing and talking and playing music like families are meant to do. Willie and Sam could each bring a friend if they wanted to. We could even go searching for real estate. That would keep you busy. We could look for the perfect section to build a beach house. What do you think? It seems so long since we had a proper family holiday.'

Roger was silent until they reached Cremorne Junction.

'Well?' she asked brightly.

'I don't have time.'

'Make time.'

'For Christ sake, Jo, haven't you worked out what it takes to be this rich?'

At Cremorne Junction the lights started to turn red as she approached and she decided to run them. Oh, there were lots of things that she could have chosen to say. She could have said that time was the only thing that children wanted, not to be rich. She could have said that the richest gift in the world was the knowledge that your father harboured a lifetime's letters from your mother; that you found yourself to have been wanted after all. She could have said that only when you felt sorrow lift could you begin to understand what you had missed all your life.

But instead, she took a deep breath and said: 'So how was your day?'

70.

Mosman

The flood lights that lit the sandstone pillars at the entrance to the Mosman house were on the same electronic timer as the sliding wrought iron gates which Joanne had activated from the controller clipped to the sun visor of Roger's car as she approached and the up-lights that lit the Phoenix palms lining the driveway were triggered by the infrared sensor that picked up the car as it entered. There had been much discussion with Frank-the-Gardener as to what sort of timers these lights should be on and Joanne, having a natural predilection for economy, had thought that three minutes was time enough for people to park and get out of their car while Frank, no doubt wanting guests to be given longer to take in the full effects of his sub-tropical landscaping, had argued for fifteen. They compromised at ten, though of course the timers could be over-ridden by a control switch at the front door whenever guests were expected.

Joanne's first words as she entered the kitchen from the garage were an acknowledgement to herself that Albert and Samantha were not yet home. Perhaps she expected them to be immediately behind them, for otherwise it would have been more usual for her to go into the hall and turn the outside lights on manually so their taxi could see the house as it approached and Samantha would be able to operate the gate's keypad opener without having to take out her cell phone to illuminate it (the one fault in the system that didn't take account of people arriving at night without a gate controller). Or perhaps she was just distracted by thought. For whatever reason, after offering tea or coffee to Roger and receiving no reply, she went straight upstairs to her bedroom and ten minutes later the outside lights went out leaving the garden in darkness.

Roger went into his study and turned on his desk lamp, then closed the door. He wasn't in a mood to have to engage in conversation when his daughter and father-in-law came home and his closed study door was a well recognised signal in the Saville household.

While he had been conscious of a sea change taking place in his affairs he knew that his inability to completely control events did not mean that he had to accept disaster. Butch Astor may or may not elect to buy in to Whiteman's Creek but his ability to take advantage of the depressed share price was not available to him now that he had been compromised by possession of the unpublished valuations which Roger had handed him. Butch was not a threat, merely an opportunity; and if that opportunity didn't eventuate there was bound to be another because, as he so often tried to remind people who didn't understand business, the desire to do deals and acquire wealth rose uncontrollably in men, mostly men, just like the desire to conquer.

On Roger's desk, within the pool of light cast by the brass shade of the Hungarian desk lamp he had retrieved from his father's office, were two framed photographs. One was of his wife and children in the cockpit of their Beneteau on a summer's day when Willie was about eleven and keen to catch every fish in the ocean, dangling a flathead on his line in his little sister's horrified face while Joanne, blond, brown and mouth wide open showing her long white teeth, shrieked with delight, unaware that her pubic hair had crept outside her bikini line (a photograph which she had tried many times to force him to remove from display).

The second photograph was of another young boy with dark hair and an expression of unbridled delight, standing beside his sailing dinghy with a wild sea behind him. This was the picture he picked up and examined most often. It had been a challenge that he had set himself: to sail out around Shark Island in a stiff breeze and back in under an hour. No-one else was involved and he hadn't told anyone he was going. The wind was due north and Shark Island was north-north west of the boat club on Percival Park where he set off. He was convinced if he could point high all the way he would be able to get around the island without tacking and then run before the wind all the way home, but two thirds of the way up the beat he was hit by a violent squall that nearly knocked him flat and forced him to bear away. Rather than abate, the squall set in and strengthened. The sensible choice was to turn and run, but he was tantalisingly close to the Shark Island jetty. If he could tack away towards Vaucluse and then come back again he might be able to get around the northern headland of the island as planned, but as he dragged the tiller towards him he lost hold of the mainsail sheet and it flew overboard leaving the dinghy floundering. Luckily, with the wind spilling out of his mainsail he didn't capsize. With just the small staysail under his control he was able to point the bow momentarily into the eye of the wind and, at that moment, the mainsail flew back towards him and he grabbed at the sheet. This, then, was the moment to turn and run for home. But he didn't.

It took him two hours.

The only moment of fear he experienced was when he saw the tall figure of his father, hands on hips, standing on the wharf at the Woollahra Sailing Club as he approached. He hadn't said what he had intended doing and for that he knew he would be in serious trouble, but when he beached the dinghy there was no sign of his father. He unclipped his sails from the halyards and folded them up slowly while filled with dread. Just as he was about to remove his life jacket he heard his father's voice shout out.

'Hold it there, young man!'

He looked up to see his father with a group of friends. They were smiling and his father had his old Leica camera in his hand.

'Give us your best smile,' he shouted out, 'and I won't tell your mother.'

As Roger put the photograph back on the desk the house telephone rang. He waited for Joanne to answer it upstairs but when she failed to do so after four rings he picked it up.

'Dad..?'

Roger frowned and sat up.

'Willlie..?'

'Dad, you have to come. Something's happened.'

His voice was high and close to breaking.

'What is it? What have you done?'

Perhaps it was the memory flowing from the photograph on his desk; perhaps it was the wild oscillations of his own emotions over the previous twenty four hours that had primed him for response; or perhaps it was just natural paternal instinct, but Roger's fear as he heard the fear in his son's voice was not for himself.

'It's Grandad,' Willie pleaded: 'there's been an accident. You have to come.'

'Where? What sort of accident? Where are you?'

'He was hit by a car on Oxford Street. It's bad, really bad. You have to come.'

'I don't understand. Where are you now?'

'St Vincents Hospital. He's in Emergency. We brought him here. I saw it happen and the hospital was right nearby, Dad. I was right there. I was right there when it happened.'

Roger stood and tried to calm his son with his voice, making motions with his hand as he spoke.

'Alright, alright, that's good. Stay calm. Tell me about Sam. Tell me she's with you and she's OK.'

'She's with me. She wasn't hurt.'

'And Grandad; what are they saying? How bad is it?'

'They said if we hadn't been there, if we hadn't been so close, and we hadn't got him to the hospital straight away he could have died.'

'But he's not going to die: is that what they're saying?'

'I can't believe it Dad. I can't believe I was right there. How could that happen?'

As far as Roger was able to tell Willie was not high or drunk but he was not entirely clear headed either.

'Willie, listen to me. I need to be able to tell your mother. Are they saying that he will live or die?'

In the pause that followed Roger could hear an announcement over an intercom, presumably the hospitals, and he imagined Willie turning away, perhaps to Sam, whose voice he thought he heard also.

'Willie ..?'

'They said he'll be alright because we got him here quickly. We saved him. They said we saved his life. But you have to come.'

'Alright; that's all I needed to know. Stay there and we'll come as quickly as we can.'

'Dad ..?'

Willie's voice was calmer now, the anxiety abating and a tired resignation starting to take over.

'I want to come home.'

It didn't need an answer.

As Roger put down the phone, opened his study door and climbed the stairs to the bedroom, it was the other photograph that he had in mind: the photograph that had his long legged wife with her head thrown back in joy and his two children laughing with pleasure and not a care in the world on a summer's day on the Hawkesbury River. For Joanne, he knew that all that was needed to make that photograph perfect again would be the inclusion of Albert Strange.

THE END